Every Man a Prophet

Every Man a Prophet

Stephen C. LeSueur

GREG KOFFORD BOOKS
SALT LAKE CITY, 2025

This is a work of fiction. Names, characters, incidents, and dialogue are products of the author's imagination and are not to be construed as real, with the exception of references to the book *Mormon Doctrine* and its author, Bruce R. McConkie, and the short axioms at the top of each chapter, which come directly from the *Missionary Handbook* and related proselytizing materials.

ISBN: 978-1-58958-826-4 (paperback)
Also available in ebook.

Greg Kofford Books
P. O. Box 1362
Draper, UT 84020
www.gregkofford.com
facebook.com/gkbooks
twitter.com/gkbooks

Library of Congress Control Number: 2025930971

To Kathy, Sam, and Danny

It is the privilege of every man in the Church who holds the Priesthood to have revelation from God for himself. You can have your minds enlightened; you can have the Spirit and power of God rest upon you. It is not necessary that you should preside over the Church, or that you should be one of the Twelve, to have such gifts and blessings as these.

Apostle George Q. Cannon

Chapter 1

You are no longer young men and women without responsibilities, but to the contrary; you have accepted one of the most important responsibilities which will ever come into your life.

Conduct of a Missionary

Bjørnstjerne Bjørnson Toressen rises every morning at 5:15 a.m. to a ringing alarm. A brisk shower, hot then cold, awakens his senses. He shaves too quickly for a resistant stubble. He bleeds easily. After wiping his chin and blotting nicks, he selects a dark woolen suit he will wear with a white shirt and tie until he returns to bed at half past midnight. The suit, though crisply pressed, hangs loosely from his body. In the past six months, he has lost nearly fifteen pounds from an already slight frame. Kristina Toressen says the weight loss comes from overwork, under exercise, poor eating habits, distractibility, and loss of sleep, all of which have become increasingly pronounced since the Toressen family moved into the Oslo mission home at Drammensvein 96G. Sister Toressen believes—and reminds her husband constantly—that his lifestyle choices are piling stress on a weak heart fitted with a pacemaker only twenty-two months earlier. Still, Bjørn, as his wife and American friends call him, is cheerful, irrepressibly so, and blessed with an ability to discern the good intentions in most everyone he meets. His eyes sparkle, even as his clothes sag.

After dressing, President Toressen goes straight to work, entering the mission office through a side door that connects his family's apartment to his office. The wall separating his office from his home hardly muffles the sound of everyday family life that will grow louder as the day progresses, but when Toressen steps from one side of the wall to the other, it's like stepping through a veil into sacred space.

As president of the Norwegian Mission, he is responsible for the physical and spiritual care of one hundred and twelve young men and women proselytizing for The Church of Jesus Christ of Latter-day Saints, and for overseeing nearly two thousand Norwegian church members who struggle to maintain their faith in the face of scornful neighbors and an unfriendly government that classifies Mormonism as a non-Christian sect. Having served as a missionary himself before immigrating to Utah, President Toressen clearly understood the challenges he would face in his native land, but he views his calling today, two decades later, as a divine charge to which he was foreordained. He had anticipated a fierce battle against the religious superstitions that have ensnared the Norwegian people. He

1

had anticipated hostility. He had expected, even relished, the contentious debates over Christian doctrines and principles. What he had *not* anticipated was the neediness of his missionaries, the insistent nurturing they required, and the constant struggle to keep their spiritual energies focused on converting the Norwegian people to the true gospel of Jesus Christ. He pushed that rock up a towering mountain.

On this Wednesday, as he did every Wednesday, President Toressen began the morning by reviewing the missionaries' weekly reports. Elder Hickson was requesting a transfer from Kristiansand because his senior companion neglected morning studies and companion prayer. Sister Morgan complained that her companion was spreading false rumors among members of the Drammen branch, saying she was moody and lazy because she had stayed in bed for five days with menstrual cramps. Elder Jackson wanted advice on how to handle Elder Simpson, who, newly arrived from the states, was refusing to go door-to-door tracting. The district leader in Stavanger reported that Elder Bender had once again been spotted—this time by one of the members—exchanging prolonged kisses with sixteen-year-old Erne Boe. President Toressen wrote "Transfer Elder Bender Immediately" on the top of the report and underlined it for his assistants to see. Elder Conley, who had been a model missionary for the first eleven months of his mission, now wrote that he was burnt out and asked to be transferred to the mission home. "The thought of another year of tracting is driving me crazy," he wrote. "Please, President Toressen, let me come work in the mission office. I'll take any job or do whatever you want." President Toressen wrote, "Mission Printer—let's talk about this," on Elder Conley's report, and set it aside for the assistants.

President Toressen pulled out the report from Elder Kinney, who last month began submitting blank reports to protest his unhappiness with the Norwegian Mission. Kinney's complaint? The elders and sisters with whom he served did not fulfill his idealized expectations. Three weeks into his mission, he had called President Toressen and demanded, "Where is the enthusiastic preaching by missionaries on street corners and the contending with false teachers? Where are the spiritual experiences and the baptisms returned missionaries tell us about in their homecoming talks? I haven't seen any such activity here in Trondheim. The mission work is stagnant. Everyone accepts lack of success as inevitable, and some elders have become quite cynical, joking about stupid Norwegians and blaming the socialist government for making the people complacent and lazy. Our district leader has all of the leadership qualities of a dried fig." Kinney also detailed these observations in a letter home to his bishop, who forwarded it to church authorities in Salt Lake City. Toressen eventually received a letter from Apostle Joseph F. Prichard asking him to look into Kinney's charges that the Norwegian Mission was suffering from spiritual lethargy. "As you know, we normally do not interject ourselves when missionaries send such complaints, but instead instruct them to engage in prayerful reexamination of their own lives and commit themselves to supporting rather than undermining their priesthood leaders. This we have done with Elder Kinney," Prichard wrote. "But given the recent problems in the Norwegian Mission, I felt it prudent to make you aware of his complaints, if you were not already, so they can be addressed as appropriate."

"Oh, yes, I am well aware of Elder Kinney's complaints. I have a few of the same complaints about the missionaries myself," Toressen said, chuckling to himself. Now, staring at Elder Kinney's blank report, Toressen pondered how to help the troubled young missionary grow into the man he wanted to be.

For all of their complaining, missionaries tended to blame themselves more than anyone else. Some days, Toressen's waiting room would fill with elders and sisters who, one by one, tearfully revealed shortcomings, both real and imagined, that were undermining their efforts to convert the Norwegian people. "I slept in past 6:30 a.m. two times last week. . . . I can't make myself read the Book of Mormon. . . . We went to the movies instead of tracting. . . . We listen to rock music while studying the scriptures. . . . I don't love my companion enough." Many confessed to sins committed before their missions, hoping to cleanse themselves of lingering impurities hampering success, and so they unburdened their consciences of past transgressions, such as cheating on a college exam, shoplifting, drunkenness, or committing a sexual sin. A confession of sexual intercourse would require Toressen to notify church authorities to adjudicate; such confessions typically prompted strong condemnation as well as stern warnings not to repeat the offense. Sexual activity in the mission field would trigger automatic excommunication. Toressen was thankful he never had to deal with that. Not yet. Masturbation, however, was a common problem among the elders, and Toressen regularly took their confessions, urging self-discipline, scripture reading, and prayer as the most effective antidotes. Only one female missionary, Sister Larkin, had ever admitted to masturbation. Toressen sat through her confession more red-faced than she while the young sister, despite his efforts to guide her toward generalities, recounted her self-pleasuring fantasies, believing a full disclosure of such details was necessary to secure forgiveness.

Toressen could have been excused for losing faith in the missionaries or castigating them or, as he was sometimes tempted to do, admonishing them to grow up, buck up, and get along. But he recognized that hidden beneath their insecurities and unhappiness was a longing to please God. It was easy to stumble under a mission's grinding demands, especially for those who arrived with quixotic dreams of missionary glory—whose patriarchal blessings promised countless baptisms and lives changed for the better—and then to labor in a cold, dark land where many served entire missions without a single conversion. "I know who I am," President Toressen said, but the burden fell heavy for young men and women who were just discovering their own true selves.

"Elder Tanner and Elder Pedersen are definitely gone," Elder John Ward announced.

"AWOL," Elder Brent Sorensen said. "Completely off the reservation,"

President Toressen looked up from his papers to see his two assistants standing solemnly in the doorway. "Ah, good morning, Elder Warden. Good morning, Elder Bearensen," he said, inviting them in with a smile.

Elder Ward grumbled a "*god morgen*" and, frowning, added, "Our names are Elder *Ward* and Elder *Sorensen*, sir."

"You don't say?" Toressen said.

"We know you're kidding," Elder Ward asserted, "but these nick-names are undermining our authority among the missionaries. They hear you say them and now they've started calling us by these names. It shows disrespect for our calling as your assistants."

Toressen had sensed a growing irritability in his senior assistant but, until now, was unaware of its source. He called many of the missionaries by slight variations of their names. It wasn't because he was trying to be clever or funny. He just couldn't remember their names. In their training sessions, the mission presidents had been counseled to learn the names of all their missionaries. "There's nothing anyone likes more than to hear the sound of their own name," Apostle Johnson told the newly called mission presidents. "It will show the elders and sisters you love them and care about them." When Toressen first arrived at the mission home, he brought photos of the missionaries with him to bed every night, staying up late to connect faces and names, but many didn't stick. He started giving them nicknames as a mnemonic device and, suddenly, as if by inspiration, the names and faces came together. Unfortunately, in many instances, he re-membered only the nicknames. Elder Sorensen was bulky and tall like a brown bear, and so Elder Bearensen seemed to fit. President Toressen had no idea why he turned the stern-faced Elder Ward into Elder Warden. "It's a real challenge for me, remembering all of your names," he told the missionaries. "When the Lord was handing out spiritual gifts, this is not one he gave to me." Still, he liked giving the elders and sisters nicknames, seeing their faces brighten because of the special recognition the names gave them, but that same magic didn't work on his churlish assistant.

"You're certainly in a hurry today, Elder *Ward*," Toressen said with cajoling cheer. "You, too, Elder *Sorensen*. What's all the excitement about?"

Elder Ward spoke first. "Fru Kjelberg said she hasn't seen them for at least three weeks."

President Toressen looked puzzled. "Fru Kjelberg?"

"She's their landlady," Elder Sorensen said. "Elder Tanner's and Elder Pedersen's landlady, and she said—"

"She hasn't seen them in weeks—"

"The mail's piling up outside their door—"

"The elders live on the second floor above Fru Kjelberg, so she'd be able to hear them walking around."

"But she hasn't heard any noise up there lately."

President Toressen's eyes widened. He scratched his chin, trying to think about what to do, but then felt a small piece of toilet paper stuck to his skin. Ever since he'd started on the blood thinner, little shaving nicks would dribble blood uncontrollably. One or two always appeared, no matter how carefully he shaved. He used dabs of toilet paper to stop the bleeding, but he often forgot to take them off. He peeled a makeshift patch from his chin and gently touched it to make sure it had dried. "Every day, it's like the little Dutch boy and the dike with my face, only I use toilet paper instead of fingers," he told the assistants. "Do you know the story of the Dutch boy and the dike?"

Elder Ward didn't hide his impatience. "This is serious, President Toressen. We don't know where Elders Tanner and Pedersen are or how long they've been gone."

President Toressen forced a smile. Elder Ward had become increasingly bold in recent weeks, talking to him as if *he* had been called to direct the mission and Toressen was his assistant. In truth, Toressen was alarmed by the disappearance of the two missionaries. He had transferred Elder Tanner and Elder Pedersen to Harstad two months ago, despite the misgivings of his assistants, who doubted these two missionaries possessed the inner strength required to work in the isolated island town two hundred miles above the Arctic Circle. Missionaries assigned to Harstad labored with little outside support. The town's only adult church member, Jann Harald Brevik, worked for the Norwegian military and was often deployed on NATO missions in the Barents Sea. The closest missionaries—the district leader and his companion in Narvik—visited Harstad only once every four to six weeks. Yet, President Toressen had felt moved to team up Tanner and Pedersen and transfer them to Harstad. Both elders expressed apprehension about their new assignments, but Toressen was adamant. "You need a new start," he told them.

Perhaps he should have noted something amiss when, about three weeks previous, their weekly reports arrived several days late. But late reports from the missionaries were not uncommon. *(How often have I been late sending my reports to Salt Lake City? Did anyone think I had run away?)* Besides, the reports now coming in from Elders Tanner and Pedersen were filled with enthusiastic descriptions of their interactions with the people, strengthening Toressen's confidence that the inspired pairing of these elders would pay dividends for both young men. Consequently, he was completely surprised when Bror Brevik called on Monday to say he had not seen the missionaries since returning from his latest NATO assignment, and they had missed church on Sunday. It was only then that the assistants reminded President Toressen of the late reports, prompting Toressen to have his assistants call the elders' landlady. Staring at his hands, Toressen pondered what to do. He dreaded informing Apostle Prichard, the regional authority overseeing the Scandinavian missions. *Would the apostle understand what I was trying to accomplish? And what would he tell the boys' parents?* President Toressen asked the assistants to kneel as he said a short prayer asking for God's inspiration and guidance in locating the missionaries.

"Amen," the three men said at the conclusion of the prayer. The assistants rose but President Toressen remained on his knees, asleep, overtaken with weariness. In the silence, the assistants could hear the feint *click, click, click* of his pacemaker.

"You've got bolters," Apostle Prichard said matter-of-factly.

President Toressen tried to read the apostle's mood over the long-distance connection. Following the prayer with his assistants, Toressen had felt a calm assurance that the missing elders were safe, but the disappearance of two missionaries definitely needed to be looked into. It could not be easily explained. If this were part of God's plan to help Elders Tanner and Pedersen develop their spiritual gifts, well, this was beyond Toressen's understanding. Apostle Prichard seemed persuaded the boys were in no physical danger, but still, leaving Harstad without permission! Depending on the circumstances, Elders Tanner and Pedersen might be sent home and even excommunicated from the church.

"Bolters?" President Toressen asked.

"It happens occasionally," Prichard said. "A missionary gets homesick or depressed and just ups and leaves. A few are tormented by immorality they failed to confess before leaving. Sometimes they turn up at home, especially if they're serving stateside. But usually they don't get far because their companions alert their leaders. They often wander around for a few hours and then turn themselves in. But three weeks? That's a long time to be missing without anyone noticing. What's going on up there?"

Static interrupted the connection. "Are you still there?" President Toressen asked, straining to hear.

"I'm here."

"I'm sorry, I didn't hear what you said."

"I said I'm still here," Apostle Prichard replied, his voice impatient.

"No, before that."

"What's going on up there, President? How can two elders go missing for several weeks without anyone noticing?"

President Toressen reminded the apostle that the missionaries in northern Norway are spread far apart and receive only periodic visits from their district leaders. "We had no idea they had left because they kept sending in their weekly reports. In fact, we're still getting them, all post-marked from Harstad."

Apostle Prichard was skeptical. "It could be one of those tricks where the missionaries have already filled out their reports in advance and are having their landlady send them in each week. We've had that happen a few times."

"No, we checked with Fru Kjelberg. Their reports seem to be genuine," Toressen said, lobbying subtly for the boys. "I feel in my heart that Elders Tanner and Pedersen are still studying, proselytizing, and obeying all of the mission rules."

Apostle Prichard snorted dismissively. "I wouldn't get my hopes up. Disobeying an important rule like this one usually portends even more significant transgressions. It's all very odd in my opinion, their being gone weeks without anyone noticing. A lot of missionaries *think* about leaving, but real bolters? That's pretty rare. And I've never heard of two companions leaving together. A good mission president can sense which of his missionaries are having problems, and he would know never to put two of them together."

Chapter 2

Wherever you are and whatever you are doing, in the eyes of the beholder, you are the Church. People of the world are judging the Church by you—measuring your behavior, your conduct, your actions, and your deportment much more critically than by your teachings.

Conduct of a Missionary

Elder Ward leaned his forehead against the airplane window and stared at the mountain landscape below. Odd-shaped patches of cultivated farmland were carved haphazardly into hillsides and along rivers and fjords. A few had cattle and sheep, just handfuls in number, grazing lazily below the surrounding cliffs. The farms with their red barns and brightly painted houses were pitifully small compared to the pastures and fields that stretched across western Iowa and into Nebraska, where Elder Ward had been raised. The accidental mosaic created by the Norwegian farms, though colorful, struck Elder Ward as mindless and inefficient until Bror Langeland showed him a construction site in the Oslo suburb of Sandvika. Backhoes, bulldozers, jackhammers, and dynamite took turns scraping and blasting away the hardened rock that lay beneath a thin layer of soil. "Norway is big giant rock," Bror Langeland explained, speaking English. "Beautiful rock, but still, rock. We make farms wherever we can."

Next to Elder Ward, Elder Sorensen slept, his right cheek pressed flat against his fist. The assistants were flying to the Narvik airport, and from there they would take the bus to Harstad to lead an on-the-ground search for Elders Tanner and Pedersen. Although the elders' disappearance was a crisis that could easily turn to tragedy, the incident infused the assistants with a sense of importance. Ward felt a measure of pride in the fact that he had foreseen trouble in putting Tanner and Pedersen together in the northern district, thus affirming his prescience, even spirituality. He would never say "I told you so" to President Toressen, at least not so bluntly. Possessing such an uncharitable thought would be unbecoming for an assistant to the president. And yet, that's essentially what Elder Ward said when Apostle Prichard interviewed the assistants before they left for the airport. Elder Ward had spoken not out of malice or pride but of duty.

Soon after being called as President Toressen's assistant, Elder Ward had begun to question the president's Lilies-of-the-Field leadership approach, which had already yielded a few minor mishaps, though none as serious as this one. Elder Ward had also grown increasingly impatient with Toressen's stream-of-consciousness decision-making style, which he initially welcomed as refreshing but now regarded as time-wasting. The other missionaries would not envy the assistants' close relationship with President Toressen if they had to sit through ten-hour meetings simply to decide where to send eight newly arriving missionaries.

Elder Sorensen did not feel as strongly as Elder Ward on the subject of Toressen's shortcomings, but during the interview with Apostle Prichard, Elder Ward had dominated their time and, in Sorensen's view, claimed too much credit for himself. Hadn't he also warned against sending Elders Tanner and Pedersen to Harstad? After waiting for a chance to join the conversation, Sorensen finally barged in with some observations that may have come across as more critical of the mission president than he intended. Still, he had only spoken the truth.

Apostle Joseph F. Prichard had flown to Oslo from Copenhagen, where, following several assaults on the sister missionaries, he had been coordinating the transfer of all Danish sisters to new missions. Upon reaching the Norwegian mission home, Apostle Prichard asked to meet with the assistants before their flight to Harstad, and went directly to their office, a windowless basement room that could barely fit their three chairs. A former college basketball player, Prichard still looked athletic and trim, even at sixty-four, with a rugged chin and confident bearing. He asked the assistants about their families, his voice like a smile, and then scooted his chair close to the young men until their knees almost touched. "What can you tell me about Elders Tanner and Pedersen?" he asked.

Elder Ward, who inherited his burnt-red hair and sense of justice from a Norwegian grandfather, went first. "Elder Pedersen was my companion when he was a greenie," Elder Ward said, then catching himself, explained, "I mean when he was a new missionary. I was his first companion after he arrived in Norway."

"I know what a greenie is, Elder Ward. I was a missionary once, too, you know," Prichard said.

Elder Ward's cheeks flushed. He was flattered that an apostle would talk with him, asking his opinion, man to man, one priesthood leader to another. His voice deepened as he continued. "Elder Pedersen was quiet and timid when we went tracting, not just at first, but even after a couple of months."

"Was he afraid?"

"Not exactly." Ward paused to think. "It was more like he was uncomfortable. He could speak the language extremely well for a greenie, picked it up fast, and he liked talking to the members, but he had trouble fitting in with the other missionaries. Not the sisters, though, just the elders."

Prichard's eyes narrowed. "Was he paying *too* much attention to the sisters or the Norwegian girls in your branch?"

"At first, I thought so, but . . . no, there wasn't anything going on. We tried to bring Elder Pedersen out of his shell by playing one of our missionary pranks on him, you know, the kind of practical jokes you play on greenies. We had a member pretend to be an investigator, but Elder Pedersen didn't take it very well."

"How so?"

"He cried." Ward wondered whether he should have mentioned this incident. He didn't want an apostle thinking he was frivolous. "We weren't trying to be light-minded. I had the same practical joke played on me, and I thought it was funny. All the missionaries did, and the members too. Everyone except Elder Pedersen."

Apostle Prichard nodded sympathetically. "What about the mission rules? This is my most important question, so think carefully about it. Did Elder Pedersen obey the mission rules?"

"Yes, sir," Ward said without hesitation. "During the three months we were together, he followed all of the rules and did everything I asked. He never complained, either. What I do recall is he prayed a lot, particularly in the afternoons when we had our *middag* supper and at night after we finished tracting. I got the impression he was homesick. You know how greenies are. Norway can be a rough mission when you're getting rejected all day long and no one invites you in or shows any interest. It takes some time to adjust."

"Did he?"

"Eventually, yes, but here's the funny thing. At first, he was very introverted and sensitive, but in recent months he's been like a ball of fire when tracting and teaching, even raging at people on their doorsteps and inviting controversy. A real Dr. Jekyll and Mr. Hyde situation. But this is the first time he has caused any problems."

Apostle Prichard gave the young man's knee a gentle squeeze. "Thank you, Elder Ward, you've been very helpful. I can tell you were a considerate companion." He straightened back in his chair, his eyes still brimming with concern. "Now tell me about Elder Tanner."

"I'm the one who knows Elder Tanner best," Elder Sorensen said. "I wasn't his companion, but we served in the Oslo District together."

"You know the most important question," Apostle Prichard said. "Did he follow the mission rules in their entirety?"

"Following the rules was never a problem for Elder Tanner."

Apostle Prichard evinced surprise but continued. "Did he get along with his companions?"

"I'd say yes. At least, there weren't any problems we knew of."

"Diligent and hard working?"

"Yes, but . . . I don't know . . . ." Sorensen struggled to explain. "This is going to sound strange, but Elder Tanner was too hardworking."

Apostle Prichard lifted an eyebrow.

"He was obsessed," Elder Ward interjected. "He didn't just follow the mission rules, he went beyond them, as if simple obedience weren't enough. He always had to go the extra mile."

"Except with Elder Tanner, it was the extra ten miles," Sorensen said. "Instead of getting up at 6:30 a.m., as the rules require, he would get up at six, and then five thirty, and so on, until eventually he was getting up at four thirty. If the district leader set a goal of giving out ten copies of the Book of Mormon for the week, he would have to hand out twenty, and if the goal were fifty hours of tracting and teaching, he had to do sixty or seventy."

"It was unhealthy," Ward asserted.

"Indeed!" Apostle Prichard paused as if choosing his words carefully: "Did he seem in any way mentally ill or emotionally unbalanced?"

The assistants mulled the question. Finally, Sorensen spoke. "He wasn't crazy or irrational. It's just that he had to be better than everyone— work harder, be smarter, you name it—and excel at everything. And he was a real know-it-all, too. At our last quarterly conference, Elder Tanner got real upset when he lost the Scripture Chase."

"I thought he was having a nervous breakdown," Elder Ward said. "I really did."

Elder Sorensen nodded in agreement. "It was something we were doing to build team spirit and help the missionaries learn their discussions and scriptures in a fun way. But Elder Tanner took it way too seriously."

"His father fancies himself to be some kind of Mormon intellectual," Elder Ward added, "and so Elder Tanner is always correcting the missionaries if they quote one word from the scriptures out of place. And he likes to school the other missionaries on the 'true' meaning of church doctrines and teachings, as if only he and his dad understand what it all means. It's like the scripture says: 'When men are learned, they think they are wise.'"

"Well, I do know something about Elder Tanner's father and his so-called faith-promoting pamphlets," Apostle Prichard observed, his face suddenly pinched. "So tell me, given the problems you so clearly saw in Elders Tanner and Pedersen, why did you put these two elders together as companions and then send them to one of the most difficult areas in Norway?"

Apostle Prichard's tone was soft and inquisitive, not accusatory, as if he were trying to understand a complicated riddle. When the assistants hesitated, Prichard grasped each by the knee. "Don't worry, Elders, I'm not looking to cast blame. I just want to understand the situation here, so we can find the missing elders and give them the help they need. We need to get this mission back on track. That's our purpose here."

Elder Ward spoke first. "To be honest, it was President Toressen's idea."

"He was trying to help the elders," Elder Sorensen said. "He thought the challenge would give them a shot in the arm. Boost their confidence."

"I could see it wouldn't work out," Ward continued. "You send only your best missionaries to northern Norway. That's what I told the president. I could see—"

"We both could see," Sorensen said pointedly, "that the conditions in Harstad would make their problems worse, not help solve them."

"Ah, I see," Apostle Prichard said, encouraging the assistants to elaborate. And they did, but the more they talked, the more puzzled he became. No matter where Apostle Prichard went in Norway, whether in the cities with thriving branches or the little towns with only a handful of members, the Norwegian Saints adored President Toressen. Sure, they recognized his shortcomings, particularly his chaotic management style and penchant for arriving late to meetings and then allowing them to run overtime, sometimes more than an hour. Prichard did hear complaints from a few local leaders about "Toressen Time," as they called it. But even they professed love for the man, and the old-timers called him the most inspirational leader ever sent by church authorities to Norway. And the missionaries! They called Toressen the prophet of Norway, the Lord's spokesman in this land, the man called by God to receive revelation on behalf of the Norwegian people. Toressen never claimed this mantle for himself, but he freely shared his visions and prophecies in a way that invited adoration by the missionaries. *Is this his goal?* Prichard had seen many promising leaders, particularly BYU religion professors, bring themselves to ruin by promoting their own brand of spirituality, as if they had found a missing key to drawing near to Christ, when it was only the apostles themselves who had the keys to heaven. Sadly, many resisted correction and, like the parable of the seed, their faith withered and died. Much to Prichard's dismay, Toressen had recounted his visions in public settings and interviews in the Norwegian press, making Mormonism appear backward and superstitious, an image the church was trying desperately to erase. Toressen cared passionately about people, especially about the young missionaries in his charge. At least, he claimed to. And yet, for unfathomable reasons, President Toressen had paired together two struggling elders and sent them on an assignment they were destined to fail.

Chapter 3

Avoid temptations. Don't play with your emotions, you may not be as strong as you think. Don't make foolish mistakes which can ruin your entire life here and for eternity.

Conduct of a Missionary

Elder Eddie Pedersen stared at the shadows fluttering across the ceiling. He rolled over and reached for his portable clock: 12:57 a.m. Barely three hours before his alarm was set to ring. *Will I be able to get back to sleep?* Eddie fluffed up his pillow and lay back down, wondering what Barry would think about what he and Elder Tanner were planning: Barry Williams with his bravado and cynicism; Barry with his insouciant charm; Barry who knocked him out and made him forget his own pain and shame. Eddie had adopted Barry's sardonic indifference to help him get through the rough days of his mission, but he discovered that it only masked the pain, preventing others from seeing what he so keenly felt. He was in a better place now. *So why am I leaving my proselytizing area? Is it an act of faith to prove my worthiness before God or simply an act of defiance, a middle finger to a seemingly cruel and indifferent God?* He and Elder Tanner had carefully planned their little adventure so it wouldn't be discovered. But if it were, would they be sent home? Eddie wasn't worried about himself. It was the straight-arrow Elder Tanner whose standing would be jeopardized. Eddie had already decided to confess everything about his present "condition" to President Toressen after they returned, and so he expected to be sent home regardless. A burst of arctic air whistled through the window. He tucked his toes under his duvet and pulled it tightly to his chin. He mulled over what he intended to tell President Toressen. As he began crafting the words in his head, his mind drifted back to the warm summer afternoon when Joey Singleton asked him to rub lotion on his sunburn.

It was August 1962. Eddie and Joey shared a two-man pup tent at Camp Kennikee in the San Bernardino Mountains. The green canvas tent, a gift from Eddie's parents, smelled fresh with the promise of adventure. As the youngest of five brothers, Eddie had waited enviously for his turn to go camping and begin earning merit badges, as each of his brothers had done. He was still physically immature and not nearly as strong as the other Boy Scouts, nor as experienced in tying knots and building campfires. That was to be expected. After all, he had only been a scout for six months and this was his first week-long camp.

Before the trip, Eddie read every page of the camp guide and day-dreamed about the heroic lifesaving skills he would learn. He practiced stripping off his clothes down to his underwear so he could quickly dive into the water to rescue a drowning swimmer, achieving a best time of forty-three seconds. At Camp Kennikee, he awoke to the smell of pine needles and bacon frying on a greasy skillet; after KP duties, he filled his mornings with classes where he learned to apply tourniquets to bleeding limbs, set broken legs using a thick branch as a splint, find lost hikers, send urgent messages using Morse code, and other crucial life skills. In the afternoons, while the other boys took advantage of their free time to canoe or hunt for snakes and lizards, Eddie would return to camp and study the class manuals. The cozy solitude of reading inside the sunbaked tent made him feel as content as a baby inside the womb.

On the day in question, Eddie was studying semaphore, picturing how he would signal for help from a mountain top, perhaps after sucking rattlesnake poison from the leg of a fellow scout. Lying on his stomach, Eddie stretched across the smooth canvas floor of the tent, resting on his elbows as he read. His wet bathing suit cooled the warm air flowing from one end of the small tent to the other.

Joey Singleton, who was a year older than Eddie, usually spent the afternoons lounging on the dock by the lake. Having attained the rank of Star Scout to please his parents, Joey had no interest in earning additional merit badges. Eddie liked Joey. Despite his waning interest in Scouting, Joey wasn't a complainer, nor did he deride Eddie's enthusiasm. Joey happily showed him a few tricks for remembering some of the more complicated knots. Most days, Eddie had the tent to himself, but today Joey returned earlier than usual. "I'm roasting out there," Joey said, lifting the tent flap and crawling in. He showed Eddie his bright red arms and back. "I'm getting an awful sunburn."

Joey stripped off his suit and examined the tan line across his waist. "Put some sunburn lotion on me, will you? I'm burning up." Eddie looked up as Joey pulled a bottle of Johnson's lotion from his duffel. "Hey, you're pretty red yourself," Joey said, pointing to Eddie's back. "I'll put some on you first."

Joey squirted the lotion across Eddie's shoulders and back, gently kneading the cool liquid into his flesh. Joey chatted pleasantly as he worked his way down Eddie's back and then up his leg from his ankles to his thighs, talking about the raft being constructed by the boys from the Riverside troop, who offered to let him have a turn with it when they were done. "You should come with me," he said. When he reached Eddie's swimsuit, Joey said, "I can't rub any of the lotion into your legs up here because your suit's wet and dripping water. Take off your suit and I'll get the rest of your legs."

Without hesitation, Eddie wriggled out of his suit. Looking back, he realized how naïve he had been—or, at least, about how it must have appeared to Brother England. It had not seemed unusual at the time. At home, the five Pedersen brothers shared two rooms. They neither asked for nor gave privacy. The first time Eddie went to the YMCA with his father, he was shy about taking off his clothes in front of others until, after swimming, his father marched him naked into the shower, where he saw a dozen other men completely exposed and scrubbing their private parts with soap, oblivious to the others around them. Camp wasn't any different. All the boys stripped and changed clothes in view of their tentmates. In the outdoor showers by the lake, many of the older boys took off their suits and rinsed them out while standing naked under the streaming water. Tuesday night before taps, the boys held an unofficial polar bear swim where they swam naked in the moonlight, laughing and showing off their budding manhood as they jumped spread-eagle from the dock into the lake. No one at camp was the least bit shy about asking other boys or men to apply suntan and sunburn lotions. It was an all-male camp. Who else were you going to ask? If Eddie felt any discomfort, he recognized that the older boys like Joey—having endured mandatory group showers in junior high gym class—regarded prudish modesty as a sign of immaturity. Eddie thought he was being grown up.

Joey squirted the lotion onto the upper part of Eddie's thighs and continued his cheerful banter as he rubbed in the lotion, moving higher and higher, caressing Eddie's inner thighs. Eddie felt a bracing pleasure that years later he would realize was sexual arousal, but Joey was so nonchalant, so absorbed in his own conversation, and the emerging sensation was so new, that Eddie attributed the delight to the lotion's sweet aloe fragrance.

"Okay, my turn for the lotion," Joey said, wiping his hands on his thighs. Eddie exchanged places with Joey and started on his shoulders. Although Joey was just a year older, Eddie could feel the firmness in Joey's shoulders and arms; and in contrast to Eddie's smooth skin, Joey's legs were already sprouting little blond hairs. Eddie also felt the strength of Joey's calf muscles. He was absently tracing a line with his finger, connecting freckles on one of Joey's thighs, when the tent flap suddenly opened.

"Okay, boys," a voice called from outside the tent. "You've got KP duty tonight." Eddie looked up to see Brother England peering into the tent, dark astonishment in his eyes.

15

"Jesus Christ! What the hell are you two boys doing," cried Brother England, an inactive church member who had been recruited as assistant scoutmaster in hopes of luring him back to the fold. Joey grabbed his swimming trunks and scrambled naked through the back of the tent. Eddie's face reddened with the immediate realization of what Brother England thought they were doing.

"I was just putting lotion on Joey's sunburn, Brother England," Eddie said, slipping on his swimsuit as quickly as he could. "Nothing happened. Honest."

Did something happen? No one accused Eddie or Joey of anything. Brother England and their scoutmaster, Brother Wilmeyer, talked for an awfully long time outside Eddie's tent, whispering ominously, as Brother England told the troop's scoutmaster what he had seen. Brother Wilmeyer alluded to something about "homosexual behavior" and later Brother England said, "Joey had a little erection when he ran out of the tent." Brother Wilmeyer gasped and asked, "Do you think—?" Eddie couldn't hear the rest of Brother Wilmeyer's question, but he heard Brother England's hoarse laugh when he replied.

"Every teenage boy gets about a thousand erections every day. They can't help it," he said. "I remember getting a big one in math class while my teacher was doing quadratic equations on the chalkboard. My God! Quadratic equations. I wouldn't think much of it."

After some additional discussion, the two men persuaded themselves that Eddie's explanation—"we took off our swimsuits because they were wet"—was entirely reasonable, and so concluded with much relief that although the boys' judgment was questionable, they had not behaved inappropriately. Brother Wilmeyer would counsel Joey, who at that moment was sitting on the dock, dangling his feet in the water and watching the other boys swim. Brother England would talk to Eddie.

"Come on out, son," Brother England called to Eddie, and then put his arm around the boy as he emerged from the tent. Brother England was a large man with hairy arms and a gruff voice, but he spoke as gently as he could. "I'm sorry I overreacted the way I did when I saw you and Joey in the tent. I shouldn't have cursed. That's never right. But it looked like . . ." Brother England didn't finish his thought. "Listen, Eddie," he said. "You and Joey are good kids. You didn't do anything wrong. But the next time you guys rub sun lotion on each other, keep your trunks on. And do it outside of your tent, where everyone can see you. That way no one will get the wrong impression. Okay?"

"Yes, sir," Eddie replied.

"Good boy. We won't say anything more about it," Brother England said cheerfully. But after dinner, Brother Wilmeyer switched Eddie and Joey as tent mates, and put his own son, Carl, in the tent with Eddie. Carl resented the change and complained loudly to his friends about having to babysit a tenderfoot scout, causing Eddie to wonder what Carl had been told. The next day, Brother Wilmeyer told the boys they would not be allowed to join the other scouts in Friday night's polar bear swim, because it was inappropriate for boys their age to swim nude in public. "Why are we the only troop forbidden to join in?" one of the boys asked.

"Because Mormons are different, and we know better," Brother Wilmeyer said. "Modesty applies to boys as well as to girls, and we must set an example." The scouts let out a collective groan and Eddie looked at his feet, certain all eyes were on him.

If Brother Wilmeyer mentioned anything to Eddie's parents, they never let on. A few weeks later, after Eddie felt enough time had safely passed, he asked his older brother Todd what the word "erection" meant. "Jeez, Eddie, why are you asking me?" Todd sputtered. "You need to talk to Dad about something like that." Todd's disapproving tone warned Eddie he shouldn't even bother asking what "homosexual" meant, though he found out soon enough when Sean Allenteer was accused of getting a boner in the shower after gym class. For the rest of the school year, the older boys taunted him by calling him "homo" and pretending to speak with a lisp whenever they said his name. Eddie felt sorry for Sean but eventually joined in the fun, calling out, "Hey, Sean Allenteer. Rhymes with queer." Sean merely shrugged at the juvenile insult, but the other boys laughed and slapped Eddie on the back. Eddie regretted his cowardice but felt compelled to signal his normality, as if it were suspect.

It was. Not by other boys, but by Eddie himself. "Nothing happened," he told Brother England, but he knew otherwise. He realized he liked being with other boys, the pleasure of walking together, arms over each other's shoulders, wrestling on the grass, winning their admiration and praise. Such attraction was normal in elementary school, where boys played almost exclusively with other boys, and only sissies played with girls. But in junior high, his friends suddenly acquired a crude obsession with girls, making lewd observations about who was flat and who was stacked, and who let the boys feel her up. Eddie shared none of their curiosity or passion. *Why would I want to touch a girl's breasts?* He thought a lot about Joey Singleton and daydreamed about going to Scout camp again and rubbing suntan lotion on each other's naked bodies. Eddie looked for

Joey at church and school, but he hung out with older boys and showed no interest in Eddie.

Eddie's best friend, Pete Kelley, talked nonstop about girls. Eddie listened and feigned the same desires, but what Eddie really wanted was the athletic, handsome Pete. Eddie joined Pete's recreation league basketball team and threw his friend passes and compliments in equal measure, hoping to win his affection. Eddie invited Pete to a family outing at Santa Monica beach and the two boys went off by themselves to dive in the waves and tan themselves. They played with a football, passing it back and forth and taking turns tackling each other in the sand. When Eddie chased Pete into the water to wash the sand off their bodies, he marveled at Pete's smooth skin and muscular frame and wondered if Pete looked at him in the same way. The boys returned to the beach and threw themselves onto their towels. "Pete, your back and legs are bright red," Eddie said.

Without asking, Eddie squirted a line of lotion on Pete's upper thighs and began rubbing it in. Pete immediately turned over and pushed Eddie's hand away. "What the hell are you doing?" he shouted.

Pete's outburst nearly brought Eddie to tears. "I-I-I'm sorry. I was just trying to be helpful."

"Well, here. I can do it myself." Pete stood and started rubbing in the lotion himself, looking around as if to make sure no one had seen Eddie rubbing his legs.

Eddie's affection for Pete eventually waned, but not his infatuation with other boys. Eddie recognized that his attraction to boys—and his disinterest in girls—would have triggered the strongest condemnation if his feelings were known. He fretted whether he should confess his desires to his bishop, so implacable were God's pronouncements against homosexuality, so unforgiving His judgments. Church leaders often spoke of moral depravity and perversion rather than homosexuality, fearful the term, if spoken aloud, would encourage its practice. But Eddie had not actually done anything wrong or committed any sins. He had also learned in his health and hygiene class that same-sex friendships were common among boy and girls. "It's quite normal for pre-adolescent males to have little 'boy crushes' on their best friends," the teacher said amid much tittering among Eddie's classmates. "The same is true for pre-adolescent females. Sometimes these same-sex crushes are accompanied by minor sexual experimentation as males and females prepare for adolescence and adulthood." The lesson persuaded Eddie his feelings were normal, not sinful. He was simply moving into adolescence at a slower pace than others. This was also normal, his teacher explained. Eddie's attraction to boys was not entirely guilt-free, but he foresaw a time when his body and mind would respond to girls. He was a male version of the flat-chested tomboys waiting for puberty to begin. All would be sorted out in high school.

Except it wasn't. The boy crushes continued. Eddie, who would later be voted best-looking senior boy, had a date most weekends and even a steady girlfriend, Sheila, throughout his junior year. But when they parked and made out, Eddie felt no sparks or passion, except when he thought about some of the boys he liked or fantasized about that day in the tent with Joey Singleton. Eddie looked for signs that some of his male friends also felt a similar attraction. *Am I the only one?* Once he rubbed the arm of John Prince in a way to signal his interest, but he was afraid of being too obvious after the reaction he got from Pete. He never forgot Brother England's advice: "Don't give anyone the wrong impression." Greater than his desire for a boyfriend was his fear of discovery.

Not that any of his fellow students would have guessed. Few were more admired than Eddie. He played piano in the school jazz band, ran on the cross country team, and played two years of varsity basketball, making the all-league third team as a guard his senior year. No one was more popular with the girls. Eddie had the conventional appeal that comes with wavy blonde hair and droopy blue eyes, but it was his smooth, boyish face that made him appear vulnerable and alluring. After breaking up with Sheila, he began dating regularly again but never dated the same girl more than two or three times, creating an aura of mystery that added to his appeal. Each new girl was determined to be the one who broke through his shell to claim the real Eddie for herself. At the end of his senior year, Eddie won an academic scholarship to Brigham Young University. His application touted his Eagle Scout Award, athletic achievements, YMCA Leadership Award, 3.8 grade point average, and Silver Star in the Foothill Regional Piano Competition, whose judges lauded not just his exceptional technique but also his expressive playing style of uncontrolled passion.

"It's like you're a different person on that stage," his mother said, tussling Eddie's hair.

His father nodded approval. "You can really let it fly when you want to."

Eddie's accomplishment brought deep satisfaction, but they were hollow victories. *Would people still like me if they knew the real Eddie, not the one with all the awards?* He knew the answer. Who was the real Eddie, anyway? Was he the one who devoutly beseeched God to remove this burden, or was he the one who devoutly wished another boy would love him back?

To outsiders, Eddie was following a well-worn Pedersen path. His father, Donald Sr., managed a thriving insurance business and had served, at one time or another, as president of several major civic associations representing San Fernando Valley. He started his business during the last years of the Great Depression, coaxed it through the war years, and then rode it to financial success during the post-war economic boom. He met his wife, Marie, at Los Angeles City College, where they both got their two-year degrees; she went on to finish at UCLA with a bachelor's degree in English, while he established his business. Marie relished her role as a civic-minded mother of five spirited boys and eventually won a seat on the school board as the champion for Glendale parents who wanted to reverse the decline in academic standards and growing power of the teachers' union, two trends that seemed to go hand in hand. She was reelected handily in subsequent elections. Don and Marie were among the most prominent Mormons in the city, and they never faltered in their church duties in public or at home. They felt deep pride in Eddie's accomplishments and told him so on many occasions. Eddie recognized he was only doing what his older brothers had already done before him.

All of the Pedersen boys had hoped to receive mission calls to one of the Scandinavian countries, given their Norwegian and Danish ancestry, but each embraced his specific assignment as divinely inspired. Even Skip expressed enthusiasm for his mission call to Texas, which many young men would have found unbearably mundane, particularly in comparison to the more exotic foreign missions they envisioned for themselves. "It must have been foreordained," Skip said after reading the letter from church headquarters, "because I had never even heard of a Texas Spanish-speaking mission before." Eddie saw his future stretch out before him in his brothers' lives: college, mission, marriage, and children.

Eddie dived into his academic studies his freshmen year at BYU. His favorite course was introductory biology. The professor, Brother Downy, melded science and religion in his lectures, and did not back down when students challenged his contention that evolution is consistent with revealed church doctrines. "I'm not here to criticize the Brethren or take away anyone's testimony," Brother Downy said when a student read a statement by a Mormon apostle condemning evolution. "I have a firm testimony of Joseph Smith and the church, and I believe we will continue to receive more insight—from both scientific study and our prophets—pertaining to the earth's origins."

It was also in this class that Eddie met his best friend, Barry Williams, when the two were assigned as lab partners. Barry was the complete opposite of Eddie: he dressed indifferently in jeans and T-shirts, neglected shaving for days at a time, and violated university standards by letting his hair grow over his ears and the collar of his ragged coat. Barry's personality differed from Eddie's as well. Whereas Eddie was circumspect and cautious, Barry was expressive both in gestures and language, impulsive, and prone to sarcasm and witty asides. After a student told Brother Downy that new evidence suggests carbon dating is flawed, and so dinosaurs could actually be 6,000 years old, just like the Bible says, Barry proclaimed for all to hear, "That incontrovertible fact and inspired conclusion was brought to you by a Utah public education." He turned icy stares into laughter by quickly adding, "I should know, that's where I got my education."

Eddie noticed a change in his own behavior when he was with Barry. He was less self-conscious, more confident, more willing to express his thoughts and feelings. Not that he was saying anything profound, but that was the point. He didn't have to. Barry's friends, most of them drama majors like Barry, also drew him out with their eccentricities. "I need some PDA," one of them would say when feeling depressed, referring to the university policy against Public Displays of Affection. This would be the signal for the other young men and women to offer hugs, which, if they were feeling silly, would evolve into a boisterous group hug. "It's the closest Mormons will ever get to group sex," Barry said, "unless you're a Mormon fundamentalist. It's worth looking into fundamentalism for that reason alone."

Several of them were performing in a university production of the new musical, "You're a Good Man, Charlie Brown," and they entertained each other singing and acting out the different parts when eating lunch or hanging out together by the library. They clearly enjoyed showing off. "It's good publicity for the show," said Caroline, a tiny coed who did cartwheels on the lawn. At Barry's insistence, Eddie attended the show on closing night and left feeling so inspired by the actors' exuberant performance that at the cast party afterwards, Eddie sat down unbid at the piano and played a rousing accompaniment as Barry encored Snoopy's dance number. And then to the surprise of all, he joined Barry in tapping out the final dance steps. Eddie's improvised routine, though unpolished, was so buoyant and carefree that everyone agreed it perfectly captured the essence of Snoopy's character.

"I need some PDA," Barry said when he and Eddie were alone and getting ready to part for the night. As Eddie opened his arms for a hug, Barry stepped in and kissed him full on the lips, then signaled his intentions by pulling Eddie's hips close to his own. Startled, Eddie ignored the signal. He quickly released himself from the embrace, then smiled awkwardly and said goodbye. As he walked the moonlit campus back to his dorm, he tried telling himself that nothing happened, the kiss wasn't what it seemed, and neither he nor Barry had any intentions beyond the PDA that all members of their group freely exchanged. But Eddie couldn't explain his joyful beating heart, nor the elation resulting from reciprocated affection after so many years of silent longing and unrequited desire. Eddie was in love.

Eddie felt a curious shyness and dizzy anticipation as he waited for Barry the next day in biology class, then a rush of excitement when Barry walked through the door and took a seat beside him. Barry lightly stroked his arm and they exchanged conspiratorial glances. Eddie blushed, delighted. In many respects, their relationship continued as it had before. Lots of bantering in biology class and the lab. Group outings with their theater friends. Around others, neither Eddie nor Barry indicated by word or gesture they were more than the friends they always had been, but at the end of the day, when they were alone and it was time to go to their separate dorms, their passion grew increasingly unrestrained. "I need some PDA," Barry would say, looking around furtively to make sure they wouldn't be seen, and then the kissing would begin. Eddie no longer pushed away when Barry pulled him close, inciting arousal evident to both.

Eddie never dreamed he could be so happy. He thought about Barry constantly and found excuses to walk by Deseret Towers, where Barry lived. He vied for Barry's attention with their friends, and felt requited elation when Barry sent him a smile or touched his arm in a way that affirmed his affection. He waited impatiently for the evenings when they were together and he could run his fingers along the muscles on Barry's arms and feel the softness of Barry's lips on his. Finding time together alone on campus was difficult, and so they began meeting under a large oak by the Brimhall Building on the far edge of campus. The grounds there were poorly lit and only the most dedicated student scientists walked the paths or haunted the old campus buildings after dark. The giant oak, twisted and bent, cast an eerie shadow across the quad as Eddie and Barry hid beneath its branches and leaves. But even in the heat of passion, they listened for footsteps. The slightest noise would cause them to jump back and feign animated conversation. Once, while locked in embrace, they were caught unawares by a young professor creeping silently by.

"Hey, you two," he cried out. "You're in violation of university rules." The startled young men stumbled into the light and stared at the professor, open-mouthed and afraid to answer. "You know it's against the rules to walk on the grass," he shouted. "Get off now, before I report you."

Eddie and Barry looked at each other, relief on their faces, and sprinted away from the professor, laughing. "We're sorry, sir," Eddie called out as they fled. Barry bounded onto the paved walkway doing his Snoopy dance. Eddie skipped merrily behind.

"Some babies are born with the physical characteristics of both male and female," Brother Downy observed during his lecture on sexual anatomy. "In some cases, the male penis may be small, almost imperceptible, or the female clitoris may be abnormally large, the size of a small penis. Internally, these babies might have both ovarian and testicular tissues. They may not identify as either male or female until they are adults, if ever. We call these intersex babies."

"We call them perverts," a student whispered, causing a titter among those around him.

Brother Downy didn't dwell on the issue, though in answer to a question, he said doctors and parents often had to make the determination of the baby's sex, with surgery following birth to correct the defect.

"Snip, snip," the student said amid more laughter.

Eddie pondered the lecture for days. There was certainly no question regarding his sexual anatomy: his penis and testicles were the proper size. At puberty, hair began sprouting on his arms and legs, and by age eighteen, he was shaving. His aggressiveness and skill in sports evidenced the requisite levels of testosterone. Wet dreams came on schedule. In every aspect, his physical and emotional development as a male proceeded as normal—except for attraction to the opposite sex. He had never outgrown the boy crushes that were typical of pre-adolescence. *Is this somehow related to the same issues that caused intersex babies?* Eddie's biology textbook did not mention intersex, and so he searched the library's card catalogue file, where he found several books on the subject. However, when he went to the fourth-floor stacks, he found the books locked behind metal cages where rare and controversial books were shelved. He would have to ask a librarian for permission. Rather than face the prospect of answering embarrassing questions about why he wanted to view the book—and still being denied access—Eddie consulted Brother Downy.

"Your question about the causes of intersex among humans has a scientific answer, but of course, at the Lord's university, there's also a theological component mixed in as well," Brother Downy said. Long-faced and freckled, the biology professor spoke with no hint of judgment or suspicion of Eddie's motives in coming to him. "Most students want to know how intersex fits into God's plan of salvation. If we're already assigned a sex or gender in the preexistence, and then are sent to earth to find a mate of the opposite sex and raise children, how can God allow someone to be born who is neither fully male nor female and, therefore, lacks the necessary capabilities to fulfill God's commandment to multiply and replenish the earth?"

"Could one explain it as a genetic variation, the kind of random mutation that underlies evolution?" Eddie asked.

"Yes, it could be a mutation, but not one a scientist would call a good mutation. There are some examples of hermaphrodites in the animal kingdom, but for humans it serves no discernible purpose—in an evolutionary sense, that is."

"So how do you explain it?"

"I look upon it like a deformity, something gone haywire in the genetic code, like being born with a withered or non-functional limb. That occurs randomly too."

"And mental retardation?"

"That's clearly a defect. There's no advantage to it."

"But whether we call it a mutation or a defect, it's all part of God's plan. Is that what you're saying?"

"Ah, now you're getting into the mysteries, Eddie. Are you familiar with the parable of Jesus and the blind man in the gospel of St. John?" Without waiting for an answer, Brother Downy stood and pulled a worn copy of the Bible from his bookshelf. He quickly found the passage he was looking for and, still standing, began reading. "And as Jesus passed by, he saw a man who was blind from his birth. And his disciples asked him, saying, Master, who did sin, this man, or his parents, that he was born blind? And Jesus answered, Neither hath this man sinned, nor his parents, but that the works of God should be made manifest in him."

Brother Downy's voice quivered with emotion as he finished. He sat back at his desk, still holding the Bible. "As I've openly acknowledged in class, I believe God works through eternal laws and that evolution is one of those laws. Consequently, genetic variation, mutation, and natural selection are the divine means by which this earth and all the flora and fauna, including mankind, developed over the eons. These evolutionary processes sometimes produce non-standard, even undesirable outcomes. I can explain to you scientifically why some people are born blind or mentally retarded or sexually ambiguous, but I can't explain why God allows it to happen."

"But as Jesus said, it's not the fault of those people. Right?"

"Of course not. I would not want to be born with mental retardation or some other defect, nor would I want my children to be hindered in this way. And yet, parents of such children describe them as a blessing and gift from God. Our job is to love them."

"And accept them as they are?"

Brother Downy frowned. "Not necessarily," he said. "After all, Jesus healed the blind man. We also should do everything in our power to fix the defects people are born with and help them, as much as possible, to live the kind of lives that God would have all of us live."

"But not everyone, not every defect, can be fixed. What if we can't fix them?"

"Then we still love them," Brother Downy said. Eddie had his answer.

In the days following his meeting with Brother Downy, Eddie became increasingly emboldened by the sweet pleasure of Barry's embrace, lingering over kisses, exploring Barry's face and lips with the light touch of his fingertips. Maybe it was desperation, but with the end of the school year only a month away, the thought of separation ignited passion and panic. Short, furtive hugs and kisses behind darkened walls or under a tree, once ecstasy, now frustrated Eddie. He gently pushed Barry against the old oak.

"Don't, please," Barry said as Eddie reached inside Barry's shirt and moved his hand across his chest.

"Don't you like it?" Eddie purred.

Barry grasped Eddie's wrists and pushed them away. "Of course I do," he said. He carefully tucked in his shirt. "But this is too risky."

"Then let's go somewhere where we don't have to worry about being seen."

"What do you mean?"

"Up the canyon or to the mountains," Eddie said. "We could borrow someone's car. There are plenty of guys in Stover Hall who'd lend me a car."

Barry stepped away. "I don't know, Eddie. If we got caught, that'd be the end of everything."

"But we won't get caught, not if we're far enough away from campus."

Barry lowered his eyes. "It's not just that. It's . . . it's that what we're doing right now is bad enough. If we start going further, we'll be disfellowshipped or excommunicated. They'd never let a homosexual serve a mission."

Eddie blanched. In all their conversations, neither he nor Barry had ever uttered the word "homosexual." They had been sitting together at a university assembly when BYU President Ernest L. Wilkinson publicly castigated homosexuals and invited those harboring homosexual proclivities to leave the campus, pledging full refunds. "Get out now, before we kick you out," he declared. A short, stocky man with a gnome-like face, Wilkinson asked the 13,000 students packed in the bleacher seats to signify their support for the university's rules by standing. Eddie rose from his seat, trying to persuade himself that the university president wasn't really speaking about him. Barry stood with him. Eddie wondered if Barry felt the same ambivalence, but he was afraid to ask, afraid to assign that name to their relationship. But the assembly had occurred many months ago, and Eddie had grown more comfortable with their friendship, especially since talking with Brother Downey. Still, hearing Barry say the word aloud—"homosexual"—made it seem degraded and obscene.

"Do you think what we're doing is wrong?" Eddie asked.

"We both know it is."

"Listen, Barry, I talked to Brother Downy, our biology teacher, and he says—"

"You talked about us?"

"No, no. We talked about intersex humans."

"We're not intersex."

"Will you shut up and listen to me," Eddie said. "Of course, we're not intersex. But it's the same principle. Something went wrong, maybe not at birth, but at puberty, when we were supposed to start liking girls, but we kept on liking boys."

"Did Brother Downy say that? Did he say that about homosexuals?"

"Well, no. But it's the same principle as intersex, you see—"

"I don't want to talk about it," Barry said, hanging his head.

Eddie lifted Barry's chin. "Look at me. I love you. How can that be wrong?"

Barry started to cry. "Don't say that, Eddie. Don't ever say that. We can't be in love. Not us."

"Who says we can't?" Eddie said, quietly at first, then forcefully. "Who says we can't?"

"Everyone. Our parents, our friends, our church leaders, the Bible, and God Himself. Our Heavenly Father says it's wrong."

Eddie stared at Barry, angry but unable to speak. He was angry with Barry for refusing to accept his logic, for refusing to accept his love, but mainly because Barry was right. Theirs was a homosexual relationship. There was no escaping the guilt or shame. And with that acknowledgment, years of inner turmoil and angst burned at his throat. "So why did God make us this way?" he shouted, his mouth twisted with resentment. "If God didn't want us to be like this, then why—"

"I don't know."

"Look at us, Barry. Is there really something wrong with us?"

Barry looked up, quivering. He fell into Eddie's arms and both men sobbed, leaning together as they slumped against the old oak, now full of budding leaves. A warm breeze caressed their tears, announcing the approaching summer. The clouds shifted, revealing a darkened sky, and Eddie gazed at the halfmoon lighting the mountains overlooking the university. He was surprised not by the depth of his sadness but by his anger—at the church, at God, and even at Barry. It was the brash, unconventional Barry who had qualms about their relationship and worried about consequences, while he, Eddie, always the essence of propriety, wanted to push it to the precipice. Just then a group of students walked by and Eddie pulled Barry closer, as if to make his point, before they broke apart.

"I never thought you'd be the reckless one," Barry said, wiping his eyes.

"Or you the man in the gray flannel suit," Eddie replied.

Barry shook his head ruefully. "Yeah, now you know. My carefree, jovial smile is a mask for heartbreak. I'm really like everyone else, a normal human being with a combustible mix of secrets and insecurities eating up his insides."

"If we were a boy-and-girl couple, no one would care about what we're doing and there'd be no problem or question of allowing us to go on missions," Eddie said.

Barry's eyes brimmed with sorrow. "Yeah, but we're not."

The next weeks passed quickly as finals week approached. Their friends talked of submitting their mission papers, joking awkwardly about confessing their sins to their bishops before getting approval. Someone claimed you got put on probation for three months for heavy petting. "Confess now, so you can go on your mission by the end of the summer," he said. "If you went all the way with a girl, well, you're in deep trouble, because you have to wait a whole year after confessing to sexual intercourse before they'll let you go."

"What about making out?" Eddie asked. The others laughed. You're good to go, they said. You don't even have to bring it up in confession. Eddie knew the pre-mission confession weighed heavily on Barry. He had been less animated and playful, more pensive, and, especially, less affectionate in recent days. Eddie couldn't wait to tell him they were in the clear.

The next time their group got together, Kenneth, a new boy from Barry's dorm, joined them in the lounge after dinner. It was evident from the way Kenneth and Barry whispered and laughed conspiratorially, exchanging witticisms with their friends, that this was not their first time together. *Is this why Barry had seemed so remote*, Eddie wondered. *Has he found a new boyfriend or is he trying to make me jealous?* If the latter, Barry was succeeding. Eddie felt crushing misery as Barry directed smiles toward Kenneth, entertaining him with flirtatious gestures and intimate asides normally reserved for Eddie. Eddie tried to get Barry alone, saying he had something important to tell him. "I found out we don't have to worry about confessing. All we did was kiss. We can go on missions just like everyone else," he said.

Eddie looked expectantly at Barry, certain he would be buoyed by the good news. Instead, Barry gave him a blank stare. "Hey, Eddie," Barry said loudly for everyone to hear. "Play Snoopy's song on the piano. I want to teach Kenneth the dance steps."

"I can't play it without the music," Eddie replied sullenly. It was a lie. Eddie had memorized it the night after he and Barry had danced together. He regarded it as their song.

Barry laughed. "Oh, well," he said, turning away. "Come here, Kenneth. I need some PDA."

Eddie, who had never before had a boyfriend, never given his heart to another, experienced the jolting agony of a lover spurned. He watched Kenneth wrap Barry in a tender hug and say something in Barry's ear. Barry laughed and whispered something back. Eddie couldn't make himself look away. A scalding bile, frothy with resentment, welled up inside. As he quietly left the room, he saw Barry peering at him over Kenneth's shoulder. Eddie pounded the walkway with righteous fury as he crossed the campus to his dorm. Too angry to cry, he counted the numerous ways Barry had humiliated him. Barry didn't just break up with him; he had tried to hurt him. Eddie determined to hurt him back, so he wrote a short note demonstrating he could end the relationship with even sharper clarity than Barry had. He agonized over each draft, vacillating between vindictive outrage and sad resignation before settling on calculated indifference. He handed Barry the note when he arrived at biology class the following Monday:

Barry:

I have immensely enjoyed our friendship, but as the semester comes to an end, I realize other matters rise to higher importance. As you know, I have always planned to go on a mission at the end of the current school year, and so now I need to concentrate on my mission preparations while also making sure I do not neglect my studies. Also, I know you have some serious personal problems that need attention without the complications of our friendship. Consequently, it would be for the best if I curtail my current association with you and our group, so outside activities do not distract me from my responsibilities and plans.

I wish you luck in your future endeavors.

Best regards,

Eddie

Eddie's throat tightened when he saw Barry and he had to choke back a sob, but once he handed over the note, he felt cool satisfaction. Eddie realized now he had let his heart overrule his head and put his church status in jeopardy. While he had not felt an overwhelming desire to serve a mission, he knew there would be no explaining to his parents a decision not to go. He would hear not end of it from his brothers and friends, not to mention his church leaders, all of them questioning the depth of his testimony. He also knew—as he had always known—that homosexuality was wrong. Fortunately, he told himself, his relationship with Barry had not ventured into forbidden territory; ending the relationship put him back on his preordained gospel path after a misguided but inconsequential detour. It had been a dalliance. Nothing more. A person is what he does, not what he feels, and he had done nothing that would make him unworthy for a mission.

Barry rarely came to biology class after receiving the note, and when he did, he sat on the opposite side of the auditorium. Eddie pretended not to notice. He looked forward to a long summer at home before his mission to help him forget the whole experience, but on the last day of class before finals, Barry dropped a note onto Eddie's desk: "I must talk with you before you leave. Please meet me tonight at 10:00 p.m. under the large oak by the Brimhall Building. I won't pressure you. I only want to talk." Eddie looked up to see Barry standing in the doorway, his eyes pleading for an affirmative answer. Afraid of the confrontation that might arise if he declined, Eddie nodded yes.

Eddie's apprehension in meeting with Barry soon gave way to an unexpected feeling of elation. Barry wanted him back! Eddie could see it in Barry's hang-dog face and forlorn eyes. Eddie felt vindication, his wounded feelings salved, his pride restored. Would he take Barry back? No, that would be impossible, not now that Eddie had accepted the fact he must go on a mission. He couldn't let anything jeopardize that. Besides, he had not forgotten his humiliation. From now on, he would closely guard his heart—from Barry, from everyone. Still, it wouldn't hurt to hear what Barry had to say. Let him lay out his feelings and make himself vulnerable before shutting the door to further contact. Eddie dressed smartly, wanting to look his best, a crooked smile on his face as he combed his hair. The feeling was as satisfying as love itself.

Eddie left Stover Hall shortly before ten o'clock and made the long walk up the dark ramp overlooking the baseball diamond and past the president's residence to the Brimhall Building. He carried an umbrella, but an overcast sky, backlit by the moon, was all that remained from a drizzling evening rain. The gnarled oak, its leaves glistening in the mist, cast a jagged shadow stretching across the dewy grass like a bony finger beckoning to Eddie. He could see Barry standing beside the tree, hands in his pockets, one leg bent and resting against the trunk. Eddie's heart jumped at the familiar sight.

"Hello, Eddie," Barry said with a smile, insouciant and disarming.

Eddie's angry intentions instantly melted away. "Oh, Barry. Why do I find you so charming?"

"Come here, Eddie. I need some PDA."

"You *are* an irresistible rogue," Eddie said, laughing. He grabbed Barry by the hips and pulled him close, eager to feel their mutual arousal. They kissed passionately. Eddie had lost himself completely in the emotional and physical excitement when suddenly he heard rapid footsteps and opened his eyes to see a bright light shining in his face.

"Edward Pedersen," a voice growled, "You're under arrest for soliciting homosexual activity on the university campus. Do not try to flee. You will only compound your trouble. Other BYU security officers are nearby to prevent your escape."

The security officer gestured to Barry, who hurriedly walked away. "Barry! What's happening?" Eddie shouted, shielding his eyes from the light. The sound of sirens brought flashing red lights. Doors flung open. Hard shoes pounded against the pavement and onto the grass.

"Get down on the ground and put your hands behind your head where we can see them."

"Barry," Eddie cried again, tears starting to flow. He kneeled on the wet grass as university security officers from the patrol car gathered around him, congratulating themselves on another successful bust. One of them handcuffed Eddie's hands behind his back. Two others lifted him by the elbows from the ground. "Nothing happened," Eddie insisted. "I'm innocent. I only came to talk."

The officers led Eddie across the grass. One of them put a firm hand on top of his head and pushed him into the back seat of their car. Eddie was sobbing uncontrollably but couldn't wipe his eyes or nose. His stomach ached as if shards of glass were churning inside. "I didn't do anything," he screamed over and over. The door slammed shut and he was gripped by suffocating panic. He swung his head back and forth hysterically, flinging tears and saliva in every direction. He kicked his feet violently against the front seat, trying to get the officers' attention, trying to make them understand. "I didn't do anything!" he cried.

Eddie marveled at how his mind wandered. Eddie had awakened to anxious thoughts about leaving his proselytizing area, but while trying to get back to sleep, he somehow had traveled to the darkest regions of his memory, where he relived his most humiliating experiences. He tried to imagine how Edvard Munch would depict him as he lay there. Munch would probably paint Eddie's blue duvet with vague outlines, alluding to its folds with a few brush strokes here and there, while focusing a light—perhaps the reflection from his alarm clock—on Eddie's face, whose grotesque features, as painted by Munch, would personify Eddie's alienation and shame. *Eddie Pedersen as the subject of an Edvard Munch painting! It's enough to make me want to scream,* Eddie thought, smiling ruefully to himself.

Chapter 4

Watch your personal appearance. Be conventional in hairdos and the clothing you wear. Let your sincere personality as a testifier of Jesus Christ attract desirable attention, not your antics or undesirable appearance.

Conduct of a Missionary

Elder Orrin Tanner listened to his companion's rhythmic breathing, steady and calm. *Was Elder Pedersen really unfazed by the thought of leaving their proselytizing area?* Leaving had been Orrin's idea; if Elder Pedersen had objected to going, Orrin would not have pressed the issue. Now that the day had finally arrived, Orrin was seized by nervous, feverish excitement, perhaps wishing that his companion had objected. Still, they would be gone only one week, two at the most—too short of a time to be missed. Harstad's lone church member was deployed to the north along the Barents Sea on a NATO assignment and wouldn't return for three weeks. Orrin and Elder Pedersen would be back before anyone noticed they were gone. Orrin wondered whether his decision was inspired. *Can a person be inspired to break a mission rule when the mission rules themselves are inspired?*

Orrin decided to write down the question while it was fresh in his mind. He rolled out of his duvet and placed his bare feet on the ice-cold floor, immediately regretting the decision he and Elder Pedersen had made to keep their bedroom window slightly ajar and their room unheated like many Norwegians they knew. He walked briskly to the living room, which, though only slightly warmer, was at least tolerable. He pulled his Inspirational Thought Book from his briefcase. The idea for the Thought Book came from the assistants. "You have every right to receive inspiration for your investigators," Edler Ward had said as he handed the missionaries small notebooks that were to serve as their Thought Books. "The Lord has given you stewardship over your assigned proselytizing area just as the prophet has been given stewardship—and the right to revelation—over the church. Magnify your calling by keeping a record of your inspired thoughts."

Much to Orrin's chagrin, Elder Ward had criticized his first entry. Orrin wrote: "We as missionaries must be as open to new ideas and truths as we expect Norwegians to be when we knock on their doors." Orrin had been so pleased with his axiom that he shared it with Elder Ward, who frowned, his eyes narrowing, after reading Orrin's so-called inspired thought. "If a person already has the truth, as we in the church surely do, then anything new or outside of that truth can only come from the devil,"

Elder Ward said. "And we certainly don't want to be open to that, do we?" Orrin felt obligated to agree. "Obedience to the existing mission rules and church doctrines, not openness to new worldly ideas, is the surest way to mission success," Elder Ward added.

What is mission success? Orrin wondered. *Is it baptisms or, alternatively, personal inspiration?* He jotted down the question in his Thought Book but this time did not show it to Elder Ward. Orrin would have preferred to experience inspiration rather than baptisms, though he knew that would be selfish. It didn't matter, though, because he had experienced neither. Still, he had not given up his quest for divine revelation. Ever since Orrin had heard the story of the biblical prophet Samuel, he had longed to receive similar revelation—to hear God's audible voice speak to him, as God had spoken to Samuel.

Orrin was ten years old when he first learned how the young Samuel had earned God's favor. Recognized as one of Israel's greatest prophets, Samuel appointed his people's judges and kings while guiding them with wisdom and commands coming directly from God. "This Samuel, this man who was mighty in the Lord," said Sister Beemer, Orrin's Sunday School teacher, "received his first call to service when he was but a boy. One night, while fast asleep, Samuel was awakened by the voice of God calling his name. 'Speak, Lord, for thy servant heareth,' Samuel replied, and God revealed many wondrous things to him."

Shy and lacking confidence, Orrin seized upon Samuel's story as a roadmap for his own life, a life of purpose in which he played a central role in God's eternal plan. And why not? If God numbers every hair on a man's head, and if not even a sparrow falls to earth without God taking notice, then surely, young Orrin thought, God knew him, watched him, prepared for him the way ahead. Holding up a picture of the devout Israelite boy bathed in God's gleaming light, Sister Beemer suggested that Samuel was no older than the ten-year-old boys and girls sitting in the classroom when God called his name. Samuel's story fired Orrin's soul with the expectation that someday he, too, would receive a heavenly manifestation of God's existence. Did God not promise revelation to all who obeyed His commandments?

Despite his lofty ambitions, Orrin Andreassen Tanner lived what people in the town of Seth would call a normal childhood. Normal meant going to church every Sunday and singing hymns and handing out the Sunday School programs as ward members entered the chapel. It meant being ordained to the priesthood when you were twelve and ironing your suit pants and carrying the sacrament trays and memorizing scriptures so you could earn your Duty to God Award. Most of all, it meant saving money for a mission. All the Mormon boys planned to go on missions. Not a week went by without someone reminding them of their future calling. "Every worthy young man with a testimony should serve a mission," Bishop Pulsipher told the teenage boys. They sat together on the front row of the chapel, backs pressed against the unforgiving benches, and listened to the bishop thump the pulpit. "And if you don't have a testimony, you should still go," he said. "There's no better way to get a testimony of this church than to go on a mission."

The Vietnam War was heating up. The boys watched the reports on the nightly news, and they glanced occasionally at the newspaper photos of American soldiers hauling wounded comrades to safety, but none anticipated having to fight. And none ever did. Not from Seth, anyway. No one Orrin knew was ever drafted or enlisted. Mormon boys were ordained to a higher calling, and God prepared a way through missionary deferments for them to carry scriptures instead of guns. That's not to say the people of Seth didn't support the war. They backed it one hundred percent. There were no draft dodgers or conscientious objectors among them. "We believe in being subject to kings, presidents, and rulers, and in obeying the laws of the land," Bishop Pulsipher declared. A short, stout man, the bishop viewed the world through a lens circumscribed by Seth's small-town boundaries. "Keep your hair cut short," he told the young men. "We're not protesting anything."

While others of their generation were either marching off to war or protesting against it, Seth's young men prepared to become missionaries. "Be in the world, but not of it," Bishop Pulsipher advised.

Orrin's mission to Norway was foreordained by God, even before Orrin was born. That's what Orrin's Grandpa Heber said. Orrin was born on June 17, 1951, in Seth. The small town located almost precisely in Utah's geographic center had been settled by his great-grandfather a century earlier. Orrin's parents, Anson and Sarah Tanner, named him after Grandpa Heber's younger brother, Orrin, who was killed in a bank robbery. Anson had vied with his brother, Porter, to be first to name a son after their much beloved Uncle Orrin. Grandpa Heber said the Lord must have intended for Anson to have the honor because Porter had nothing but daughters until Orrin was born. Thereafter, Porter had nothing but sons. After Grandpa Heber baptized Orrin on his eighth birthday, he brushed the wet hair from Orrin's face and, suddenly tearful, lifted the boy from the water and brought him close to his face. "Everyone who knew my brother Orrin said he would have accomplished extraordinary things—even become an apostle—had he not been called to a mission in the spirit world. You are destined for the earthly missions my brother could not fulfill," Grandpa Heber said, his lone eye blazing with conviction. Orrin shivered in his white baptismal clothes.

"Isn't that right, Dad?" This was Orrin's constant refrain when he discussed church history and doctrine with his father, who taught classes full-time in the church's seminary program, which allowed students at local high schools to go off campus and attend daily, one-hour religious courses. Anson also published numerous pamphlets untangling knotty issues relating to Mormon history and doctrine and was gaining a following among rank-and-file church members who used the pamphlets' inspirational stories to supplement Sunday School lessons and church talks. At dinner, Orrin's father would review with his young son some of the issues discussed in his pamphlets or questions he got from students, much to his mother's dismay. "Orrin's too young for the mysteries," Sarah would say. Anson scoffed at the notion, while Orrin begged his mom to relent. "I can understand. Isn't that right, Dad?"

Orrin's growing knowledge of esoteric church teachings and history gave him confidence and pride, as if his father were inviting him into a secret club. In truth, Orrin was diffident and self-conscious, even among friends, often stumbling over his words when trying to make himself heard. His gospel expertise set him apart, at least in his own eyes, as someone with merit, even as he stood on the sidelines watching fellow students gather together in cliques and gossip about who liked whom or debate which rock band was the best. Religious doctrine ranked low on the list of teenage conversation topics. However, Orrin's expertise became handy—and brought him a much praise—when he competed in Scripture Chases with fellow students. Everyone wanted Orrin on their team for the Scripture Chases, which were essentially trivia contests testing their gospel knowledge. The contests gave Orrin a sense of belonging, though he still hovered around the edges of the teenage cliques at church as well as at school. He admired his father's erudition and wanted to be like him, a confident, respected gospel scholar who attracted more than a hundred people to his gospel lesson courses for adults. When Orrin gave talks in Sunday School, he would push back his wavy, dark hair and strike an orator's pose not unlike his father's. And in those talks, after quoting a scripture or offering doctrinal insights, he would turn to his father and give him a look that said, "Isn't that right, Dad?"

In Orrin's junior year, he became friends with Joe Prichard. Handsome and with a rogue smile, Joe was a natural leader whose willingness to flout the rules made him appear daring and mature, qualities that drew other boys to him. Orrin felt his status was tenuous, and so he hung quietly, careful not to say or do anything that might get him expelled from Joe's tight circle of friends. Joe's crowd shared an instinctive love of amusement, leading to diverse temptations. Together they sneaked away from a Scout Jamboree and smoked hollow reeds by the swamp, feigning sophistication as they puffed smoke rings. At the church welfare farm, they knocked down ladders and left their friends stranded in apple trees. As deacons, they put salt in the sacrament water and wrote insults in the margins of the Sunday School programs they passed out to the congregation: "Hey, cheapskate, your tithing check bounced" and "Your husband has a secret plural wife." Orrin hesitantly joined in, despite fears these pranks might jeopardize his standing with God, but his desire for belonging trumped his youthful pangs of conscience. He also feared his father's disapproval should he find out. He never did.

At fourteen, Orrin felt the first urges of manhood. They did not come as soon or as strong as they did with the other boys, who, when among themselves, freely speculated about whose breasts were larger and who they would like to do it with. Orrin was unsure whether "do it" meant going all the way. Like everything else, Orrin stood on the sidelines, not particularly concerned with sex and quite baffled by his friends' obsessions. He was waiting for the right girl whom he could impress with his gospel knowledge, but the girls, like the boys, talked only of unfathomable, superficial things. Orrin felt guilty listening to the boys' banter. Even talking about sex brought him into conflict with the scripture in Proverbs: "As man thinketh in his heart, so is he." God had commanded against committing adultery or "anything like unto it," a phrase understood to include necking and petting. Some church authorities also forbade goodnight kisses. "A slippery slope," they said. Orrin's priesthood leaders set the bar high, expecting their youth to stand as a bulwark against the free-love heresy sweeping the nation. "God judges us not by our actions alone, but by our thoughts and desires as well," Bishop Pulsipher told the young adults at a Saturday night youth conference. "Immorality of the heart is a grave sin."

Orrin never acted on these desires—not that he ever had the chance. He never asked a girl out on a date, and the one dance he attended, he stood silent with other wallflowers, passing the time by fantasizing about which girls he would like to dance with. Many of his friends had steady dates. Joe had a new girlfriend each month. The boys listened with cool teenage indifference to the stern warnings from church leaders denouncing sexual immorality. Joe developed an elaborate philosophical justification that got him around the Church's broad definition of sexual activity. "The only thing that's really a sin is sexual intercourse. That's what church leaders are trying to prevent," he explained. "And so they put up all of these fences around it. No kissing, no making out, no petting. No whatever. But sex is the only thing that's really a sin in all of this. The rest are just firebreaks. That's why you don't see anything against kissing or petting or any of that other stuff in the Bible."

Joe suffered none of Orrin's ambivalence about sexual matters. He could tell a dirty joke or speculate about which girls might "do it" without a trace of guilt. Saturday nights he specialized in necking and petting, but Sunday mornings he rose early to prepare and bless the sacrament, showing no awareness of the conflict between the spirit and the flesh. The two enemies coexisted peacefully in his soul. Orrin found comfort in this aspect of Joe's character. Joe's easy conscience and ability to reconcile God and mammon helped alleviate the contradictions preying upon Orrin's mind.

Despite his adolescent turmoil, Orrin knew where his future lay. His destiny never was so clear as the night when he turned sixteen and his father ordained him a priest. They both spoke at sacrament meeting. Orrin talked about sustaining the prophet and the blessings of obedience, with scriptures and stories from church magazines his parents helped him find. He had grown to nearly six feet, with a stout build like the Tanner men, but with his mother's dark features, including her coal-black, curly hair, and his father's unusually square jaw. Orrin spoke deliberately, trying to sound authoritative, nervously pressing his heavily waxed hair to stop it from retreating into tightly wound coils. Everyone agreed he would make a fine missionary.

His father, Anson, spoke on the subject of prayer. The stories he told were personal, especially concerning his desire to have a large family. Anson and Sarah initially had trouble conceiving. They fasted and prayed, saw medical specialists, and Sarah received a special blessing from Grandpa Heber promising her a fruitful womb. Finally, after three years, Sarah became pregnant with Orrin, and they thought the Lord's blessing of a full quiver would follow. But it was not to be. Anson told the congregation that while preparing his talk, he reflected upon his desire for more children, and before going to bed asked the Lord why his righteous prayer had not been answered. "That night I had the most vivid dream," he said. "I dreamed I was picking apples from a gloriously white tree. I set aside three of the apples by the tree, looked away momentarily, and when I turned around, I saw two men holding a newborn baby. The first man was my grandfather, Lars Andreassen, who cradled and rocked the baby and then passed it on to the next man, my father, Heber Tanner. My father cradled and rocked the child and then handed it to me. The child was my son, Orrin.

"Lars pointed to my baby and said, 'This young spirit is a child of God and precious in His sight. Unto whom much is given, much is required. Watch over this child, nurture him, and raise him in the ways of truth, that he may become mighty and strong in the Lord.'"

The dream ended and Anson awoke. "The answer to my prayer," he told the congregation, "was right before me all along." He turned and looked tenderly at his son. Orrin's chest heaved with a vague sensation that it was filling with light.

That night, before retiring, Orrin knelt by his bedroom window and ruminated on his father's dream. Myriad stars shone in the cloudless sky. God seemed more real to Orrin than anytime he could remember. And more than anything, he wanted revelation—visions and dreams and a thunderclap of voices from heaven. He wanted to be like the Prophet Joseph Smith and Lars Andreassen and Grandpa Heber and his dad and all those who proclaimed certain knowledge that they had been chosen for a special mission.

A shooting star disappeared over a mountain peak. To the west a lone star burned radiantly above the others. Was this Kolob, the place where the Prophet Joseph said God dwelt? "Here I am, Lord," Orrin said, his eyes fixed upon the star. "Speak, for thy servant heareth."

Kolob pulsed with fire and life.

One evening, Orrin overheard his parents in loud argument. "That was long ago," Anson said, his voice rising. "I see no point in rehashing the issue."

But rehash it they did. Orrin learned that his father's older brother, Porter, had initially tried to break up Anson's engagement to Orrin's mother, Sarah. She had grown up in a series of Midwest foster homes and had no idea who her parents were. Porter thought Anson, then a young Army private fresh out of gunnery school and bound for Europe, was rushing into marriage. Porter worried that Sarah had converted to Mormonism without conviction and, even worse, had unknown and possibly defective lineage. "What happens if you marry her and later find out she has Negro ancestors?" Porter asked. "Where will your posterity be then?"

Anson lashed out at his brother. "You're a bigot!"

"No," Porter replied calmly. "I'm just being realistic."

Suspicions were not allayed until Orrin's Grandpa Heber gave his mom a patriarchal blessing proclaiming that she was born through the sacred lineage of the ancient biblical prophets Ephraim and Joseph—the same as the Tanners. The blessing placated Porter and cordial relations were subsequently established, at least for appearance's sake, but Porter's bruising accusation occasionally burned in Sarah like an old scar, as did the doubts he had sown about her ancestry.

"What if Porter was right?" Sarah sobbed. A tall, large-boned woman with a dark complexion and sturdy in every regard, she rarely showed emotion, but that night her tears flowed.

Anson crossed his arms impatiently. "You're being irrational, Sarah. My dad is satisfied—I'm satisfied. Even Porter is satisfied. You should be too." Anson gave his wife a stiff hug.

A week later, when Orrin knew his father was alone in his study, he approached Anson at his desk. "Is Mom a . . . am I," Orrin stammered. "Are Mom and I Negroes?

"What!? Why would you even ask such a question?"

"I overheard you and Mom arguing about it, about what Uncle Porter said."

Orrin expected his father to answer with the same measured equanimity that he discussed church doctrines and practices with Orrin. Instead Anson's face darkened and he spoke in a harsh, disapproving tone. "Stop it! Stop your ridiculous questioning right now! Thanks to your uncle, I have to deal constantly with your mother's obsessive fears regarding this issue. I will not have you also unsettled or consumed by Uncle Porter's thoughtless remark, so please put this out of your mind. Grandpa Heber's patriarchal blessing settled it. Do you understand? He settled it. I want you never to ask me about this again."

Orrin nodded his agreement, persuaded at least momentarily by his father's emphatic assertion. But his father's uncharacteristically violent outburst left the impression that something else must be wrong, perhaps related to a nascent controversy over his father's church pamphlets, which his father later would be forced to publicly disavow. Even worse, Orrin thought, maybe there was something wrong with Orrin himself but which his father was loath to reveal. Orrin retained his fervent desire for revelation and indisputable knowledge of God's approval, but his father's tirade opened a gulf between father and son, the beginning of a trust broken, and planted seeds of self-doubt that plagued Orrin whenever he felt himself falling short of the mark.

Orrin closed his Inspirational Thought Book and placed it back in his briefcase. Tomorrow he would ask Elder Pedersen whether he thought God would inspire a person to undertake an action that placed that person at odds with another of God's commandments. Could it not be similar to a person breaking a law—say, for example, speeding on the interstate to rush a critically injured person to the hospital—to save a life? A higher law supersedes a lesser law. Orrin hurried back to his bed and burrowed under his duvet, pulling it over his head to hold inside his warming breath. A minute later, he poked his nose out from his duvet and fell into a disquieting sleep.

Chapter 5

You cannot afford to disappoint your companions or loved ones by becoming a failure, or by doing less than your best at all times.

Conduct of a Missionary

President Toressen swept his desk clean, using his hand to push the last dinner crumbs into the waste basket. After wiping his hands with a handkerchief, he took a sheet of paper from the drawer and began jotting notes for the points he wanted to make. Beside the number one, he wrote, *They are wonderful boys.* He thought a moment, then crossed it out and wrote, *You have raised a wonderful son. You should be proud.* Toressen crossed out this one too. *I should say something more specific about their sons, something to give them hope,* he thought. Take Elder Tanner, for example. The hardest working missionary in Norway. Completely dedicated and never causing any problems (except for his out-of-character meltdown at the last district conference). And Elder Pedersen, such a generous, self-effacing companion to every missionary with whom he has served. Yes, his unique problem still troubled him. *Maybe if the church would leave boys like him alone, they might more easily find their way; of course, that's not for me to decide, but the important thing is that your son remains on the strait and narrow path to redemption.*

Pounding at the door aroused President Toressen from his reverie.

"Bjørn! It's eleven o'clock. Time for bed," his wife called from the family quarters. She was emphatic but not irritated. *A good sign,* Toressen thought. Still, he couldn't delay any longer. He picked up the phone and dialed the number given to him by the mission secretary.

"Hello?" It was a man's voice.

"Ah, hello," Toressen said cheerfully. "Is this Brother Anson Tanner, father of Elder Orrin Tanner?"

"Yes."

"This is President Bjørnstjerne Toressen of the Norwegian Mission. It is a pleasure to talk with you, Brother Tanner. I have read all of your publications and just by knowing your son, I feel like I know you very well."

"Thank you."

"And I must tell you, Brother Tanner, your son is surely one of the most dedicated missionaries it has been my pleasure to serve with. Did you know that Elder Tanner—I mean Orrin, of course—accompanied me on my last conference tour as my personal scribe, just like Oliver Cowdery, the church's first scribe. Not that I'm Joseph Smith, not by any means. Nobody who has seen me try to lead this mission would mistake me for Joseph Smith. That is certain."

"Orrin did tell me about serving as your secretary," Anson said. "It's been one of the highlights of his mission. His mother and I appreciate the unique opportunity you gave him."

"Did he tell you why I asked him to write down my talks? I wanted to record my visions and spiritual experiences the Lord has blessed me with—and surely, they are a blessing. They might be appropriate for publication as one of your faith-promoting pamphlets. You see—"

"Bjørnstjerne!" The door to President Toressen's office flung open and Sister Toressen scowled in the doorway. Tube-shaped curlers surrounded her head like a pink helmet. "Don't you know what time it is?"

"Shhhhhh." President Toressen put his hand over the receiver and whispered, "I'm talking to Elder Tanner's father . . . from Utah."

"Why is he calling at this hour?"

"*I* called him," Toressen said, still whispering. "He is the father of one of our missing missionaries." Sister Toressen's face softened and she mouthed *sorry* before quietly leaving the room.

When President Toressen returned to his call, Anson said, "I'm sorry, President, but I'm not publishing my pamphlets anymore. I thought Orrin told you. He was pretty upset about it, so maybe he was waiting for the right moment to say something."

Toressen was momentarily quiet, surprised, wondering why Orrin would be upset. "Oh, that's okay," he said at last. "My stories get a lot of people riled up anyway."

"How's Orrin doing?"

"That's why I called," Toressen said, still sounding cheerful. "He is a fine missionary, one of our best, but we haven't been able to locate him lately."

"What?"

"I'm sure it is nothing to be alarmed about."

"You mean you don't you know where he is?"

"He has been sending in his reports regularly, so I don't think we need to worry, but he and his companion appear to have left their assigned area and—"

President Toressen heard Brother Tanner shouting to someone in the background, "Get on the phone. Get on the phone. It's the mission president. Orrin's missing. Get on the phone!"

Sister Tanner joined the conversation from another line and President Toressen explained from the beginning the circumstances that led him to conclude Elder Tanner and Elder Pedersen had left their tracting area. "Has Elder Tanner mentioned anything in his letters to you indicating where he might be working?" Toressen asked.

"No, we got a letter Wednesday"—it was Tuesday, his wife said—"Okay, Tuesday. We got a letter on Tuesday from Harstad. Isn't that where he's supposed to be?"

"Yes, but the problem is, he and his companion aren't staying at their Harstad apartment anymore, but they haven't told us where they've gone."

Brother and Sister Tanner began talking at once, their voices a cacophony of concern. President Toressen spoke calmly, assuring them that their son was okay, that there probably was a mix-up of some kind or maybe Elder Tanner and his companion thought they had good reason for proselytizing in a new area. "We tell our missionaries to follow the spirit, and that is probably what your son is doing," Toressen said. He truly believed it. "If you gave me one hundred missionaries like Elder Tanner, why, we could—"

Toressen stopped, and his voice came through the line like a wistful song, "You know, when the missionaries go out tracting, they like to encourage each other by saying, 'Knock 'em dead.' I know it's just an expression, but I tell the missionaries, 'We're not in the business of killing but of restoring life, eternal life.' I tell them, I say, 'Elders and Sisters, you are not knocking on doors. You are knocking on hearts.' And so, if I had one hundred missionaries like Elder Tanner, I could—"

"Bjørnstjerne! Get off the phone and come to bed."

President Toressen turned in his chair to block out the pounding on the door and glanced at his watch. "I am sorry," he told Brother and Sister Tanner, "but it is nearly midnight here and I have another phone call to make, but don't you worry, we'll get to the bottom of this. I am sure Elder Tanner and his companion are fine. We'll let you know first thing when we hear from him." Toressen started to hang up and then remembered his scribbled note. "You have raised a wonderful son. You should be proud," he said before pushing down on the receiver.

President Toressen's second call did not go nearly as well. He spoke only with Elder Pedersen's father, who feared his son may have instigated the trouble. "I only hope he hasn't brought down another missionary with his . . . moral problems," Brother Pedersen said. He expressed skepticism there could be any good reason for the two missionaries to leave their area. Perhaps it was due to the late hour, but Toressen suddenly felt exhausted. He was relieved when Sister Toressen stormed into the office and threatened to end the conversation herself.

"It is getting late and Sister Toressen wants me to come to bed," President Toressen said with as much pleasantness as he could muster. "It surely was a pleasure to talk with you, Brother Pedersen. I already know so much about you and your family, just from knowing your fine son."

"I'm not so sure Eddie exemplifies the best of the Pedersen family," his father replied. "He was a fine boy once, but . . . I don't know what happened to him."

"Don't lose hope. Based on what I know, you have raised a wonderful son. You ought to be proud."

Apostle Prichard insisted on meeting with President Toressen the next morning. Toressen did not share the details of their conversation with his wife, but she was sitting outside his office door, reading the latest issue of *Lys over Norge* when Apostle Prichard began speaking. Sister Toressen knew she shouldn't eavesdrop, but as Prichard's voice grew increasingly loud and impassioned, she couldn't help but hear, not everything, but enough. "Sending those two elders north together was an incomprehensible decision . . . true inspiration does not violate common sense . . . yet another example of your lack of discipline . . . the boys' moral standing is in jeopardy. . . . This may yet be the last straw."

Bjørns's replies were too muffled to hear, but did it really matter? Sister Toressen saw the writing on the wall. Unlike the biblical king Belshazzar, she didn't need an interpreter. The Brethren had lost patience and were preparing to cut short her husband's mission. She had feared this outcome from the beginning. No one was more devoted to his calling than Bjørn, but the administrative duties overwhelmed him. Scatterbrained and impulsive, he paid scant attention to the church's reporting requirements, nor to the metrics and goals used to measure his success. The apostle's tirade reminded her of a similar scolding Bjørn received from his mission president twenty years earlier in the very same office. Elder Bjørnstjerne Toressen, then a young Norwegian missionary, had organized a large meeting for investigators but neglected to make the advance arrangements. It wasn't until the morning of the event that he thought to notify the mission president.

Sister Toressen, who was then Sister Kristina Nielsen, had been sitting outside the office door on that occasion as well, waiting for her exit interview before returning to Salt Lake City. "Do you know how bad this will make the church look when investigators show up and nothing is prepared?" the mission president shouted before dismissing Bjørnstjerne.

"Help me, please. Help me," Elder Toressen murmured as he walked shame-faced out the door, clutching the planned program in his hand. He was pleading with God, but Sister Nielsen, seeing no one else in the outer office, thought he was talking to her.

"Give me that," she said, grabbing the program from Elder Toressen's hands. "Get downstairs and tell the printer to get the plates ready." Elder Toressen started to protest. "Go," she bellowed. "I'll be down in ten minutes."

Sister Nielsen quickly typed up the program agenda, noting that Elder Toressen had made himself the main speaker, and hurried to the mission printer's office. When the printer started arguing about protocol and priorities, Sister Nielsen pointed out that investigators were the mission's highest priority, then turned and left without hearing the printer complain about sisters who acted like they held the priesthood. Sister Nielsen had spent her last twelve months working in Oslo's central district, and so she knew well the inner workings of the local branch. She made a flurry of phone calls, and by mid-afternoon she had rounded up the chapel's custodial staff and launched a Relief Society effort to bake refreshments and organize a musical number.

Elder Toressen arrived at the chapel just as the program was slated to begin, smiling and unfazed by his tardiness. When it was his turn to speak, Sister Nielsen braced herself for an embarrassing performance by the bumbling elder. What she heard was a man transformed. He stood before the congregation as God's oracle, and through his voice the scriptures became song, rich in texture and powerful in the subtle refrain of his message. "If anyone will come after me, let him deny himself and take up his cross and follow me," Elder Toressen said, quoting the Savior. "For whosoever will save his life shall lose it, but whosoever will lose his life for my sake shall find it." Never before had Sister Nielsen felt so moved, so inspired to believe in herself, so desirous not just to be good but to do good. Clearly, God could make weak things strong.

She flew home the next day and did not see Bjørnstjerne again until he showed up at her doorstep six months after her husband died. Sister Nielsen, now Kristina Kelley, had been married less than a year when her husband was killed in a helicopter training accident at Fort Bragg. Bjørnstjerne wanted to marry her. "I need you," he said, reminding her of that day in the mission home when she rescued him from failure. "God has great work for me to accomplish, but I cannot do it without you."

Kristina frowned. "I hardly know you."

"I can give you children. I know you want children, children who will be your own in the eternities."

"But if you marry me, they won't be yours. They will belong to me and my first husband. You will have none."

"I know who I am," he declared.

This was a strange reply from a strange man. But the strangeness added to Bjørnstjerne's aura of divine favor. As he pressed his case, Kristina was moved by the same spirit she had felt when she heard him preach in Oslo. She believed God had, indeed, foreordained Bjørnstjerne to a special mission, and she wanted to be part of it. And she did want children. Bjørnstjerne immigrated to the United States and they were married three months later by their ward bishop.

As he had promised, Bjørnstjerne gave her children—five of them. He also needed her help, lots of it. She served as the de facto office manager in his remodeling business. He had a knack for bringing in customers, but she balanced the books, paid the invoices, and made sure the subcontractors showed up on time. When Bjørnstjerne was called as ward bishop, Kristina worked behind the scenes to manage the bureaucratic side of saving souls. Bjørnstjerne inspired his congregants to look beyond themselves and tackle life's challenges with optimism and faith, but it was Kristina who saw to it that impoverished families received church welfare assistance and unemployed men found jobs through the church's employment services. She took justifiable pride when, under her husband's guidance, many of the wayward returned to the fold and the chapel reverberated with the joyous singing of hymns. Bjørnstjerne endured his wife's insistent nagging and acknowledged his myriad imperfections. "I am thankful God loves even the sinner, because surely I am one," he said.

Kristina embraced the idea of being Bjørnstjerne's life partner in raising a family and performing good works, but even on the day they married, she questioned whether she really loved him—at least, in the way a wife is supposed to love her husband. As she listened to Apostle Prichard berate her husband, the question again crossed her mind. Had it been worth the trouble, all these years, only to see Bjørnstjerne abruptly dismissed as the Norwegian mission president? It would be compassionately done, of course. Perhaps the Brethren would publicly reference an unexpected worsening of Bjørnstjerne's heart condition. A suspicious mind might think Elder Prichard's severe tongue-lashing was purposely designed to trigger such a cardiac event, after which church leaders could justifiably release Bjørnstjerne from service and call another to his place. The humiliation would be exquisite.

Chapter 6

Pray always lest you enter into temptation. Remember there is no personal problem so serious in your life that good hard work and prayer won't overcome.

Conduct of a Missionary

Elder Ward took off his glasses and squinted impatiently at the bus schedule posted by the curb, calculating the wait time. A stinging wind whipped his reddened cheeks. Wet snow collected on his eyebrows. "Fifteen minutes," he said after consulting his watch. His fingers ached with a sharp, icy pain despite a new pair of gloves.

Elder Sorensen stood next to him, still pale and shaken from the landing at Evenes Airport, with his woolen scarf pulled over his mouth and nose. A snowy gust had rocked the jet on its approach, causing it to drop precipitously into a jolting halt. The Norwegian passengers didn't flinch, but Elder Sorensen had started to shout "Jesus Christ" and then caught himself. "Flip, flip, fliiiiiiiiiiip," he screamed until the wheels stopped skidding. "The Lord protected us," he told his companion while they waited for the bus that would take them from the Narvik airport to Harstad. When the bus finally arrived, the assistants dragged their duffel bags to the back row and slept the entire way.

"Welcome to outer darkness," Elder Jenkins, the Norway North district leader, proclaimed with mock solemnity when the assistants arrived at the Harstad bus station. Elder Jenkins and his junior companion, Elder Wootson, had arrived from Narvik the day before to help investigate the disappearance of the Harstad missionaries. Wootson took the assistants' bags and carried them up the long hill to the hybel. Jenkins and Wootson both wore fur caps with the flaps pulled tightly over their ears and tied under their chins, while the assistants suffered with fedoras that exposed their ears to the frigid air. They were protected somewhat from the wind by the eight-foot mounds of snow that snowplows had pushed to the side of the road. "Can't blame Tanner and Pedersen for running away from a place like this," Jenkins said.

Elder Ward offered a wincing smile. It was Elder Jenkins's way of reminding the assistants that he hated his current assignment. A few months earlier, Elder Jenkins thought he was next in line to become a zone leader. Instead, he was transferred to Narvik, a challenge he regarded as more suited for a promising missionary than a proven leader. He arrived in Narvik just as a bruising winter descended on the region. When the sun disappeared in December for more than a month, Elder Jenkins persuaded himself the assistants had purposely banished a rival to the far reaches of outer darkness reserved only for the worst of Satan's minions. The coming of spring had brought welcome sunlight but not, even in early May, relief from random snowstorms and sharp Arctic chills. Elder Jenkins had served his time and wanted out.

"If you help us find the missing elders, we'll send you anywhere you want to go," Elder Ward said. "Bergen, Halden, Lillehammer. You name it."

"I hear Kristiansand is delightful in the summer," Elder Jenkins suggested.

"President Toressen is in such hot water, he'd probably make you the next assistant," Sorensen added. The four missionaries laughed as they stomped the snow from their feet and slipped off their rubber overshoes before entering the hybel.

Once upstairs, the assistants began a thorough inspection of the three-room apartment, starting with the kitchen. "Who cleaned the refrigerator?" Elder Ward asked.

"We did," said Elder Jenkins.

"You shouldn't be touching anything."

"We can put the lutefisk back in there if you want."

"That's not funny, Elder. This is no time for lightmindedness," Elder Ward snarled.

"Don't get your garments in a bunch," Elder Jenkins shot back. "We had to clean the refrigerator. It smelled to high heaven. But everything else in the refrigerator and kitchen is just as they left it. We found jars of mayonnaise and mustard in the refrigerator. Also a few sticks of butter, one half used. All the dishes were washed and put away. They left nothing on the counters. They even swept the floor before they left."

The two assistants opened the cupboards and drawers. They found the dishes and utensils as Elder Jenkins had described. In the pantry were partially consumed boxes of oatmeal and rice, half a jar of peanut butter, and an unopened packet of bean stew mix. "Okay, let's look at the living room," Elder Ward said.

The living room was modestly furnished: small couch, green upholstered chair, two end tables, a floor lamp, and a coffee table with a runner. Every piece bargain basement. The elders stared at the furniture. "What, exactly, are we looking for?" Elder Jenkins asked. "Not blood stains, I hope."

"It's possible."

"Yeah, and it's possible that Elder Tanner and Elder Pedersen were visited by the Three Nephites and translated directly to the Spirit World,"

Elder Sorensen said in a mocking tone, "but that's not the first thing on our list of clues to look for." Ignoring his companion, he turned to Elders Jenkins and Wootson. "The main thing is we're trying to figure out whether Elder Tanner and Elder Pedersen made plans to leave. If so, we're looking for clues telling us where they might have gone," he said. He lifted a couch cushion and then set it back into place.

"It was planned, all right. No doubt about it," Elder Jenkins concluded. "Look at the kitchen. Clean as a whistle. The living room too."

The young men filed into the bedroom. The furnishings were spare: two single beds, mattresses stripped of bedding; one wooden dresser; and two end tables and lamps. Elder Sorensen pulled open the dresser's drawers and pawed through the clothes. "Let's see, several pairs of socks, some garments, and a few T-shirts."

Elder Ward called from the closet. "I see two suits, several white shirts, a handful of ties, and two pairs of shoes. And here's their hats. Wouldn't they have taken their hats with them?"

"Those are fedoras, like you're wearing," Elder Jenkins said. "Here in the north, they would have taken their fur hats, not these."

The missionaries continued their search and then made a final inventory. Missing from the apartment were the missionaries' suitcases, duffel bags and bedding, discussion books, flannel board, and scriptures, as well as most of their clothing. But still remaining were a half dozen copies of the Book of Mormon, weekly report forms, pens, and personal correspondence, such as letters from home, as well as some of their clothes and a few items in the pantry and refrigerator. "It seems clear to me Elders Tanner and Pedersen made plans to leave for an extended period of time," Elder Ward said.

"Yeah, but look at the stuff they left behind," Elder Sorensen said. "They also intended to come back."

"In either case, they didn't abruptly vanish but planned this all out in advance. I think they moved to a new proselytizing area," Jenkins asserted.

Elder Ward frowned. "But why didn't they tell anyone?" The elders continued opening drawers, inspecting furniture, and peeking behind doors and curtains, looking for additional clues, but no one had a good answer to Elder Ward's question.

Elder Jenkins and his companion returned to Narvik the next morning. Elder Ward was glad to see them go. Jenkins had complained incessantly about being stationed in a small town with only a handful of active church members and a seemingly endless winter. "Be sure to tell President

Toressen how helpful I've been," Jenkins said, pounding his hands together as they waited for the bus. "I'll look for my transfer in the mail."

"You've got to look at your assignment as an opportunity," said Elder Sorensen.

"The Lord hates a complainer," added Elder Ward.

"You ought to know," Jenkins replied as he and his companion carried their duffel bags onto the bus. The assistants stood silently in the morning darkness and watched the bus drive away, its tires slushing in the melting snow.

Apostle Prichard's instructions to the assistants had been explicit on one point: keep the search low-key. "Don't draw attention to yourselves. If people ask, tell them you have come to Harstad on church business," he said. "And when you inquire about the missionaries, don't suggest they are missing or have run away. The church's enemies could do much harm by publicizing such information."

Elders Ward and Sorensen started their search for Elders Tanner and Pedersen at the police station. All missionaries are required by law to register with the local police if they plan to stay in a city or town for more than a short visit and so, the assistants reasoned, they could make a few innocuous inquiries when they registered. Their questions would be discreet and indirect. After morning scripture study and a run-through of the fifth discussion, the assistants dressed warmly and headed into town. The sun, though low on the horizon, shone brightly across the snow-packed streets. The temperature had already climbed above freezing, and the melting snow carved little streams of ice-blue water that rushed along the curbs and through the small fishing town that was just awakening from winter. Upon entering the police station, the elders were greeted by a tall, friendly man with thick lips and a short beard.

"Ah, you must be the Mormons who have come searching for the missing missionaries," he said, extending his hand. "I am Police Captain Aksel Hansen."

Elder Ward looked as if he had swallowed a bucketful of fish brine. "Nei," he said, feigning nonchalance. "No, we have come to register."

Hansen was puzzled. "You are not looking for them?"

"We want to know where they are, of course," Ward said.

"Do *you* know?" Elder Sorensen asked.

"No one knows. Isn't that why you are here? I cannot help you if you are not honest with me," Hansen said.

Ward's shoulders slumped. "Yes, we don't know where they are, but we don't want to bring a lot of publicity that will embarrass the missionaries or their families."

"Well, that is unfortunate, because publicity is the best way to find missing persons. But, yes, I understand," Hansen said. He scratched at his beard, looking bemused. "Anyway, everyone here is already on the lookout for your missing Mormons. I do not think anything bad has happened to them. This is a nice place. Nothing bad happens here."

"Takk," the assistants said in unison after signing the registration papers.

"Will you be staying long?" Chief Hansen asked.

"Just until we finish our church business," Ward replied.

"Ja vel," said the chief, who pointed to the elders' slim fedoras. "Your ears are going to freeze if you wear those hats here."

The assistants, not knowing how to reply, quietly put on their gloves. Elder Sorensen wrapped his scarf high around his neck, so it covered the bottom half of his ears. "Ha det," they said, leaning into the wind as they pulled the door shut.

Chief Hansen turned to the clerk. "Ah, slik er det med sektene. This is how it is with the sects."

Bror Brevik's wife finally answered the door after some persistent knocking by the assistants. Dressed in a flannel nightgown and faded slippers, she had the look of a once-attractive woman who no longer kept up appearances. "Come in," she said, balancing a toddler on her hip. She called upstairs, "Jann Harald, the new missionaries are here." Søster Brevik swept a handful of children's blocks from the couch and invited the elders to sit.

"These elders are here to look for the missing missionaries," Bror Brevik told his wife.

"Who's missing?

"Elders Tanner and Pedersen. No one knows where they are," Brevik said. Turning to the assistants, he said, "I am not surprised the police chief already knows about the missing elders. Their landlady is telling everyone they ran away."

Elder Ward frowned. "This is bad publicity for the church."

Bror Brevik shrugged. "We cannot worry about that right now. The important thing is to find the missionaries."

"Wait a minute," his wife said. "The missionaries—Elder Tanner and Elder Pedersen—told me they were going to start working in a new area."

Elder Ward jumped up from his seat. "What? When did they tell you this?"

51

"A few weeks ago, I think. It was right after Jann Harald went on deployment. Elder Tanner and Elder Pedersen came to the house and said they would not be dropping by for a while because they were going to try a different area."

"Why did you not tell me they had gone to a new area?" Bror Brevik said, looking displeased.

"You never told me they were missing."

"Did they say where they were going?" Elder Ward asked.

"Not that I recall, but I thought it was going to be temporary, maybe a week. They work in so many different areas, I did not think it remarkable. You mean they did not tell *you* where they were going?"

"They did not tell anyone," Bror Brevik said. "We think they ran away."

"Oh, those are good boys," his wife said. "They would not do that." When asked why, she said, "They seemed very happy, like they were enjoying their work together. When I last talked to them, I did not get the impression they were planning a jailbreak. Of course, I would not blame them if they have run away."

"You mean because of the weather?" Elder Sorensen asked.

"Because of the church."

The assistants gave Bror Brevik a quizzical look. "Ingrid, my wife, she is not Mormon," Brevik whispered, and the assistants nodded with understanding. While Søster Brevik left to help her older children get ready for school, Bror Brevik suggested that the assistants visit the bus station, harbor, taxi company, and other places where the missionaries might have gotten transportation out of town. "Let us see if someone at those places can tell us where they went," he said. After the trio finished their planning, Bror Brevik announced he was leaving to help the assistants with their search. Søster Brevik stood in the doorway, her half-dressed daughter still on her hip.

"Sure, leave me here to look after the children while you are off with your church business, just like you always do," she said, glaring at her husband.

The assistants stared uncomfortably at their shoes until Bror Brevik finally broke the silence. "You are right, Ingrid. I will stay," he said.

Søster Brevik's face suddenly softened. "No, I was wrong to be angry, Jann Harald. Of course, you should look for those boys. You know how much I like them. Now I am worried too." She kissed her husband and shuffled back into the hallway.

A full day of driving around Harstad brought few answers. Everyone they talked to was friendly and eager to help. "Oh, they came to our house," said one man unloading fish from his boat into a large metal bin. "They had that funny little board, what do you call it—?"

"A *flannelltavle*," Elder Ward said. "Flannel board."

"Yes, a *flannelltavle* with those little pictures they put on it—"

"When was that?"

"Oh, sometime in early April, I think. We told them—"

"Was that the last time you saw them?"

"Well, no, we saw them here a week later, at the butcher's shop, buying whale beef. They said hello and asked when they could come back. I said anytime. Of course, we are not interested in joining a sect. We were born, baptized, and confirmed in the State Church, and we will die in the State Church. But they were nice boys."

All the conversations followed the same pattern: people knew the missionaries and had seen them regularly in town. Many had invited them in for dinner or to talk. None considered themselves investigators—some were downright dismissive of Mormonism—but everyone liked the missionaries, especially Elder Pedersen, who was quite the entertainer with his piano playing. The Norwegians enthusiastically speculated about where the elders might be. One person saw them at the bus station with their display of religious posters. Another saw them talking to Peter Reissmann, the old man who runs supplies to the island villages along the coast. Most suggested the young men temporarily moved south to escape the relentless darkness and cold. "It has been an ugly winter, even for us," said a stoop-shouldered fisherman. His leathery skin suggested decades at sea. "I would leave, too, if I could."

They had received some good leads, Bror Brevik said. They would definitely want to talk with Herr Reissmann and the manager at the bus station. But the assistants returned to the hybel that evening tired and discouraged, bones aching with cold and thoughts as dark as a Norwegian winter. The people in northern Norway were friendly, friendlier than the people in Oslo and other large cities. Everyone professed a genuine willingness to help, and several invited the assistants to drop by anytime, including for middag supper. If the missionaries were nearby, they would easily be spotted and reported to the assistants. And that's what was so troubling. No one reported seeing missionaries since mid-April.

Before going to bed, the assistants went downstairs to ask the landlady if they could use her phone and quizzed her again about when she had last seen the missionaries. "Three weeks perhaps, I do not know. I already told that to the other missionary, Elder Jenkins," Fru Kjelberg said. "I did not know I needed to keep track of them."

"We do not blame you," Elder Sorensen said.

Fru Kjelberg cocked her head and squinted her eyes, as if she were about to reveal a secret. "I will tell you something very curious. After they left, I have been setting the missionaries' letters on the table outside their door, but ten days ago all the letters were gone and they had left an envelope with this month's rent."

"So they came back," Elder Ward exclaimed.

"I supposed so at the time, but I did not see them come or go. That is why I say it has been several weeks since I have seen them. Maybe they did run away."

The assistants eagerly passed on the news to President Toressen. "Elders Tanner and Pedersen must be close by if they returned to pick up their mail and pay their rent," Elder Ward said. "Still, it's peculiar that everywhere we go, people here tell us how much they like the missionaries, but no one knows where they are."

Toressen tried to buck up his assistant. "The friendliness of Harstad's people toward the church is truly inspiring," he said cheerfully. "Perhaps the Lord is using the missionaries' absence to soften the hearts of the people. I don't think they have disappeared. They are just absent. You have done good work. Your next step is to find out where the elders went proselytizing. We will keep you in our prayers."

After hanging up, Elder Ward put five Norwegian crowns in the bowl by the telephone. Before going to bed, the assistants prayed together and then separately, each asking for guidance in finding Elders Tanner and Pedersen.

Chapter 7

Don't go into the mission field with unconfessed sins in your mind and conscience—if you do, you cannot become a strong, effective missionary.

Conduct of a Missionary

Eddie heard Elder Tanner climb out of bed and walk rapidly to the living room. Unable to sleep, Eddie intended to join his companion, wondering whether Elder Tanner was also having misgivings about their plan to leave their proselyting area. But after putting his feet on the icy floor, Eddie jumped back into his warm bed. Eddie decided that if they got caught, he would take the blame upon himself. No one would doubt that a homosexual would also lead his companion astray. When first confronted with Eddie's homosexuality, his dad's wan, unyielding face exuded a disappointment and disdain that suggested he expected that continued transgressions, not redemption, lay ahead for Eddie. Even Eddie was beginning to think of himself as a lost cause. Eddie checked the time: 1:30 a.m. He tried willing himself to sleep but once again found himself back at Brigham Young University.

Eddie Pedersen blinked and rubbed his eye. The slight motion of his arm caused the wires to become detached from the leather strap wrapped around his bicep.

"Careful," Brother Orlan said as he reattached the wires. "You don't want to break the connection." Eddie sat in a green plastic chair, which Brother Olan's assistant had brought from a nearby classroom. The setup felt makeshift, like kids playing doctor. Curtains were drawn around Eddie, while a few feet behind, Brother Orlan, an associate professor who led the university's Institute for Reparative Therapy, was attaching wires to the electrical panel and calibrating the machinery. "What setting would you like?" Brother Orlan asked.

Eddie asked for the maximum, 1600 volts. Brother Orlan tried to persuade him to start at a lower voltage and then work his way up, but Eddie was adamant. He wanted to show everyone his desire to change was sincere. Brother Orlan turned out the lights and the slide projector started to hum. Eddie stared at the blank screen, waiting for the slides to drop. The room smelled faintly of formaldehyde. Eddie's left eye was red and itchy from an erupting stye, but he resisted the temptation to rub it, and instead squeezed his eye tightly in hopes of reducing the irritation. He had electrodes attached to his biceps, thigh, and groin. The reparative therapy treatment called for Eddie to view slides of naked men and women in erotic poses. If aroused by the seductive photographs of men, Eddie would receive a punishing shock, thus training his mind and body to have a natural aversion to homosexual thoughts and desires. Eddie considered himself blessed to have this chance to make himself right with the God.

The projector rattled and whirred as the first slide fell into place. Eddie braced for the shock of 1600 volts of electricity, enough to burn and scar the flesh. "Thy will be done," he said in whispered prayer.

Eddie had been despondent following his arrest by the campus police. The Office of University Standards was notified, as well as his BYU bishop. The security officers threatened him, saying he would be expelled and lose all of his first-year credits unless he confessed and provided the names of other homosexual partners. Running away or driving a car off a cliff seemed his only options. Eddie seriously considered the former and wished he had the courage to do the latter. Bishop Perry, a history professor, came immediately to visit Eddie in the dorms the next morning. Seeing Eddie's humiliation and shame, Bishop Perry embraced the distraught young man and assured Eddie he loved him—and God loved him too. Eddie could overcome his compulsion, the bishop said. They remained behind closed doors for the next two hours as Eddie confessed everything: the episode at Scout camp, his many boy crushes while growing up, his romance with Barry, and his arrest. "I wish I could die and start my life over," Eddie said, gulping between sobs. Bishop Perry, a round-faced man with crooked teeth and a compassionate smile, shed nearly as many tears as Eddie.

"Homosexuality is a grievous, ruinous sin," Bishop Perry said. "But you showed great resolve and self-control. Like Joseph fleeing Potiphar's wife, you abandoned your relationship with Barry before it became truly egregious. You've taken an important step in the repentance process by acknowledging and confessing your sin. Now let's get you back on track to go on your mission."

At the end of their meeting, the two men knelt in prayer and Eddie asked God's forgiveness and help in overcoming his problem, saying he recognized that his arrest was the Lord's way of getting him on the straight and narrow path. Eddie's sincerity moved Bishop Perry, and he became Eddie's advocate with school authorities. Bishop Perry argued that the physical acts committed by Eddie did not reach a level of severity requiring harsh punishment, and with this reasoning he persuaded University Standards officials to take no action against Eddie. When BYU's security chief resisted, saying Eddie had clearly violated the university's honor code, Bishop Perry became incensed. "The spirit of the Gospel calls for us to help rather than persecute Eddie. Let he who is without sin cast the first stone," Bishop Perry said.

The burly security chief finally agreed to drop the charges, but he was irritated by Bishop Perry's condescending tone. The chief knew better than anyone about recidivism among sexual deviants, and so he spit back a scripture of his own. "The dog returns to its own vomit, and the sow, after washing herself, returns to wallow in the mire," he said as the bishop walked out the door.

Eddie's arrest forced him to honestly admit to himself what he had long evaded and even attempted to repress: he was inexorably attracted to members of his own sex. It was not some physiological flaw like, say, bedwetting, that one eventually outgrows. Somehow, inexplicably, it had become part of who he was, apparently at an early age. That much was clear. In high school, he had parked at the valley overlook and made out with some of his high school dates, but it had always been at their subtle urging. He felt no passion in the deep kisses, only emptiness and, at times, boredom, as he pondered his own lack of ardor. *It must be because we're not in love*, he told himself. But the kisses he later exchanged with Barry, though simple and chaste, aroused sensations of both contentment and desire. For days after, Eddie could feel the sweet memory of Barry's lips. He had been fooling himself, of course, in thinking his attraction to men could be justified before God. The depth of his sinfulness horrified Eddie, filling him with self-loathing and guilt. The public humiliation of his arrest only intensified those feelings.

Nevertheless, confessing to Bishop Perry had lifted a weight Eddie had carried since childhood. Acknowledgment brought relief. He no longer had to rationalize or pretend but accept and change. *I want to marry, raise children, and be a family man, a breadwinner, just like my older brothers.* With Bishop Perry's guidance, Eddie handed over his burden to God. Not that it would be easy. But the prospect of change buoyed Eddie's hopes and, despite the awful events of the past few days, awakened an unexpected feeling of spiritual renewal.

Young men and women who committed sexual transgressions were typically required to go through a repentance process lasting one year before they could go on a mission. But while Eddie had not engaged in sexual activity, Bishop Perry did not know whether his homosexual experimentation merited a similar repentance regime. He arranged for Eddie to drive with him to Salt Lake City for an interview with Apostle Joseph

F. Prichard, who was known for his knowledge and experience in handling moral issues, having written several books on the subject, including "Living a Chaste Life in an Unchaste World."

"How long have you been smoking dope, son?"

Eddie stared across the desk, his hands cupped on his lap. His sandy blonde hair was trimmed around the ears and tapered short in the back, so it didn't rest on his collar, just the way Bishop Perry had instructed the barber to cut it. "How long . . . how long have I *what*, sir?" Eddie stammered, uncertain whether he had heard the question correctly.

Apostle Prichard laid the folder on his desk and leaned closer. Eddie could see an uncut whisker where Prichard's chin turned at a severe angle. Prichard eyed Eddie with the exasperated look of a man who had seen and heard it all. "How long have you been on weed or grass or Mary Jane or whatever you're calling it these days?"

He must have me mixed up with someone else, Eddie thought. He pulled at his tie, trying to loosen the stranglehold around his throat. "I'm not here because of marijuana. I'm here because—"

"I know why you're here," the apostle said, glaring impatiently. It was said Apostle Prichard could stare into your soul and know your every thought. "The repentance process requires you to put all of your cards on the table, and I would advise you to do that now, while we can still do something to help you. That's the only way it works."

"I've never smoked marijuana or done drugs of any kind or drank or smoked cigarettes or broken the Word of Wisdom. I haven't had sex or done anything more than kiss someone."

"Have you kissed a girl?"

"Yes, sir."

"Have you kissed a boy?"

"Yes, sir, I'm here because—"

Apostle Prichard slammed his hand on the desk. "I don't understand how, after kissing a girl, you would ever have any desire to kiss a man. Were you experimenting?"

Eddie felt his armpits starting to drip. "I don't know why I did it, sir. I liked it, I guess. I know I'm not supposed to, but—"

"No!" Apostle Prichard slammed the desk again. "You didn't really like it. Tell the truth, didn't it make you feel dirty and vile and disgusted with yourself?"

Eddie hesitated, unsure. The heat of the apostle's glare urged an answer. "That's how I feel now," Eddie replied. "The thought of doing it again fills me with revulsion."

58

"Of course, it does. That's because it's a compulsion, a nasty habit, like smoking or alcoholism or being hooked on drugs. You know it's bad for you, but you can't stop. I know it's fashionable for so-called experts to say people are born homosexual and there's nothing we can do about it, but this is a malicious and destructive lie. I testify as an apostle of the Lord Jesus Christ that a loving God would never do that to anyone. It's a habit, that's all, a filthy, selfish, sinful habit. It's very addictive too. After just one homosexual experience, boys and men are soon craving more. But you can beat it, son, if you want to. It's not easy. We've learned through years of dealing with men and women—though it's hard to believe a sweet sister would indulge in this habit—that you can beat it. The Lord will help you if you want to. Do you want to, Eddie?"

Eddie's face brightened. "Oh, yes, more than anything in the world."

When his parents drove up from California to bring him home for the summer, Bishop Perry was waiting with Eddie in his dorm room. "You have to confess your sin to your parents," the bishop said, "because you have sinned against them as well as God." Eddie's heart nearly stopped at the thought. "It will make a man of you," Bishop Perry assured him.

"Are you all packed?" Eddie's father asked when they arrived. Eddie felt deceitful leading them up the stairs to his room. All the time his mother chattered merrily about how everyone was looking forward to his return, while his father said his brother Skip had already arranged a summer job for Eddie bussing tables at Bob's Big Boy restaurant. "If you start Monday, you can probably get in three months of work before you put in your mission papers."

Once they reached his room, Eddie introduced his parents to Bishop Perry and closed the door. His whole body quivered and he felt dizzy and out of breath, barely able to speak or hold back the tears, but he spoke anyway, taking the first step off the cliff. "Mom, Dad, Bishop Perry is here because I've sinned, a bad sin. I kissed a boy. That's all I did, but it's a homosexual act. I just kissed him, that's all. But I know what I did is wrong and I am repenting, and I confess to you my sin, because I know you taught me better and I am very sorry."

As Eddie's words spilled out, his mother's face turned ashen. His father stood stiffly, his jaw tightening, and pulled his wife close. Eddie had been counseled to admit his sin but not to say he was a homosexual. One can commit homosexual acts, but there is no such thing as a homosexual person. That's a myth, the devil's trick. And when it appeared Eddie might never stop talking, Bishop Perry interrupted and said, "Your son is a thoughtful and brave young man and is doing all of the right things to repent and live the Lord's commandments."

Bishop Perry told Brother and Sister Pedersen about BYU's Institute for Reparative Therapy, which was one of the nation's leading programs for helping young people overcome their homosexual addictions. "Our program combines inspired gospel truths with rigorous academic research. It has achieved the highest success rates of any program of its kind in the nation. Many researchers are coming here to learn how the university does it," he said. Because Eddie had not committed a sexual transgression, he did not have to wait a full year to be forgiven and go on his mission. "The good news is that if Eddie stays at BYU this summer and successfully completes reparative therapy, he will be eligible to go on a mission in September just as you and he have planned. And he will remain a student in good standing with the university as well," the bishop said.

The arrangements had already been made for Eddie to stay in a group home and work with a university landscaping crew over the summer while undergoing treatment. Bishop Perry would remain his spiritual advisor to guide him through repentance. Amid hugs and tears, Eddie's parents readily agreed to the proposition, and after an awkward dinner in which Eddie and his parents referred only obliquely to his "problem," they returned home early the next morning. They told Eddie's brothers and friends he was staying the summer at BYU to prepare for his mission.

Chapter 8

The things of God can be understood only by the power of the Spirit.
Seek Truth. Avoid Contention. Leave the mysteries alone.
Search The Scriptures: A Missionary Study Guide

The Language Training Mission, or LTM, as it was known, offered the normally reserved Orrin Tanner the chance to take the spotlight. Orrin arrived at the Ricks College LTM eager but worried how he would fit in among the Scandinavian missionaries during their eight weeks of language and religious training at the Idaho school. The raw confidence exuded by many of the other missionaries intimidated Orrin, who retreated to familiar defenses, hiding behind a wall of feigned indifference amid the hubbub and scramble among missionaries thrown together in a new, intense environment. Those accomplished in sports, music, drama, or other pursuits seemed natural leaders and acted as such. Consequently, Orrin had resigned himself to playing his usual sideline role when, much to his delight, his exceptional knowledge of Mormon doctrine brought him prestige and respect.

"Elder Tanner, are you by chance related to the Mormon scholar, Anson Tanner?" asked President Hyrum Clark, who presided over the language training program.

Orrin beamed with pride. "Yes, sir. He's my father."

"Our missionary library holds all your father's pamphlets from both his *Tanner's Faith-Promoting Series* and *Tanner's Guide to Mormon Theology.* Of course, we encourage the elders and sisters to focus their studies on the standard works, but your father's pamphlets serve as valuable resources for our instructors when they teach about some of our, shall I say, more problematic issues."

President Clark soon learned that Orrin, like his father, possessed an in-depth knowledge of Mormon history and doctrine. When he arrived at the language training facility, Orrin had already read and studied the church's four standard works of scripture. He had also memorized the six missionary discussions and all 165 scriptural verses used to teach and persuade people of Mormonism's truthfulness. All missionaries would eventually learn to recite word for word the six discussions during the course of their two-year missions, but few could recite all 165 scriptures. Many never learned any of them. President Clark had never encountered a missionary who entered the LTM with such a firm grasp of the scriptures. "Of course, Elder Tanner will need to relearn it all in Norwegian, but that shouldn't be too difficult for someone with his dedication and talent," Clark remarked to one of his counselors.

Anson Tanner's publishing business, which was now garnering both father and son some notoriety, came about almost by accident. Anson began the faith-promoting series with an account of Grandpa Heber Tanner's vision of the spirit world. Anson had intended to publish only Grandpa Heber's story, but the pamphlet sparked a flood of mail from people who told Anson their own stories of miracles and faith—about a lost girl rescued by the Three Nephites; about an Indian who gradually turned white after being baptized; about a faithful tithe payer who, even when unemployed, always had enough to pay his bills. "I should publish these stories," Anson told his brother, Porter.

Porter was skeptical. In fact, he had objected to printing Grandpa Heber's story. "Dad's vision is a sacred experience. You don't cast your pearls before swine," he warned.

Grandpa Heber scoffed at Porter's concerns. "It's our duty to bear witness to God's hand in our lives," he said. "The pure in heart will recognize the truthfulness of our spiritual experiences. Those who mock and scorn will have to answer to God." That settled the matter. Anson continued publishing the faith-promoting stories of others based on the same philosophy: those who have eyes to see, will see; and those who have ears to hear, will hearken.

Anson's decision to publish *Tanner's Guides to Mormon Theology* also arose in a roundabout way. Anson taught high school seminary classes while aiming, eventually, to secure a position in the BYU Religion Department where Porter was a tenured professor. Anson had originally intended to write a book analyzing Mormonism's unique doctrines. He believed (unrealistically, Porter said) such a book would be his ticket to securing a university position, but he kept getting mired down in the details. Did Brigham Young teach that Adam was God? Absolutely. What did he mean? Depends on which church authority you ask. Did President Woodruff's Manifesto ban new polygamous marriages? Not really, despite what orthodox Mormon histories taught. Most problematic was the church's ban against Negroes holding the priesthood or entering the temple. "Our prophets have been very clear in teaching that God cursed Negroes with a dark skin, just as He did the Indians," Anson said, "but our early history is quite murky on when the ban originated." Sarah regularly asked Anson when he intended to finish his book. "I still need to do more research," he would reply.

Anson's effort to find definitive answers stretched into years, his notes filling up rows of filing cabinets that had taken over the garage. Anson dusted the cabinets daily. He even painted them once, giving them a shine reflecting his bright hopes for cataloging divine truths. His ambition of teaching in BYU's religion department rested on the planned book. Then someone beat him to it. In 1958, Elder Bruce R. McConkie, a member of the First Council of Seventy, published the encyclopedic *Mormon Doctrine* addressing the same topics and questions. "That's your book," Porter said, shaking his head. "You waited too long."

Anson reluctantly agreed, but after reading *Mormon Doctrine*, he concluded that McConkie had short-changed a few topics and skirted around complications in others. Some sections were flat-out wrong. Anson never said so. Not explicitly. Criticizing Elder McConkie or any Mormon leader was not in his nature. Nevertheless, he decided to publish his own interpretation of various topics in a series of scholarly pamphlets called *Tanner's Guides to Mormon Theology*. The pamphlets raised eyebrows among Mormonism's academic elite, but rank-and-file members, who were already familiar with *Tanner's Faith-Promoting Series*, poured over the new tracts, which invited them to participate as equals in the ongoing debate of Mormonism's practices and teachings. *Tanner's Guides* soon found their way into Sunday School classes and church talks. Anson produced more than twenty pamphlets, building an academic catalog he hoped would win him a coveted university teaching job. "These pamphlets are the equivalent of several doctoral dissertations. That ought to count for something," he said.

Anson put Orrin to work setting type on the printing press installed in the garage. Orrin's duties also included proofreading, correcting typographical errors, and fact-checking the footnotes. Orrin initially resented the work and manufactured excuses to run off with friends, but over time it sparked an intellectual awakening and thirst for knowledge. Like his dad, Orrin began to thrill in the discovery of an obscure quote by a church authority that illuminated a gospel principle or gave insight into a heretofore unknown church historical event. The knowledge he gained boosted his confidence, that he was someone of merit, and fueled quixotic dreams of receiving revelation like the young prophet Samuel. Orrin saw himself as an apprentice to the same exclusive group of Mormon scholars to which his father sought membership and to which Uncle Porter already belonged. Anson encouraged his son's curiosity with a father's pride. "Ask, and it shall be given you; seek, and ye shall find; knock, and it shall be opened unto you," Anson said, quoting scripture. Father and son often worked together, quietly, into the night.

Porter, who already had misgivings about Anson's publishing ventures, disapproved of the way his brother allowed Orrin to engage in Mormonism's knottier issues. Finding Anson alone in the garage, Porter pressed his point while Anson was finishing a day of printing. "A boy his age shouldn't be studying the mysteries. It will only confuse him when he reads that one apostle says one thing about evolution and another says the exact opposite. Topics like these—evolution, the Adam-God theory, polygamy, and such—we don't even discuss them with our college students," Porter said. "Don't pit Brethren against each other, Anson. It makes it appear as if they're in the dark, just like everyone else."

Anson took a greasy rag hanging from a nail on the garage wall and began wiping printer's ink from his hand. He scrubbed vigorously the folds between his knuckles where black stains had taken up residence in the tiny cracks of his skin. "That's about as clean as I'll get them," he said, inspecting the blackened grooves crisscrossing the backs of his hands. He looked up at Porter. "I reject the notion of mysteries," Anson said, placing the rag back on the nail. "There are things we don't yet understand, but, ultimately, there are no inconsistencies or contradictions that cannot be reconciled with more research and study. Besides, the truth never hurt anyone."

Porter scoffed. "It's the height of arrogance for anyone to think they're an oracle of truth."

"Every person who humbles himself before God and obeys His commandments is entitled to divine knowledge through inspiration, even revelation," Anson countered. "Such wisdom isn't reserved for Joseph Smith or the apostles and prophets alone. It's everyone's birthright."

"Pride cometh before a fall," Porter said, lecturing his younger brother as if he were one of his students. "Our duty is to follow the prophet, not try to be one. Mark my words, the path you're on will lead to ruin not just for you, but for Orrin as well."

"Now look who's setting himself up as a prophet," Anson replied. As long as Anson could remember, his brother had acted unbid as his guide. Porter had questioned his engagement to Sarah and, even though he eventually came to appreciate Sarah's strengths, Anson had never forgiven his brother's meddling. And rather than supporting Anson's desire to join him in the university's religion department, Porter offered only nitpicking discouragement. It bothered Anson that his wife often defended Porter—"Listen to him, Anson, he understands how universities work"—as if she had forgotten the insulting suspicions Porter had voiced when they first met. Anson turned out the garage lights. The two brothers scowled in the darkness.

"There are two keys to success, both here and in the mission field," President Clark instructed the elders and sisters at an early morning orientation over breakfast. The room smelled of bacon and eggs and syrup. "The first is obedience. Follow the mission rules to the letter, which have been given to us by way of inspiration. Similarly, always obey your mission leaders, who have been selected by inspiration and ordained to guide you. If knowledge is light, then obedience is the light switch that turns on the learning and intelligence you seek."

"The second key to success is to keep yourself morally clean. That means staying an arm's length away from the opposite sex. The devil lays no more cunning snare than the lure of sexual attraction." President Clark paused and looked directly at the half dozen female missionaries sitting together near the podium. "And Sisters, you have a special responsibility to dress and behave in a way that helps the elders cultivate wholesome thoughts and does not distract them from their work. And to all of you, I promise that if you adhere to these two divine principles—obedience and moral purity—you will be blessed with the gift of tongues enabling you to learn the language of the foreign land to which you have been called."

Despite this promise, Orrin struggled to learn Norwegian. He especially had trouble detecting the subtle differences between some of the vowels. "Listen again," his instructor said, repeating "i" and "y" over and over, but they sounded the same to Orrin. The other Norwegian elders also experienced various degrees of difficulty replicating the Norwegian language, but eventually they started making sense of the new syllables and sounds. Not so Orrin, who worried something was wrong with his hearing and visited the health clinic to have his ears tested. "Some people have a knack for languages," the doctor said after informing Orrin his hearing fell within the normal range. As his instructors had predicted, Orrin eventually began hearing the nuanced sounds, but he lacked the ability to reproduce them with either clarity or consistency. He could understand Norwegian, but his spoken words were a jumbled soup that made sense to no one but him.

Orrin could not help but compare himself with the others. He did not begrudge the quick fluency of the elders who came from Norwegian homes, but everyone was outpacing him. One missionary in particular, Elder Edward Pedersen, drove him to distraction. Pedersen would sit hunched over the manuals, holding his hands against his face like blinders, contorting and shaping his lips as he practiced saying the words.

During orals, Pedersen stood in front of the class and flawlessly recited the lessons. Despite having no previous training in Norwegian, Pedersen quickly mastered the language's distinctive accent, speaking in lyrical sing-song sentences that sounded to Orrin's ear as if spoken by a native speaker. "How do you do it, Elder?" Orrin asked.

Elder Pedersen shrugged. "It's my musical training, I guess. My ability to play songs by ear enables me to hear all of the individual sounds in the Norwegian language." He tried to demonstrate for Orrin by playing different chords on the piano, sixths and sevenths, majors and minors. "Hear the difference?" he said. "With practice, you can hear each individual note as well as the distinctive blend of each chord." Pedersen replayed the chords, this time striking each note separately before playing the notes together in a single chord.

"I still don't get it." Orrin forced a laugh, trying to hide his frustration.

"I should get back to my memorization," Pedersen said.

What arrogance, Orrin thought. Elder Pedersen seemed like a bloodless automaton, more concerned with achieving his own goals than with helping a fellow missionary. A cold fish too. Pedersen kept largely to himself, rarely conversing with his LTM companions or joining in their mealtime banter. When the eight Norwegian elders returned to their apartment late at night, Pedersen undressed by his closet, quickly and furtively, then climbed silently into bed after a lengthy nighttime prayer.

Orrin's prayers were lengthy, too, and filled with pleading. Like Jacob wrestling with the angel, Orrin wrestled with the Norwegian language and wondered why God had singled him out for this challenge.

Four weeks into his language training, Orrin received a special blessing from President Clark asking God to loosen his tongue so he might speak Norwegian with fluency and clarity. President Clark and the LTM instructors were as puzzled as Elder Tanner was discouraged.

"You're a strange case," President Clark observed as he put away the consecrating oil. "We've never before had someone who could understand both the written and spoken language but who could not, at least with elementary proficiency, speak the language himself."

"I don't understand it myself," Orrin replied. "I'm sure your blessing will help loosen my tongue."

It did not. Orrin's instructors reported that a native Norwegian meeting Elder Tanner for the first time would find his words incomprehensible, prompting President Clark to call Orrin into his office for a confidential interview.

"Elder Tanner, is there something weighing on your conscience, something you wish to confess?" Clark asked. When Orrin hesitated, Clark continued. "Missionaries who struggle with the language are often struggling with the guilt they justifiably feel over past transgressions. Confessing your sins will wipe the slate clean and remove the stumbling block to speaking the language."

Orrin was not shocked by the question, because he also had wondered whether an unacknowledged sin lay as an obstacle in his path. Doubts that had been raised by Uncle Porter but angrily brushed aside by his father came to mind. He dismissed them, as his father instructed, and instead told President Clark about his lightminded banter with friends and their pranks, such as salting the sacrament water and smoking hollow weeds at a Boy Scout Jamboree. Reaching back for something to confess, Orrin concluded, "I laughed at dirty jokes."

President Clark shook his head. "There must be more, something else. Have you been chaste with the young ladies?"

"Yes, sir. I've never even been on a date."

"So you've never—

"Even kissed a girl, though I would like to some day."

President Clark stood, indicating the interview was over. "Elder Tanner, the Lord is pleased with your sincere confession," he said, shaking the young elder's hand. "And don't worry, you will have plenty of time for kissing girls after your mission."

Anson Tanner advised his son to have faith in himself. "You're an intelligent young man. It will come," he wrote in reply to Orrin's letter that detailed his frustration. "If God is testing you, as you suggest, then you should demonstrate your faith by focusing on the talents you bring to the mission. You have a knowledge and understanding of the scriptures that can help the other missionaries. Be generous with your talents and God will accept your sacrifice, as he accepted Abel's sacrifice." Orrin embraced his father's advice and asked President Clark if he could teach some of the gospel doctrine lessons. Clark readily agreed. He was eager to take advantage of Elder Tanner's scholarship, which would set a good example for the other missionaries. He did not know Anson Tanner had fallen into disfavor among church leaders.

Orrin selected the preexistence for his first lesson. "You may not know this, but many religions don't believe we lived with God as spirits before coming to earth," Orrin told the assembled missionaries. "Some people may challenge you, claiming the Bible says nothing about the preexistence. But the evidence is there." Orrin instructed the missionaries to open their Bibles to chapter nine of the Gospel of John. He read the first three verses: "And as Jesus passed by, he saw a man which was blind from his birth. And his disciples asked him, saying, Master, who did sin, this man, or his parents, that he was born blind? Jesus answered, Neither hath this man sinned, nor his parents: but that the works of God should be made manifest in him."

"Here's the key," Orrin said. "The disciples asked whether the beggar had been cursed with blindness because of sin. He had been blind since birth, so the only time he could have sinned was in a preexistent life."

A Danish sister raised her hand. "But couldn't someone argue that the disciples were wrong in making this supposition. Jesus never explicitly endorsed their assumption."

"Yes, but it's important to note he did not reject it," Orrin replied. "The disciples spoke as if the concept of the preexistence was common knowledge and accepted among the Jews, which it was. Thus, there was no need for Jesus to remark on it. Instead, Jesus spoke to the question of why this man was born blind. The answer was—"

Elder Pedersen, suddenly animated, interrupted Orrin. "By that logic, Jesus also implicitly accepts the notion that we, as spirits, could sin in the preexistence."

"Well, I don't know if one could say—"

"That's the implicit logic, Elder Tanner," Pedersen insisted. "And not only could we sin in the preexistence, but as a result, we could be punished with a physical disability or flaw when we come to earth."

"Negroes sinned in the preexistence," said a Swedish elder.

"They were less than valiant. That's not really a sin," Orrin corrected.

President Clark, sitting at the rear, frowned. "You are letting the missionaries get off topic, Elder Tanner."

Elder Pedersen persisted. "Isn't this question relevant to understanding our earthly existence? Are some people born with disabilities or predispositions such as alcoholism by random chance or because of some sin on their part in the preexistence?"

"Those are good questions, but—"

President Clark interrupted loudly. "You're veering further off topic." He continued talking as he walked to the front. "Still, this is a good object lesson for Elder Tanner and all of you. When investigators want to explore doctrines and practices beyond the scope of the discussions, like say polygamy or temple worship, you must develop techniques for steering them back to the discussion's main points."

Clark was now standing in front of the room. "Thank you, Elder Tanner," he said, signaling the end of the gospel lesson. "I'm sure you will do better next time." Turning to Elder Pedersen, President Clark wagged a finger, saying, "And you, Elder, should focus your time and attention on the gospel's basic principles, instead of hypothetical questions that will lead you and your investigators down a rabbit hole of confusion and doubt."

Orrin reluctantly shoved his unfinished presentation into his coat pocket and stepped down from the dais, regretting he had not delivered a similar harsh rebuke to Elder Pedersen. *What was Elder Pedersen trying to prove with his pedantic questions, questions he surely knew no investigator would ever ask?* Orrin's irritation increased as he thought about the ease with which Pedersen learned Norwegian. The unfairness gnawed at his gut. Orrin realized his uncharitable feelings toward Pedersen undermined the spirituality he needed to be a successful missionary. That made Orrin dislike him even more.

Chapter 9

Cultivate self-discipline, self-control, self-mastery.

Conduct of a Missionary

"Whoa, what's that?" Tom grimaced as he pointed at the dark purple bruise encircling Eddie's bicep.

Eddie looked down at his arm. He had forgotten how nasty the bruise looked. "Oh, I burned it on the exposed tailpipe of a dune buggy."

"Does it hurt?" Tom reached out a hand, but Eddie shied away.

"Yeah, a little."

"You ought to have it looked at."

"If it doesn't get better, I will," Eddie said. The dune buggy tailpipe was a lame excuse. He had seen a couple of dune buggies making noise in the street, but he didn't actually know anyone who owned one, and so he was relieved Tom didn't ask any more questions. He would have to be careful undressing in front of Tom and his other housemates.

Dr. Orlan had warned about the bruises, especially at the voltages Eddie had requested. "It can't be avoided but, still, it's all for the good," Dr. Orlan explained. "The psychological principles guiding our reparative therapy program are quite simple: human behavior can be molded by rewarding desired behaviors and punishing behaviors that are not. Just as chimpanzees, pigeons, rats, and other animals can be induced to perform complex tasks or even abandon instinctual activities, so, too, can human behavior be modified by intelligently designed systems of reward and punishment."

In Eddie's case, the punishment was the shocks. If aroused by the slides of naked men, he would receive a high-voltage shock lasting three seconds, and the shocks would continue in ten second intervals until Eddie pushed the plunger to bring up slides of naked women. He received no shocks when viewing the women. This was his reward. "See, Eddie," Dr. Orlan concluded. "You will develop an aversion to homosexual behavior while over time, we hope, you will develop an attraction to women."

The bruise had formed on Eddie's arm after just a few weeks. He occasionally felt the sting of the electrode, a phantom pain, when he was sitting at his desk or watching television. This would be followed by dull throbbing. He took to rubbing his arm, almost as an unconscious reflex. It was while he was getting dressed for church that Tom noticed the reddish-blue bruise peeking out from under Eddie's sleeve.

The fabricated story about the dune buggy wasn't the only lie Eddie told his housemates. He made up excuses whenever he had a reparative therapy session or a counseling appointment with his bishop, leaving the townhouse quickly after saying he was off to see a friend. "Who are these unnamed friends?" Tom finally asked. "We've never seen you with anyone but us—and you're not around here very often." Eddie said nothing, hoping their interest would fade. Eventually, Tom became convinced Eddie had a girlfriend, and teased him in front of the others. Eddie smiled, encouraging them to believe it was true,

The summer campus buzzed with rumors about the therapy program. "Shock-cock treatment," Tom said amid laughter from the housemates. "My psychology professor told our class all about it."

"They really shock 'em?" Gil asked.

"Right on their nuts. They show them a picture of a naked man and then—ZAP!"

Eddie's housemates grabbed at their crotches, gleefully feigning pain. Eddie felt shame and alarm. Was the program now public knowledge? He wanted to find out more but didn't want to draw attention to himself by asking too many questions.

"Why do they call it 'shock-cock' if they shock them on their nuts?" Fred said.

"Because 'shock-nuts' doesn't rhyme, idiot."

"Does the shock-cock treatment really work?" Gil asked.

"It's still experimental," Tom explained. "It's called aversion therapy, supposedly based on B. F. Skinner's reinforcement theory and some work by a Russian doctor. You can train pigeons and rats to do just about anything."

"I'm going soft just thinking about it," Eddie said, prompting more guffaws. Eddie asked whether Tom's professor said who was conducting the program or where it was taking place.

"No, it's sort of hush-hush. Our professor wouldn't tell us anything else, other than pointing out that the program shows how you can apply psychological principles to help people overcome mental problems."

"Man, you've got to be a real pervert if you need the shock-cock treatment," another housemate, John, said. A returned missionary from France, John recounted how a missionary companion made a pass at him while they were sharing a bed. "I slugged him in the nose and reported him to our mission president. He was on the next flight home. I wasn't the first one he tried to get funny with."

"He's probably getting the shock-cock treatment right now."

The banter continued, with Eddie adding a few derogatory observations about homos and fags. When Gil commented sympathetically about those undergoing the treatment, Tom said, "It sounds like you need the shock-cock treatment," which elicited more laughter. For the rest of the summer, whenever anyone got overly dramatic or did anything less than manly, someone would remark, "It sounds like you need the shock-cock treatment." Eddie felt himself blush whenever anyone said it to him. It stung when he said it to others.

"These results are exceptional, Eddie. I am very pleased," Brother Orlan said, fingering a stack of Eddie's read-outs on his desk. "You should be pleased too." He looked up from his papers and pushed back his glasses, waiting for Eddie's response.

Eddie looked past Brother Orlan to a tree branch scratching at the office window, as if searching for a way inside. Its leaves were cheerless and brown, despite a mid-summer rain. On the way to his appointment, Eddie had spotted Barry walking across the quad toward the library. His heart trembled with sadness and desire. Eddie had no thoughts of saying hello. That would certainly call into question his desire to change. But his lack of animosity toward Barry surprised him. Barry had betrayed him in the coldest, most despicable manner, yet Eddie felt only sorrow and loneliness when he saw him. Seeing Barry, Eddie realized that in all of the conversations bouncing around in his head—about homosexuality, the reparative therapy program, his interview with Apostle Prichard—he was having imagined conversations not with himself but with Barry. Barry would understand. He would laugh and joke and sneer at the absurdities. "Shock-cock," Barry would say. "Sounds to me like they're trying to cure heterosexuality as well as homosexuality. No more sex for anyone."

"You're right," Eddie would tell Barry. "I'm not getting aroused by women."

"Jesus Christ," Barry would reply. "How could anyone feel arousal with 1600 volts of scorching electricity surging through his flesh?"

Brother Orlan snapped Eddie back to the present. "You're rather quiet, Eddie. Do you have any questions about the program thus far?"

"I was wondering about the photographs of women."

"Yes?"

"Am I supposed to be aroused? I know I don't get shocked, but . . ."

Brother Orlan smiled. "Don't worry about that, Eddie. We're just getting your body and your mind sensitized to the idea that homosexual desires bring pain. We're not worried about building up your heterosexual desires because, well, those are natural. Everyone has them. Once we eliminate your homosexual urges, then your desire for women will kick in, like instinct."

"But do you know what causes these urges—I mean the homosexual ones?"

"I don't know and I don't care," Brother Orlan replied. "That's the beauty of reinforcement theory. You don't need years of expensive analysis telling you that you have an oral fixation on your mother because she stopped breastfeeding you too soon or too late or whatever absurd theories psychiatrists are positing these days. Everyone's got an opinion about what causes homosexuality. Some of them might even be right, but to me, it doesn't matter. I don't speculate about what goes on in your mind. I only care about how you act."

"That sounds logical, I guess."

"It's more than logical, Eddie. Reinforcement theory is based on divine principles. What does the Doctrine and Covenants teach us about God's spirit, about what happens when we sin?"

"He withdraws his spirit."

"And when we do what is right, when we obey God's commandments?"

"He blesses us with his spirit."

Brother Orlan slapped his hand enthusiastically on the desk. "Yes, yes, that's absolutely correct. God blesses us with a warm feeling, even a burning in our hearts, telling us our behavior pleases him. That's reinforcement theory in a nutshell. God reinforces the right behaviors by rewarding us with his spirit when we obey, and he punishes us by withdrawing his spirit when we disobey or displease him. See how that works?"

Eddie nodded yes. Brother Orlan offered a comforting smile. "Based on the results during your first eight weeks of therapy, Eddie, you're making great progress developing the behaviors that will enable you to become the person you want to be."

Even if Brother Orlan didn't care what caused homosexuality, Eddie did. He wondered if he had been wrong in believing his homosexual impulses had a biological origin. *Perhaps I latched onto the intersex phenomenon as a way to justify my unnatural behavior as natural,* he thought. *I was trying to rationalize behavior I knew was wrong.* Still, the question bothered him: what caused him to be attracted to members of his own sex? When Eddie wasn't working, he searched the library's catalogue files and combed through its collection of psychology books and journals. He would start by perusing a book's index to see whether it dealt with homosexuality, and then quickly scan the relevant pages. Eddie didn't check out any of the books. He had heard rumors that BYU Security monitored students who checked out salacious materials; besides, he didn't want to bring home books for his housemates to see. His research brought no insight or satisfaction. Psychiatrists almost universally regarded homosexuality as a mental illness, but they disagreed as to its causes and treatment. After noting that a Salt Lake City psychiatrist was cited extensively in academic books and articles about homosexuality, Eddie made an appointment to see him.

Dr. Frank Carlton's office was spare. He sat in a large black leather chair opposite Eddie, whose chair, though not quite as large, was equally comfortable. Dr. Carlton held a notepad on his lap. He rolled a ballpoint pen between his fingers while a half-smoked cigar smoldered on an ashtray. "I know I'm attracted to men," Eddie said, "but nothing I've read and no one I've talked to can explain why. None of it makes any sense to me."

Dr. Carlton chomped pensively on his cigar, rolling it from one side of his mouth to the other. "You'll never learn a thing in that reparative program your church has dragooned you into. You don't cure neuroses by shocking people. If you want to know the truth, I think this medieval torture being inflicted on you is clear evidence your church leaders are trying to repress their own sexual urges. It says more about them than it does you. You know, Eddie, I sometimes use surrogates to help my patients overcome their fear of women. For some men, all it takes is three or four sessions. A carrot is much more effective than a stick."

"I could never do that. The church wouldn't allow it," Eddie said.

Carlton smiled scornfully. "And yet, a barbaric shock regimen is perfectly fine."

"Fear of women. Is this my problem?"

"It might be. Nearly all of my homosexual patients have come from homes with domineering mothers who were overly demonstrative and smothering in their affection, while their fathers were weak and emotionally detached, even hostile, and often absent from home. You see, the homosexual's unsatisfactory relationship with his father feeds an unhealthy identification with the mother. Our goal will be to get you to de-identify with your mother and re-establish your identification with your own sex."

"But none of my brothers are homosexuals. Why did I turn out differently?"

"How do you know you are different from your brothers? Families have a way of keeping such things hidden, you know."

"I can't believe that."

"I bet your brothers don't know anything about you, do they?" Dr. Carlton rubbed out his cigar amid a cloud of smoke. "But that doesn't really matter, anyway. You're the one who's here, not them. What is it you want to get from therapy, Eddie?"

Eddie leaned forward in his chair. "I want to be like everyone else.

I want to get married, raise a family, and not spend the rest of my life wondering why I'm different. I can't imagine spending the rest of my life as a homosexual."

"You want to be normal. That's good. And you are right to want to understand what caused this. That's an important step in addressing mental disorders. I can help you get at the nub of your underlying neurosis and then overcome it, so you can live a normal life."

A timer buzzed, announcing the end of the fifty-minute session. Eddie stood and thanked the doctor. Dr. Carlton instructed Eddie to schedule another appointment with his receptionist, but as the two men shook hands, each knew Eddie wasn't coming back.

Near the end of the summer, the gospel doctrine teacher in Eddie's ward showed a slide presentation of ancient ruins in Mexico and Peru. He had recently returned from a BYU-sponsored tour of both countries, where university professors had lectured on the similarities between the Book of Mormon civilizations and the once-dominant Aztec and Incan peoples. "I want to show you some of the fascinating discoveries our scholars have made in pinpointing the cities we read about in the Book of Mormon," the teacher said. The lights went out and the slideshow began.

Eddie was as eager as anyone to see the presentation, but at the familiar sound of the whirring projector, he felt the queasy taste of lunch in his throat. His face flushed and perspiration ran down his forehead. As each new slide dropped into place, he felt the sting on his arm and on his leg and on his groin. He looked at his surroundings, trying to convince himself he was safe. The room grew warm, then unbearably hot. His lunch climbed higher in his throat. Finally, Eddie excused himself and rushed to the bathroom, and vomited into the sink and onto the floor. When the nausea passed, he wiped his mouth and chin with a paper towel. He hardly recognized the pale, sweaty face staring back at him in the mirror.

The shock-cock treatment wasn't working. That's what Eddie started calling it, just like his friends, just like he knew Barry would. "Looks like you could use the shock-cock treatment," he would say to himself when feeling low, gallows humor that barely disguised his contempt for himself and his disillusionment with the program. Slideshows now filled him with dread and nausea. But naked men? Not so much. He was done with Barry, but he longed for someone like Barry, someone who cared for him and understood him and jolted him—*yes, that's the right word*, he mused to himself—jolted him with pleasure and filled him with an excitement that made him look forward to tomorrow. Such desires were wrong. He knew it and loathed himself for it. But he no longer believed Brother Orlan or the shock-cock treatment or psychiatrists like Dr. Carlton could help him.

Eddie concluded that his condition was a Job-like test. Just as God had cursed Job with boils and all manner of afflictions, He had cursed Eddie with homosexual desires to see whether Eddie would succumb not just to carnal temptation but also to despair and apostasy. The hardships and humiliations he had suffered—his arrest by BYU security, his confession to his bishop and parents, the painful shock-cock treatment, and being forced every day to hide his condition and shame from his friends—were all part of this test. Eddie vowed he would not curse God and die, but persevere. He remained in the treatment because, after all, wasn't this one of the trials he had been given, a cross he must humbly bear? Eddie no longer worried whether he would be allowed to go on a mission because he believed a mission, too, was part of God's plan. If Eddie fulfilled an honorable mission while resisting temptation at every turn, he would prove himself worthy and God would lift the burden of homosexuality from him.

Eddie's faith was rewarded. Upon completing the twelve-week therapy regime, he received an enthusiastic endorsement from Brother Orlan, who commended Eddie for meeting every program metric. Two weeks after Bishop Perry submitted Eddie's mission papers, he received a call to Norway. His parents drove to Provo for his missionary farewell and drove him to the mission home for a three-day orientation before he began language training at the Ricks College LTM. While Eddie chatted with his parents during the ride to Salt Lake City, his mother noticed Eddie massaging his arm. "You were rubbing it constantly during church yesterday, even while you were giving your talk," she said. "Is there something wrong with your arm?"

"No, it's just a little sore from the therapy. Dr. Orlan says it will subside."

Eddie's mother turned and faced Eddie in the back seat. "Let me look at it."

"It's nothing, Mom."

"You're going to be gone for two years. You should see a doctor before you go, just in case."

Eddie continued resisting until his father, pinched and angry, pounded the steering wheel with the palms of his hands. "For God's sake, Marie," he shouted. "Stop treating Eddie like a weak little flower. We agreed we would treat Eddie like the man we want him to be."

Eddie's mom turned back in her seat and stared at the traffic ahead.

"I'm okay, Mom. Really," Eddie assured her. That was the last thing anyone said before they arrived at the mission home. On the sidewalk, Eddie's father shook his hand vigorously and his mom gave him a tearful kiss, though she was careful not to hug him too closely. Suitcase in hand, Eddie walked up the steps, desperate to bury the past.

Chapter 10

Develop no intimacies, affections, or love affairs of any kind. Have no unauthorized correspondence within the mission.

Conduct of a Missionary

"Coffee?" The silky voice shook Apostle Joseph F. Prichard from his reverie. "Coffee, sir?" the flight attendant asked. She held a tray of empty cups in one hand, a coffee pot in the other.

Prichard smiled. "No, thank you. I'm a Mormon," he said, scanning her name tag. "We don't drink coffee, Tammy. Do you know anything about the Mormons?"

"The Mormon men who fly with us are always dressed in white shirts and ties. Is this a requirement?"

"No, it's because we want to look our best, as befitting representatives of our Savior, Jesus Christ." Prichard smiled again, but the flight attendant's eyes wandered ahead to the next row. "What else do you know about the Mormons, Tammy?"

"I know not to offer you a cigarette when I come back," she replied, laughing, and then moved up the aisle, careful not to look back. "Coffee?" she asked the passengers in the next row.

Apostle Prichard adjusted his glasses and returned to his report, searching for the precise words to convey his sense of betrayal. Righteous anger flowed from pen to paper. He had spent nearly forty-eight hours in Oslo advising President Toressen and his assistants on how to handle the situation with the missing missionaries, but it wasn't until he was boarding the plane for home that he realized one of those elders was the homosexual boy he had counseled the previous summer. Was President Toressen so obtuse that he didn't recognize this was a salient piece of information? Even worse, had Toressen purposely kept this information from him in an ill-conceived effort to protect the young man?

It would not be the first time Toressen had coddled a troubled missionary. He routinely gave the poor performers and malcontents jobs in the mission office, hoping they would catch the spirit of work from President Toressen and other mission leaders. Instead, they infected the mission headquarters with their cynicism and flagging faith. It was the number one rule for mission presidents: don't bring your problem elders into the mission home. President Toressen acted as if he was somehow different. Most shocking was Toressen's indiscriminate sharing of his visions and prophetic dreams during a speaking tour across Norway a few months earlier. Every member of the Twelve agreed Toressen had been indiscreet, though none endorsed Prichard's suggestion that Toressen be relieved following a particularly disastrous speech to newspaper reporters. "If we brought home every mission president who somehow fell short of perfection, we'd quickly run out of mission presidents," said Apostle Hiram G. Bingham, president of the Quorum of the Twelve. "He needs your loving support and guidance."

After hearing Prichard's complaints, some of his fellow apostles joked that he was jealous of the charismatic Toressen, who inspired adulation among the church's small band of Norwegian faithful. "It's the opinion of the non-Mormons I'm worried about. He's making us look like a superstitious cult," Prichard said. He shook a disapproving finger and glowered at the others, making it clear he did not appreciate friendly teasing, even from senior apostles.

The truth was that he had never liked the ebullient Norwegian. Upon meeting Apostle Prichard for the first time, President Toressen had enthusiastically recounted a vision in which he foresaw that he would be called as the Norwegian mission president, despite a massive heart attack his doctor warned would preclude any type of stressful activity for the rest of his life. "I know God has a special calling for me here in Norway because of the spiritual experiences with which I have been blessed," Toressen said. "I'm sure you know what I am talking about."

Apostle Prichard nodded his agreement, but Toressen's comment resurfaced dark thoughts Prichard had long ago sought to bury. Prichard had never aspired to apostleship, never considered it as a possibility. He was an educator and looked upon the church's Institute and seminary programs as his true calling. He rose quickly to a leadership role and traveled willingly to the farthest outposts to instill the church's teachers with his philosophy. "Our goal as instructors is to strengthen the testimonies of the church's young people. Everything we teach—every scripture we read, every story we tell, every lesson we plan—should be aimed toward that goal," he said, adding that the corollary is also true. "You must never ever teach anything that would undermine or in any way harm the testimonies of our precious youth."

One of the program's senior instructors spoke without raising his hand. "But what if a student asks about a controversial subject, clearly showing they understand the topic? Don't we owe it to them to have a frank and open discussion?"

Prichard glared at the man. "What part of 'never ever' don't you understand?"

Prichard heard grumblings among the old guard. When word reached Prichard that the malcontents were calling him "Brother Never Ever," he embraced the epithet, even putting it on his name tag at their next quarterly Institute conference. "Never ever harm the testimony of our young," he proclaimed during his keynote. "Never ever." Sensing continued resistance to his message, Prichard reassigned some of the older instructors, including those who thought their seniority made them untouchable, and removed them from plumb positions at the larger universities. Several found themselves teaching in remote towns where they were the only faculty. This prompted the usual complaints, but the Brethren supported the moves. A few of those reassigned retired or quit. "This is the optimal outcome," he told his wife.

When Prichard was called to lead the Eastern States Mission, some in the Institute's old guard interpreted this as a rebuke for his overreaching, and indeed, several of those exiled by Prichard were allowed to return to former positions. But when Prichard completed his three-year assignment, not only was he tapped to oversee the church's entire education system, but he also was called to the First Council of Seventy, strengthening his institutional clout in shaping the instruction to his liking. He anticipated he would serve the rest of his life in the First Council of Seventy directing the church's education and Sunday School programs. He smiled with satisfaction when he learned that some of the newly minted Institute teachers were calling themselves "Never Evers." The teachers would now police their own.

Everyone had anticipated his call to apostleship but Prichard himself. He felt worthy but not chosen. After all, an apostle is supposed to be a special witness of Jesus Christ, but he had not seen the Savior or experienced a unique revelation of Christ's mission, the kind of revelation he believed each apostle was privileged to receive. He pleaded with the Lord, hoping to receive the witness before he was ordained an apostle. When that day came and passed, he fasted and prayed, locking himself in his study for more than twenty-four hours, most of the time spent on his knees. Still no sign. He wondered, *What does it mean to be an apostolic witness for Christ? Does it require a personal visitation, that you see and speak to him face to face? Or does this make you a Doubting Thomas, demanding proof before you become a witness?* He wanted to ask the other apostles whether they had revelations or visions affirming their calling to the Twelve, but he felt it improper to ask them to reveal something so personal and sacred, and he was embarrassed by his own lack of witness to his new calling. He never doubted the church or his testimony of Joseph Smith's prophetic role, but he began to doubt his own call to apostleship.

"Do you think we made a mistake?" Apostle Bingham asked.

Prichard stared across the desk of the church's senior apostle. Three months into his calling as an apostle, he finally broke down and confessed his feelings of inadequacy to Elder Bingham. He had expected disappointment, perhaps alarm and a scolding, but not the wry amusement in Bingham's voice. "I can't perform my responsibilities as an apostle of our Lord Jesus Christ without the special knowledge to which I will bear witness," Prichard said. "I want—I need—what you and the other apostles have."

"And what is it you think we have?"

"I-I don't know, exactly, but I don't think it proper for to me ask what witness you've got."

"Nor would I tell you. That's between me and the Lord," Bingham said emphatically.

"So what do I do? How do I get the assurance I need?"

Apostle Bingham roused himself in his chair. Ninety-three years old with a shock of white hair draped over an otherwise bald head, he pointed a long, bony finger at Prichard. "God most assuredly called you to apostleship. I can testify to that because I was there when the decision was made. Elder Prichard, you should know you have been carefully vetted by the Twelve, and we have every confidence you have the knowledge and intelligence and managerial skills needed to succeed in your calling. The Lord prepared you for this mission. Now, regarding the spiritual confirmation you seek, remember what we tell our young men, the ones who are hesitant to go on missions because they don't yet have a testimony."

Prichard beamed with sudden understanding. "We tell them to go anyway."

"Because going on a mission—"

"Because going on a mission is the best way to gain a testimony of the church," Prichard said, completing Bingham's statement.

Bingham leaned back in his chair. "And serving as an apostle, devoting yourself to the Lord with all your heart and being, is the best way to gain the apostle's witness you seek."

Apostle Prichard felt his burden lifting. "I understand," he said, tears flowing. "I understand."

Apostle Prichard never again allowed himself to doubt his calling. Instead, he became an ardent witness of Christ, believing that each time he bore his testimony of Christ's saving grace, it brought him closer to gaining an unequivocal spiritual witness. His willingness to abandon his doubts and give himself over was not only a test of faith but also a lesson in how to develop faith, a lesson he imparted whenever he spoke. To a group of missionaries arriving in Salt Lake City to begin their two-year sojourn, he said, "We know from experience that many of you have come to the mission home still harboring doubts—doubts about yourselves and the church. I say to you, cast away your skepticism and disbelief and distrust and fear. Embrace faith, and God will reward your faith with the loving embrace of his spirit."

A sister missionary with pale skin and a neatly pressed skirt hesitantly raised her hand. "I want to be strong, but I'm not sure what you mean. How do I embrace faith?"

Apostle Prichard gave an encouraging smile. "Obedience. You embrace faith by demonstrating your willingness to obey all of your priesthood leaders and, of course, all of the mission rules. Obedience builds faith."

More questions followed as the young elders and sisters eagerly sought wisdom and inspiration before embarking on their assigned missions. The intimate back-and-forth with one of the Lord's apostles did more to strengthen their testimonies than a hundred hours of scripture reading. "Remember who you are," Prichard counseled. "You represent me and all of the Twelve Apostles, we who bear special witness of Jesus Christ."

A nineteen-year-old elder in an ill-fitting green suit and mismatched tie shot up his hand. "I know it's important for each of us to gain our own testimony through the warm feeling in our hearts," he said. "But is it true that the apostles, because of your special calling, have actually seen Christ? Is that what it means to be an apostle?"

An eerie silence swept through the room, as if the Holy Spirit itself had suddenly made its appearance known. The missionaries leaned forward, necks straining, hoping to hear an answer that would not only inspire in the moment but would also carry them through their missions and serve as a faith-promoting story they could recount over and over in testimony meetings and in family gatherings when they had children of their own. Prichard shifted on his feet but offered only a weak smile while he pondered how to answer the question. "The Book of Mormon and Bible contain many awe-inspiring stories of miracles and visions in earlier times, and so you might think it natural to inquire whether those of us in the Lord's service today have experienced those same blessings," he said. Prichard spoke softly at first, but his smile slowly became a scowl, and his calm voice growled with stern indignation. "However, such an inquiry is not only unnatural but also impertinent. Like a Doubting Thomas who must see and feel the Lord's wounds, you want me to reveal my most sacred experiences—my sacred communion with the Lord—to bolster your own faith. I give you this advice now so you will never forget it. Do not inquire into the mysteries to satisfy your own misguided curiosity. It is demeaning to me, to the Twelve, and to God."

Apostle Prichard wondered if he had spoken too harshly. A tearful apology from the young missionary followed, but Prichard couldn't reignite the uplifting spirit that had prevailed before the exchange. For this he blamed the elder, but out of kindness, the apostle thought it best not to reprimand the boy further, and so accepted his apology.

Still, it was this obsession with answering the unanswerable and knowing the unknowable that had to be nipped in the bud, not only among the church's young people but also among—especially among—the church's academic elite. He had fought that battle as the head of the church's education department, and he continued to fight it as a member of the Twelve. That's why he was so rattled by the Norwegian mission president, Bjørn Toressen. It was bad enough that Toressen spoke openly of his visions and sacred experiences. Nobody did that, not even his fellow apostles. If you are blessed to peer beyond the veil, keep it to yourself. Toressen was such an absent-minded administrator that Prichard was beginning to question the man's fitness to serve and whether he was exaggerating his spiritual experiences (not that some General Authorities didn't embellish a little, but they did so to promote faith, not themselves). There was something vaguely threatening about Toressen's self-assured spirituality, though he couldn't say why. Prichard was sitting on the stand when Toressen told a Norwegian congregation of his calling to become president of the Norwegian mission. It was humbling but no surprise. "The Lord knows who I am," President Toressen proclaimed.

"I sure wish He'd tell me," Prichard muttered to himself after the flight attendant cleared away his tray. "What a strange man."

Chapter 11

Be anxiously engaged in saving souls. The Church is here to bless the people and you are its minister. The reward is to rest with those souls in the Kingdom of God.

Conduct of a Missionary

Orrin prided himself not only on being the most prepared missionary called to serve in Norway, but also the most enthusiastic and confident in his ultimate success. Having not forgotten the story of the young prophet Samuel, he laid this offering before God: Orrin would demonstrate his faith by turning himself into the most hardworking and obedient missionary in Norway, and God, in return, would reward him not only with baptisms, but also with the spiritual breakthrough he had long desired. His inability to effectively speak the language had been discouraging. Still, by the end of eight weeks of language training, his instructors had declared him ready to preach, assuring him that time and practice would refine his speech.

Orrin arrived tired but wide-eyed with anticipation at Oslo's Fornebu Airport on a snowy November morning. Orrin and his fellow missionaries wandered aimlessly through the airport, unable to decipher the instructions barked out over the airport's public address system. But soon they heard the exuberant shouts of elders from the Oslo mission home, who greeted the new missionaries with handshakes so friendly they hurt Orrin's fingers. "Velkommen til norge, greenie," said an elder wearing a brown fedora and a neon smile. "Welcome to Norway." He gave Orrin a portentous wink and a slap on the back, as if the fate of the Norwegian mission were being passed directly into his care.

After shepherding the arriving missionaries through baggage claim, the mission home elders piled everyone into a van and drove them to mission headquarters. They assured everyone they would love President Toressen and they would love the work and love the Norwegian people and they would never work harder but never be happier, because the Norwegian mission was the best mission in the world. Exhausted but content, Orrin stared absently at the road. The chattering missionaries could not disturb his reverie. Trucks cleared the way, pushing aside mounds of snow as their headlights bounced on the icy highway ahead. Snowflakes flew against the window, then melted into a hazy blur. Although it was seven o'clock, the sun would not rise for another hour. As they passed a valley blanketed in glistening snow, Orrin thought of the scripture that says that the field is ripe and ready to harvest. The next morning, Elder James Flossen, Orrin's senior companion, picked him up at the mission home, and together they rode the Kjelsås line streetcar to their hybel, or apartment, in Oslo's Grünerløkka district.

Elder Flossen was tall with a thin face and long nose that gave him a bird-like appearance. His dark blue suit had an ironed shine, particularly at the knees and elbows, but he carried himself with confidence and chatted comfortably with the mission home elders. Sister Toressen, the mission president's wife, greeted Elder Flossen heartily, suggesting he was a top performing missionary; however, Orrin was disappointed that during the streetcar ride to their hybel, Elder Flossen did not engage the Norwegian passengers in conversation, as the missionaries were instructed. Rather, he sat quietly and read the *Dagsblad* newspaper. Orrin scanned the car, having determined to dive into the work. Except for a group of teenage girls who talked and laughed among themselves, the Norwegians read newspapers or stared ahead, avoiding eye contact with fellow passengers. At the next stop, an older man wrapped in a scarf and coat smiled at Orrin as he took a seat two rows ahead. Orrin jumped up and took the seat next to him.

"*Jeg er en mormonmisjonaer,*" Orrin said. "I am a Mormon missionary."

"I have been to America many times," the man replied in English. "It is a nice country."

Orrin persisted in Norwegian, asking the man if he had heard of Joseph Smith. The man ignored or misunderstood the question and continued in English. "Seattle and San Francisco. I work on a boat. I was, how do you say, merchant marine."

The conversation continued in this manner, each man insisting on speaking the language of the other, each talking increasingly louder, as if this would help the other to understand, until Orrin looked up to see Elder Flossen standing above him. "The next stop is ours," he said, sliding Orrin's suitcase across the aisle. "I've got your duffel bag with your duvet and bedding. We've got to be ready when I pull the cord."

"Shouldn't we be speaking Norwegian?" Orrin asked.

"You just asked me that question in English."

Orrin grinned sheepishly. He turned to the Norwegian man and handed him a pamphlet. "I know Joseph Smith was a true prophet who restored the true church of Jesus Christ," he said in garbled earnestness. Elder Flossen pulled the cord and the two missionaries exited onto Toftes Gate. Orrin watched the streetcar's lights vanish into the snowy fog.

During the short walk to their hybel on Helgesens Gate, Orrin's hands stiffened in the cold. "You're going to need better gloves," Flossen observed. The elders passed inside a courtyard of what appeared to be wooden storage sheds and walked in silence up four flights of stairs. The stairwell smelled faintly of boiled cabbage. "Home sweet home," Elder Flossen said, pushing open the hybel door with a shove from his shoulder. He smiled sadly and switched on a lamp.

The two-room hybel—a bedroom and a kitchen—offered reasonably comfortable furnishings, including two dressers, two tables, a bookshelf, two kitchen chairs, and a sitting chair whose seat cushion was held together with strips of black tape. The kitchen had a hot plate with two burners, a toaster, and a large basin with a cold-water spigot. The apartment once had a refrigerator and oven, Elder Flossen said, but they kept shorting out the electricity, so the apartment manager made the previous missionaries get rid of them. Their hybel faced the street, overlooking a park. The large windows offered a generous view of the cars and people scurrying home from work along the sidewalk below. Elder Flossen turned on a small electric floor heater—the apartment's only heat—assuring Orrin the hybel warmed up quickly, though he kept his coat on while Orrin unpacked his suitcase and put away his clothes.

"Hey, where's the bathroom?" Orrin said as he got out a toothbrush and razor.

"Outside, in the courtyard. I thought you saw them when we came in."

"You mean the storage sheds . . . ?"

". . . are outhouses, Elder Tanner."

Orrin stared at Elder Flossen. Was it really true? Senior companions often played practical jokes on greenies fresh from the LTM. "We share the first row of outhouses with the other people in our stairwell," Flossen explained in a tone indicating he wasn't kidding. "If you want to brush your teeth or wash your hands, you do it in the kitchen basin. But if you want to use the toilet, that's outside. The key is hanging by the door. And by the way, always take toilet paper with you. They're supposed to provide it, but it's never there when you need it."

Orrin tromped down the four flights of stairs into the courtyard. The outhouse was damp and the floor slick, but the walls and seat were clean. It smelled only mildly unpleasant. He felt a frozen wetness on his neck and looked up to see snowflakes falling through a hole in the ceiling. Orrin had come to Norway with romantic visions of serving under extreme hardship, perhaps in a desolate northern village where he could prove his Job-like faith and good character. Oslo had been a disappointing first assignment, but Orrin was beginning to see Grünerløkka's possibilities. The wind whistled through the cracks and Orrin steeled himself for the icy air awaiting outside. "Welcome to Norway," he said, shivering but not unhappy, and locked the outhouse door behind him.

"Wanna take the first door?" Elder Flossen asked. Orrin stepped forward and pushed the buzzer. Hearing footsteps approach, he swallowed, moistening his throat, and rocked forward on his toes, suddenly alert with nervous excitement.

Orrin had awakened that morning to the sound of screeching brakes and muffled voices outside the window. Elder Flossen rolled over and opened his eyes when Orrin's feet hit the floor. "It comes by every morning at five fifty-four," he said, yawning. "You get used to it." On the street below, Orrin watched a dozen hardy Norwegian commuters climb onto a downtown bus. The doors closed and it disappeared in a cloud of black smoke. Elder Flossen pulled his pillow over his head and rolled on his side, but Orrin did not fall back to sleep until just before the alarm rang a half hour later. The two missionaries rose and shuffled across the cold wooden floor to the kitchen, where Elder Flossen filled two pans with water and set them on burners. "We'll use this one for shaving after the water heats up," Flossen said, pointing to one of the pans. "I'll make oatmeal in the other."

Hanging above the basin sink was a mirror with several cracks, a survivor of numerous drops and falls. While Orrin shaved, he studied the mission schedule tacked on the kitchen wall next to the sink:

6:30	Arise and dress
7:00	Breakfast
7:30	Personal study
8:00	Study with companion
9:00	Final preparations/travel
9:30	Proselytize
3:00	*Middag* supper
5:00	Proselytize
9:30	Return to hybel
10:30	Sleep

This will be my schedule for the next twenty-two months, Orrin thought to himself. He would have a half day free on Saturdays to take care of personal business, such as writing letters and doing laundry. A portion of each Sunday would be spent attending church. Otherwise, he was expected to be constantly engaged in their work and putting in a minimum of fifty-five hours of proselytizing each week, not including travel time.

Orrin memorized scriptures during his personal study and worked on his door approach during companion study. Much to his annoyance, Elder Flossen frequently interrupted him to correct his pronunciation and grammar. "That's how I pronounced it in the LTM, and my instructors said I was pronouncing the words correctly," Orrin insisted.

"They were just trying to be encouraging," Flossen replied. He had Orrin repeat several words and phrases over and over, and then combine them into sentences. "Don't worry, it takes time," he said sympathetically. "Once you're out talking with Norwegians, you'll start imitating their words and accents without even thinking about it."

While Elder Flossen visited the outhouse one last time before they began tracting door to door, Orrin tried on the new black fedora he had purchased the day before. The Norwegian elders were required to wear hats from October through March, a rule designed to keep the young men warm against their better fashion judgment. It was common knowledge among the missionaries that people lose up to ninety percent of their body heat through the top of their heads, an assertion that, like the mission rules themselves, no one challenged. Orrin thought the fedora made him look either pretentious or silly, he couldn't decide which, but like white shirts and ties, it served as a signifying feature of missionaries. After Flossen returned, the two missionaries put on their heavy coats and overshoes and packed their briefcase with pamphlets and copies of the Book of Mormon, then knelt in prayer before they left. "Guide us to find the pure in heart who seek thy word," Orrin said.

"*Goddag, vi representerer Jesu Kristi Kirke av siste dagers hellige, ogsa kjente som Mormonkirken*," Orrin said cheerfully. "Good day, we represent The Church of Jesus Christ of Latter-day Saints, also known as the Mormon Church."

The woman at the door, coffee cup in hand, gave Orrin a puzzled look, then said something he didn't understand. Elder Flossen stepped forward and repeated Orrin's introduction, to which the woman frowned. "*Ikke interessert*," she replied, and started to close the door. "Not interested."

"Would you be interested if we told you God speaks to living prophets today, just as He did in biblical times," Elder Flossen said. He reached into his coat pocket and pulled out a pamphlet with Joseph Smith's portrait on the front. "I testify that this man was called by God to restore his true church to earth."

A bemused look swept across the woman's face, as if Elder Flossen had said something terribly funny. "I will take your pamphlet, but I was born, baptized, confirmed, and married in the State Church, and I will die in the State Church," she said, sounding apologetic. "I'm sorry, but I am not interested."

Elder Flossen started to reply but stopped as soon as the door clicked shut. He took out a spiral notebook listing the names and numbers on each door of the apartment building and calmly noted "Reject" next to the woman's apartment number.

"I didn't get a chance to bear my testimony," Orrin said, not a little disappointed, given it had been his first door.

"Sometimes they close the door faster than we can talk." Flossen finished writing the name and number of the next door in his tracting book. "I'll take the next door and we can alternate the rest of the day. Talk a little more slowly. She couldn't understand you. She thought you were selling something, which is why I had to jump in. But don't worry, you'll get it." Elder Flossen was already ringing the next doorbell before Orrin had a chance to respond.

The rest of the day brought more of the same. Many people merely peeked through the eyehole before walking away without opening the door, and those who did open up spoke reluctantly with the elders. Orrin was largely a bystander. Few could understand him, regardless of how slowly he spoke. After Orrin delivered his basic approach, which lasted less than thirty seconds, Elder Flossen would take over the conversation. Within an hour, the excitement that had carried Orrin through the early morning hours began to fade and he was overcome with an aching weariness. Once he fell asleep while Elder Flossen argued at length with a born-again Christian about whether man is saved by faith or works. Orrin woke with a start when the man shouted that the elders must accept Jesus in their hearts. After each of Orrin's turns at the door, Flossen would offer suggestions, invariably finding a word or phrase that needed correcting. "Your accent's wrong here" he would say matter-of-factly, or "Say '*dere*' instead of '*du*.' It's not polite to use the familiar form." Desperately tired, Orrin responded with resentful grunts. He was quite willing to be chiseled and molded into perfection by the Lord, but he was not prepared to accept Elder Flossen as the instrument for this task.

They stopped for an hour at noon to share a chocolate bar and watch ice-skaters in the park. Later, when they returned to their hybel for afternoon *middag*, Elder Flossen cooked bean soup from a mix and put a fried egg on top for extra protein. "We'll alternate cooking breakfast and *middag* once you've settled in," he told Orrin. They left in darkness at five o'clock to resume tracting, mounting the same streetcar and working the same apartment complex with the same results. By the day's end, they had knocked on nearly one hundred doors, talked to fifty-three listless, lacka-daisical people, none for more than five minutes and most less than two, handed out seventeen pamphlets, and sold one Book of Mormon. Upon arriving back at their hybel, Orrin stopped first at the outhouse, then changed into his pajamas, brushed his teeth, said his prayers, and climbed into bed while Elder Flossen was still writing in his mission journal. Orrin fell immediately into a deep, dreamless sleep.

Orrin's ability to speak and understand Norwegian improved slightly in the days that followed, though the main words he heard were "not inter-ested" and "we belong to the State Church." Elder Flossen continued to do most of the talking, but he would signal Orrin with a slight nod for Orrin to bear his testimony. Orrin felt a surge of accomplishment each time he testified of Joseph Smith's prophetic mission, even though the doors were fast closing and sometimes shut before he finished. Unlike Orrin's first day, they engaged in a few lengthy conversations, and one man even invited them in. He was wearing a sweater and tie and had short-cropped hair, not unlike the missionaries, and Orrin tried to envision the man in white bap-tismal clothes, as they had been taught to do, but the man turned out to be a Jehovah's Witness who wanted only to argue scriptures. "Where does it say in the Bible you can have multiple wives," he demanded. Orrin was eager to respond, having memorized numerous scriptures on that point from the Old Testament, but he only knew how to recite them in English. Elder Flossen merely said the church stopped practicing polygamy in 1890, which didn't really address the man's objection.

"Actually, the church didn't really stop until 1904," Orrin whispered to his companion.

Elder Flossen gave Orrin a confused look. "What are you talking about?"

"President Joseph F. Smith issued a second manifesto in 1904 offi-cially ending polygamy once and for all. My father wrote about it."

Elder Flossen turned to the Jehovah's Witness and handed him a Joseph Smith pamphlet. "Please read this pamphlet about a modern-day prophet."

"There are no prophets today," the man countered, refusing to take the pamphlet. "The Bible contains everything God has revealed to his prophets."

When riding on the streetcar, Orrin tried to draw out the commuters with genial smiles, but few reciprocated. Bundled in burly overcoats and scarves, they stared straight ahead and avoided eye contact with Orrin as if he were a snake-headed medusa. All of his attempts to engage them were met with frozen silence except for one couple. The young man and his blonde companion at first seemed resistant but perked up when Orrin tried a new tactic. Rather than recite his spiel about Joseph Smith, he talked enthusiastically about finding joy in life and happiness in the gospel. "*Med mormonene, dere can bli likegyldig,*" he said.

The young man and his girlfriend looked momentarily stunned, then looked at the title of the pamphlet Orrin had given them, "You Too Can Be Happy." Their eyes widened and, laughing, they said, "*Vi skal bli likegyldig. Tusen tak.*" They were still smiling when they pulled the cord and got off at the next stop. Elder Flossen was smiling too, apparently pleased with Orrin's small triumph.

"That's how you get Norwegians out of the doldrums," Orrin said, sliding back into his seat.

"It sure is," Elder Flossen observed, unable to stifle a laugh. Sensing something amiss, Orrin demanded to know what was so funny. "You mispronounced the word 'happy,'" Flossen said. "It's '*lykkelig.*'"

"What did I say?"

"You said *likegyldig.* That means indifferent or apathetic. You told those people that Mormonism can make them become apathetic."

"How do you know what I said?" Orrin demanded.

"Because you talked so loudly. Everyone on the streetcar could hear you," Flossen replied, still chuckling. Orrin slumped in the seat, his humiliation surpassed only by his anger at his companion, who seemingly reveled in Orrin's failure. He imagined Elder Flossen regaling the other missionaries with the story of Orrin's moronic blunder and making it part of Norwegian mission lore. When they got to their stop, Orrin stared straight ahead, avoiding eye contact with his fellow passengers, who undoubtedly had overheard the discussion. He sensed an uncharacteristic gleam in their eyes as he shuffled down the aisle and out the door.

The only people who seemed really happy when the missionaries showed up at their door were Norwegian church members. Bror and Søster Magnussen, converts with two teenage children, hosted the missionaries for dinner and family home evening every Monday. Søster Magnussen fussed over the missionaries, feeding them Norwegian treats, teasing and insisting that Elder Flossen was much too thin to withstand Scandinavian winters. The Magnussen children were mainly intent on practicing their English, and fifteen-year-old Astrid, a blossoming redhead, made it her goal to wheedle laughter and praise from the young Americans. Erik, who intended to attend Brigham Young University in Utah after he finished normal school, had memorized bits of dialogue from Hollywood movies. "What we have here is a failure to communicate," he would say when a missionary mispronounced a word. Everyone was keen on helping the new greenie learn Norwegian, but Orrin wasn't sure whether they were laughing with him or at him.

When the elders visited Søster Laaksdahl, she greeted each with a grim handshake and then burst into tears. A lifelong member, she had married a non-Mormon because, as she explained, many of the most devout Norwegian men often moved to Utah, leaving behind a dearth of eligible Mormon men. Her husband, Lars, was a good man but had resisted all efforts to bring him into the fold; so now, after fifteen years of marriage, Søster Laaksdahl had finally recognized that Lars would never join the church. "It has been difficult, because we never had children," she said. "I fasted and prayed for that blessing many, many times. If we had children, I would have someone to accompany me to church and be with me in the celestial kingdom."

Orrin thought of his own mother, Sarah, who had sought unsuccessfully for years to conceive, wondering whether God was punishing her for some unrecognized sin or character flaw. She, too, had fasted and prayed, as had Orrin's father. This occurred before Orrin was born, of course, but he later overheard hushed conversations between Uncle Porter and his father about his mom, who was adopted and never knew her parents. After a miscarriage, she worried that she had not been valiant in the pre-existence, and so childlessness was her curse. Sarah was not assuaged until Grandpa Heber gave her a patriarchal blessing that not only proclaimed she belonged to the house of Ephraim and Joseph, but also blessed her with a fruitful womb. That his mother's fruitful womb produced only one child did not diminish her belief that a miracle had occurred. When Søster Laaksdahl asked the missionaries for a blessing, Orrin's heart leapt at the thought they might offer her a similar promise of offspring, that he might even be the voice in delivering the miraculous news. But he didn't know Søster Laaksdahl's age and felt uncomfortable making such a pronouncement without an overwhelming surge of inspiration—one he had never felt before—and besides, God would have to put the words in his mouth, because he certainly had no idea how to say them in Norwegian. It was just as well, then, that Elder Flossen spoke the blessing, telling Søster Laaksdahl the Lord was pleased with her faith and good works. "Please bring thy comforting spirit into her heart and home," Elder Flossen said.

The elders had a standing invitation every Thursday afternoon at one o'clock with Søster Halversen, an eighty-seven-year-old widow who had converted to Mormonism a few years earlier. White-haired and stocky, Søster Halversen clapped her hands gleefully when they arrived and reached out to hug them. When Orrin leaned back, thrusting out his hand to shake instead, she laughed and, winking at Elder Flossen, said, "We will have to teach this greenie that it's okay to hug an old woman, unless he thinks he might like to take me back to America as one of his wives. I don't give you any bad thoughts, do I, Elder Tanner?"

Orrin's cheeks reddened. "*Uffa meg. Uffa meg for deg*," she said. "Oh, my. Oh my, for you."

She helped the elders take off their coats and scarves and led them into the living room where a coffee table was loaded with more food than two missionaries could eat. Orrin counted at least a dozen varieties of Norwegian open-faced sandwiches, called *smørbrød*, topped with shrimp, ham, hard-boiled egg slices, cucumbers, beef, and other meats and vegetables. "Eat, eat," she insisted as she poured two cups of herbal tea. Orrin watched Elder Flossen shovel spoonfuls of sugar into his tea, and so he did the same. Søster Halversen said she and her husband, Hans, had lived together in this apartment and raised their two sons here without much thought about religion, but when Hans died she felt a spiritual emptiness that needed filling. She started attending services at the State Church but found herself sitting alone each Sunday feeling as empty as the chapel pews. "But when the Mormon missionaries came to my door, I felt the joyful spark missing from my life and when they took me to church, I was greeted by a community of believers who took me in as one of their own," she said. "So I decided to take the missionary lessons. The missionaries have been coming every week since."

"Did you get a spiritual witness by reading the Book of Mormon?" Orrin asked.

"*Uffa meg*," she said. "I am too old to read such a ponderous book. I took the missionaries' word for it. I believe and I am happy. I feel contentment when I attend church services and the radiance of youth when you elders visit my home."

Her sons had tried to stop her from being baptized, thinking their octogenarian mother was suffering from dementia. The church's tithing requirement also raised suspicions. "The Norwegian people do not pay taxes to support your generous retirement pension so you can give money away to a fanatical sect that isn't even Christian," said her oldest son, Jens. Her boys backed down after Søster Halverson's physician signed a written statement affirming she was of sound mind, though he might not have done so had he known it was to support her intention to join the Mormon Church. She had told him she needed the statement to show she could control her own finances, which was technically one of her sons' key concerns. The Oslo branch president, a sober-minded executive well-respected in the business community, further allayed concerns by telling her sons they could attend tithing settlement with their mother, so they could have a full record of her donations. "I love my sons, but sometimes they act like *idioter*," she said.

Søster Halversen asked the elders many questions about their activities, prompting frowns. "Few people want to speak with us, let alone invite us in to teach them the discussions," Elder Flossen said.

"And no one can understand me, no matter how slowly I speak," Orrin said.

Søster Halversen nodded sadly. "*Uffa meg. Uffa meg for dere.*"

Orrin took a bite of what looked like creamy white pudding. "Hmmm. What is this, Søster Halversen?"

"*Risgrøt.*"

"Rice porridge," Elder Flossen said.

Søster Halversen smiled. "It is made with rice, milk, sugar, cinnamon, and some of my own special spices. Do you like it, Elder Tanner?"

"I love it," Orrin said, spooning himself another bowlful.

"Then I will make *risgrøt* for you every week." At the end of the afternoon, Søster Halversen packed up sandwiches and snacks for the elders to take home for supper, but when they arrived back at their hybel, Elder Flossen was so stuffed that he lay down and took a two-hour nap while Orrin practiced the first discussion. At five o'clock, Elder Flossen awoke, and after restocking their briefcase with pamphlets and copies of the Book of Mormon, the two elders headed out to knock on more doors.

On Saturday, after prayers and study, Orrin and Elder Flossen carried their soiled clothes to a laundry three blocks from their hybel. They washed their temple garments in the kitchen sink, because a laundry had once sewn up the sacred markings on the garments, thinking they were holes. This incident occurred many years before, Elder Flossen explained, but he had been told by his first companion that all missionaries should wash their own garments or have them washed by church members. After placing their wet garments on hangers to dry, Orrin and his companion hopped on the Kjelsås streetcar to the mission home. Because it was their day off, at least for the next eight hours, they dressed in casual clothes, leaving Orrin relaxed, like he was off duty. Still, he slipped a few pamphlets in his coat pocket, just in case. The streetcar bustled merrily with shoppers and students heading downtown to museums and stores, but they avoided eye contact with Orrin, apparently recognizing he was a Mormon missionary even without his coat and tie. Perhaps it was his fedora, which only missionaries and older Norwegian men wore.

The mission home was also abuzz with activity. Two missionaries flew past as Orrin entered, hurrying to set up a Book of Mormon display at the bus station. Orrin said hello to the elders who picked him up at the airport when he arrived in Norway, and while following Elder Flossen up the stairs, he ran into President Toressen outside of his office. Toressen's face lit up in recognition. "Oh, Elder Tanner, it's so good to see you again. How was your first week?" he asked, shaking Orrin's hand.

"Great! I love the work," Orrin said, smiling through his lie. Toressen's exuberance and warm greeting aroused such a feeling of good cheer that Orrin, in the moment, really did feel great—or, at least, not despised and defeated.

President Toressen was still pumping Orrin's hand when Elder Flossen called from ahead. "Hurry up, Elder Tanner, we've got a lot to do today."

"Elder Flossen likes to keep the trains running on time. That's good," President Toressen said. "You're fortunate, Elder Tanner. We've paired you with one of our best missionaries. I wish I had a hundred more just like him."

Toressen released his grip and as Orrin walked away, several other missionaries rushed up to speak to the mission president. Upstairs, Orrin changed out of his clothes and took his first shower since leaving the mission home six days earlier. Never had a shower been so needed or felt so satisfying. He turned the faucet to get the hottest water he could stand. Enveloped in a curtain of cleansing water and steam, Orrin emptied his pores of a week's worth of grime and his mind of the unexpected disappointments of mission life. *Is this what missionaries call the best two years of their lives? One week in and I'm already looking forward to the end. How will I survive the next twenty-two months?* These and other dark thoughts that had plagued Orrin's mind slowly washed away and he emerged from the shower refreshed and ready to begin anew. God had given him a challenge and Orrin vowed to show himself worthy. After getting dressed, he and Elder Flossen did their grocery shopping for the week and then returned home to fill out their weekly reports and write letters home. At five o'clock, both were dressed and ready to proselytize for the rest of the evening.

Rejuvenated and eager to win over the Norwegian people, Orrin refused to accept "not interested" as a final answer, always pressing with an earnest smile that conveyed the good news he sought to impart. He again tried to envision people dressed in white and ready for baptism. The results were largely the same, though more people smiled back at them and several complimented Orrin on his efforts to speak Norwegian after only a week in the country. Orrin even placed two copies of the Book of

Mormon with prospects who promised to read them. Each time Orrin bore his testimony, he felt a strong sense of accomplishment and love for the person hearing his words. A young mother with a baby on her hip, exhausted by Orrin's persistence, asked him to come back when her husband was home, a triumph that could not be spoiled by Elder Flossen's prediction the couple would not be home when the missionaries returned on the appointed night.

One man in particular sparked hopes that they had finally found a golden contact. The man, dressed casually in slacks and a button-down shirt, greeted the elders politely, saying he had seen them around the apartment complex and wondered who they were. He liked Americans, he said, and had always hoped to visit the country one day. He had the milk-fed look of a Mormon. Elder Flossen did most of the talking and though much of their conversation was incomprehensible to Orrin, he felt a strong prompting to bear his testimony. He hesitated, not wanting to interrupt the flow of conversation, and waited for Elder Flossen to give him the discreet nod telling him to jump in. It never came. Before Orrin had a chance to speak, the man had closed the door and Elder Flossen was writing "reject" in his tracting book.

The elders knocked on several more doors, but Orrin's mind was pre-occupied with the missed opportunity a few doors earlier. As they walked between buildings, Orrin told Elder Flossen he had been prompted to bear his testimony to one of the men they had talked with.

"Which man?" Elder Flossen asked.

Orrin took the tracking book and flipped to the page. "This one," he said, pointing to the "reject" next to the man's address. Elder Flossen still looked puzzled, so Orrin added, "He's the one who was very friendly and said he liked Americans."

"He rejected us, Elder Tanner. I tried to bear my testimony, but he cut me off, saying he wasn't interested."

"We have to go back. I feel like I should do this, that God wants me to do this."

Elder Flossen, clearly annoyed, pushed back his hat and rubbed the red line across his forehead. "Okay, I've got an idea. Let me go first and I'll signal when it's time for you jump in with your testimony."

They walked back to the apartment building and up to the fourth floor where the man lived. Orrin rang the doorbell, jittery with excitement. He could see the pamphlet shaking in Elder Flossen's hand. When the man answered, he looked at the missionaries with surprise. "We are sorry to bother you again, but we wanted to give you this pamphlet about our church," Elder Flossen said, handing the man the Joseph Smith pamphlet. Flossen nodded to Orrin.

"I know this man, Joseph Smith, was a prophet of God and The Church of Jesus Christ of Latter-day Saints is God's true church on earth today," Orrin said, heart pounding and face radiating goodwill. The man thanked them, implying he would read the pamphlet, and politely closed the door as he had done before. As they walked back down the stairwell, Orrin felt indescribable elation, a confirmation that God had a purpose in sending him to Norway. He had taken a chance, making himself vulnerable, and for the first time since entering the mission field, felt he was succeeding in his assigned task. He savored the feeling, listening quietly to the echo of their footsteps in the stairwell.

When they reached the main floor, Elder Flossen turned to Orrin and said, "Elder Tanner, please don't ever do that to me again." Elder Flossen opened the door to exit the building and, pulling his scarf over his beak-like nose, leaned a shoulder into the wind.

Chapter 12

Learn to pause in your discussion. Do not rush. Take time to let the investigator ponder what you say.

The Message and the Messenger

Elder Eddie Pedersen entered the Language Training Mission at Ricks College in a dark fog of despair. Twelve weeks of shock therapy had left him physically wasted and emotionally traumatized. The scarlet bruises on his bicep and inner thigh served as visible reminders of the psychological wounds and disorienting shame. The reparative program had successfully extinguished his attraction to members of his own sex, at least temporarily, but in the process, it had broken his spirit and made him distrustful not only of himself but of everyone around him. He realized now no one loved him, not really, not for who he was. Not his friends or his bishop or Brother Orlan or even his mom and dad. Eddie saw the disappointment and undisguised revulsion in his parents' eyes when he told them his secret. A lifelong bond obliterated in a second. Despite all his awards for music and athletics, despite his faithful attendance at church and performance of his religious duties, despite his academic achievements and good humor, they didn't love homosexual Eddie. They couldn't. It wasn't allowed. They were permitted to love only the heterosexual Eddie they prayed he would become. Until he became that person, Eddie trusted no one. Intimacy brought pain. Perhaps he should have blamed God, even hated God for his misery, but he couldn't. Eddie was counting on God for deliverance. That was the deal. *For the next two years, I, Eddie Tanner, will obey every mission rule and faithfully perform every task set before me, never questioning and never complaining, always doing my duty. In return, you, God, will lift the burden of homosexuality from me so I can regain my self-respect and the love of my family, friends, and church.* Eddie began and ended each day on his knees, beseeching God to abide by the deal.

Eddie's desire to hold up his end of the bargain enabled him to bury his heartbreak and focus with feverish intensity on his language training and missionary studies. With a natural ear for music, he quickly picked up the Norwegian sing-song of syllables and sentences. And while other missionaries were easily distracted by letters from girlfriends and thoughts of home, Eddie poured himself into the work, often sitting alone reciting passages from the discussions while fellow missionaries lingered over meals or tossed around a frisbee between classes. He understood that the other Norwegian missionaries considered him disagreeable and aloof, even arrogant, but that was a price—even a punishment—he was willing to bear. Didn't this prove his commitment to the deal? Eventually, the other missionaries stopped inviting him to join in their activities. The more Eddie distanced himself from the others, the more praise he received from his instructors and the mission leaders. "Look at Elder Pedersen," said LTM President Hyrum Clark during a meeting of the Scandinavian missionaries. "He's already memorized the first four discussions and we still have three weeks left. If you put in the effort, the Lord will bless you with the gift of tongues."

Whether the other missionaries were envious or resentful of his rapid progress, Eddie couldn't tell. He liked the other Norwegian missionaries, bore them no ill will for his predicament, and did not begrudge them for enjoying their mission callings when he could not. He wanted to be liked, even if actual friendship was not possible. The exception was Elder Tanner, a know-it-all who exuded unusual confidence in his gospel knowledge. *Am I envious of Elder Tanner?* he wondered. *Or am I justifiably offended that Elder Tanner condescendingly dismissed my questions during our gospel study lesson?* Eddie had risked exposing his secret by asking whether God punishes people in this life for something they may have done (or failed to do) in the preexistence, only to be slapped down for daring to ask the question. Eddie chided himself for his uncharitable feelings toward Elder Tanner. He would need love and forbearance to be a successful missionary, and he had already concluded that mission success would be measured in baptisms. Baptisms would be a sign of God's commitment to the deal. Eddie decided to forgive Elder Tanner, just as he hoped God would forgive him.

On a rainy mid-November morning, Eddie watched his senior companion get ready for their first a day of tracting together. Elder Ward had been in Norway for nine months, six months in Bergen, and kept everything he needed at his fingertips. In his right front suit pocket was their flannel board and illustrations for teaching the discussions. His left front suit pocket contained their tracting book, a small spiral notebook in which he recorded the names, addresses, and responses of the people they visited. Next to the tracting book, Elder Ward slid in his stack of 165 scripture cards, grouped according to topic, such as signs of the true church, nature of the Godhead, biblical references to the Book of Mormon, and scriptural proofs that God requires baptism by full immersion. Under his suit coat he wore a "book holster," a vest-like contraption that held two copies of the Book of Mormon like revolvers, one under each arm. In his left back pants pocket, he carried a Norwegian address book and calendar to record appointments to teach discussions, and in his right back pocket he kept his missionary business cards. On one side of the business cards was his name and the mission home address printed over a photograph of the Salt Lake City temple; on the other side were the church's thirteen Articles of Faith, the *Trosartikler*, printed in Norwegian. Also stuffed into a back pocket was a well-used map of Bergen with the schedule and routes of each bus and streetcar. Elder Ward arranged all of these accoutrements in such a way that no one would know he was carrying anything on his person except a pen (right breast pocket), a wallet (left front trousers), and change for the bus (right front trousers). Even when fully packed and ready to go, Elder Ward looked slight and anemic, given his pasty face. He walked with military precision, as if he always knew where he was going and wanted to get there fast.

"Hey, greenie," Elder Ward told Eddie. "When people see me reach into my pocket and take out the flannel board, their mouths fall open like they've seen me pull a rabbit from inside my coat. It's real showmanship and adds to our mystique. Jehovah's Witnesses can't do anything like this. All they've got are those amateurish comic books they hand out."

Eddie was pleased with his first assignment. President Toressen told Eddie that Elder Ward was a top missionary. "This will get you off to a great start, Elder Pedersen," Toressen said. "We received an outstanding report from your LTM leaders, one of the best I've read. To whom much is given, much is expected. You have a bright future ahead."

"Thank you, president," Eddie said, almost smiling. "Do you know my background—I mean, about before my mission?"

President Toressen paused, then closed his eyes, as if searching for the right words. Eddie heard a faint clicking sound and waited, uncomfortably. Had Toressen fall asleep? Toressen finally opened his eyes, his face aglow. "All that matters is who you are now. A mission is a place where elders and sisters find themselves, their best selves. I'm not saying it will be easy"—Toressen chuckled to himself—"*uffa meg*, to hear some people talk, I make more mistakes in one day as mission president than I have in my whole life up to this point. Maybe they are right. But it doesn't matter, because I know who I am. Remember this, Elder Pedersen, the truth will set you free."

Elder Ward and Eddie took the bus from their Fyllingsdalen hybel to Laksevåg, where Elder Ward let Eddie take the first door. A young housewife in jeans answered. Her jaw tightened and her lips pursed when she saw the elders. She was already closing the door when Eddie began, so he hurried through his door approach, certain he was mispronouncing or forgetting key words. Could she see his hands shaking? Peeking behind the door, the woman said something Eddie didn't understand, so he replied with a phrase he had memorized during language training. "*Beklager, men jeg har nettopp kommet til Norge, så jeg snakker ikke språket så godt,*" he said. "I am sorry, but I have just arrived in Norway, so I do not speak the language very well."

"How long have you been in Norway?" she asked.

"This is my first day talking with people?"

The woman's eyes widened. "Your first day. And you can already speak like this? That is not possible."

"I had eight weeks of language training before coming here."

"Still, that is remarkable," she said, inviting the elders in and apologizing for the meager furnishings. "I am in school studying to be a nurse and my husband recently started teaching, so we have been collecting odds and ends for our home. Can I offer you tea?"

"Herbal tea, thanks," Elder Ward said as the elders took seats together on the couch. She introduced herself as Marie Beckstad; while she poured the tea, Elder Ward deftly produced the flannel board and pieces, saying they would like to tell her more about their church. They taught Fru Beckstad part of the first discussion, alternating discussion points while sipping tea. Eddie again impressed, speaking his memorized portions of the discussion as if he were speaking extemporaneously. They left a Joseph Smith pamphlet and set up a time to return when Fru Beckstad's husband would be home.

"Fru Beckstad is golden," Elder Ward exclaimed afterwards. He put his arm around Eddie's shoulders. "Elder Pedersen, this is the beginning of a beautiful friendship." Eddie smiled weakly, recognizing the movie phrase, but he ducked away, not sure how to interpret his companion's affectionate embrace. Elder Ward laughed. "Don't be modest, Elder. You've devised probably the most effective door approach in the history of the Norwegian mission."

For the rest of the day, Eddie and Elder Ward looked for ways to mention that it was Eddie's first day in Norway, usually by apologizing for a mispronounced word or Eddie's inability to understand everything people said. Their strategy worked. Many people, after expressing astonishment at Eddie's command of the language, saw the elders' visit as an opportunity to share their views of American politics and culture. Older Norwegians who had lived under Nazi rule during World War II praised Americans and treated the elders as if they were representatives of the soldiers who helped rid their country of Germans, but younger Norwegians, though enamored with American movies and rock music, offered scathing assessments of President Nixon's escalation of hostilities in Vietnam. And while the elders typically avoided arguments about the Vietnam War or racial injustice, Elder Ward strongly disputed the contention of one man that Americans were either very rich or very poor—and that most were very poor, especially the Negroes. "We Norwegians believe in social and economic justice," he said as he stood at the door talking with the missionaries. "Everyone has a right to education, healthcare, and good wages, regardless of their occupation."

"We believe in freedom, not socialism," Elder Ward responded. "You cannot force people to do what is right. That is the devil's plan." Eddie understood little of the ensuing debate, so while the two men argued, he mulled President Toressen's admonition: "The truth will set you free." Eddie knew this was a quote from Jesus in the Gospel of John, but he could not recall the context, nor what Jesus meant by "truth." *Was it that Jesus was the Son of God, the Savior whose sacrifice made possible the forgiveness of our sins? I certainly have need of that.* Eddie's reverie continued until a woman from inside the apartment yelled something about sects and ordered her husband to shut the door and finish eating his dinner. When he didn't comply, she stomped to the door and shut it herself, still muttering about sects.

Most discussions were congenial. Eddie and Elder Ward were invited in twice to discuss Mormonism, which allowed Eddie to further astound his hosts by reciting, with impeccable precision, whole sections of the missionary discussions. "You do not speak with a Bergensk accent," they would say. "Yours is like a southern Norwegian accent."

"One of my language instructors was from Kristiansand."

"Ah, yes," they would say, delighted with their ability to locate his dialect.

But if they said Eddie had an accent that sounded like Norwegians from Østfold along the eastern shore of the Oslo fjord, Eddie would say, "One of my language instructors came from Halden." By the end of the day, he and Elder Ward had handed out twenty-three pamphlets, sold five copies of the Book of Mormon, and made four appointments to return and teach the discussions.

They adopted the same strategy for the rest of the week. Eddie's language skills were impressive whether he had been in Norway one day or five. Elder Ward consulted the Mission Comparative point system and tallied up the results with evident delight:

Each hour of tracting: 1 point
Each hour of general conversation and teaching: 5 points
Selling or placing a Book of Mormon: 5 points
1st Discussion: 10 points
2nd Discussion: 20 points
3rd Discussion: 30 points
4th Discussion: 40 points
5th Discussion: 50 points
6th Discussion: 60 points
Baptism: 100 points (for each person baptized)

The Mission Comparative had been designed by the previous mission president, President Larsen, to motivate the missionaries while also measuring their performance. Baptisms, of course, were the ultimate goal, but they were rare events. Even with more than fifty missionary pairs working round the clock, the number of converts fell well below one hundred most years, sometimes dipping to fifty. Some missionaries labored their entire missions without converting anyone. Given the low likelihood of baptism success, President Larsen wanted the missionaries to have a feeling of achievement in other aspects of their daily work. "What missionary pair wouldn't want to see their names atop the Mission Comparative?" President Larsen said. "This offers a way for them to feel good about themselves and their work, even if their efforts don't lead directly to baptisms."

The point system also helped Larson keep track of slackers, though most missionaries embraced the competition. The assistants published the totals for each missionary pair in the *Gospel Net*, a weekly newsletter sent from the mission home to all the elders and sisters. After hearing some grumbling among the elders and sisters that the point system undermined the spirit of their work, President Larsen likened the Mission Comparative to keeping statistics in baseball. "A single or double doesn't always lead to a run scored, and a run scored or an RBI doesn't always lead to a win, but all are necessary to winning the game," he said. "Our point system helps build each missionary pair into a winning team."

Elder Ward was excited not just about the points, but also the prospects. He made a list of all of the callbacks and taped it to the refrigerator, predicting an explosion of baptisms in Fyllingsdalen. Eddie nodded in agreement but hesitated to show enthusiasm or any type of emotion. Of course, he was pleased with their success, which was due in no small part to his contributions. He wanted to believe that already God was rewarding him for his genuine remorse and humble submission to every necessary requirement for forgiveness laid out by church leaders. And he desperately wanted to interpret the week's events as a sign God intended to lift the burden of homosexuality from him. But when he undressed at night, the purplish stain across his bicep also served as a sign God was not yet done with His punishment, and when Eddie knelt in prayer, he sometimes felt a throbbing in his arm that revived his shame. Elder Ward's optimism gave him hope. On Saturday evening, after completing their reports and personal business, the two missionaries set out for an appointment to teach the first discussion to a family Elder Ward proclaimed was golden.

Eddie and Elder Ward took the bus to the Grøndahls' apartment in Laksevåg. The entire family greeted the elders heartily. Herr Grøndahl shook Eddie's hand vigorously, complimenting him on his Norwegian and welcoming him to their home. "I still have trouble understanding some of the accents I hear," Eddie said.

"That is because we do not come from Norway. We come from Bergen," Herr Grøndahl said, chortling as he explained that Bergen residents proudly proclaim a unique place in Norwegian history and culture.

Herr and Fru Grøndahl looked to be about forty-five years old and had two sons, ages seventeen and fourteen, and a ten-year-old daughter. Their faces were round and pale, their hair various shades of red. Fru Grøndahl brought out a tray with a pot of tea while Elder Ward set up the flannel board on the coffee table. As the tea was poured, Elder Ward asked if they could call them Brother and Sister Grøndahl. Yes, please, they said. "Bingo," Elder Ward whispered to Eddie from the corner of his mouth.

Elder Ward took the first point in the discussion, which was to convince the Grøndahls—or, at least, get them to agree—that prophets are needed today just as much as they were needed in biblical times. He began by alluding to the confusion among the many Christian churches. "Take a teaching like baptism, for example," Elder Ward said. "Some churches believe it is necessary, while others do not. Some believe it has to be done by immersion, others do it by sprinkling. Back in ancient times, when there were living prophets upon the earth, how did the Lord give men the answers to questions like this?"

Bror Grøndahl gave the obvious answer. "He spoke to his prophets."

Elder Ward smiled approvingly. "Back in those times, why was it so important to have living prophets on the earth?"

This time Søster Grøndahl answered. "Because the people needed God's word."

"I am sure that is right. And why are the statements of living prophets more reliable than our own opinions?"

"Their teachings are inspired by the Lord and are not just their own opinions," Søster Grøndahl replied.

"You are right again." Elder Ward paused to make eye contact because he was bringing them to the central conclusion of the discussion's first point. "Bror and Søster Grøndahl, as you think about the confusion among the churches, what is one reason we need a living prophet?"

"To answer our questions," said Søster Grøndahl.

Bror Grøndahl leaned forward. "And teach us the truth about religion."

Elder Ward placed another figure on the flannel board and crossed his legs, his signal that the point was established and Eddie should take his turn. Eddie flushed and spoke haltingly, nervous despite a week's worth of practice. The Grøndahls indeed appeared special, and he didn't want to misspeak any of his lines. "Bror and Søster Grøndahl, the reason we have gathered here today is to tell you about a prophet called by the Lord in our own time by the name of Joseph Smith. In 1820, Joseph Smith, then fourteen, wanted to join a church, but as he visited those in his neighborhood, he found this same confusion among churches about which we have been talking. So he prayed and asked God which of the churches was right. As he was praying, he saw a pillar of light that descended gradually until it rested directly over his head. In the light, he saw two personages in the form of men whose brightness and glory defied all description. One of them called Joseph Smith by name and said, pointing to the personage beside him, "This is My Beloved Son.""

"Bror and Søster Grøndahl, I know Joseph Smith did see the Father and the Son. In fact," Eddie said, gesturing to his companion, "he could see them as clearly as you can see Elder Ward and me." Eddie crossed his legs and Elder Ward smiled in approval. Eddie tingled with excitement. It felt good to tell Joseph Smith's story, to speak Norwegian, to be a missionary and teach. He belonged.

Eddie and Elder Ward continued taking alternate points. Eddie marveled at how well the conversation flowed. Each time the elders asked a question, the Grøndahls gave answers that moved the discussion forward toward its major conclusions. Even their children joined in, making observations that aligned with relevant gospel principles. It did not raise suspicions that Bror and Søster Grøndahl responded with answers closely following the hypothetical dialogue in the missionary discussion manual. Rather, it strengthened Eddie's testimony that God's inspired hand had guided the creation of the discussions as a means to lead people to gospel truths. He could see the Grøndahls' faces light up with fresh understanding.

"If there was an apostasy from Christ's original church, then it means our church is false," Søster Grøndahl said.

"And our baptism in the State Church is invalid." Bror Grøndahl's voice trailed off, as if he were considering the implications of his assertion.

"Now the beautiful thing we are going to tell you about today," Eddie said, "is that the Lord has restored his true church and the priesthood back to earth again." Eddie paused, just as Elder Ward had instructed him in their practice session, and with all the sincerity he could muster, gave them the baptismal challenge. "Bror and Søster Grøndahl, when you come to know in your own hearts that this is true, will you be baptized by someone who has the priesthood?"

Husband and wife looked Eddie straight in the eye. "Ya, Elder Pedersen," they said.

"We hold regular baptismal services in the church. We shall be having a baptism in six weeks," Eddie said. "Will you prepare for baptism by studying, praying, and attending church with us during this time?"

Bror Grøndahl and his wife and children talked briefly among themselves. Bror Grøndahl spoke for his family. "Elders, you have touched us with your spirits. We already believe."

Eddie's heart jumped and for the first time in months, he allowed himself an unabashed smile. Elder Ward gave an approving nod. Eddie fought back tears as he thought of the scripture, how great will be your joy if you should bring many souls into the kingdom of God. But for Eddie, it was more, much more, than the joy of bringing someone into the church. The Grøndahls' conversion served as evidence God had deemed him a worthy vessel to carry His spirit and preach His gospel, that the Lord had indeed accepted Eddie's acts of contrition. The deal was intact. Eddie started to bear his testimony, his eyes welling, when Bror Grøndahl interrupted him to ask if they could be baptized sooner, adding something Eddie didn't understand. The entire family pressed him to agree. "Ya," Eddie said, nodding amicably, still in the throes of happiness.

Elder Ward, turning suddenly pale, said something to the Grøndahls Eddie did not understand. Bror Grøndahl gestured excitedly with his hand and opened his Bible to a passage in the Acts of the Apostle. Elder Ward read it silently, then made a counter explanation. Elder Ward was trying to remain calm, but desperation crept into his voice.

"What's going on?" Eddie whispered in English.

"You told them they could be baptized tonight?"

"Wait. What?"

"They asked you if they could be baptized tonight. And you said yes."

"I didn't realize. . . . Tell them we can't."

"What do you think we've been arguing about," Elder Ward said, exasperation on his face. "They say the apostles in Christ's original church baptized people immediately upon conversion." As the elders conversed back and forth, the Grøndahls looked on, puzzled though still eager for baptism.

"Listen, Elder Pedersen, this family is golden," Elder Ward said. "I don't want to lose them over a silly misunderstanding. I'm going to call our district leader and see what he says to do." He asked if he could use the Grøndahls' telephone and hastily excused himself. "Stall them until I get back."

Eddie smiled weakly at the Grøndahls and took a sip of tea. Its bitter taste stung his throat. Eddie's armpits felt hot and sticky. How he wished he could take off his coat, but the mission rules didn't allow it. The Grøndahls repeated their desire to be baptized and Eddie tried to explain they could not arrange a baptism so quickly. The local church authorities had to be notified, the Grøndahls had to be interviewed, papers had to be filed. Hampered by a limited vocabulary, Eddie used elaborate pantomime to emphasize it would be impossible to open the church building and fill the baptismal font at this late hour. "No water at church," Eddie repeated several times. Eventually, the Grøndahls understood the problem and their expressions of confusion turned to comprehension. "Ah, I see," said Bror Grøndahl, smiling and nodding.

"Elder Ward," Eddie yelled, relieved. "It's okay. They understand now."

As Eddie stood up to find Elder Ward, Bror Grøndahl took his arm and led him to the bathroom where Bjørnar, the oldest son, was filling up their bathtub. He grinned broadly and swished his hand gently in the water. Elder Ward walked in and asked, "Did you want me?"

Bror Grøndahl pointed to the tub. "We are going to be baptized here."

Elder Ward yanked Eddie into the hall. "What did you tell them?"

"I didn't tell them anything. They—"

"I've still got Elder Johansen on the phone. This time don't do anything until I get back."

"Please . . . don't leave me," Eddie pleaded, but Elder Ward hurried down the hall without answering. Bror Grøndahl, seeing the bewildered Eddie standing alone, called him back into the living room, where he was talking with Søster Grøndahl.

"We are ready," he said.

"What?"

Bror Grøndahl pointed to his three children, who danced into the room wearing brightly colored swimsuits. Elder Ward returned in time to see the children skipping around the coffee table. "Why are they wearing swimsuits?" he demanded.

The oldest son stepped forward. "We are ready to be baptized."

"Did you tell them to put on their swimsuits?" Elder Ward said, pointing angrily at the children.

"No, I—"

"We can't baptize them in swimsuits."

"I didn't tell them we could."

"Well, what are we going to do now?" he said.

"Maybe you could explain—"

"I'm going to call Elder Johansen back. Don't let them get into the tub."

Eddie followed Elder Ward part way down the hall, his throat tightening. He was beginning to hate the Grøndahls and Elder Ward. *Was this family crazy or merely stupid? And why has my companion left me alone with them?* Eddie returned to the living room determined to sit quietly and not say anything, but when he got there, Bror Grøndahl was grinning clownishly and holding up a large pair of green-striped swimming trucks. At first, Eddie thought Bror Grøndahl intended to wear the trucks himself, but by his gesturing, Eddie realized that Grøndahl wanted him to put them on. The bathtub water turned off.

"It is ready," the oldest son hollered. Bror Grøndahl stepped forward and pressed Eddie to take the trunks. The Grøndahls' round faces beamed menacingly. Eddie grabbed the trunks and bolted down the hall shouting for his companion.

"Elder Ward. Elder Ward!" Eddie flung open the door where Elder Ward was supposedly calling their district leader and found him sitting with four other missionaries, their faces stretched thin to keep from laughing. Eddie stared at them, uncomprehending, until one of the missionaries, a pimply faced elder, erupted in laughter that spread like contagion to the others. Seeing their ruse had finally been discovered, the Grøndahl children ran down the hallway hooting and shrieking triumphantly. Still stunned, Eddie turned and saw Søster Grøndahl standing at the door.

"Welcome to Norway, greenie," she said, giving him an enthusiastic bear hug. His emotions whipsawed and raw, Eddie collapsed into tears on Søster Grøndahl's shoulder.

Eddie could see everyone was trying to make him feel better. "I went just as far as you did before I figured out what was going on," said Elder Johansen, the acne-scarred district leader.

Bror Grøndahl, who was the first councilor in the Bergen branch presidency, had been an accomplice to six such "greenie baptisms," as he called them. They had become a Grøndahl family tradition, much like a holiday pageant the children especially looked forward to, each enthusiastically playing his or her part whenever a greenie came to Bergen. "They are disappointed if they cannot fool the new missionary or get them to believe in our story, at least for a little while," Bror Grøndahl said. "So you see, you have made my children very happy."

"One time, the greenie even put on the swimming trunks," Søster Grøndahl said.

"You are not so gullible, after all," Bror Grøndahl added.

The six missionaries crammed together in the Grøndahls' living room. Sitting on the sofa and chairs brought in from the kitchen, they pulled themselves close to the coffee table and took large helpings of *smørbrød* and sweets prepared by Søster Grøndahl for the occasion. Cups of tea flavored with generous spoonfuls of sugar were passed among them. The colorful array of meats, toppings, and Norwegian pancakes with whipped cream and strawberries enlivened the happy banter of the Grøndahls and their guests.

"Eat. Please eat," Søster Grøndahl said, hovering over the elders like a robin with newly hatched chicks. The Grøndahls reveled in their camaraderie with the young American elders. In turn, the elders basked in the unconditional acceptance they rarely experienced as they went door to door among the Norwegians.

Søster Grøndahl had shooed the missionaries out of the room when Eddie broke down. After he stopped crying, she left him alone to compose himself. "You come out and eat with us when you are ready," she said. After rejoining the group, he understood they had meant no harm, that they had not intended to embarrass him or make him play the fool. They tried with compliments and cajoling to put him at ease and erase his shame for falling for their prank, but they were mistaken in believing this was what had upset Eddie. Something deeper, darker gnawed at Eddie, something he couldn't begin to name. He hid his turmoil behind a grim smile, furtively rubbing his arm as he listened impassively to their festive chatter.

Chapter 13

Wherefore, now let every man learn his duty, and to act in the office in which he is appointed, in all diligence. He that is slothful shall not be counted worthy to stand, and he that learns not his duty and shows himself not approved shall not be counted worthy to stand.

Conduct of a Missionary

"I don't think I ever saw him smile."

"Who? Who didn't smile?"

Elder Ward stopped to knock snow from the low-hanging branch of a thick pine. He ducked under the branch, then pulled it back and held it so Elder Sorensen could walk through. "I'm talking about Elder Pedersen," Ward said. "He never smiled, not a real smile anyway. He would sort of grimace, like it was painful trying to force his face muscles into a smile. But he couldn't quite do it."

"You're exaggerating. In those three months you were together, he never smiled once?"

"Well, perhaps once. But that's it," Elder Ward said. After Elder Sorensen stepped clear from the tree, Elder Ward let the branch fly back into place, spraying snow as it crashed against other branches. "President Toressen agrees with me. When we were talking about Elder Pedersen once, President Toressen said, 'We've got to figure out a way to get Elder Pedersen to smile. He's got a beautiful smile, if only he'd let people see it.' And I was like, 'How do you know it's beautiful if no one's ever seen it?'"

"You really said that?"

"No, but I was thinking it. I mean, maybe Elder Pedersen is just hiding crooked teeth."

Elder Sorensen snorted. "President Toressen thinks everyone has a beautiful smile."

Elder Ward and Elder Sorensen walked out of the forest and into a moonlit valley covered in several feet of snow, following a crusty path through Harstard's *Folkeparken*, or People's Park. The icy snow crunched noisily underneath their feet. During the past week, they had visited villages on Hinnøya island, taking buses to Evenskjer, Lødingen, and Borkenes to investigate whether the missing elders were proselytizing in those places or in the nearby countryside. No one had seen the missionaries. The assistants were beginning to believe they had been sent on a fool's errand when they received a tip from the butcher that Elders Tanner and Pedersen had talked of visiting the homes along Kilhusveien just beyond the city park.

They caught a pair of buses to the rural district, seeking information about the missing elders while carefully avoiding any mention that this was the real purpose of their visit.

"We have just arrived at Hinnøya island, and so we are visiting some of the areas surrounding Harstad to talk about our religion," Elder Ward said after climbing the steps and knocking at the door of the first home. "However, we do not want to impose if our missionaries have recently visited here."

"We would not want to become nuisances by visiting too often," Elder Sorensen added.

"Oh, it is not a bother," said a ruddy-faced man who introduced himself as Olav. "We are pleased to have you visit us. It is cold outside. Please come in."

The assistants unwrapped their scarves and hung their coats on an entryway peg. "Have you talked with Mormon missionaries before?" Elder Ward asked.

"Oh, yes, some of your missionaries have been here and talked to us with their *flannelltavle.*"

Elder Sorensen leaned forward, asking nonchalantly, "Oh, that is interesting. Was it long ago?"

Olav tilted his head back and looked at the ceiling, as if counting the days backward in his head. However, he was not really trying to recall the precise date, because, in fact, he knew the missing missionaries had not visited their part of the island since their disappearance more than three weeks ago. That's what he really wanted to say. But he knew from talking with friends who lived in town that these new missionaries, Elder Ward and Elder Sorensen, became uncomfortable, even upset, when people suggested that Elders Tanner and Pedersen were missing, and so, being loath to offend his guests, Olav pretended he didn't know the missionaries were missing. "Vigdis," he said, calling for his wife, "when was the last time those Mormon missionaries came here to our house?"

"They came with their *flannelltavle,*" she replied, emerging from the kitchen with a teapot and cups.

"Yes, but when was it? Perhaps a month ago, right?"

"Yes, it was the night of the aurora borealis," Vigdis said.

"Yes, that is right," Olav concluded. "It was one of our most colorful displays of the northern lights in years."

"Yes, those missionaries have since moved on to proselytize in other areas," Elder Ward said, hoping the Norwegians might volunteer where they had gone.

"Yes," the Norwegian couple said.

"They may have talked of going north to Andenes," Elder Sorensen offered by way of suggestion.

"Yes, that is a nice town," Olav said, nodding agreeably.

"Or maybe south to Svolvær," Elder Ward suggested.

"Yes, that is also a nice town."

In more than a dozen homes, the conversations proceeded in a similar fashion, as if the assistants and Norwegians were reading from prepared scripts omitting the word "missing." The friendly rural folk eagerly invited Elders Ward and Sorensen to come inside and chat over tea. When one of the assistants raised the question of when the other missionaries last visited, the husband might make a show of rubbing his beard or chewing on his pipe while his wife blew cold air on her tea, as if both were pondering their answers. Elder Ward estimated he and his companion drank upwards of two quarts of tea each during their futile attempt to discover the missing elders' whereabouts. The couple at the last home they visited was so insistent on treating them to hot tea and warm bread that the assistants missed the 10:00 p.m. bus back to Harstad, the last of the night. The man offered to put on his boots and coat and show them the shortcut through the *Folkeparken*, but Elder Ward said if he would point the way, they could manage on their own. "It is very simple," the man said, pointing up the forested hills with his pipe. "Just follow the trail people have already made over the frozen lake and it will lead you directly back to Harstad."

"Do you really think we're walking over a frozen lake?" Elder Sorensen asked as they crossed a wide valley of snow. "Maybe Elders Tanner and Pedersen fell through walking back and we're going to be next."

"Don't be ridiculous. If the Norwegians are walking over these trails, then it's got to be all right." But even Elder Ward got a little worried when they took a wrong turn and headed down an embankment and into a flat expanse unmarked by footprints. Every crunch of snow under their shoes sounded like a sharp crack of ice, and both elders trod gingerly until the trail reemerged. Now they quickened their steps. Their path was lit by a bright moon, but gray, misty clouds threatened to obscure the night sky, and so they hurried to get out of woods before the moonlight disappeared.

"Do you think the people we talked to suspect the elders are missing?" asked Elder Sorensen, whose his warm breath crystalized into a moist fog as he spoke.

"Yeah, I'm pretty sure they know, just like the people in town."

"So they were pretending not to know?"

"Yeah."

"And you pretended not to know they knew?"

"Yeah. So?" Elder Ward said with mounting exasperation.

Elder Sorensen was quiet. Both elders were panting, their legs growing heavy from the snow encrusted around their ankles and shoes. Finally, Sorensen stopped. "Do you think they knew that we knew they knew we were pretending the elders aren't missing?" he asked. Elder Ward continued marching ahead without answering. "Well, do you?" Elder Sorensen said, resuming pace and hurrying to keep up. "Do you?"

"I think I'm going to pretend I don't know they know I know you're a moron," Elder Ward said.

They walked in silence the rest of the way, not slowing until they saw a sign pointing the way out of the park. Upon reaching their hybel, the elders stripped off their wet clothes and collapsed on their beds. "You know, if something had happened to us tonight, they would have said it was because we broke the mission rules and stayed out past our curfew," Elder Ward observed.

After catching his breath, Elder Sorensen, said, "Elder Ward, let's not ever do this again." The elders said their prayers and burrowed under their down duvets, falling immediately into sleep.

Chapter 14

Be obedient. Follow the instructions of your Mission President and all those who supervise your labors.

Conduct of a Missionary

The day after President Toressen informed the Tanners their son was missing, Anson booked a flight to Norway. Sarah tried to talk him out of it. "We don't have extra money to spend," she said. "Besides, how will you be able to help? You don't even speak the language."

Anson didn't have a rational answer. "I'll just feel better being there, knowing I'm close by in case Orrin needs help."

"And what about me? You're going to let me stay here and answer all the questions about why you've suddenly flown to Norway? You're just trying to avoid facing the embarrassment you've already caused here at home?"

"Do you think I'm to blame for Orrin's disappearance?"

"I didn't say that. But you need to address the problems we've got here. If there is any connection, that's the best way to help Orrin."

If there is any connection? The truth was Anson had lain awake all night, turning on one side and then the other, seeing the many ways his troubles and Orrin's were connected. He didn't know for sure, of course. But just in case, he needed to go to Norway and explain to Orrin. He knew Sarah was also awake. He sensed it by the sound of her breathing, like a sigh, but they said nothing to each other, lying side by side, mulling dark thoughts. He arose at six o'clock, showered and dressed as if going to work, then announced he was going to Norway.

His troubles—their shared troubles—began shortly before Orrin left on his mission. The issue was so minor that Anson didn't even consider it controversial. In his pamphlet narrating the journey of his father, Heber Tanner, into the spirit world, Heber had said he was guided by a "guardian angel." The pamphlet had circulated for years without objection, and in fact, Mormon educators routinely referred to his father's experience in church talks and classroom lessons as evidence of revealed Mormon doctrine regarding the afterlife. But recently someone had sent the pamphlet to church headquarters with a note pointing out that Elder Bruce R. McConkie's *Mormon Doctrine* emphatically states the concept of guardian angels is "an old and false sectarian tradition." Anson subsequently received a letter from head of the church's education system, Apostle Joseph F. Prichard, asking him to correct the offending passages. "It is especially important that you, as an instructor in our high school seminary program, align both your writing and teachings with revealed gospel truths," Prichard wrote. "Let me know at your earliest convenience that the error has been rectified."

Anson brought the issue before a family council. Grandpa Heber angrily resisted making any changes. "The angel told me himself he was my guardian angel. That's how he introduced himself," Heber said, pounding the floor with his cane. "Elder McConkie doesn't know what he's talking about. Tell them you won't do it."

"It's a minor change, Dad. All we're doing is taking out the word 'guardian.' We're still describing him as an angel," Porter said.

"It's the principle of the thing. If we make the change, it's like we're saying I made a mistake, that I misremembered."

"No one's saying you made a mistake."

"Then why do we have to make the change?"

Grandpa Heber and Porter went back and forth, Porter acting as the voice of reason, trying to remain calm in the face of their father's anger. Anson listened carefully and then offered what he thought might be a compromise. "Let's keep the pamphlet as it is, but insert a footnote, explaining the possible conflict with Elder McConkie's book, but also including a further discussion of the topic."

"Further discussion," Porter said mockingly.

"It would be respectful," Anson insisted.

Porter exploded in anger. "Don't you get it, Anson? After the Brethren have spoken, there's no such thing as 'further discussion.'"

"But—"

"I've seen this happen dozens of times at BYU, sometimes in the history department but usually in the religion department where professors set themselves up as experts in some aspect of church doctrine or teachings. And when they get a letter like this, they think it's a request or an opportunity to start a dialogue. It isn't a request. The Brethren don't want more enlightenment from you. Apostle Prichard isn't asking you to consider making this change. He's telling you to do it. Don't resist counsel, Anson."

Sarah usually chafed at Porter's overbearing manner, especially the way he often bullied and spoke condescendingly to her husband, and while she didn't like Porter's tone, she felt in this instance to voice agreement with him. "Let's do what Porter recommends," she said. "When in doubt, always follow the Brethren."

Sarah was right. Anson knew it was just his pride, but it hurt to hear her take Porter's side. Even worse, making the change violated the principle that had made his pamphlets popular: their fidelity to truth. Still, obedience trumped all, and so he agreed to make the change, eventually persuading his father to accept it, even if he didn't like it. And Anson still had one more card to play, though he kept it to himself. Apostle Prichard was a longtime family friend with deep roots in the area, his grandparents having helped settle Seth with the Tanner family. Anson wrote to Apostle Prichard, stating he would comply with his request but also asking if he could meet with the apostle the next time he was in Seth. "I would like the opportunity to explain my research and the purpose of my pamphlets, and see if, in the future, there might be compromise language satisfactory to all that could be adopted. I have a few suggestions in that regard," he wrote.

Apostle Prichard grabbed Anson's shoulder while vigorously shaking his hand, welcoming him into his office with a familiarity reserved for old friends. "How is your father? He must be well past ninety, isn't he?" Prichard asked. "Please, take a seat."

"Ninety-three."

"Feisty as ever, I hope."

"Too feisty, sometimes. Some days he's got more energy than Sarah and me have combined."

"Ah, yes, Sarah. How's the little woman? You rang the bell and won the prize when you married her, Anson. Converts make our best members, I always say. They know what it's like to be without the gospel. Makes them appreciate it more."

"I won't disagree with you about Sarah. She's been the helpmeet I've always needed and more. I couldn't have managed my pamphlet business and all my teaching responsibilities without her, that's for sure. Dad says she has more business sense than any of the Tanner men, especially me." Apostle Prichard laughed but said nothing more, a signal for Anson to continue. Prichard's cordial greeting told him he had been right to approach the apostle. "The reason why I wanted to meet with you, Apostle Prichard," he said, "is I wanted to explain my purpose in printing my pamphlets. You see, it's always been my desire to move up from teaching high school seminary to teaching at the college level, perhaps at Brigham Young University or at one of our Institute programs adjoining a major college. I see my pamphlets as my passport—a scholarly credential, so to speak, like a dissertation—that can give me entry into the academic world. Given your position as head of the church's education system, I thought it might be helpful for you to hear my side, so as to avoid any future misunderstandings."

Apostle Prichard gave a frowning, confused look. "Misunderstanding? Is there a misunderstanding about the change you were supposed to make? Were we not clear about that?"

"Oh, perhaps 'misunderstanding' is the wrong word. What I meant was to clarify—"

"Clarify? Again, our position is clear. And didn't you agree to make the change?"

"Oh, yes, absolutely."

Apostle Prichard picked up a letter from his desk and straightened his glasses to help him focus. "Then what I don't understand, Anson, is why in your letter to me, you suggested we might reach some 'compromise language' in your pamphlet. If you're making the change, why would there be any need for compromise language. Isn't the matter settled?"

What is happening here? Anson wondered. In his head, he could hear his brother's voice telling him to quit trying to explain, just admit he had been wrong, acknowledge Apostle Prichard's preeminent priesthood position, pledge compliance with whatever he required, and then shut up. He knew that's what he should do, but he tried one more time. "Well, you see, I thought—"

Apostle Prichard held up a hand. "Anson, our families have a long and storied history working together in building the kingdom, a pioneering history we both can be proud of. But Brother Tanner—and here I must call you Brother Tanner because I cannot let our friendship interfere with my responsibilities overseeing the church education program—and so, Brother Tanner, while I appreciate your desire to rise in the ranks, you cannot count on our friendship to gain any special consideration."

Anson wiped the perspiration from his forehead. "Oh, that was not what I intended."

"I'm sure it wasn't. But ever since this question of guardian angels arose, your other pamphlets have received additional attention that is raising eyebrows among the Brethren. These aren't topics you should be discussing in high school seminary courses. You understand that, don't you?"

"Yes. It's never been my intention—I have never discussed these pamphlets in my classes."

"That's good to hear, Brother Tanner. Now, if you have your sights set on progressing in the church educational system, I counsel you to focus on your current position as a seminary instructor and not go looking beyond your position with pamphlets and research that take you into areas best left to the General Authorities. In the meantime, always aim to inspire your students and strengthen their testimonies and never, ever teach anything that would damage the fragile testimonies of our church's youth. Do you understand me?"

"Yes, yes, I do."

Apostle Prichard stood to indicate the meeting had ended. "Brother Tanner, thanks for coming in. Please give my best regards to Sister Tanner and your father."

"You only had to say one thing: 'I will make the change you requested.' That's all you had to say."

"I know. I know that now, Porter."

"Then why did you suggest a meeting for 'further discussion' and some kind of 'compromise'? What were you thinking?"

Normally, Porter's contemptuous scolding would have raised Anson's hackles and forced him to defend even the indefensible, but not now. Anson was so distraught, uncertain how to make things right, he embraced Porter's withering assessment of his actions. "I-I-I understand now what you've been saying about not drawing attention from the Brethren. It was a mistake. I blundered."

"What are you going to do now?"

"That's the thing. I don't know. I don't know what Apostle Prichard wants me to do."

"Well, you should have asked him."

"He seemed to think he had made himself clear."

While the two brothers argued, Sarah offered her advice. "You need to show him you're taking his counsel to heart. Tell him you won't publish any new pamphlets. No more new pamphlets."

"None? Ever?" Anson asked.

Sarah spoke calmly. "Just until the Brethren are satisfied and comfortable with what you're doing."

"But my goal of teaching at a university level—"

"You won't ever be promoted to a university level if they're not on board with what you're doing, so you're not really giving up anything," Porter said.

"Dad, what do you think?" Anson asked.

"I think Apostle Prichard is a pompous ass," Heber exclaimed.

"Dad! You can't disparage the Lord's anointed that way," Porter said. "That's worse than cursing."

"He's certainly not acting like an apostle, in my opinion. Anson's printing company is a private business, and certainly none of his business. I say we should ignore him."

"But—"

"And put 'guardian' angel back into my story. I know what the angel told me."

Anson may have been unsure what Apostle Prichard wanted him to do, but Bishop Pulsipher was not. The next Sunday after priesthood meeting, Bishop Pulsipher called Anson into his office. "Now Brother Tanner, what's this business going around about you and your pamphlets?" the bishop asked before Anson had a chance to sit down. Anson's throat tightened. He thought this was a matter between Apostle Prichard and himself. Why was the bishop inserting himself into this? He liked Bishop Pulsipher. Frank had been his second counselor when Anson served as bishop. Anson and Sarah hosted his counselors and their wives once a month to dinner, a tradition that helped Anson mentor and nurture the men who served with him. Though not well-educated and sometimes harsh in his judgments, Frank was earnest and dependable, something Anson valued in a counselor. When asked whether he thought Frank would make an effective bishop, Anson emphasized his positive qualities, saying he would work tirelessly and grow into the position. Now Anson wondered whether he should have been more forthcoming about Frank's weaknesses.

"It's just a misunderstanding, Frank. Not as serious as it might appear."

The bishop's face turned suddenly dark and Anson realized he had made a mistake by not referring to him as Bishop Pulsipher. "Brother Tanner, I hope you understand I'm not meeting with you as your former counselor or friend, but as your bishop and spiritual counselor."

"Yes, Bishop. I'm sorry. I meant no disrespect. It's, well, I appreciate your concern. I've already talked over the issue with my family and we've decided that to avoid any further misunderstandings, I won't write or publish any new pamphlets until Apostle Prichard and his colleagues decide everything is in order."

"Yes, that sounds like an acceptable sacrifice to lay before the Lord, Brother Tanner. But in a matter like this, it's important to go the extra mile, beyond what might be asked, to make clear your loyalty to the church and the Brethren."

"Now wait a minute," Anson said with more heat than he intended. "No one's questioning my loyalty, not after twenty-five years of teaching seminary and seven years of faithful service as bishop, which you had the privilege to observe firsthand."

Bishop Pulsipher's jaw stiffened. "Brother Tanner, you don't seem to understand how serious this is. This matter was brought to my attention by stake leaders because you teach the gospel doctrines class in our ward. As you know, I've never been a fan of your pamphlets. Too much mucking around in the mysteries for my taste, though I know some people like that kind of thing. I like gospel discussions that are straightforward and focused on basic gospel principles, not on speculation and half-baked theories. If I've learned one thing while serving as bishop, it's that church members would virtually see all of their troubles disappear if they stopped worrying about extraneous things like who said this or that about some obscure doctrine and simply obeyed their leaders. That's the lesson here."

Knowing that Bishop Pulsipher would continue talking if not interrupted, Anson said, "And so what are you saying?"

"Brother Tanner, it's not enough to stop writing new pamphlets. You've got to stop publishing your older pamphlets as well. Make a clean slate and show the Brethren you're one hundred percent behind them. That will help you concentrate your energies on what's really important."

"But Sarah and I depend on those pamphlet sales to supplement our income."

"Then it will truly be a sacrifice worthy of you," Bishop Pulsipher said. "And for my part, I won't have to worry about anyone complaining about your teaching our seminary students or our gospel doctrine class. I can vouch with utmost confidence for your testimony and commitment."

"I'm not going to lose my teaching position, am I?"

"Heavens, no. Not if you take these actions. You have my word on that."

"Thank you, Bishop. Thank you." Anson, feeling dizzy, grabbed at the chair's arm as he stood, steadying himself. "I'll do as you recommend."

"I never doubted you would." Bishop Pulsipher smiled, satisfied, as he and Anson shook hands. "You know, it's been a long while since we've had you and Sarah over for dinner. I'll have Pearl give Sarah a call, so our better halves can make the arrangements. It will be fun."

Chapter 15

Be careful of designing persons. You may find yourself trapped in embarrassing situations. Avoid the very appearance of evil, and don't seek it or attempt to test your strength of resistance. You may be weaker than you think!

Conduct of a Missionary

Three weeks into his mission, Eddie and his companion began teaching a homosexual man. Elder Ward never suspected, the thought never crossing his mind. Elder Ward called the clear-eyed man with short-cropped hair, neatly pressed shirts, and polite manners a "dry" Mormon. "Not yet baptized," he explained. So how did Eddie know the man was a homosexual? He couldn't articulate or pinpoint what it was about the man. He even tried to talk himself out of his suspicions. "Just because Tom Haugen is an unmarried man in his forties who works as a nurse's aide doesn't mean he's a homosexual," Eddie told himself. "Was it the way Bror Haugen fussed over the missionaries when they entered, taking their coats, insisting they remove their shoes as well as overshoes, and then pouring each elder a cup of tea with fastidious charm, warning them not to burn their tongues, and jumping up with exaggerated concern when Elder Ward dripped jam on his tie?"

Oh dear, let me help you, Elder Ward," Bror Haugen said, dipping his napkin in ice water and gently dabbing at the stain on Elder Ward's tie.

Bror Haugen seemed more curious about Mormonism than interested in joining. He quickly caught on to the way the discussions led him to the inevitable conclusions the elders wanted him to believe were his own. "Well, if you say it that way, then of course, we need prophets today," he would say, or "Yes, according to your logic, the Catholic Church fell away from the original church established by Jesus Christ. Of course, that assumes Jesus actually organized a church." Even if Bror Haugen chafed at being force-fed the conclusions, he continued inviting the elders to return. As a non-smoker, he readily agreed with the ban on cigarettes and other tobacco products mandated by the church's health code, called the Word of Wisdom; however, he insisted he was not ready to give up alcohol or coffee, which were also prohibited. Elder Ward thought if they could only persuade Bror Haugen to attend church, he would feel right at home among Norwegian Mormons, who were just like him. Elder Ward foresaw that the next discussion—number four—would be a crucial turning point, because it contained the baptismal challenge.

"This could be the kick in the pants he needs to become a more serious investigator," Elder Ward said as the two missionaries climbed the steps to Bror Haugen's apartment. "I have a feeling he's been waiting for us to give him this push."

Their visit began with the usual chitchat while Bror Haugen served the tea and insisted the missionaries try the Norwegian *mandelbunn*, a type of almond cake, he had baked for them. Elder Ward pushed aside some of the plates to set up the flannel board, but before beginning the discussion, he excused himself to use the bathroom. As soon as the door to the bathroom shut, Bror Haugen looked directly at Eddie and said in English, "You are homosexual, is this not true?" The color drained from Eddie's face and he nearly spit out his tea. "Did I say it correctly?" Bror Haugen said. "Homosexual? It is the same word, '*homoseksuell*,' in Norwegian."

"Are you asking if Elder Ward and I are homosexuals?"

"No, darling, just you."

Eddie swallowed and tried to speak, but he couldn't think of what to say, in English or Norwegian. Seeing Eddie's confusion, Bror Haugen continued, "You know I am homosexual, right? And you? You are homosexual too. I can tell. Do not ask me how, but I can tell. Am I right?"

"I was, as you say, '*homoseksuell*,' at one time," Eddie said. Pronouncing the word in Norwegian made it sound even more ominous. "But I have been in treatment and now I am in remission. Please do not say anything to Elder Ward. He does not know. No one in Norway knows, except my mission president."

"Remission?" Bror Haugen said. "Being homosexual is not like having cancer."

"I know, but I have gone through a program. I am normal now." The toilet flushed. Elder Ward would soon rejoin them. "Listen," Eddie said, whispering, "our church does not condone homosexuality. You cannot join or be a member, so why are you listening to the discussions?"

"My church does not accept homosexuals, either. I thought maybe your church does."

"What would make you think that?"

"Well, your church believes in polygamy, does it not? At least, it did at one time. That shows a certain tolerance for nonconventional sexual relationships. And when I saw that you were serving a mission, I thought . . ." Bror Haugen's voice trailed off. "Obviously, I was wrong."

"I am sorry. You are a nice man."

The bathroom door clicked opened. Bror Haugen leaned across the coffee table and spoke sympathetically. "Okay, but now you listen to me,

Elder Pedersen. There is no treatment for homosexuality. There is no remission. This is who you are."

He reached over to pat Eddie's hand. "It is liberating once you accept the truth."

Eddie instinctively pulled away. "I am cured," he insisted, and Bror Haugen was left waving in the air. He gave Eddie a sad look and sat back in his chair as Elder Ward arrived.

"Elder Pedersen, you look very pale. Are you feeling all right?" Elder Ward said.

"It is just a bit of indigestion. Those sausages we had for *middag* did not quite agree with me," Eddie replied, and then excused himself to go to the bathroom. He felt wretched. Looking into the mirror, he stared at himself through dull, empty eyes. *Is it so obvious what I am?* All of the traumatic memories from his treatment—and the associated nausea—came flooding back. *Is Bror Haugen right?* Eddie splashed cold water onto his face, took several deep breadths to relax himself, and repeated over and over, "I am not a homosexual. I am not a homosexual. I am not a homosexual."

During the subsequent discussion, Bror Haugen said nothing to give away his conversation with Eddie. In fact, he participated with more interest and fervor than in previous discussions, raising Elder Ward's hopes he was poised to accept the baptismal challenge. "I think he's going to go for it," Elder Ward whispered to Eddie as they read scriptures describing the meaning and purpose of baptism. However, when the missionaries asked Bror Haugen whether he would agree to be baptized if he gained a spiritual witness, Bror Haugen announced he was finished investigating Mormonism and was satisfied with his own religion. Elder Ward pressed Bror Haugen to continue the discussions, bearing his testimony over and over, emphasizing that he knew the church was true, but to no avail. Eddie also bore witness but with considerably less enthusiasm, knowing Bror Haugen would not be persuaded and wishing only that Elder Ward would relent soon enough for them to catch the 9:15 p.m. bus back to Fyllingsdalen.

Envy gnawed at Orrin like an unshakable affliction whose symptoms were guilt and shame. He wanted desperately to prove himself as a missionary, but week after week, he and Elder Flossen were among the lowest-scoring missionary pairs in the Mission Comparative. It did not help that Elder Pedersen and his companion, Elder Ward, regularly stood at the top of the missionary scorecard. Had it been anyone besides Elder Pedersen, Orrin might have felt at least grudging admiration for the many teaching hours they logged each week, but he was unable to let go of the rivalry and resentment Elder Pedersen had stirred during their time in language training. One of the reasons Orrin and his companion scored so poorly was the inordinate amount of time they spent visiting Norwegian members, which garnered no points. The warm fellowship Orrin enjoyed in the members' homes did not stop him from complaining to Elder Flossen that they were spending too much time with members. The mission rules, after all, directed the missionaries to keep member contacts to a minimum and, most importantly, said they should stay no longer than fifteen minutes with each member family—just long enough to get referrals for potential investigators. It was a rule they routinely violated. "Shouldn't the local branch take charge of visiting the members?" Orrin asked. "Don't they have home teachers and Relief Society visiting teachers just like we do at home?"

"They do, but it's a struggle with so few members to fill those positions," Elder Flossen said. "Norwegian branch presidents depend on the missionaries to supplement church programs and help keep the members active."

"But the mission rules—"

"All I know, Elder Tanner, is the members like our visits and I like visiting them. It's fun," Elder Flossen said, his tone suggesting their discussion was ended.

It was the fun that made Orrin feel guilty. He hated knocking on doors all day long. It was a mind-numbing task. He and Elder Flossen sometimes went days without being invited in. After one hour, he was bored and wanted desperately to stop. Or to visit a member. The two hours they spent with Søster Halversen each Thursday were a respite from hard labor. She welcomed them with a big smile, delighted in serving them *smørbrød* and *risgrøt,* and listened sympathetically to their daily travails. Before one of their visits with Søster Halversen, they knocked on the door of an enraged woman who, before the elders had a chance to speak, scowled and hurled a stream of invectives. "Jehovah's Witnesses," the hatchet-faced woman screamed. "You were here two weeks ago. We have the State Church in Norway and don't need Jehovah's Witnesses. Please go away and leave us alone." The door slammed.

As Elder Flossen was writing "Reject" in his tracting book, Orrin felt a twinge of doubt. "She thought we were Jehovah's Witnesses. She didn't realize who we are."

"She rejected us, Elder Tanner."

"No, she rejected Jehovah's Witnesses. No one likes Jehovah's Witnesses."

"I'm not going back."

"Well, I am," Orrin said. Perhaps this was just a test to prove his faithfulness and persistence. How many missionaries, after weeks and even months of failure, finally succeeded because they went the extra mile? Orrin climbed back up the stairs and silently rehearsed what he was going to say. He nervously rang the doorbell while Elder Flossen, hiding in the stairwell below, listened.

The woman opened the door looking more terrifying than before, but her surprise at seeing Orrin rendered her momentarily speechless. Orrin seized his chance. "Pardon me for returning, but you mistakenly thought we are Jehovah's Witnesses. We are not Jehovah's Witnesses but representatives of The Church of Jesus Christ of Latter-day Saints, also known as Mormons," Orrin said. He reached into his coat pocket and showed her a Joseph Smith pamphlet.

"Mormons?"

"Yes," Orrin said, smiling hopefully. "We are Mormons."

The scowl returned to the woman's face. "Mormons are even worse than Jehovah's Witnesses," she shouted, refusing the pamphlet. The slamming door echoed up and down the stairwell.

"*Uffa meg*," Søster Halversen said, her false teeth clicking with laughter, when the elders told her the story. She put a hand to her mouth to push her dentures back into place. "*Uffa meg for dere.*"

Orrin had felt quite depressed after the incident, but Søster Halversen's sympathetic laughter took away the sting. It made the raging woman, and not Orrin, the object of ridicule. And that's why Orrin liked visiting Søster Halversen and all the church members in their district: the members treated the missionaries as heroes, the same kind of heroes missionaries had envisioned themselves to be when they came to Norway. "*Uffa meg for oss,*" Orrin said, joining in the merriment.

Still, Orin's frustration grew into despair, clammy and cold like Norway's gloomy winters. *How is it,* Orrin wondered, *that every missionary except me wakes up with an eager smile and determination to make it a great day?* Not wishing to admit failure, Orrin dutifully put on the missionary mask each morning, telling Elder Flossen he knew today was the day they would find a golden family. Could he keep this up for two years? Missionaries like Elder Pedersen picked up the language without any problems and enjoyed immediate success, while Orrin struggled to make himself understood. Not that it mattered. Eyes clouded over and doors slammed regardless of whether they understood him. Elder Flossen seemed unperturbed by the constant rejection. Day after day he headed out, not exactly with a desire to set the world on fire, and usually without strict attention to the handbook's proselytizing schedule. He marched to the beat of his own drum, bantered pleasantly with the members who lived in their area, often dropping by their homes when he knew the comedian Fleksnes was going to be on television. He also came perilously close to flirting with fifteen-year-old Astrid Magnussen, while spending precious time talking about American movies and music with her older brother, Erik, not at all feeling the momentous weight of the missionaries' calling. Orrin envied and resented Elder Flossen as much as he did Elder Pedersen. "Please, Lord, purge these uncharitable feelings from my soul and help me become a successful missionary," Orrin prayed.

At a Sunday meeting of the Bergen District missionaries, Elder Ward presented a new way to track the missionaries' interactions with Norwegians. "Experience shows that ninety-nine percent of all Norwegians will reject us," Elder Ward said.

"Make that ninety-nine *point nine* percent," Elder Stevenson remarked to knowing laughter.

"You're probably correct," Elder Ward said. "And so it makes you wonder: Why are we here? Why do we go out day after day, hour after hour, when the inevitable result is rejection?"

"It's to gather the few, like in the parable of the shepherd," said their district leader. "We're trying to find those few who have the courage to join the church."

"That's true too," Elder Ward continued, "but we carry our message not only to them but also to those who reject us. We're a voice of warning, just like the Bible says. When we testify that Jesus Christ has restored his true church to earth through the Prophet Joseph Smith, we are delivering God's message of warning to the Norwegian people. And so, we need to note that in our tracting books, that we delivered the message."

Elder Ward showed the other elders and sisters his tracting book. Next to the word "Reject," he had also written "DM" for "delivered the message," indicating the homes where either he or Elder Pedersen had born their testimonies. Pointing to the tracting book, he said, "This will serve as a record in the next life when the newly deceased stand before the judgment bar. Jesus can pull out tracting book and say, 'Well, it says here the missionaries delivered my message, and you rejected it.'"

"Does this mean we need to save our tracting books?" one of the sisters asked.

"We throw ours away when they get full," an elder said.

"No, no. God will keep track, just like He keeps a record of all our activities, good and bad. But delivering the message is such an important part of our work that I'm going to propose that DMing become part of our missionary scorecard, so missionaries get rewarded points for delivering the message, because even when we get rejected, we're still fulfilling our purpose as Norwegian missionaries. It will be a great motivator."

Three weeks later, the assistants reprinted Elder Ward's presentation in the mission's weekly newsletter and all the Norwegian missionaries began recording "DM" in their tracting books. Even Elder Flossen, who often disparaged suggestions from other missionaries, said Elder Ward's idea was a good one, though he didn't think much of Elder Ward himself. "I served with Elder Ward in Trondheim," Elder Flossen said. "He wants to be an assistant so badly his teeth hurt."

Chapter 16

Conversion comes only through the Holy Ghost. Your contacts feel
his presence strongest as you bear testimony.

A Uniform System for Teaching Investigators

"What's going on in there?" a young elder asked Elder Blake, the mission secretary. The elder, a newly arrived greenie, was sitting outside the
president's office waiting with five other missionaries to talk with President
Toressen. Behind the closed door to the president's office, they could hear
impatient scolding and murmuring acquiescence.

"As usual, President Toressen is a little behind schedule with his interviews, and, well, I think Sister Toressen is trying to get him back on track,"
Elder Blake said.

Sister Toressen emerged from the office a few minutes later, her face
pinched and frazzled. "President Toressen is ready for his next interview,"
she said, barking out the name of one of the seated missionaries. The elder
dutifully stood and ambled into the office. Sister Toressen handed Elder
Blake a portable clock. "Here, set the alarm for ten minutes," she said.
"When it rings, knock on the door and tell President Toressen it's time to
end the interview."

"But Sister Toressen, he never listens to me."

"Just do it. If he doesn't listen, come get me. I mean it. It's the only
way he's going to get through all of his interviews. Ten minutes. That's it."

Orrin had come to the mission office with Elder Flossen for their
weekly showers, but seeing that President Toressen was conducting interviews, Orrin asked that his name be added to the list. "I can't guarantee
you'll get in," Elder Blake said. "You know how it is. Take a seat and let's
see what happens."

President Toressen largely adhered to his wife's tight schedule, sometimes stretching out the interviews to fifteen minutes, but Sister Toressen
was needed only once, and she banged on the office door so loudly that
the frightened missionary promptly scampered from the office. As Orrin
waited his turn, he couldn't help but notice the contrast between when the
missionaries entered Toressen's office and when they left. Many of those
waiting to see the president looked as tired and defeated as Orrin felt, but
after a short session with President Toressen, they emerged with straightened shoulders, vigorous smiles, and eyes that sparkled with enthusiasm.
Toressen often followed the missionaries out the door, continuing a story
or beginning a new one, before reluctantly returning to his desk.

"He's truly an inspired man," a sister missionary said after emerging from the office, her face beaming.

"A new dawn is breaking on the Norwegian mission," proclaimed an awestruck elder after his interview. "Nothing can stop us now."

The assistants interrupted one of the interviews to get approval for a conference presentation, and then lingered in the office, talking in whispered conversation with Elder Blake. "It's not like when President Larsen was here," one of the assistants said. "The mission was a well-oiled machine. Everything worked like clockwork."

"Yeah, but President Toressen carries a wonderful spirit wherever he goes. Not that there was anything wrong with President Larsen's style, but everyone is happier working with President Toressen."

"Everyone but Sister Toressen," the assistant said, his eyes filling with laughter. Just then, the alarm went off and Orrin was called into the mission office.

"Elder Tanner, it's so good to see you again," President Toressen said. "The last time I saw you was when you arrived about three months ago. We assigned you to work with, uh, Elder Flotsam, right?"

"Flossen, sir. Elder Flossen."

"Yes, yes. A fine elder. And so, how have you been enjoying your mission so far?"

Orrin knew President Toressen was going to ask this question. He had been asking himself the same question every day since he arrived in Norway. The answer was too painful to acknowledge even to himself, so how could he tell the mission president? How could say he had never been so miserable and discouraged? That he was homesick and missed his family and friends? That he couldn't understand why he was having so much trouble learning the language? That everybody was telling him how great Elder Flossen was, but he seemed rather pedestrian and uninspiring? That he hated the monotony of door-to-door tracting and couldn't understand why the Lord had sent him to Norway in a fruitless search for converts? If he revealed any of these thoughts, he would also reveal himself to be an unworthy missionary who lacked the proper spirit.

"I love the work and the Norwegian people," Orrin said, repeating what he thought good missionaries were supposed to say. Hoping to give President Toressen a hint of his true feelings, Orrin added, "Still, I wish Elder Flossen and I were experiencing more success. We hardly ever get invited in and don't have any promising investigators."

"The Norwegian soul, like the Norwegian soil, can be difficult to penetrate," President Toressen said, looking beyond, lost in thought. Suddenly, he turned around, as if remembering something, leaned over and picked up a large cardboard box, somewhat worn, and placed it on his desk. "You'll never guess what's in here," he said. He eagerly opened the box and, reaching inside, pulled out a stack of pamphlets and piled them in front of Orrin. "It's *Tanner's Guide to Mormon History and Doctrine* and *Tanner's Faith-Promoting Series*," Toressen said. I never realized it was your family until I was reading the pamphlet on plural marriage and I saw not only your father's name, but also your name. Did you help write these articles?"

"I mainly did the proofreading and typesetting after the articles were written, but sometimes I helped with the research."

"Elder Tanner, your father, Anson Tanner, is one of our church's most distinguished scholars. And you're a real scholar, too. I have every Tanner pamphlet and brought them with me to Norway. I'm getting set for a speaking tour at the quarterly conferences, and so I got out the pamphlets to help me prepare, never thinking I had one of *the* Tanner authors right here in Norway."

"These are two of my favorite pamphlets," President Toressen said, pointing to "Heber Tanner's Visit to the Spirit World" and "Lars Andreassen's Remarkable Life on the Arizona Frontier."

"Heber Tanner is my grandfather and Lars Andreassen is my great-grandfather," Orrin explained. "Grandpa Heber married Lars's daughter, Sonya. Lars Andreassen was born in a small island town in Norway before he joined the church and immigrated to Utah. I think it says the name of the island in the pamphlet."

Orrin hurriedly skimmed the pages, looking for a reference to the island. "Here it is," he said, after finding the page. "It's Riksøy." But when Orrin looked up, President Toressen was asleep, his eyes closed and his chin resting on his chest. Other missionaries said this sometimes happened. One elder thought President Toressen was having a revelation, eliciting mocking laughter from the other missionaries. Toressen wouldn't sleep at all if his wife didn't make him come to bed, the senior elders said. Still, Orrin was unnerved that President Toressen had fallen asleep during his interview.

Click, click, click. Orrin heard the ticking of the president's pacemaker. *Is this normal or a sign something's wrong?* The clicking continued, increasing Orrin's anxiety. *Should I get help?* Orrin's decision was made when the alarm clock rang loudly outside the office. President Toressen's eyes popped open and he smiled, refreshed. "Elder Tanner, how would you like to accompany me as my scribe on my speaking tour?"

"Scribe, sir?"

"Yes, I need someone to record my talks. I'd like to have a written record, like the Tanner pamphlets, of my first conference tour through the Norwegian branches. With your editing experience and knowledge of church history and doctrine, you'd be perfect for the job."

Elder Blake banged on the door and poked his head in. "Times up, President Toressen. It's time for your next interview."

"Come in, come in, Elder Blake. You're just the person I want to see. I want you to arrange for Elder Tanner to accompany me on my conference tour. Let the assistants know so they can make the adjustments in our next scheduled move of the missionaries."

"Yes, President."

President Toressen stood and shook Orrin's hand. "Elder Tanner, it looks like you and I are going to be companions in a few weeks. I hope you don't mind a little snoring. Elder Blake, please send in the next missionary."

Orrin left with a smile stretched across his face, much like the previous missionaries who had met with President Toressen.

The first tour stop in Bergen began disastrously. The chapel overflowed with missionaries and members who had come from surrounding towns and cities as far away as Stavanger to meet the mission president for the first time. At the appointed time, President Toressen was nowhere to be found. Orrin had arrived with the mission president thirty minutes before the scheduled start, but neither he nor the assistants could find him anywhere in the chapel. Everyone stayed clear of Sister Toressen, who tore through the building like a raging bull, calling Bjørnstjerne's name. Orrin finally took a seat in the front row while the assistants consulted their watches and amid shrugging shoulders, discussed with the local branch president whether to begin without Toressen. At half past the hour, a commotion in the hallway caused a turning of heads. "Bjørnstjerne, where have you been?" his wife cried, her shrill voice ringing in the rafters. Despite the turmoil, President Toressen entered the chapel with the relaxed demeanor of someone who did not realize or did not care he was late. A slight man barely five and a half feet tall, he disappeared in the crush of people who converged around him. Some of the taller missionaries had to bend over to shake his hand as he walked down the aisle. He pushed ahead, smiling and saying hello to members he knew, and then went straight to the podium.

"I apologize for being late, but I have just returned from visiting the home of the Norwegian composer Edvard Grieg," he said. "When I listen to that man's compositions, I can feel God's spirit in his music, and I know as assuredly as I stand here before you that God inspired him, stirred his heart, so Grieg could put into musical form the spirit and character of the Norwegian people. All of our American missionaries should listen to Grieg's compositions, so you can gain an understanding of the true Norwegian soul. Before speaking to you today, I wanted to visit Grieg's home, to see what he saw, to hear what he heard, and to feel what he felt, because that is what I want to give to you today. I want to sing to you"— and now he laughed and assured the congregation he wouldn't actually sing, that all of his brothers and sisters had lovely voices, and his brother Haakon won national awards for his singing, but he, President Toressen, had a gift for a different kind of singing—"but as I was saying, I want to sing to you of Norway's sacred heritage. I want my words to be a tone poem you embrace and hold in your hearts, so you see, as I foresee, the marvelous destiny that lies in store for the Norwegian people. You, my fellow brothers and sisters"—and here he digressed to expound on the principle that we are all the spiritual brothers and sisters of our Lord Jesus Christ—"you are a part of this destiny."

President Toressen spoke in this manner for two hours. The timbre of his voice was smooth and pleasant, his eyes a reassuring caress that enchanted and enthralled. He quoted scriptures and Norwegian writers, including his namesake, Bjørnstjerne Bjørnson, and Nobel Prize–winning author Knut Hamsun, and then reviewed his people's history from their forced conversion to Christianity by Saint Olav to the sequence of events leading Bjørnson to write the Norwegian national anthem, "*Jeg, Vi Elske Dette Landet*" ("Yes, We Love This Land"). He introduced his wife, Kristina, and told the story of how they met at the mission home while serving as missionaries. He backtracked to tell of his conversion to Mormonism, the subsequent conversion of both parents and all six brothers and sisters except his older brother, Ole, who had drowned three years earlier at age nineteen.

Orrin scribbled furiously, trying to keep up with the meandering speech. Toressen spoke without notes, leaping back and forth between scriptures and stories. Missionaries and members alike had trouble following his discursions and several dozed through portions of his speech. But Orrin, who was forced by the nature of his task to follow every rhetorical thread, found that buried within these seemingly disconnected stories of faith and history were recurrent themes that, like the variations of a melody within a symphony, could be discerned by those who had ears to hear.

"Twenty months ago, I suffered a severe heart attack, and while lingering near death, I was rushed by ambulance to the University of Utah hospital to receive a pacemaker for my heart," President Toressen said.

"While undergoing surgery, I dreamed I was back in Norway, standing on a large hill in one of our beautiful island towns, preaching the gospel to a multitude of my fellow countrymen. The people looked gaunt and jaundiced, as if they had been sick or starving, but despite their deplorable condition, they listened with rapt attention and even fought to get close, so they could hear what I was saying. However, I soon grew tired and had to stop speaking. 'Please continue,' the people shouted. 'I am sorry, but I cannot,' I said. 'I do not have the strength.' But as soon as I said those words, a thunderclap exploded overhead and I heard a voice from heaven say, 'Bjørnstjerne Bjørnson Toressen, your mission in Norway is not yet finished.'"

The Bergen congregation trembled and gasped. President Toressen wiped his brow and continued. "When I awoke from surgery, the first thing I told Kristina was, 'I'm going to be called as the Norwegian mission president' and recounted to her my dream. Sister Toressen said I was still woozy from the anesthesia—she was careful not to say I was hallucinating—and here let me say there is always a danger when you are a visionary man, though I am not claiming to be one, because, like the Prophet Lehi's sons, people may say your visions are the foolish imaginations of your heart, just as people attributed Joseph Smith's visions to epileptic hallucinations, and so I assured Sister Toressen this was a genuine dream, and my good wife believed me, and we kept this to ourselves until six months later when Apostle Joseph Prichard called and asked me to meet with him at church headquarters. 'I bet you can't guess why I asked you to come,' he said, a big smile on his face, and I said, with an even bigger smile, 'I know exactly why you called and I bet you can't guess who's already packed and ready to go to Norway.'"

Hearty laughter swept through the congregation. "And here I am today," he said, spreading his arms wide. "God has designed his plan, and while we cannot always discern His intentions, if we remain faithful and trust in Him, eventually He will fulfill all of His promises, just as he fulfilled His promises to the children of Israel, to Lehi and his sons, to Joseph Smith, and now to the Norwegian people."

President Toressen stood like a lion at the pulpit, vigorous and glowing with confidence. And like a symphony composer whose music builds to a climax reverberating with the strains of earlier movements, Toressen's stories gathered in power and fixed themselves indelibly in the hearts and minds of his listeners. All Norwegian history had been leading to this point in time—from the Vikings and St. Olav to Bjørnstjerne Bjørnson, Edvard Grieg, and now President Toressen—when God would soften the hearts of the Norwegian people and The Church of Jesus Christ of Latter-day Saints would flourish. Those hearing President Toressen's inspirational words—missionaries and members alike—were united in their belief that under his leadership, they would have the privilege of ushering in Norway's impending religious renaissance.

President Toressen and Orrin traveled to three more cities—Kristiansand, Trondheim, and Moss—sometimes stopping in smaller towns to commune with congregations of fewer than a dozen people. Just as he had done in Bergen, Toressen inspired missionaries and members with his boundless enthusiasm and vision for the work. The Norwegians especially loved him because he was one of their own, and because he spoke of Norway as a chosen land and of Norwegians as a chosen people. In the out-of-the-way towns, the members clung to the president, recounting how they had been disowned by parents and ostracized by friends while they struggled to keep their children interested and active when only eight souls met each Sunday for church services. They told of the minor miracles and spiritual experiences that led them to Mormonism, and they took strength from President Toressen's assurances that Norway stood on the precipice of change. Orrin marveled at the faith of the rural Norwegian Saints and felt ashamed of the indulgent self-pity and pessimism he had allowed himself.

Orrin's task was made more difficult by the fact that President Toressen never gave the same speech twice, always speaking without notes in a meandering style characterized by numerous scriptural references, comical musings and asides, anecdotes from his missionary days, and peppered with stories of people in the audience with whom he had served. He also filled his talks with tales of his visions and dreams, adding new information or elaborating on certain details to illustrate the particular theme for each day's speech. During his speech to the Trondheim members, President Toressen said that on the day he performed the temple ordinances in proxy for his deceased brother, he saw Ole watching the ceremony from the back of the temple auditorium, and so in this way he knew his brother had accepted the gospel in the spirit world. In Drammen, he testified that the marriage in Cana described in the gospel of St. John—the marriage where Jesus turns the water into wine—was actually a polygamous ceremony in which Jesus himself was married.

"We have only one prophet over the church, but we each have God's spirit to guide us in our church callings and our individual lives," President Toressen asserted. "Revelation is the birthright of every man and woman. The miracles and heavenly visitations experienced by Joseph Smith and the early Saints were not one-time occurrences but harbingers of God's love and spirit He is pouring forth in the latter days, even unto the Saints in Norway."

With the mention of Norway, President Toressen digressed to talk about his homeland. "By virtue of our harsh environment, we have been tested, shaped, and strengthened by God, and as a reward, He has given us this beautiful nation, a steadfast rock—like the rock of Peter—of grand mountains, shimmering rivers, verdant forests, and breathtaking fjords. We did not conquer the land, but neither did it conquer us, and now we live together as one with the land. We are this land."

Briefly overcome with emotion, President Toressen paused. The audience grew silent, the only sound being Orrin's frantic scribbling across his notebook. With all eyes upon him, Toressen gathered up his energy. "A new day is dawning on Norway and you are called to labor in the Lord's field," he said, growing in stature as he spoke. "Do not hesitate or be afraid. 'Ask, and it shall be given you; seek, and ye shall find; knock, and it shall be opened unto you.' Each of you has the gift of revelation. Each is a prophet over his realm and calling."

After this speech, missionaries and members began calling President Toressen the prophet of Norway. Norway was his realm and calling. President Toressen never called himself the prophet of Norway and, in fact, tried to discourage any type of adoration by acknowledging his failings and fallibility, especially as an administrator and husband and father, saying he was repenting daily and trying to do better, and was thankful for a wife who helped lift him when he stumbled and was strong where he was weak, praising her as the perfect helpmeet. Still, the people swarmed him after his speeches, shaking his hand and staying near, lingering, absorbing his spirit and holding it tight.

These events drained Toressen. The people didn't see it but Orrin did. By the end of the evening, after the last smile and embrace and heartfelt goodbye, the vigorous color vanished from his face. In Trondheim, President Toressen stumbled as he walked down the steps from the dais and would have fallen had not Orrin grabbed his arm and held him steady. As it was, Toressen hit his head on the railing, and though it was a minor bump, it began to bleed due to the blood thinner he was taking. Sister Toressen, who had been present for the speech, rushed forward, scolding her husband while dabbing at the cut with a Kleenex taken from her purse. "Honestly, Bjørnstjerne, you're going to give yourself another heart attack," she said.

"Perhaps I will give you one first." Toressen kissed his wife and winked at Orrin, who held a firm grip on his arm.

After each speaking engagement, Orrin would write up his notes while sitting outside the president's office and in this way, he became acquainted with many of the missionaries as they waited their turn to see the president. Most struck Orrin as sober and eager to succeed, while also wearing the missionary mask of ready-to-conquer-the-world optimism. "No different than me," Orrin thought. Orrin also saw that, like him, an unnamed dissatisfaction lurked beneath the mask. Some confided in Orrin their troubles, but often he discerned the cause of their unhappiness based on a remark President Toressen or the assistants made in his presence. Some missionaries could not get along with their companions; others were disappointed they had not been promoted to senior companion or district leader as fast as other, allegedly less competent missionaries; one was distraught over his parents' impending divorce, which he hoped to prevent by working harder; and many were simply homesick or discouraged. While waiting to see President Toressen, Sister Allison complained bitterly to Orrin about the endless drudgery of tracting. "I didn't come on a mission just to knock on doors for twelve hours every day," she said.

Orrin recognized himself in many of their complaints, but now, having traveled with the president and observed the behind-the-scenes work of the mission office, he was seeing mission life from a different perspective. The missionaries' problems, while certainly distressing, seemed relatively minor in the overall scheme of their work. If the church were true, as the elders and sisters claimed, what did it matter if your companion chewed with his mouth open or a dog chased you over a fence and tore a hole in your pants or the police confiscated your passport because you forgot to register at the city headquarters? "There are no problems in this mission," President Toressen would say, "only challenges." That's not to say he minimized or dismissed the missionaries' anxious concerns. He poured every ounce of his physical and emotional being into his interviews, taking the missionaries' burdens upon himself, and in the process, lifted them up and restored their hope. The missionaries emerged from his office buoyed and confident they could move whatever mountains were standing in their path and, most importantly, feeling that President Toressen was pleased with their performance and, whatever misgivings they had about themselves, he regarded them as the best missionaries in the world. The transformation Orrin witnessed in the countenances of some elders and sisters, from the time they went into the president's office to the time they came out, was nothing short of miraculous.

Norwegian members received the same rapt attention and concern. All day long came a steady stream of people hoping to discuss a pressing question or problem. Some just wanted to converse with the prophet of Norway. Missionaries also brought investigators to meet with Toressen, confident that nonmembers couldn't help but feel his irrepressible spirit. President Toressen turned no one away and carried on lengthy conversations amid a flurry of assistants and secretaries running in and out of his office, asking for his signature on reports or approval for invoices or action on myriad administrative responsibilities, all needing his attention. Orrin witnessed the exasperation of the missionaries called to serve in the mission office. They had become accustomed to the rigid efficiency of the previous mission president and chafed at President Toressen's insouciant regard for the nuts and bolts of running the mission smoothly.

"Salt Lake City says if we submit another late financial report, they'll have to get the accountants involved," the mission treasurer said as he shoved a handful of papers onto the president's desk.

"I trust they'll find our finances are in order as a result of your excellent stewardship, Elder," Toressen said, signing the papers cheerfully before handing them back to the treasurer,

At the end of the day, President Toressen was completely used up. When it came time for Orrin to review his notes with him, Toressen would slump lifelessly in his chair, his eyes dull and his face dark with weariness. Orrin would read to him a portion of the text, and he would nod, pretending to agree with the transcript, but his mind had gone into hibernation. Sometimes he would stop talking mid-sentence and close his eyes, then sit motionless for a minute or longer. Orrin waited patiently, listening to the clicking of the pacemaker. After a brief rest, President Toressen would open his eyes and begin speaking as if he hadn't been sleeping. None of the other missionaries, not even the assistants, realized how exhausted President Toressen became, because he always managed to recharge himself overnight and regain the spirit that infused the mission. Sister Toressen, of course, understood the strain the mission activities placed on her husband. She worried constantly, often taking charge of his schedule, shouting "Bjørnstjerne" and barking out furious orders, much to the horror of the missionaries. But President Toressen, his mind on loftier matters, accepted criticism from his wife and others with cool equanimity, too happily engaged in his Father's work to allow minor irritations to dampen his spirits.

Orrin saw President Toressen lose his temper only twice. The first time came after the president arrived back from the Trondheim conference.

Elder Blake met the president at the door and began badgering him about a statistical report, scolding Toressen as if he were a child, telling him he was neglecting his duties, warning that church authorities were displeased with him, and enumerating the tasks needing immediate attention—in essence, telling the president how to run the mission. Elder Blake's advice was well-intentioned, and because he had probably borne the brunt of Salt Lake City's displeasure while Toressen was absent, Toressen listened patiently to his secretary's tirade, agreeing to get on the reports right away. But as they headed upstairs, the president received a phone call from Sister Langerud, an old friend, who wanted Toressen to give her husband a blessing before he went in for eye surgery the next morning. President Toressen assured her he would come at once.

"You can't go now," Elder Blake said, waving papers in front of the president's face. "You must address these issues immediately."

President Toressen tried to make a joke. "Well, Elder, when the cow's in the mire, then you've got to—"

"Can't someone else go?"

"That will be enough, Elder Blake!" President Toressen said, shaking an indignant finger under the missionary's chin. The uncharacteristic outburst silenced Blake. Calming himself, Toressen finished his lecture in a quiet, piercing tone. "I appreciate what you are trying to do for me, Elder, but don't tell me how to go about my business." President Toressen took the keys to the mission van, saying he would be back in thirty minutes to work on the reports. He returned two hours later.

Chapter 17

Develop good work habits. These same traits will carry over into your life. Good work habits will become part and parcel of your character. If you are inactive and asleep, Satan will come and sow tares in your soul.

Conduct of a Missionary

After serving three months as Eddie's companion, Elder Ward received a call to be Bergen's district leader, and so Eddie was assigned a new senior companion, Elder Charlie Jensen. Eddie noticed immediately a difference in the proselytizing styles of the two elders. Elder Ward always got straight to the point. He introduced himself and then announced he had news about living prophets and the restoration of the true church of Jesus Christ. He delivered the message. He eschewed discussion of the United States and politics. If the people good-naturedly began conversing in English, he forged ahead in Norwegian as if he hadn't heard them. He told Eddie he did this because he spoke better Norwegian than they did English and he didn't want them to misunderstand when he delivered the message, but Eddie suspected the real reason was that Elder Ward took it as a personal affront when people spoke English, as if they thought his Norwegian was lacking. Elder Ward also didn't like to waste time at the door and would reject people quickly if they didn't seem interested. "We're a voice of warning," he would say as he wrote "DM" next to their name. Whenever a page of their tracting book became completely filled with rejects, he scrawled a large "X" through the page with the enthusiasm of an artist putting his initials on a finished painting.

In contrast, Elder Charlie Jensen adopted a folksy, even lackadaisical approach, as if door-to-door missionary work were nothing more than a spontaneous lark by two untrained American boys who, since they happened to be in the neighborhood, decided to drop by to see if anyone wanted to talk about Mormonism or any other subject that struck their fancy. "As I am sure you can hear by my accent, we are Americans," Elder Jensen would say, grinning broadly with his fresh-off-the-farm baby face. In fact, Elder Jensen grew up on a southwest Texas farm and spoke with a heavy Texas drawl, which he did not try to hide. He could not roll his r's and had long ago given up trying, but he disarmed Norwegians with his friendliness, and he obliged anyone who wanted to show off their English.

"I have lived in America four years," a ruddy man said in barely comprehensible English during Eddie's first day of tracting with Elder Jensen. "I have the degree in engineering from Minnesota University."

"Ah, it is colder there than in Bergen, is it not?" Elder Jensen replied in English.

"Yes." The man ran his tongue along his mustache and then delved into a lengthy discussion with the elders about Minnesota and the cultural differences between the countries. The man was not interested in Mormonism, but he invited the missionaries to come back anytime. "America is land of the big opportunities," he said, shaking their hands.

One morning they tracted up two long-haired young men, Ole and Bjørn, who played in a Norwegian band. Upon hearing Elder Jensen speak, they invited the missionaries in and asked them to help with a country-and-western song they were composing in English. The song, "On a Mountain," had a pleasant melody, but Ole and Bjørn could not create the country sound. Eddie, spotting an electronic keyboard, asked if he could try playing the song back to them and help them discover how to fix it. After a few pass throughs, Eddie was able to play the song's chords and then, making a small adjustment, gave it a country feel.

"What did you do?" Ole asked.

"I changed it to major chords," Eddie said, showing them the chords on the piano. "See, with country, you want to make it simpler by playing the major chords, the first, fourth, and fifth." Ole and Bjørn strummed along with Eddie, huge smiles on their faces as they played the new chords. "Okay, the other thing you must do is sing it with a twang. I'm not really sure how to do that. Maybe we can figure it out by having Elder Jensen, who comes from Texas, sing it for us."

Elder Jensen enthusiastically sang the verses, putting on a thick drawl, and sure enough, he gave it a genuine country-and-western sound, but they were uncertain what, precisely, he was doing. The four young men went back and forth, taking turns singing and listening until Bjørn interrupted, shouting, "I've got it. I've got it!" The problem, he pointed out, was they had been giving a hard pronunciation to the second syllable of the words "mountain" and "courting." Instead, these words should be pronounced "mount'n" and "court'n." So they tried it like this:

> On a mount'n where the wildflowers grow
> On a mount'n where the cool waters flow
> I went court'n my true love
> Miranda, my sweet baby rose

This discovery so excited Ole and Bjørn that they had the elders sing with them several of their other compositions, noting the changes in pronunciation and chords that gave their songs an authentic country-and-western flavor. After two hours, Elder Jensen said it was time to go, but left behind pamphlets and a Book of Mormon, which Bjørn purchased. "Come back any time, my cowboy friends," he said.

With the coming of spring, the Bergen missionaries set up an outdoor Book of Mormon display each Saturday morning at the central bus station, a place bustling with shoppers scurrying about with packages of fresh fish, flowers, and other weekend purchases. Buttonholing the Norwegians was a cat-and-mouse game in which the missionaries tried a variety of stratagems to engage shoppers in conversation as they hurried by with their packages, while the Norwegians, in turn, employed their own countermoves to avoid eye contact or even acknowledging the missionaries' presence, lest they be corralled into discussions of golden plates and ancient American ruins. Those who were too polite to ignore the missionaries sometimes purchased a copy of the Book of Mormon as a way to end the conversation. The missionaries understood this, but they believed every Book of Mormon sold offered the possibility of conversion, however remote, regardless of the purchaser's motivation. Plus, a sale garnered them five points in the Mission Comparative.

After closing down the display, the missionaries gathered at Elder Ward's downtown hybel for supper and to play a card game they called *Trosartikler*. The mission rules prohibited missionaries from playing with regular face cards, so they took their missionary business cards and created four suits, each numbered from one to thirteen, like a deck of cards, and played Gin Rummy. They called the game *Trosartikler* because their business cards had the church's Articles of Faith—"*Trosartikler*"—printed on the back, and because some of the elders and sisters recoiled at the idea of playing a game called Gin Rummy, even if it didn't have anything to do with drinking alcohol. "It isn't appropriate for those called into the Lord's service," Elder Ward said amid nods of agreement. *Trosartikler* provided the missionaries with a lively diversion from their work, although the quick-tempered Elder Jones would occasionally throw down his cards and storm out of the hybel if he lost too many hands in a row.

The games were noisy affairs, punctuated by laughter and conversations about girlfriends and families and home. The sisters didn't care about winning and good-naturedly played the sacrificial patsies when Elder Jones wasn't mired in a losing streak. Sister Hansen often played the wrong cards because she misread the markings, provoking more merriment than angst. Eddie enjoyed the camaraderie of the sisters, who brought a feeling of home to their gatherings. The sisters, being older, had reputations as old maids who, unable to find husbands at home or in college, had come on

141

missions as a desperate last resort. Eddie considered this a misperception, having observed that the sisters were more effective than the elders, perhaps because they understood the importance of fellowshipping people into the church rather than browbeating them with scriptural arguments. Their approach to missionary work sprang from an intrinsic desire to nurture as well as teach, as if driven by instinct to bring investigators baked treats and flowers, to socialize and draw investigators out with sincere interest in their lives, to revel in conversation and fun, to make others feel special. Their laughter and geniality almost made Eddie smile.

Occasionally, the conversations at the Saturday night gatherings turned to more serious topics. One night when Elder Jones complained about how his temple garments were riding up his rear, Elder Ward immediately rebuked him for lightmindedness. "Never joke about garments, Elder."

Elder Jones scowled resentfully, but he knew he had gone too far, especially in front of the sisters. The missionaries stared awkwardly at one another until Elder Jensen broke the silence. "Did you hear about what happened to the missionaries in Mexico?" he said. "On their P-Day, some of the missionaries from the mission home went to a local gym to play basketball. After they finished, two of the elders discovered they had forgotten to bring a clean pair of garments. So, while the others changed into their garments and street clothes, those two had to wear their basketball clothes back to the mission home. On the way, their car got in a terrible accident. Everybody survived without a scratch except for those two missionaries. One was thrown from the car and had his head decapitated at the neck, right at the spot where his garments would have come to."

The elders and sisters nodded knowingly. Elder Parnell asserted that his father's garments had protected him from bullets during the war, and Elder Jones said an older cousin had been in a serious fire, but the only place he got burned was on his arms below his garments. "I hear that every missionary has at least one experience with the devil on their mission," Elder Jensen said. The missionaries again nodded in recognition. The somber looks on their faces suggested some had already been tested.

"Joseph Smith said the devil has control over water," Elder Ward said. "When did he say that?"

"It's in the Doctrine and Covenants. That's why we're not allowed to go swimming or ride in boats."

Satan was as real to the missionaries as the actors who played Satan in the temple ceremony. The devil was always trying to hinder their work by filling the elders' minds with sexual thoughts and arousing their desires for young girls. If that didn't work, he used lightmindedness to distract them from their sacred callings, which is why Elder Jones received such a strong rebuke. Elder Parnell told of a missionary in Australia who, as a joke, bestowed the Holy Ghost on a fire hydrant. "As soon as he invoked his priesthood, he was struck mute and paralyzed. His companion had to carry him back to their apartment."

"I heard the exact same story," Elder Ward said, "but I heard it happened in Japan."

"What happened to the missionary?"

"He died the next day."

The missionaries silently mulled over Elder Parnell's story. The talk of Satan and his powers conjured up a dark spirit, both fascinating and foreboding, as if an evil force were poised to crash through the window. Suddenly, Elder Jones blurted out, "I had an experience with the devil." He looked to Elder Ward to see whether it was appropriate to continue. With a turn of his head, Elder Ward gave silent approval, and Elder Jones continued.

"Remember the time we were playing *Trosartikler* at the Minde hybel, and I got mad and ran outside. I was upset, not just about the game, but about a lot of things. I was homesick and discouraged, you know how it is, and so I decided to go back to our hybel by myself. I knew we're not supposed to go anywhere without our companions, but . . . I'm not like the rest of you. I'm not smart and I have trouble speaking Norwegian and no one listens to us anyway. I thought about packing my bags and running away.

"When I first started walking down the street toward the bus stop, there wasn't anyone around. But after only about a minute of walking, I noticed a man on the other side who seemed to be watching and keeping pace with me. When I sped up, he sped up; and when I slowed down, he slowed; and when I stopped, he stopped too. It was real eerie. He was dressed in dark clothes, all black, and he wore a black hat and gloves. Although I couldn't see his face clearly, I could see he had very dark skin.

"Anyway, when I got to the end of the block, the man stopped and looked at me like he knew where I was going and he was waiting for me to cross the street. When I hesitated, he raised his arm and waved for me to come over to his side. A real bad feeling came over me, like this man was evil and I shouldn't be there, so I raised my hand and commanded him to depart in the name of Jesus Christ, like Peter does to the devil in the temple, and then I ran back to you guys as fast as I could. I didn't look back except once, just before I got to the door, but when I turned around, there was no one there. The street was deserted again."

Elder Jones closed his eyes somberly and squeezed his hands into tight fists. Bluish veins bulged from under his skin.

"I knew you were in trouble," Elder Parnell told Elder Jones, "when we were out tracting and you got mad and said there was no such thing as the devil. Do you remember saying that?"

"Yes,"

"That's as good as inviting him in. You never want to say something like that."

"I've learned my lesson," Elder Jones said meekly. He was pale and quivering, and at that moment, the devil's presence seemed dangerously close. No one dared speak, lest they inadvertently summon his spirit. Finally, Elder Ward suggested the missionaries kneel in prayer, which dispelled the foreboding atmosphere, and the elders and sisters wrote letters and read the scriptures until it was time for everyone to return to their hybels.

Elder Jones had been surly and discontented much of his mission. Twenty months out and he was still a junior companion. He harbored anger at his companions, the Norwegians, and most of all, his parents, whom he blamed for pressing him to go on a mission. After that night, however, Elder Jones's tantrums and outbursts diminished. It wasn't just the recounting of his story with the devil, but also the revelation of his anxiety and frustration, feelings the other missionaries shared, that enabled them to view him more sympathetically. He, in turn, felt more accepted. It helped that he had only a few months left on his mission, so he could see the end on the horizon. But more than anything else, his experience with the devil validated his missionary credentials. He repeated the story on several occasions, including a dramatically embellished account he told to all the missionaries at the next conference. After hearing the exaggerated versions, Elder Jensen remarked to Eddie that he had some doubts the episode happened exactly as Elder Jones related, but neither Eddie nor his companion voiced this opinion to others. As a matter of etiquette, missionaries did not question another missionary's faith-promoting story.

Is the devil as real as Elder Jones contends? Eddie wondered. Church leaders plainly thought so, warning the elders and sisters to constantly be on guard, lest they fall prey to the whispered temptations Satan placed before them. *Is this the source of my troubles? Has Satan put homosexual thoughts and desires in my thoughts that I struggle to resist? If so, why can't I purge them from my mind?*

This line of thinking—that the devil made him do it—was incomprehensible to Eddie. His homosexual tendencies had presented themselves at an early age; he could not remember a time when he was not attracted to other boys. *Did Satan lay claim to me from the beginning. If so, why? If Satan is real, then he certainly would be trying to discourage me, undermine my faith in the deal, encourage me to act on my desires and break my part of the bargain.* But was the devil the original cause of his homosexual desires? Eddie did not think so. That riddle remained unsolved.

Chapter 18

Stay with your companion and never go anywhere alone. There is
safety when you are together.

Conduct of a Missionary

When Orrin's service as President Toressen's scribe ended, he was reassigned as the companion to the district leader in Halden. A gray, overcast
April sky blanketed Oslo on the day Orrin departed the city. Before leaving, he collected the rest of his belongings from the Kjelsås hybel, where
he learned that Elder Flossen had left the day before, having been transferred to Grorud as Oslo's new district leader. Elder Morris, who had taken
Orrin's place in Kjelsås, greeted Orrin as if they were old friends. "Ah, so I
finally meet the illustrious Mormon scholar, Elder Orrin Tanner," he said,
showing a toothy smile. "Elder Flossen sure sung your praises. He says
you're a machine."

Orrin was uncertain how to answer. During their three months together, Elder Flossen had done nothing but criticize and correct him.
Orrin didn't think Elder Flossen even liked him. "That was nice of him,"
Orrin replied, realizing he needed to say something. "Being his companion was certainly an interesting experience."

Elder Morris didn't perceive Orrin's ambivalence. "You're right. He'll
make an exceptional district leader."

Orrin stepped into the kitchen to say goodbye to Elder Morris's companion, Elder Regan. Much to Orrin's surprise, he saw Elder Regan peeing
in the sink. "Um, don't mind me," Elder Regan said, seeing the astonished
look on Orrin's face. "I'm just taking advantage of our new toilet."

Orrin exited quickly, startled by what he had seen. "I should explain," Elder Morris said. "We learned to do this from Sister Halversen.
Whenever Elder Flossen and I visited her, we dreaded going downstairs to
use the shared toilets in the basement. It was a long way, and some of the
residents gave us dirty looks when we used them, like we were bums off
the street. 'Listen,' Sister Halversen said, 'you should pee in a jar and pour
it down my sink. That is what my brother does when he visits me. And
that is what I do when I get up at night. I'm not going to go all the way
downstairs at two in the morning.' Isn't that wild? Eighty-seven-year-old
Sister Halversen pees in a jar."

"So did you pee in the jar at her apartment?" Orrin asked.

"No, we were too embarrassed. But when Elder Flossen and I got
home, we thought, 'Why not?' But rather than first pee in a jar and then

pour it down the sink, we decided to pee directly into the basin sink, which is just the right height."

By this time, Elder Regan had zipped up, so Elder Morris showed Orrin where Elder Flossen had attached a bottle of soap to the wall over the sink and placed a can of bathroom cleaning powder on a nearby shelf. "See, we squirt a little soap on our hands and spread the powder in the sink," said Elder Morris, demonstrating for Orrin. He turned on the water. "And voila, we rinse it all away,"

"You should have heard Sister Halversen laugh when Elder Flossen told her how we arranged the sink," Elder Morris said. "'*Uffa meg*. That is my American boys,' she said."

Elder Rick Thompson greeted Orrin with an open smile, showing a row of perfectly even teeth. With his neatly pressed suit and polished shoes, Elder Thompson stood out as an example of how missionaries should look. He was handsome, too—dark hair swept to the side, high cheekbones, and dimpled cheeks—just as the Oslo sister missionaries had said when they gossiped among themselves. He helped Orrin unload his suitcase, suit bag, and duffel from the train, and together they walked across the Tista River to their hybel on Svenskegata. Elder Thompson carried Orrin's suitcase, the heaviest of his belongings, the entire way. The Halden hybel was a penthouse compared to Orrin's previous accommodation. The studio apartment had a spacious living room with comfortable beds and chairs, and a separate kitchen with a stove and small refrigerator. Best of all, it had a bathroom and shower they didn't have to share with anyone. Elder Thompson prepared a lunch of *smørbrød* and cut beets and, over lunch, explained that as the leader of the Østfold District, he oversaw the missionary pairs in Moss, Sarpsborg, and Fredrikstad. They would be doing a lot of traveling to those locations. Given his responsibilities, he expected Orrin to take over much of the workload in managing their proselytizing activities in Halden. "I've heard only good things about you, Elder Tanner," he said. "This represents an important stepping stone to becoming a senior companion."

The eight district missionaries met the next week in Fredrikstad, because the elders there had a hybel large enough for all of them to gather and sleep overnight on the floor. In the morning, they practiced the discussions and exchanged ideas for innovative door approaches and new ways to contact people besides door-to-door tracting. Orrin's language comprehension had improved immensely, but he still struggled to speak clearly, and so he was heartened that two of the other elders, including a newly arrived greenie, needed even more help. *At least I'm no longer the worst one here*, he thought to himself, pleased to be in the position of giving assistance. Orrin marveled at the optimistic zeal of the newer elders, who drew from a bottomless supply of maxims to keep themselves energized. "Make it a great day." "When God closes a door, He opens a window." "When the going gets tough, the tough get going." "The greater the challenge, the greater the reward." Orrin excelled during their joint scripture study, having memorized all of the discussion scriptures in both English and Norwegian. None of the other elders came close to matching his skill in quoting scriptures or expounding on Mormon teachings relevant to the six missionary discussions. Elder Thompson, who had already served seventeen months, seemed not at all embarrassed or put out that his young companion far outshone him in this regard but, in fact, generously praised Orrin, as if he shared pride of accomplishment with him.

Back in Halden, Elder Thompson let Orrin take the lead in developing a new door approach that referenced Thor Heyerdahl, the famous Norwegian explorer who had recently returned from an expedition in which he had sailed from Morocco to Barbados in a reed boat. "Heyerdahl proved that ancient people could have sailed across the Atlantic Ocean to the American continent," Orrin said when presenting his proposed door approach to the Østfold elders. "His journey offers scientific proof supporting the Book of Mormon's claim that the American Indians sailed from Israel to America in 600 BC."

"Did he sail in the same kind of boat that the Nephites used?"

"We don't really know much about how the Nephite boats were constructed, but what Heyerdahl has shown is that is possible to build a boat using readily available, natural materials that can withstand the voyage."

The Heyerdahl Approach, as the missionaries called it, appealed to Orrin's faith in the intellectual foundations of Mormonism, that religion and science were compatible, and enabled him to engage Norwegians in a friendly discussion about religion. He sold a Book of Mormon the first time he tried it. The other district missionaries were equally successful. They found that the mention of Heyerdahl's name aroused patriotic fervor in even the unfriendliest Norwegians, all of whom knew of his expedition and regarded his accomplishments as a national triumph. In the first week, the Østfold District set a new mission record for placing copies of the Book of Mormon. Even more important, Orrin and his companion garnered several callbacks to present a slideshow, "Ancient America Speaks," describing the archeological evidence pointing to the truthfulness of the Book of Mormon. Elder Thompson directed Orrin to write an article about the district's success for the mission's weekly newsletter. "You deserve credit for making the Heyerdahl Approach really work for us," he told Orrin when the article was published in the *Gospel Net* two weeks later.

This success fueled the Østfold missionaries' enthusiasm to try another idea they called the Businessman Approach. Missionaries sought not to convert individuals but husbands and wives and families, but they primarily encountered housewives during the morning and afternoons, rarely finding men at home. "We should try to contact men where they work," suggested Elder Decker, a large and scruffy missionary. "That way, not only are we going directly to the head of the household—"

"But also to the potential priesthood holder," Elder Thompson interjected.

Elder Decker voiced agreement. "In short, we're going directly to the type of people we want to bring into the church: business executives and managers who can fill badly needed leadership positions in Norway." Everyone agreed it was an inspired idea, and so Elder Decker and his companion wrote up a proposed dialogue for a Businessman Approach and sent it out to the district missionaries.

The normal start time for knocking on doors was 9:30 a.m., but Elder Thompson and Orrin started the Businessman Approach at 8:30 a.m. when many businesses were opening up, so they could catch men before their days got too full. The goal was not to teach a discussion but simply to introduce themselves and after delivering a short message, make an appointment to visit them at their homes. Elder Thompson and Orrin took the downtown bus to the business district and began working their way up the avenue. At the first office, the receptionist refused to let them talk to her boss. At the second office, after talking their way past the receptionist, the businessman started yelling at the missionaries as soon as they introduced themselves, saying they were interrupting an important meeting. At the third office, a travel agency, the manager berated Orrin for his poor Norwegian before ordering them to leave. And at the fourth office, the manager yelled at the receptionist for allowing the missionaries to come in, and then stormed away without talking to them. His cheeks reddened, Elder Thompson apologized to the receptionist, who stared glumly as the elders exited the office.

"You know, Elder Tanner," Elder Thompson said, a wry grin spreading across his face, "perhaps the Businessman Approach isn't so inspired after all. Let's go home and get something to eat, and then go visit church members, who will be much happier to see us than these people seem to be."

In August, Orrin and Elder Thompson traveled to Moss for the baptism of Bror and Søster Larevik. The Moss elders had declared the Lareviks golden from the first day they met them. "You could see it in their faces, that they were humble and hungering for the truth," Elder Decker told Orrin as he related the story of the Larevik's conversion. After the missionaries' first visit, they had a standing invitation for dinner with the Lareviks every Friday evening, after which they taught additional discussions. Their three children, ages six to twelve, adored the missionaries who doted on them like younger siblings. The Lareviks started attending church after three discussions, which was highly unusual because most investigators, even the serious ones, resisted coming to church. Fellowshipping with Mormon missionaries in the privacy of your home is one thing, but it's quite another to publicly acknowledge your affiliation with the American sect by attending church. The Lareviks gave up alcohol and coffee without any problems, but Bror Larevik, who smoked a pipe, struggled with tobacco addiction. Søster Larevik received a spiritual witness first, saying she felt a warm, calming feeling when reading the Book of Mormon. Bror Larevik didn't receive his spiritual witness until he prayed for help to kick his tobacco habit. "I felt at once the Lord would help me, and I never smoked again," he said.

Still, he asked the missionaries if he could suck on his pipe from time to time without lighting it. "I wouldn't be inhaling the nicotine. I just like the taste," he explained. The missionaries consulted with President Toressen, who rejected the idea. Bror Larevik dutifully gave the missionaries his pipe, so he wouldn't be tempted.

The Lareviks nearly backed out of the scheduled baptism when the missionaries, while discussing with Bror Larevik his impending ordination to the priesthood, revealed that Negroes were not allowed to hold the priesthood. The Lareviks, who considered themselves to be tolerant, open-minded people, slumped on their couch, confusion and anger on their faces. "Why didn't you tell us this sooner?" Søster Larevik demanded.

The missionaries explained the church's doctrine, which held that Negroes were less than valiant in the preexistence and so had been cursed with dark skins, the mark of Cain. They showed the Lareviks the relevant scriptures from the Pearl of Great Price and assured them Negroes would receive the priesthood sometime in the eternities. "I read to them a statement from Apostle Peterson, who said if Negroes are faithful, they he will be allowed to enter the celestial kingdom as servants," Elder Decker said. The discussion went back and forth, with the Lareviks asking many questions. Elder Decker's stomach churned as he saw his golden investigators struggle, and so he asked if they could kneel in prayer, to which the Lareviks agreed. Each prayed in turn, asking for guidance and understanding. When they finished, Bror Larevik, his face softened, turned to the missionaries and said, "Well, if the prophet says so, then we must accept it."

Elder Decker brushed back a tear as he recounted Bror Larevik's acceptance of the Negro priesthood ban. "Never in my life had I seen such perfect, childlike faith."

Orrin sat behind the Lareviks at the baptismal service. Bror and Søster Larevik wore white baptismal clothes, as did Elder Decker, who would be performing the baptisms. Although the Larevik's two older children were also eligible for baptism, they wanted to wait for their father to receive the priesthood so he could have the privilege of baptizing them. The atmosphere in the chapel was solemn but joyful as the branch president scurried about to ensure the baptismal font was properly filled and that everything was in place to begin. Bror Larevik was cheerful and confident, his bright rosy beard resting handsomely against his white shirt. He stood and shook hands with the many well-wishers who paraded by on the way to their seats. Søster Larevik, however, fussed nervously with her baptismal gown and, unlike her husband, smiled weakly and barely acknowledged those offering congratulations. While Bror Larevik chatted with soon-to-be fellow Mormons, she sat alone, eyebrows knitted in contemplation of some deep pain. Orrin looked around, wondering if others were also seeing Søster Larevik's apparent second thoughts, and he was about to get up and notify the branch president when the playing of the organ signaled it was time for the program to begin. Søster Larevik's turmoil fascinated Orrin. He would not have been surprised had she bolted for the door. But when it came time for the baptism, she took her husband's hand and walked haltingly to the font.

Bror Larevik was baptized first. He rose triumphantly from the water, glowing, and gave Elder Decker a hug. Seeing his wife standing on the platform, he waded to the side, reached out a hand and helped her into the water. He gave her a kiss before climbing the stairs out of the font. Søster Larevik's face was ashen, even ghostlike, but no longer contorted in pain. Rather, she looked like she was in shock. "Surely, everyone must see," Orrin thought. Nevertheless, Elder Decker raised his hand to the square and recited the baptismal prayer. When he finished, Søster Larevik held her nose as he lowered her purposefully into the water and then raised her up. These were Elder Decker's first baptisms in Norway and his face beamed with happiness. Upon standing, Søster Larevik let go of Elder Decker's hand, sputtering and wiping the chlorinated water from her eyes, and climbed out of the baptismal font.

The branch president, Bror Hendriks, hosted a celebration afterward at his home. Nearly the entire branch membership came, everyone eager to welcome the Lareviks and make them feel part of the small community of Moss believers. The missionaries dived into the refreshments while Bror Larevik, a barrel-chested man with a booming voice, shook hands and chatted pleasantly as if he had been a member his entire life. Søster Larevik hung close to her husband, gripping his hand, her lips stretched into a tight smile and her face dazed and uncertain. While pondering Søster Larevik's mental state, Orrin felt a tap on the shoulder.

"Hello, Elder Tanner. How is President Toressen's scribe?" President Hendriks said gaily.

"President Hendriks, it is good to see you again," Orrin replied, and the two men shook hands vigorously. Orrin was truly happy to see President Hendriks, whom he had met during President Toressen's speaking tour. Of average height and physique, the Moss branch president was not a prepossessing man, but he had a kind face that put people at ease and invited intimacy. The director of a factory employing physically and mentally challenged adults, he had a natural sympathy for society's misfits. He and Orrin had developed an instant rapport at their first meeting, given their shared love of church history, and President Hendriks now began quizzing Orrin about his Norwegian ancestry.

"One of my great-grandfathers, Lars Andreassen, came from the small island town of Riksøy. It is located somewhere south of the Lofoten Islands."

"It must be very small, because I have never heard of it. Have you been there?"

"No, but when I complete my mission, my mother and father are planning to meet me here in Norway and visit Riksøy. We are hoping some Andreassen relatives might still live there."

As the two men continued chatting, Orrin watched the Lareviks make the rounds. Søster Larevik offered forced smiles; she had the downcast eyes of someone in mourning. "Do you see Søster Larevik?" Orrin asked at last. "She has a look of anguish and overwhelming despair, and she has looked that way since she entered the chapel. I thought she might not go through with the baptism."

"Your observation is correct," President Hendrik said with a deep sigh. "She is suffering a heartache known to many members here is Norway. As a result of joining the church, she is being disowned by her parents and shunned by many of her friends. Her husband, Bror Larevik, has a personality that is insensitive—no, insensitive is not the right word—that is immune to such things, but Søster Larevik sees the rough road ahead not only for herself but for her children as well. It will not be easy for them to be Mormons. Bror Larevik does not see it. Their children do not see it. But she sees it."

"But joining the church is supposed to bring joy," Orrin replied. "That is why we come here, as missionaries. If you have God's spirit with you, does that not bring happiness and joy?"

President Hendrik smiled. "You know the famous church hymn, 'Come, Come Ye Saints,' the one Utah Mormons like to sing?"

"Yes, of course. It is a favorite of Mormons everywhere."

"It is a song about people suffering and in pain, Elder Tanner." Orrin tried to interrupt, but President Hendrik held up his hand and continued. "The Mormon pioneers had been driven from their homes, and they were singing about toil and labor, bemoaning the hardships of their journey, just as Søster Larevik is grieving the loss of her old life. The song even says that if we die before our journey is through, then happy day, because we will be free from our worldly sorrows."

President Hendrik took a sip of punch, pausing to make sure Orrin understood. "So what sustained the pioneers on their difficult journey? It was their faith and their community. Now look at the people around you," he said, directing Orrin's attention to the scene before him. The Relief Society ladies were generously laying out the food they had prepared, while the young children chased each other between the chairs. Elder Bender, the Moss greenie, pretended to be a horse as two children scrambled onto his back. Clusters of people chatted and milled about. Laughter filled the hall.

"Yes, Elder Tanner, I am happy," President Hendrik said. "And Søster Larevik will be happy too. We will give her church jobs and she will make many new friends and find joy in our community and peace in God's spirit."

President Hendrik shook Orrin's hand and then left to join the festivities. Orrin thought about the scripture where Jesus told his disciples they must be willing to forsake siblings and parents, and even their children if necessary, and take up their cross and follow Him. *Take up your cross.* Orrin understood Søster Larevik's sorrow and burden, the cross she had to bear. It took great courage for the Norwegian people to invite the missionaries into their homes, to be open to new truths, and to accept the consequences of embracing them. As he watched Søster Larevik reach out a desperate hand in fellowship to the warmhearted President Hendrik, Orrin silently vowed to be as courageous and open to truth as he hoped the Norwegian people would be when he knocked on their doors, and not only that, but to accept the consequences of embracing truth, no matter the burden, as his cross to bear as a follower of Christ.

Chapter 19

Guard against familiarity with the opposite sex. There must be no courting, kissing or embracing. Your kisses should be for home consumption and be brought home (unused) to your loved ones where they belong. Kissing and hugging aside from this lead to immorality.

Conduct of a Missionary

Elder Jensen apologized to Eddie when the two were first paired as companions. "Elder Ward, he's a machine," Elder Jensen said, noting that Elder Ward and Eddie had consistently ranked among the mission's top performers. "I can't work those long hours like he does, so you might have to get used to seeing our names lower on the Mission Comparative."

"That's okay," Eddie replied, though he didn't mean it. He had joined Elder Ward in rising at six o'clock every morning—a half hour earlier than mission rules required—to get a head start on their work. Not that Eddie liked Elder Ward's arduous pace. By mid-morning, Eddie's energy flagged, and he longed to take a nap when they returned to their hybel at three o'clock for *middag* supper. But he had a deal with God. Going the grueling extra mile demonstrated his willingness to keep up his end of the bargain. *Will my past effort go for naught under Elder Jensen?*

Eddie needn't have worried. Although Elder Jensen worked without urgency, took frequent breaks, and even went home early if he "wasn't feeling it," as he remarked on more than one occasion, he and Eddie were invited in more often than any of the other Bergen missionaries, including Elder Ward. Eddie attributed their success to Elder Jensen's easygoing, aw-shucks manner and genuine affinity for people. "Let's go visit these referrals from the Temple Square visitors center," Elder Jensen said, thumbing through a stack of referrals. "How did you accumulate so many?"

"Elder Ward ignored them. He said they were a waste of time."

"Well, let's give them a try. If people have visited Salt Lake City and Temple Square, they presumably have come away with a favorable opinion of Mormons."

At the first home, a smiling housewife erupted with violent cursing when she found out the church had given to the missionaries the information she and her husband had provided at the Temple Square visitor's center. "We never asked for the missionaries to come," she said. "We never would have signed the goddamned registrar if we had known the Mormons wanted our names and addresses for this purpose."

When the next referral responded in a similar manner, though with less swearing, Elder Jensen decided that hereafter, they would not mention their visit was connected to the temple, pretending instead they were just tracting in the area. However, Elder Jensen, though a Texas native, introduced himself as coming from Salt Lake City, which prompted Norwegians to talk excitedly about their recent visit to his hometown. "What a coincidence," Elder Jensen would say, feigning happy surprise. "Did you get a chance to see the Tabernacle or temple while in Salt Lake City?" Some people mistakenly thought they had gone inside the temple, but Elder Jensen never corrected them. He was a talented actor and endeared himself to the Norwegians, who were delighted to talk with someone from the place they had recently visited, especially if it allowed them to show off their English skills. Two prospects even invited the missionaries in to hear the first discussion.

"What are we going to do if they keep taking the discussions? You'll have to tell them eventually you're not from Salt Lake City," Eddie said. "They're going to be awfully mad when they found out you lied."

"I'll tell them during the discussion on tithing," Elder Jensen replied. "They'll be so freaked out when they hear they have to pay ten percent of their income to the church, they won't care where I come from."

One of the families, the Noruds, became regular investigators. Bror and Søster Norud both had family members living in the United States, including Bror Norud's older sister and husband, who were Mormons living in Holladay, a suburb southeast of Salt Lake City. A handsome, athletic-looking couple, the Noruds represented the vanguard of a younger, cosmopolitan generation ready to throw off the nation's cautious frugality and constrictive cultural norms, as if they sensed Norway's coming explosion of oil wealth. Bror Norud, in fact, worked for an engineering firm aligned with one of several foreign oil companies seeking to establish themselves in Norway, and so he often made trips to the company's main office in Stavanger. Søster Norud taught elementary school but planned to quit when they began raising a family. Neither described themselves as religious, but they seemed intent on making friends with the missionaries and hearing what they had to say, if for no other reason than to demonstrate their broad-mindedness.

"The Norwegian people, they do not understand anything about Mormons," Bror Norud said. "They talk about Mormonism as if it were a cult, but it is really not so different from the State Church—I mean, you believe in Christ, right?"

"If they could go to Utah and see what we saw, they would see that Mormons are nice people, just like the Norwegian people," his wife added.

"My brother-in-law has done quite well there. He and my sister have five children—"

"*Uffa meg*, five children!" Søster Norud said.

"Yes, five children, two cars, and a house larger than what we could afford to buy here."

During the second discussion about the Book of Mormon, Eddie explained that a prophet, Lehi, and his family were led by God to the American continent about six hundred years before Christ. His children's families eventually feuded, with one group remaining righteous but the other falling into sin and disbelief. To keep the two groups separate, God cursed the wicked people with darker skin. "Who are the people in America today that descended from the dark-skinned people?" Eddie asked as he put up flannel board characters of Lehi and his dark descendants.

Bror Norud scratched his chin. "The American Negroes?"

"No, they are the American Indians," Eddie said. "In the Book of Mormon, they are known as Lamanites."

"And the faithful people were called Nephites, after the prophet Nephi, who was their first leader," Elder Jensen said. "The Nephites, who were the righteous, white-skinned people, built large cities and developed a sophisticated civilization whose ruins are still visible today in Central America and South America."

"Are there still white Indians in America?"

"No, the Nephites were eventually overpowered and completely de-stroyed by the dark-skinned Lamanites, but not before a white prophet, Moroni, buried an account of his people written on gold plates," Eddie said, attaching a cutout of Moroni on the flannel board. "That record is the Book of Mormon, which Joseph Smith translated from gold plates."

"Your story sounds too fantastic to be true," Søster Norud said.

Bror Norud agreed. "Do my sister and her husband believe this?"

"Absolutely," Eddie replied, "and we can show you extensive archeo-logical evidence supporting the Book of Mormon."

"But the way to find out if the Book of Mormon is true is to read it for yourself," Elder Jensen added. "Bror and Søster Norud, will you read the Book of Mormon and ask God's spirit to help you understand it and know it is true?"

The Noruds hesitantly agreed. Bror Norud left on business trips shortly after and was gone for several weeks. The missionaries visited Søster Norud during this time, but she refused to talk with them, open-ing the door only slightly and looking around furtively, as if worried her neighbors would see. When Elder Jensen asked whether she had been reading the Book of Mormon, she said, "It would be best for you to come back when my husband returns. He is the one most interested in talking with you."

In March, Eddie and Elder Jensen also began teaching the discussions to Søster Haldis Rolfsen and her thirteen-year-old son, Arne. A thin and anxious woman, Søster Rolfsen had yellowing teeth from years of smoking and an indifferent attention to dental hygiene. The ends of her fingers were also nicotine-stained, which the missionaries couldn't help but notice as she rolled cigarette after cigarette, spilling bits of tobacco on the coffee table. She smoked incessantly and was as careless with the cigarette ashes as she was with her tobacco. Once she almost caught the flannel board on fire. Arne was small for his age, blond with a face dotted with freckles, and quite shy at first, ducking behind his mother's arm and refusing to answer any of the missionaries' questions. Arne didn't have many friends at school and because he often stayed with his father on the weekends, he hadn't made any friends in the neighborhood. Still, Arne was intrigued by the American visitors; at their next visit, Elder Jensen was able to engage Arne by teaching him how to speak Texan. "Smile when you say that, pilgrim," Arne repeated in English over and over, much to his own delight. Eddie also taught him to play the bass part in a chopsticks duet on the piano. Thereafter, Elder Jensen would always start each visit by teaching Arne a new cowboy phrase in English, while at the end, Eddie would teach him a new piece on the piano. Søster Rolfsen watched contently, rolling cigarettes and filling the room with clouds of gray smoke.

"There's no way I'm going to quit smoking," Søster Rolfsen announced after the Elders told her about the Word of Wisdom. "I've tried many times, but it drove me crazy. I could not work. I could not sleep. I could not even make myself eat. All I wanted to do was smoke a cigarette. After the last time, I said the hell with it—excuse my language, Elders—stop torturing yourself, Haldis, You will never quit, so stop trying."

Eddie and Elder Jensen tried to persuade her by citing scriptural passages that God would help her, as well as pointing to medical studies demonstrating the harmful effects of smoking and alcohol.

"Oh, I know all that," she said. "I would still be married if my husband was not such a heavy drinker. But no, I vowed never to torture myself again. Really, it is no use." She rubbed her spent cigarette into the ashtray with extra force, as if emphasizing the point. While the elders read additional scriptures and testified she could overcome her addiction, Søster Rolfsen rolled and lit another cigarette, inhaling with obvious pleasure. Still, she did not discourage the missionaries from returning, nor did she object when they took Arne with them to Mormon youth activities held on Tuesday nights at the Bergen chapel. "If he makes friends and is happy there, then I am happy too," she said.

On Sundays, Eddie played the piano in junior Sunday School and the organ for a small branch choir he and Sister Hartman organized. He arrived early each Sunday to coordinate the choice of songs with the chorister, seventeen-year-old Bente Larsen. Elder Jensen sat in on their meetings, because it was against mission rules for a missionary to be alone with a member of the opposite sex. Sometimes, Bente's best friend, Kari Johannsen, joined the meetings for no other reason, apparently, than to banter and be entertained by the elders. Their laughter could be heard throughout the chapel. Eddie also planned the choir's songs with Sister Hartman. Again, mission rules required Elder Jensen or Sister Hartman's companion to be present, but usually both joined. Their cheerful noise also echoed down the hallway.

The missionaries and a dozen members spent the entire day at church. Those who stayed cooked together in the church kitchen, often preparing elaborate meals and desserts, and ate together in the cultural hall amid lively conversation. As the district leader, Elder Ward kept a close eye on the elders, sometimes issuing stern warnings against spending too much time with the Norwegian girls or sister missionaries.

"Arm's length, Elders," he said after pulling aside several elders who seemed to be having too much fun with Bente and Kari while cleaning up after their Sunday meal. "Keep an arm's length away."

Elder Jensen gave him a mocking salute and returned with the other miscreants to the kitchen. Despite the elders' claims of innocent intent, Bente and Kari were both pretty girls whose affable personalities made them worthy of the elders' attention. "Who would you choose, Bente or Kari?" Elder Jensen asked Eddie one day as they finished tracting and walked to the bus stop.

"Come on, Elder Jensen, you know we're not supposed to talk about that stuff."

"It's pretty clear Bente has the hots for you. You can see it not only on Sundays, but also the way she's always finding excuses to talk with you during youth activities on Tuesdays."

"She's just trying to be nice to Arne and make him feel included," Eddie said. "I like that about her."

"Ah, so it is Bente."

"You're the one who likes her. And probably Kari too," Eddie replied. "You're the one who's always talking about them."

"No, I've got a girlfriend at home waiting for my return, so this is just a hypothetical exercise for me. But for you . . ."

"I'm going to keep my mind on my mission and out of the gutter," Eddie said, trying to make a joke of it.

Elder Jensen laughed. "Okay, you win. But you'll owe me a hundred bucks if you come back here after your mission and marry one of those two girls."

"I'll give you a thousand," Eddie said, offering a rare smile.

Although Eddie feigned good humor, his stomach tensed whenever Elder Jensen teased him about Bente and Kari. He didn't mind that Elder Jensen and other missionaries thought something was going on between Bente and him. *At least they don't think I'm a homosexual.* Elder Ward had even cautioned him once, though it was about spending too much time with the sister missionaries. What bothered Eddie, filling him with apprehension whenever Elder Jensen mentioned the Bergen girls, was his total lack of attraction to them. He loved Bente, who was blessed with a sweet demeanor and a natural gift for drawing people out, much like Elder Jensen. She was pretty, too, with soft curls and sparkling eyes that made her as alluring as any girl he had dated. And yet, he wasn't attracted to her, not really, just as he wasn't attracted to any of the pretty high school girls he had taken to movies and concerts.

Elder Jensen was another matter. He had an outsized personality and was jovial and witty, like Eddie's friend Barry, but whereas Barry tended to be sardonic, even cutting, Elder Jensen possessed a natural warmth and tranquil temperament that attracted people to him and made them want to be his friend. Eddie had arrived in Norway emotionally broken, and his first three months with Elder Ward had only pushed him deeper into depression. But Elder Jensen's kind, confident manner had helped Eddie shed some of the self-doubt and spiritual malaise that had plagued him since his arrest and completion of reparative theory. Eddie woke up every morning eager to spend another day with Elder Jensen. Even if the work was boring, Elder Jensen never was. When they stood at someone's doorstep, Eddie would stand back and admire Elder Jensen's ability to charm and engage Norwegians with genuine respect, never treating them with condescension or disdain. He certainly charmed Eddie.

"We have no desire to talk with you about Mormonism. Religion has no interest for us," said a gravelly voiced woman, her face fast disappearing behind a closing door.

"So what would you like to talk about?" Elder Jensen asked cheerfully.

"Huh?" The door opened slightly.

"We do not have to talk about religion. Perhaps you would rather discuss politics or movies or American television or popular music. My companion here, Elder Pedersen, is an accomplished musician. If you have a piano, he can play any Beatles song you like. You know the Beatles, right? You name the song, he can play it."

Now smiling, the woman opened the door. "Okay, come in." She turned and shouted into the living room. "Hey, Lars, the Mormons have come to play Beatles songs for us."

The couple, Lars and Marit, had a small piano, though neither played. While Marit explained to her husband what the elders intended to do, Eddie shot his companion a desperate, what-are-you-thinking look. Elder Jensen chuckled. "You can do it, Elder. I've heard you playing around on the piano at church. You're good," he said. "Besides, what have we've got to lose?"

"What do you mean 'we,' paleface? I'm the one who's going to make a fool of himself." Eddie sat down at the piano, adjusted the bench, warmed up with a series of arpeggios, moving deftly up and down the keys, and then called for the first song.

"'Within You, Without You,'" Lars said, grinning mischievously. Eddie stared blankly at the piano, not knowing how to begin.

"Oh, come on," Elder Jensen said. "Nobody ever listens to that song. Pick one we can sing along with."

"'Michelle,'" Marit offered. It took Eddie only a few strokes of the keys to find the right chord progression. Elder Jensen started singing the lyrics, slightly off-key, but he soon got Lars and Marit joining in, and Eddie too. They moved from one song to the next, most of them lively and fun, such as "Yellow Submarine" and "Ob-La-Di, Ob-La-Da," but Lars insisted on singing "Yesterday" as a solo. Elder Jensen also made a few selections, carefully choosing songs he had heard Eddie playing in between meetings on Sundays. Eddie got stumped on a few songs, but his hosts didn't care. When Lars asked for "Why Don't We Do It in the Road," Elder Jensen quickly jumped in.

"I'm sorry, but Elder Pedersen will catch on fire if he tries to play that song," he said. They finished their contest with a melodramatic rendition of "Hey, Jude" that was twice as long as the original. Lars and Marit applauded enthusiastically when Eddie finished, and then invited the elders to come back the next week for dinner. "We belong to the State Church and are not interested in joining any new religion, but we will let you tell us about Mormonism," Marit said.

"How did you know I could do play those songs without the music?" Eddie asked as the two elders exited the apartment building.

"Inspiration, I guess," Elder Jensen replied with his aw-shucks smile.

"Elder Jensen, you really are inspired."

"And Elder Pedersen," Elder Jensen said, putting his arm around Eddie's shoulder, "you are a treasure."

Eddie was in love, had a full-on crush. He knew it, embraced it, savored it. He reveled in Elder Jensen's compliments and attention, just as he had reveled in Barry's. He tried his best to impress Elder Jensen, diving into his mission studies while also becoming bolder and more assertive in his door approaches, trying not to be offensive but friendly and open, even playful like his companion. He conscientiously adopted Elder Jensen's suggestions and never wavered in his enthusiasm for the work, even when tired, always looking for signs his companion returned his affection. More than once while they were changing clothes, Eddie found himself admiring the firm line of muscles stretching down Elder Jensen's calves. He daydreamed about the softness of his lips. *Are they as tender as Barry's?* It was wrong to think about such things, he knew that. *Did the elders have similar thoughts about Bente or Kari or the sister missionaries?* Eddie would never act on his desires, just as the elders never—or almost never—acted on theirs. In Eddie's case, the likely result would be a sock in the jaw, plus a plane ticket home and the humiliation of excommunication from the church. Still, every Beatles love song they had sung in Marit's apartment, he was singing to Elder Jensen.

Eddie never expected to fall in love. Hadn't he been praying each morning and night for God to deliver him from this cursed condition? He had worked tirelessly as a missionary, obeying all of the commandments and holding up his end of the deal by doing everything asked of him. *Why isn't God holding up His end?* Being in love filled him with sublime elation, but also with confusion and guilt. How could he pray for relief from his love for Elder Jensen when the feeling brought such happiness? He couldn't, not with honest conviction. It was a Job-like test. Eddie tried to reconcile his contradictory feelings by concocting scenarios in his mind where, after their missions, he and Elder Jensen would go into business together and live next door to each other, working side by side every day, like they were doing as missionaries, and then returning home to their wives and children each night. *Perhaps our love will be like that between David and Jonathan, unselfish and pure and approved by God.*

Elder Jensen continued teasing Eddie about Bente Larsen until, after they had been companions for nearly three months, he received a Dear John letter from his girlfriend. She had met a returned missionary at BYU and was engaged to be married in September. "Five months, Elder Tanner," he said, crumpling the letter in his shaking hands. "She waited nineteen months for me. Why couldn't she wait five more?" Eddie held Elder Jensen briefly while he cried, offering soothing words of encouragement, telling him he would meet someone who was worthy of his love.

"I hope you never have your heart broken by someone you love who doesn't love you back," Elder Jensen said, brushing aside a tear. Eddie simmered a pot of *risgrøt*, which he sweetened with cinnamon, raisins, and brown sugar. "Well, I guess you're going to have some competition for Bente and Kari now that I'm a free man," Elder Jensen said with forced cheerfulness as he spooned a second helping of the buttery creamed rice.

Eddie turned from the stove and gave his companion a mock salute. "Let the best man win."

A week later, Elder Jensen was transferred to Larvik. All of the Bergen missionaries went to the train station to see him off, as did Bente, Arne, and a few of the local members. The Norwegian members were used to seeing missionaries come and go, but for Eddie it was a solemn affair. He felt a tinge of jealousy when he saw Elder Jensen and Bente having what seemed like an intimate chat. *Wouldn't they be surprised to know which one of those two I was jealous of?* he thought with bitter sadness. He and Elder Jenson shook hands for the last time as Elder Jenson climbed the steps onto the train car. "Well, Elder Tanner, it looks like you'll have to be the one who tells the Noruds I lied about growing up in Salt Lake City," he said. Before Eddie could respond, he added, "You know, my transfer out of here shows President Toressen really is inspired, a true prophet of Norway."

"What do you mean?"

"Now that I'm a free man, I probably would have gotten myself into some kind of romantic trouble with Bente or Kari . . . or maybe with both of them," he said, smiling at the thought. "So you see, President Toressen was inspired to send me far away from temptation. It's your lucky day. Because now that I'm leaving, Bente is all yours. Love her well, Elder."

The train's idling diesel engines started up with a roar and the conductor signaled for everyone to get aboard. "I have something to tell you about that," Eddie shouted above the din.

"What did you say?"

"I love someone else."

"What? Tell me who it is," Elder Jensen shouted, his eyes eager and wide. Before Eddie could answer, the conductor closed the door with Elder Jensen standing on the inside, his quizzical face framed in the window.

"Goodbye, Elder Jensen," Eddie said quietly, the diesel's exhaust choking his throat. He watched until the last car rattled around the bend.

Chapter 20

Make the contact feel happy that he prayed, and express gratitude to him, even if he did poorly.

A Uniform System for Teaching Investigators

With Elder Jensen's transfer, Eddie became a senior companion and was now in charge of the Fyllingsdalen area. His new companion, Elder Dahle, flew in from Tromsø, where he had worked since arriving in Norway three months earlier. Eddie drove with Bror Madsen, Bergen's branch president, to Flesland Airport to pick up his new companion. Elder Dahle was short, slightly overweight, and already showing a bald spot. At twenty-four, he was also one of the oldest missionaries, having resisted invitations to serve a mission until his graduation from college ended his draft deferments. "It's not that I don't support the war. If I had been drafted, I would have served, but I figured I could accomplish more good carrying a Bible than a gun," he said.

"Is it difficult being an older missionary?" Bror Madsen asked.

"No, not really. In fact, it gives me some advantages over the younger missionaries. I'm more mature, of course, and I've had five more years of leadership training in my ward. And with my master's degree in business, I have a better feel for the salesmanship side of being a missionary. Hopefully, I can help you out in that area, Elder Pedersen."

Bror Madsen snuck a sideways glance at Eddie and smiled. "I could use the help," Eddie replied.

"Did you have much success applying your experience in Tromsø?" Bror Madsen said.

"Not as much as I could have. My companion was not very receptive to taking advice from a greenie and, admittedly, I didn't speak the language very well."

"Elder Pedersen is one of the most proficient Norwegian speakers of all the missionaries who have served in Bergen," Bror Madsen said. "You would do well to let him teach you."

"You bet. Elder Pedersen, you help me with the language and I'll help you with the teaching. We'll make a great team."

Bror Madsen gave Eddie another sideways glance, but Eddie didn't notice. He was staring out the window, thinking about Elder Jensen.

During their second day of working together, Eddie took Elder Dahle to visit the two country-and-western musicians, Bjørn and Ole. Elder Ward had counseled the elders to reject the Norwegian duo when it became clear they weren't interested in joining the church. "You're wasting valuable time, especially when somewhere out there are humble seekers and the pure of heart who are waiting to hear the gospel message," Elder Ward said.

Elder Jensen had continued the visits anyway. "There's no reason why we can't find the pure of heart while also visiting Bjørn and Ole," he told Eddie. "Besides, they really enjoy jamming with you, Elder Pedersen. We're supposed to be planting seeds, and that's exactly what we're doing with them."

"Sometimes I think that's all we're doing," Eddie replied. "That and DMing people."

"That's the most fun I've had tracting since coming to Norway," Elder Dahle said after an hour-long session with Bjørn and Ole. "We ought to try and write a song for them—you know, the lyrics. I bet we could. Wouldn't that be something?"

True to his word, Elder Dahle offered Eddie tips for engaging people at the door. "Whenever you can, call people by their name," he said. "It's a little thing, but it shows you care enough to learn their name." Even more important was to always smile. "Smiling is the easiest thing in the world to do. People respond better to people who appear happy and confident. When *you* smile, *they* smile."

Eddie could think of no reasons not to adopt Elder Dahle's suggestions, though he felt smarmy and false. When tracting, they looked for people's names, which were often listed on mailboxes or above the doorbell, so they could incorporate their names in their door approaches. "Good day, Herr so-and-so," and later, "Fru so-and-so, have you heard of the Mormon Church?" Or, "Herr so-and-so, would you be interested to know that God talks to prophets today, just like in biblical times?"

Elder Dahle continually reminded Eddie to smile, which made him self-conscious and unable to concentrate on their conversations with people at the door. *Should I show my teeth or keep a tight-lipped grin? Can people tell I'm forcing it?* It was quite distracting. Elder Dahle had a natural, effortless smile that actually seemed genuine, as if he were happy in the moment. People really did smile back at Elder Dahle just as he said they would, but when Eddie smiled, they stared back stone-faced and cold. "People don't respond to me the way they do to you," Eddie said after being reminded yet again to smile.

"You have one of the saddest smiles I have ever seen," Elder Dahle replied.

"What do you mean? Are you saying I'm not really smiling?"

"No, I'm saying your smiles are sad, like you're in mourning or something. You're smiling, but your smile says the opposite of happy."

"Well, I don't know how to fix that," Eddie said tersely.

"You need to practice in front of a mirror. That's what I did, and now I can flash a happy smile anytime I want. See." An effervescent smile spread across Elder Dahle's face showing two rows of smooth, white teeth, the same smile he showed at every door. "We can work on it back at the hybel, but in the meantime, it's best you don't try to smile. It even makes me sad."

The next week, Eddie and Elder Dahle were visited by Elder Ward, the Bergen district leader and Eddie's former companion in Fyllingsdalen. Elder Ward tracted with Elder Dahle in the morning, while Elder Ward's companion tracted with Eddie, and then they switched in the evening. Elder Ward knew the area well and enjoyed going around with Eddie to visit some of the investigators and members he had known. But he frowned when, at the end of the day, he reviewed the list of Fyllingsdalen investigators and saw the musicians Ole and Bjørn were still on the list. "They're PFers," he said.

"PFers?" said Elder Dahle.

"Professional Friends, people who like the missionaries and are glad to talk with us and be our friends but who aren't interested in the gospel." Eddie tried to defend his decision to keep visiting the young men, but Elder Ward cut him off. "Tell me the truth, Elder Pedersen. Do you honestly think Ole and Bjørn are serious investigators interested in joining the church?"

"No, not right now," Eddie said reluctantly, "but some day they might be."

"And when that time comes, the Lord will lead the missionaries to their door."

Elder Dahle shook his head in disappointment. "But they are so much fun to visit."

"We're not here to have fun," Elder Ward snapped.

After Elder Ward and his companion left, Eddie and Elder Dahle discussed the matter and decided to drop Ole and Bjørn as investigators. They also identified a few others who likely were wasting their time. "We'll visit them one more time to see whether they're really committed to studying and working toward baptism," Eddie said. "I hate the idea of thinking we gave up on them too soon, especially since they are so nice to us."

The two elders said little the rest of the night, spending their time in scripture reading and somber reflection. After they had said their prayers and climbed into bed, Elder Dahle whispered to Eddie in the darkness.

"It's too bad we won't be going back to see Ole and Bjørn, because I had already begun writing a song for them."

Eddie was feeling discouraged after an exhausting day with the district leader and didn't really want to extend it any longer. "Do you have to tell me now?"

"Well, I don't have the lyrics yet, but I've thought up a clever country-and-western title."

"And what's that?"

"Maybe it's more bluegrass than country-and-western."

"Just tell me, please."

Elder Dahle's voice rose in excitement. "The song is called 'Papa Held the Priesthood but Mama Wore the Pants.'" Eddie and Elder Dahle burst into laughter together. "That's a pretty good title, don't you think?" Elder Dahle asked.

"Yes, yes it is," Eddie said. "I do regret we won't be able to pitch your song to our Norwegian PFers."

When Elder Dahle heard Eddie still chuckling a minute later, he leaned up on his elbow and looked across the room to Eddie's bed. "It's too dark to see your face from here, Elder Pedersen, but if I could, I bet it would have just the smile we're aiming for."

Eddie wrote his parents a letter every week, as instructed by the *Missionary Handbook*. Eddie's letters were always upbeat and contained descriptions of his companions, detailing only their positive attributes, while emphasizing their successes. He didn't want his parents worrying about his special "problem," so he continually told them how happy he was serving a mission that was strengthening his testimony of the church. His parents also wrote regularly. His father's letters generally included instructions on appropriate missionary conduct, while his mother offered gossipy details about his brothers and their families. Eddie craved the letters from home, yet they also made him anxious. His father's disapproval and his mother's concern loomed as a subtext Eddie was always trying to decipher. In one sentence his mother would say she was extremely proud of his mission service, but in the next she would advise Eddie to go to his mission president with any problems, doubts, or temptations. *What does she mean by that?* It seemed clear to Eddie what his father meant when he wrote: "You are serving as a representative of the church, and so you shouldn't do anything that would embarrass the church or bring shame to you and the family." *Will my condition ever be forgiven or forgotten?*

Eddie's mom also shared his letters with his brothers, who occasionally wrote Eddie short missives reminiscing about their own missions and encouraging him to stay the course. "God doesn't measure success by the number of baptisms but by your faith and effort," his brother Skip wrote. "Don't let the long days of tracting or lack of progress discourage you. The two years will go by surprisingly quickly and soon you'll be home, playing the field again and searching for your eternal helpmeet. A mission also prepares you for married life (especially for the lack of sleep you get after the babies start coming)." Eddie tried to read between the lines. *Do my brothers know about me? Is Skip trying to send me a message by talking about finding a girl to marry?*

Shortly after being made a senior companion, Eddie received a letter postmarked San Francisco from a name and address he did not recognize.

Dear Eddie (or should I say Elder Pedersen?),

My name is Kenneth Hoffman. You may not remember me, but we met once at a party at Deseret Towers, where I was a friend of Barry Williams and some other people you knew. I am writing because I have sad news about Barry. He died in a car crash about a month ago. I know you and Barry were once good friends, and so I thought you would like to know—if you haven't already heard. However, that isn't the only reason I am writing, because I am painfully aware that I caused your breakup with Barry, and for that I am sorry. And you may not believe it, but Barry was too. You deserve to hear the whole story.

Barry and I continued seeing each other after the night you saw us together. After all, you had broken things off with him. He was both sad and mad, and I was more than glad to offer a consoling shoulder. Unfortunately, we were indiscreet and found out by BYU security. (We were discovered in a compromising embrace by Provo cops, who turned us into BYU security.) We both faced expulsion unless we agreed to reveal the names of other homosexuals. I didn't really like BYU (too conservative for me), and so I withdrew before they could expel me, but Barry was freaked out, given that expulsion would have revealed everything to his family and essentially scuttled his mission plans. He gave them your name but they needed evidence, and they came up with an entrapment scheme. Barry really hated the idea and he cried and cried when he told me what they wanted him to do, but he was absolutely terrified of the prospect of anyone finding out about him, and that's why he lured you into a trap with BYU security.

He hated himself. He told me he regarded betraying you as a bigger sin than homosexuality. I left Provo shortly after, but his friends said when he returned to school the following year, his self-loathing and guilt drove him to take greater risks. My own belief is he wanted to get caught. Whatever the case, he was eventually caught again, and this time, he was given a choice of expul-

sion or the shock-cock treatment. He accepted the treatment, hoping again to keep his situation quiet, but about six weeks into the program, his car skidded off the road somewhere up Provo Canyon. He wasn't killed instantly, but he died before anyone could reach him. Internal bleeding, I think.

The official story is he hit a patch of black ice, but none of his friends really believe that. They think the shock-cock treatment was too much for him. Humiliating as well as painful. It's scandalous, really, but speaking out means exposing yourself to the same humiliation, so everyone keeps quiet, myself included. I have since moved to San Francisco, where I'm part of a community of people who don't care who (or what) I am, though I'm still hiding my sexual orientation from my family and friends.

Again, I am sorry for the pain I may have caused you. If Barry were still alive, he would apologize as well—a hundred times over.

It goes without saying that you probably should tear up this letter after you read it. It probably wouldn't be helpful for either of us (especially you) if one of your fellow missionaries were to read this. I hope you have found peace and fulfilment in your mission.

Sincerely,
Kenneth Hoffman

Eddie tearfully read the letter a second time. He understood only too well Barry's fear of being found out, his self-loathing for who he was and what he had been forced to do. Barry drove himself off a cliff. *Isn't that what I wanted to do as well?* Barry was the courageous one after all. Eddie had loved Barry, then despised him. Now he forgave him.

"Are you okay?" Elder Dahle asked when he saw Eddie's tears.

"I just received news that a good friend of mine from college died in a car accident." Eddie told Elder Dahle about Barry and his over-the-top personality, how he brought Eddie into his circle of theater friends, and about their jubilant performance of "You're a Good Man, Charlie Brown."

Elder Dahle listened sympathetically, and when Eddie was finished, he said, "Well, it's comforting to know he's now in the bosom of the Lord. If he was as faithful as you are, Elder Pedersen, you'll have a joyous reunion someday in the celestial kingdom, singing all those songs from the Charlie Brown musical."

Eddie and Elder Dahle trudged through May and June with few callbacks or invitations to teach. Their only genuine investigator, Arne Rolfsen, now fourteen, attended Mormon youth activities faithfully each week. Elder Jensen was no longer around to teach him how to speak Texan, but Elder Dahle began feeding him aphorisms from the book *How to Win*

Friends and Influence People. Elder Dahle viewed the shy and socially awkward Arne as a special project for which his skills were particularly well suited. "I was also short for my age, so I know what it can be like when all the boys and girls are taller than you," said Dahle, who stood just over five feet. He acknowledged that *How to Win Friends and Influence People* wasn't one of the approved books for missionaries to read, "but its principles are consistent with gospel teachings," he said. "They can really help Arne."

Eddie knew it was unfair to compare Elder Dahle to Elder Jensen, but he couldn't help it. Elder Dahle lacked Elder Jensen's charisma and natural charm, and many Norwegians saw through his attempts to win them over through his salesman techniques. Neither was it fair to blame Elder Dahle for the fact they had fallen to the bottom of the Mission Comparative. Unlike Eddie, who interpreted every rejection as a sign of God's dissatisfaction—and even worse, that the deal was off—Elder Dahle never personalized rejection other than to search for new ways to improve his door approach. He drew from an unending store of adages to carry him through the day, and Eddie would sometimes see him standing at their mirror, rehearsing expressions of clean-cut goodwill and sincerity. He practiced one technique in which he removed his glasses and pretended to clean the lenses with a handkerchief. "I do this when I think people are about to reject me," Elder Dahle said. "The gesture makes them think I'm about to say something profound, so they wait to let me finish polishing the lenses and put my glasses back on."

Eddie cast a skeptical eye at his companion. "Does it work?"

"The problem is that I haven't come up with anything profound to say. I've already told them that there are living prophets today. What could be more profound than that?"

"How about telling them they can become gods and goddesses?"

Elder Dahle shook his head. "Too strong. Opens up a can of worms."

Eddie continued pondering the problem. "Tell them they were alive even before they were born."

Elder Dahle's face lit up. "That's it. You're a genius, Elder Pedersen," he said. He turned to the mirror and intoned to his reflection, "*Visste du at du levde før du ble født?* Did you know that you lived before you were born? We call that the preexistence. In the preexistence, we're like little chicks inside our eggs waiting to be born, and when we come to earth—that is, when we are born—we peck away at our shells and emerge . . . we emerge as ugly spiritual ducklings—"

"Some more ugly than others?"

"Well, yes, maybe, but the point is we're all ugly ducklings who, all of us, during our earthly existence, have the potential to become swans." Elder Dahle looked expectantly at his companion. "What do you think, Elder?"

"I think *you're* the genius, Elder Dahle."

"I'm just glad to be working in a city that knows what spring is," Elder Dahle said, pointing to the colorful wildflowers lining the highways and decorating the hillsides. "Did you know it's still snowing in Tromsø?"

Bergen didn't have spring snow, but it had rain. Lots of it. Eddie and Elder Dahle always took umbrellas with them just in case, and would leave their wet umbrellas at the bottom of an apartment stairwell to dry while they tracted in an apartment building. On one particularly rainy day, someone stole their umbrellas, so for the rest of the day, they ran between apartment buildings in the brief sunny moments between downpours. When their timing was bad, they got soaked.

"*Uffa meg*, you are completely wet," said a woman upon seeing the elders.

"Yes, Fru Bergsen," said Elder Dahle, making sure to use the woman's name. "We got caught in an unexpected rain."

"There is no such thing as unexpected rain in this city. Do you not know you should always carry an umbrella in Bergen?"

"We had umbrellas, but someone stole them," Eddie said, explaining how the missionaries had left them in a stairwell.

"That is terrible. Who would do such a thing?" Fru Bergsen said. "Please come in." She gave each of the elders a towel to dry their hair and made them tea to warm up. Rummaging through her closet, she found two umbrellas, which she gave to the elders, saying they could keep them. "It angers me that someone would steal your umbrellas."

"You are very kind," Eddie said. "But we would like to come back and tell you about our religion, perhaps in the evening when your husband is home. We can return your umbrellas then." Fru Bergsen agreed and the elders went on their way.

"Maybe God had someone steal our umbrellas so Fru Bergsen would let us in," Elder Dahle said in a half-joking tone.

"If she joins the church, you'll have a faith-promoting story to relate at your missionary homecoming."

"Yes, but it needs a little embellishing," Elder Dahle said. "I think I'll say that it was the Three Nephites who took them."

"God sent them all the way to Bergen just to steal our umbrellas? That's the story you're going to tell?"

"God works in mysterious ways, Elder Pedersen." The elders ducked their heads and opened their umbrellas to a darkened sky. They silently crossed the walkway to the next apartment building, dodging puddles as raindrops pitter-pattered on their umbrellas.

The last week he and Elder Dahle were together as companions, Eddie received a letter from Elder Jensen, who had been home from his mission little more than a month.

Dear Elder Pedersen:

How is everyone in Fyllingsdalen? I bet you didn't expect to hear from me so soon. And I've got news I bet you didn't expect. I'm engaged to be married. Clinched the deal last night. Cindy and I prayed about it and we both got the same answer. Celestial marriage, baby! Can you believe it? I came home expecting that for the next several years I'd be hanging around church dances searching for my one and only, but my first day at Institute class I met Cindy and . . . well, the rest is history. We hit it off right away and have been seeing each other every day since. She's prettier and smarter than my ex-girlfriend. Is that mean to say? Well, it's true. I wanted you to be one of the first to know. Of my many companions, you were my favorite, and if you were here, I would ask you to be my best man. Let's always stay friends. I hope you'll come to see us when you get home. I know you'll like Cindy.

Tell Arne and Ole and Bjørn and all the Bergen members I say hello. And be sure to give Bente Larsen a big kiss if you dare. Is she the one you love? I'm dying to know.

Best regards from your best friend,
Charlie (formerly known as Elder Jensen)

Eddie didn't know how to feel. Disappointed and sad he would never renew his friendship with Elder Jensen, that they likely would never see each other again? Or relieved he would never have to confront his feelings for Elder Jensen or struggle to contain his desire for him? Guilty because his unrequited homosexual love persisted as strong as ever? These and a host of vexing emotions welled up inside, causing physical heartache and soul-crushing torment. The spirit inside him—whoever or whatever he was—longed to get right with the Lord but could not understand why he remained unchanged. *My God, my God, why hast thou forsaken me?*

Eddie was still feeling melancholy after saying his prayers. While lying in bed and thinking about Elder Jensen, he called to his companion. "You know, my brothers also got married very quickly after they got home from their missions," Eddie said.

"It's pretty common," Elder Dahle replied. "I saw it happen quite often at BYU."

"Why is that? Why are returned missionaries in such a hurry to get married?"

"Oh, that's quite simple," Elder Dahle said, a mischievous lilt in his voice. "They're probably eager to assume another missionary position."

Eddie pondered his companion's answer only briefly before deciphering its meaning. "Ha, ha, ha, ha!" he howled. Elder Dahle joined in and the two elders roared with laughter until tears ran down their cheeks. Eddie had to cover his mouth to prevent himself from getting the hiccups.

"Elder Pedersen, I bet you have that natural smile on your face again."

Eddie wondered how a person could simultaneously feel incredibly sad and deliriously happy. "I'm smiling through my tears, Elder Dahle," he said. "I'm smiling through my tears."

Chapter 21

Don't be satisfied with your work if it is less than your potential. Find reasons for doing your work well and do not make excuses for your failures.

Conduct of a Missionary

In October 1970, fully thirteen months into his mission, Orrin finally got called to be a senior companion. Getting passed over had been discouraging, especially when Elder Pedersen became a senior companion after only six months. Orrin was being transferred back to Kjelsås, the area where he had begun his mission. Many missionaries might have been disappointed by this move, but Orrin regarded it as an exciting challenge, a chance to apply everything he had learned in an Oslo district he knew well. What's more, he had been assigned a newly arriving missionary as his companion. "We entrust only our best missionaries to train our greenies," Elder Thompson told him. "I argued strongly for you to get a greenie, and President Toressen heartily agreed. You've earned it, Elder Tanner."

"Much of what I know, I learned from you," Orrin said, hoping he sounded sufficiently humble. He was sincere. Elder Thompson, who was completing a stint as an assistant to President Toressen, had been Orrin's favorite companion. Self-assured but patient and generous in his praise, he had consistently encouraged Orrin and looked for ways to boost his confidence during their three months together in Halden. As a result, Orrin was returning to Kjelsås buoyed by the same optimism and enthusiasm he had brought with him as a greenie more than a year ago. "Just as President Toressen is the prophet of Norway, I am the prophet of my proselytizing area," Orrin reasoned aloud. "I am entitled to inspiration and even revelation on behalf of our investigators." Returning to Kjelsås renewed his heretofore unspoken deal with God: *I, Elder Orrin Tanner, will obey all the mission rules and rise above expectations to proselytize and bring the humble and meek into the fold; and God, in return, will reward me with my long-sought spiritual breakthrough.*

Elder Thompson would be returning home in a few days to a girlfriend who had waited twenty-four months for him, sending letters without fail each week, plus a variety of baked goods and knitted scarves throughout his mission. "I'm happy for you," Orrin said. "But now that I'm coming back to Oslo, I wish you were still working in the mission home. I could use your help."

"You'll do fine, Elder Tanner. Besides, Elder Ward and Elder Sorensen are stellar missionaries," Elder Thompson said, referring to the new assistants. Orrin shook Elder Thompson's hand and wished him luck. Feeling suddenly melancholic, he wondered whether he would ever see him again.

Elder Eric Gregersen, Orrin's new greenie, shared Orrin's eagerness and optimism. Nineteen and away from home for the first time, Elder Gregersen was unschooled in Mormonism's basic history and doctrines but undaunted by the anticipated challenges of mission life, confident that his desire and faith were sufficient for the task. He had a boyish face dotted with freckles, a gap-toothed smile, and the irrepressible geniality of a middle child who had the ability to get along with anyone, largely through submission to others. Above all, he was trusting. He immediately trusted Orrin's judgment, not just because of Orrin's longer experience as a missionary, but also because Orrin's reputation as a Mormon scholar had been kept alive at the Language Training Mission. The Norwegian language instructors recounted stories of Orrin's exceptional erudition to each group of missionaries that passed through the training facility, hailing his scholarship to both challenge and inspire their new charges.

If Elder Gregersen felt fortunate to be paired with such a distinguished companion, Orrin was equally happy to be given oversight of an impressionable greenie willing to follow his direction. Although Elder Gregersen did not share Orrin's burning desire for mission greatness, he unquestioningly obeyed the mission rules and adhered to the rigid work schedule. Orrin saw his task as making Elder Gregersen understand that the rules merely set the minimum expectation. Success—garnering not just investigators but also baptisms—demanded the extra mile. After all, the average Norwegian missionary might teach only one or two converts over the course of two years. Some none at all. Multiple baptisms would require enormous effort and exemplary spirituality, both in conduct and thought.

Orrin wanted to set a good example for his new companion—after all, they would be partners in this ambitious effort—and a good way to start was by proselytizing on the streetcar. As he and Elder Gregersen were riding the Kjelsås streetcar from the mission home to their hybel, Orrin slipped out of his seat and sidled up to an older gentleman near the back of the streetcar. The man knitted his eyebrows in disapproval. "Excuse me," Orrin said. "My companion and I are Americans new to Oslo. Could you tell me if this streetcar will take us to Olav Reyes plass?"

Of course, Orrin knew exactly where the streetcar was going, but he had learned never to begin by talking about Mormonism when engaging people in a public place. Put them at ease and gauge their demeanor.

The man's face softened. "Oh, yes. It's not far, maybe five kilometers. Are you a student? You speak Norwegian very well."

"Thank you. I studied the language before I came here, and I have lived in Norway for about a year now. I'm a missionary for The Church of Jesus Christ of Latter-day Saints, also known as the Mormon Church." A familiar shadow dropped over the man's face. He turned away and gazed out the window. "Thank you for your help," Orrin said, pulling a Joseph Smith pamphlet from his coat pocket. "Here, I would like to give you this. I know this man is a true prophet of God and that the church he established is the true church of Jesus Christ." Orrin stood to leave, alerting the man he would no longer bother him. The man took the pamphlet without looking at Orrin. "Thank you for your help," Orrin repeated, smiling as he left.

"I heard you bear your testimony. That's the only part I could understand," Elder Gregersen said when Orrin returned to his seat. "What did he say? Does he want us to teach him the discussions?"

"No, but I DMed him."

"DMed?"

"Delivered the Message."

"Maybe you planted a seed?"

"That's the idea, Elder. We do a lot of that in Norway."

As the streetcar approached Olav Reyes Plass, the man turned and signaled to Orrin they were approaching his stop. Orrin nodded his thanks as Elder Gregersen gathered his suitcase and other belongings. "Gee, Elder Tanner, I think you really did plant a seed," Elder Gregersen said, his voice full of admiration.

The walk to their hybel was slippery and cold. Orrin took Elder Gregersen's suitcase so the shivering elder could button his jacket and put on his gloves. Orrin welcomed the heavy flakes of snow falling from the cloudy sky. The winter sun had disappeared, despite the early hour. A misty aura surrounded the streetlamps, puncturing the afternoon darkness with a magical halo. The scene reminded Orrin of the day he arrived in Norway. And now, as he walked amid familiar cobblestone streets, he realized President Toressen had given him a chance to begin anew, to do his mission right, the way he had always envisioned. He smiled with unexpected satisfaction when they turned into the courtyard and he saw the row of wooden outhouses standing like sentinels on guard duty. The apartment was unchanged. The beds, chairs, and table were all the same, though more visibly worn, as were the curtains, mottled and drab, reeking of the hybel's clammy, stale air. A small refrigerator now sat next to the two-burner hotplate. A jagged crack had etched itself diagonally across the mirror that hung over the sink. "Elder Gregersen," Orrin said as he examined the soap dispenser and cleanser sitting by the sink. "I need to explain something to you about our bathroom situation."

"*Uffam eg*, you're back in Grünerløkka. That is bad for you, but good for me," Søster Halversen said, laughing.

"I am glad to be back. I have got big plans for this area," Orrin said.

"And you have got a greenie," she said, nodding toward Elder Gregersen. "He is just like you when you first came to my home. All smiles, not understanding anything. But look at you now, speaking Norwegian like you were born here. It is a miracle, the way you missionaries grow up right in front of me."

Søster Halversen had prepared a large spread of open-faced sandwiches, meats, and sweets, just as she had been doing every week since two elders came to her door five years ago. Orrin stole a look at Elder Gregersen, who was cautiously sipping tea for the first time in his life, probably wondering, as Orrin had wondered, if it was really okay to drink tea.

"What is this?" Elder Gregersen asked in garbled Norwegian, stabbing at piece of meat with his fork.

Orrin was about to correct him by offering a clearer pronunciation, but Søster Halversen, who had listened to countless mispronunciations in thick American accents, needed no translation. "It is *kjøttkaker*—meatballs," she explained, providing an English translation. "Try it with lingonberries."

Søster Halversen wanted to hear everything Orrin had been doing since he had been transferred to Halden ten months earlier. She delighted in his stories about traveling with President Toressen and serving as his scribe, but she liked best his accounts of missionary misadventures. With each recounting, she would let loose a high-pitch laugh while clutching at her dentures. "*Uffa meg. Uffa meg for dere.*"

Dear sweet, silver-haired Søster Halversen. She opened her home and heart to the missionaries, which made his message even more difficult to deliver. "We have to stop our weekly visits," Orrin told her. "The mission rules say we should not spend too much time with members, no longer than fifteen minutes. We are called to proselytize and preach, not visit members."

Orrin had worried about how Søster Halversen would react. She looked more chagrined than upset or disappointed. "I guess I have been selfish keeping you boys from your work," she said.

"You have been wonderful," Orrin assured her. "No one has been more blessed than the missionaries who have been serving in your area. But thank you for understanding."

"Maybe you can come by sometimes for the short visit your mission rules allow for church members. I will make for you *risgrøt*."

"Don't worry. We'll see you every Sunday at church. You can count on that."

No miracles resulted from Orrin's return to Oslo. The Norwegians living along the Kjelsås streetcar line did not suddenly become interested in Mormonism. He had forgotten that the poorer apartment buildings, ones Elder Flossen had tried to avoid, housed more than their fair share of odd, lonely people. A wild-eyed, disheveled woman, after listening briefly to their message, said she wanted to join the church but the devil, jealous of her devotion to God, wouldn't allow it. Although it was late afternoon, she was still wearing a nightgown, stained and tattered, and she scratched uncomfortably at her arms and chest. When Orrin suggested that Satan did not have that kind of power over people, she threw open her nightgown and showed the elders dark-scabbed sores on her breasts. "He stabbed me with ice picks," she said, unabashedly fingering the tiny scabs dotting her wrinkled, sagging breasts. The elders looked away, embarrassed for themselves and the woman, then turned and hurried down the stairs and knocked on the next door.

"Welcome to Norway, greenie," Orrin said as he stared at the door, waiting for someone to answer. Elder Gregersen laughed nervously, but the two elders never discussed the incident or mentioned it to other missionaries.

Søster Laaksdahl burst into tears when Orrin told her the missionaries were halting their weekly visits, assuring her he would alert the branch president to ensure she received regular visits from both priesthood representatives and relief society visiting teachers. The Magnussen children frowned petulantly when Orrin delivered the news, but Bror Magnussen, though clearly disappointed, praised the elders for their dedication. "You are still welcome to visit our home anytime," he said. "We hope you won't hesitate to call on us if you ever need anything."

To maximize their reported hours of missionary work, Orrin decided he and Elder Gregersen would engage streetcar passengers while they traveled to and from their tracting destinations. In addition to boosting their standing on the Mission Comparative, streetcar tracting would serve as a demonstration to God of their sincere intent and willingness to go the extra mile. "Don't begin by talking about religion or even mention you are a missionary," Orrin advised Elder Gregersen. "Just tell them you are an American and need help getting off at the right stop. Norwegians are friendly and helpful if they don't know you're a Mormon."

"But what if I don't understand what they're telling me?"

"It doesn't matter because we already know where we're going. When you sense they're finished giving directions, thank them and then give them a pamphlet and bear your testimony. Move away quickly if they start scowling."

Orrin and Elder Gregersen started getting up at 6:00 a.m., a half hour earlier than required, to increase their study time and ensure they also reached their tracting area by 9:30 a.m. as recommended in the mission guidelines. Elder Gregersen needed the additional study time, having forgotten nearly all of the discussion dialogue he had memorized during language training. He also struggled with the strict routines and spartan conditions of missionary life. Shaving with water heated on a burner took some getting used to—the water was either too hot or too cold—and he had trouble seeing his face clearly through the cracks in the mirror, a frustrating problem when shaving around newly sprouted pimples. Orrin spent a lot of time teaching Elder Gregersen basic cooking skills, such as frying an egg, boiling oatmeal and rice, and even stirring soup packets into hot water. Elder Gregersen's last-minute trips to the outhouse often had them running to catch the streetcar. Orrin silently counted up the irritations but said nothing, remembering how difficult his early weeks had been. Besides, Elder Gregersen reminded Orrin of his own puppy-like eagerness to please. Orrin looked for instances to compliment him and boost his spirits, as he wished Elder Flossen would have done.

On their third day together, Orrin pinned a three-by-five notecard above his bed that asserted: I am a baptizing missionary. "This is an affirmation," he explained to Elder Gregersen. The assistants had taught the missionaries about the power of affirmations at a recent conference. "The idea is to first identify the type of person you want to be and the goals you want to achieve. Next, you write them down and look at them every day. Visualize yourself as the person performing the way you want to perform and achieving the things you want to achieve. Babe Ruth hit home runs because he believed himself to be a home run hitter. Charles Lindberg flew across the Atlantic because he believed himself to be a skilled pilot. Do you understand the concept?"

"I think so," Elder Gregersen said.

Orrin offered several more examples of historical figures who believed in themselves. "The key is to repeat your affirmation and envision your affirmation several times a day, every day. You can't help but become the person you think you are."

"It sounds like magic or voodoo."

"It's inspired," Orrin said.

Elder Gregersen nodded in agreement. He took a notecard and wrote his own affirmation, which he pinned on the wall above his bed: I will serve an honorable mission.

179

Each day unfolded like another: a few crazy people, a few doors slammed in their faces, a few copies of the Book of Mormon sold, a few callbacks. Most people were polite, closing the door slowly while apologetically insisting they were not interested. The elders walked many miles each day, climbing stairs and hustling between apartment buildings to get out of the blowing snow. Orrin's tight-fitting shoes pinched his toes, eventually causing his right big toe to blister and bleed, but he said nothing, not wishing to slow their search for a golden family. Elder Gregersen remained a work in progress. At one home, he pushed the doorbell so hard that the button stuck. The buzzer rang and rang, as if he were deliberately keeping his finger pressed against the button, impatiently waiting for someone to answer the door. Elder Gregersen tried prying the button loose with a fingernail, but to no avail.

"Let me try," Orrin said. Using a penknife, he had almost dislodged the button when they heard footsteps approaching the door. Panicking, Elder Gregersen hit the bell violently with his fist, shattering the bell's plastic cover. Elder Gregersen was on his knees picking up the pieces when the front door opened and a petite woman holding a mop and rag stood facing the elders. Thinking he should be the one to explain, given that he broke the buzzer, Elder Gregersen scrambled to his feet and began speaking rapidly. A mishmash of memorized door approaches spilled out. "We are representatives of the Mormons and we have come here with a message about a prophet of God who translated a new church with living prophets who can guide us in these troubled times and . . ." Elder Gregersen sheepishly held out his hands with the broken pieces of the woman's doorbell but said nothing more because, as he later told Orrin, he didn't know the Norwegian words for doorbell, broken, or pieces.

The woman looked at Elder Gregersen's hands and then up at him. "I did not understand a thing you said."

Orrin jumped in and explained what happened. "We are very sorry."

The woman examined what was left of her doorbell, then pushed the button. It rang. "Still works," she said, then pointed at Elder Gregersen. "Was he trying to speak Norwegian?"

"He just arrived in Norway and is still learning the language. He gets flustered when he is nervous, like when he breaks someone's doorbell."

The woman laughed. "Tell him it will be easy to replace the cover."

"We can see you are busy," Orrin said, pointing to the mop, "but we would like to come back and talk with you about our religion."

The woman agreed and they set up an appointment to return in three days. "Maybe God broke the doorbell on purpose," Orrin said as the elders rode the streetcar back to their hybel. When Elder Gregersen expressed solemn agreement, Orrin did not explain he was joking.

Elder Gregersen's incompetence and naiveté wore on Orrin. He tried looking for his companion's positive traits. For one, Elder Gregersen didn't give up. He wanted Orrin's approval as much as he did God's. And although he was virtually hopeless in his efforts to engage people on the streetcar and buses, he never shirked at taking his turn. Sure enough, the next morning, Elder Gregersen was trying valiantly to talk with a young high school student on the streetcar. Orrin wrote a short note about Elder Gregersen's persistence in his Inspirational Thought Book.

The Inspirational Thought Book, like affirmations, had been the assistants' idea. "God is always trying to inspire us and guide us to golden contacts," Elder Sorensen said when introducing the concept. He showed the missionaries a small notebook he carried in his suit pocket. "Consequently, we need to be ready to listen. I carry with me this Thought Book, so I can jot down inspirational ideas that come to me throughout the day." The assistants passed out a similar notebook to each of the missionaries. As Orrin watched Elder Gregersen slide next to a pair of older women and begin his streetcar approach, despite their obvious annoyance, Orrin took out his Thought Book and wrote, "Persistence in the face of resistance is love."

Elder Gregersen proved his worth as an aspiring missionary—and, perhaps, as an inspired one too—when he suggested they leave a Joseph Smith pamphlet in the outhouse each time they used it. "Lots of people like reading material when they go," he said, "and there's plenty of room to set the pamphlets on the toilet paper dispenser. They'll stay without falling down if we wedge them in." Orrin and Elder Gregersen began leaving pamphlets in each of the outhouses assigned to their building. They wrote their contact information on each pamphlet and replaced any pamphlets that disappeared. The main question was whether to record the activity as "tracting" in the Mission Comparative. Orrin finally decided against it, fearful the other missionaries would think they were padding their statistics. Still, that didn't stop him from daydreaming about the faith-promoting story they could tell if outhouse tracting led to a baptism.

During their fourth week together, they met a young couple from Sweden who listened attentively to the entire first discussion. Neither the husband nor his wife smoked, often a chief obstacle to conversion, and both seemed to enjoy the intellectual stimulation of discussing the meaning of New Testament scriptures. "Of course, we have heard of Mormons, but we knew little about your church," the husband said as they sipped tea together. "Your church is much more grounded in reason and logic than our State Church, which remains stuck in its medieval roots of superstition and mystery." He and his wife expressed interest in learning more about Mormonism, but they balked when Orrin invited them to kneel in prayer to ask God whether they should be baptized. Panic swept over their faces, as if they suddenly realized what they were getting themselves into. No one was home when the elders returned for their appointed visit. When they finally caught up with the Swedish couple several weeks later, the man rejected them curtly, saying, "We are not interested in becoming Mormons."

One person who was interested was Siri Poulsen, the woman with the broken doorbell. She lived in Grefsen, a suburb near the end of the Kjelsås line, where she rented the bottom floor of a large frame house that had been converted into individual apartments. The doorbell cover had already been replaced when the elders returned for their appointment, but they knocked on the door anyway. Søster Poulsen, as the elders soon began calling her, had smooth olive skin, intense dark eyes, and striking auburn hair. She wore a casual pants suit and a thinning sweater. Her apartment reeked of cigarettes and loneliness.

"I am sorry my furnishings are so sparse," she said as the elders took off their hats and coats and placed them on a living room chair. "I am only renting this hybel while I study for my pharmaceutical license." She opened a cigarette case on the coffee table and took out a hand-rolled cigarette. She struck a match and started to light it, then stopped. "Excuse my manners, I am not used to having guests. Would either of you like a cigarette?"

"We do not smoke," Orrin said. "Smoking and drinking are against our church's health code."

"I am off to a bad start then," she said, lighting up and blowing smoke from the side of her mouth. "Can I get you coffee or tea?"

"We do not drink coffee or tea either," Elder Gregersen said.

"But we drink herbal tea, if you have it," Orrin added. "It is the caffeine we avoid."

Søster Poulsen excused herself and a few minutes later returned with a tray of tea for the elders and coffee for herself. She lit another cigarette, exhaling a thick stream of gray smoke as she poured the tea. "So what is this special message you had to travel all the way from America and break my doorbell to tell me?"

Orrin set up the flannel board display and the two elders took Søster Poulsen through the first discussion while she smoked cigarette after cigarette, stopping only to roll new ones. She agreed with nearly all the discussion points, saying it is logical that people would need prophets today.

"Why would God just stop talking to people?" she asserted. "That does not make sense."

The elders returned once a week after their first visit. Before moving to Oslo, Søster Poulsen lived in Mandel, a small town on the southern tip of Norway. She was older than the other students and did not socialize much. Although not exactly a recluse, she spent most of her time studying at home when not in class. "It has been hard for me to make friends," she said. "I am not used to living in such a large city. I will return home as soon as I pass my exams." Despite her friendliness, she had a permanent look of worry and talked constantly about the difficulty of her courses and exams. "Smoking is the only thing that calms my nerves," she said.

The elders suspected Søster Poulsen had invited them in because she was feeling lonely and adrift after her move to Oslo, but whatever her reasons, she proved to be an attentive investigator. She read the pamphlets left by the elders after each visit, occasionally looked up some of the recommended biblical passages relating to the discussion points, and readily agreed to kneel in prayer with the elders at the end of each discussion. She was quite excited about reading the Book of Mormon after hearing about its divine origins, but when the elders returned the next week, she proclaimed it a hard slog. "But if you tell me it is true, I will believe you. After all, I do not read the Bible and I believe it to be true," she said, smiling through a smoky haze.

Despite her busy schedule, she agreed to attend Sunday services. They met her at her home and rode the streetcar together to the chapel on Hekkveien in Grünerløkka. The church members were friendly but cautious when greeting Søster Poulsen, knowing the missionaries sometimes attracted oddballs and eccentrics who, if they joined, participated only intermittently before falling into inactivity. Søster Halversen, however, did not withhold her enthusiasm. "*Uffa meg*," she said when introduced to Søster Poulsen. "I should have known that when the elders stopped visiting me, they would find someone young and pretty to take my place." She winked at Orrin, who smiled guiltily.

Before the services began, Søster Poulsen excused herself to go to the restroom. A few minutes later, Elder Dunlop, the zone leader, tapped Orrin on the shoulder. "There's smoke coming out from under the door in the women's bathroom," he said. Orrin's first thought was that a fire had broken out, but Elder Dunlop added, "Your investigator is in there smoking a cigarette."

Orrin, who had been mingling with church members, excused himself and rushed down the basement stairs to the bathroom. Smoking in a

Mormon chapel was like serving sausage at a bar mitzvah. He hoped no one besides Elder Dunlop had noticed, but when he turned down the hallway, he saw a line of women waiting outside the bathroom. Søster Poulsen exited shortly after and Orrin escorted her past the disapproving stares and back upstairs, where they slid into a pew beside Søster Halversen. The opening services proceeded smoothly, but when the congregation dispersed for Sunday School classes, Søster Poulsen said she needed another bathroom break.

"I am sorry, but you cannot smoke in the bathroom or in any place inside the chapel," Orrin said. "It is not allowed."

"Okay, l will go outside."

Orrin followed her out the door, hoping to steer her around the corner, where they wouldn't be visible, but Søster Poulsen pulled out a cigarette and lit up as soon as she stepped outside. She tossed the match onto the stoop. "Oh, that is much better," she said, blowing smoke contentedly through pursed lips.

It wasn't long before people walking through the foyer noticed Orrin standing outside with Søster Poulsen, who wasn't content smoking just one cigarette. Orrin tried to ignore their stares through the glass doors while he asked Søster Poulsen about her impressions of the morning services. The members looked more astonished than upset. His being alone with a person of the opposite sex would surely cause talk. Meanwhile, Elder Gregersen was reminiscing with a missionary from his language training group when Elder Dunlop interrupted.

"Do you know where your companion is?" Elder Dunlop asked.

"He's with our investigator, Søster Poulsen."

"They're together all right. He's alone with her on the front steps of the church, and she's smoking cigarettes."

Elder Gregersen ran through the chapel, reaching Orrin and Søster Poulsen just as she was rubbing out her last cigarette with her shoe. "Where have you been?" Orrin said angrily.

"I . . . I didn't know."

"Never leave me again."

Elder Gregersen looked away, chastened. Søster Poulsen, unaware of the controversy, kicked the ashes and tobacco shreds over the stoop and into the bushes below, and then walked with the elders back into the chapel, heavy with the smell of cigarettes.

"*Uffa meg*," Søster Halversen said as the elders walked by. "*Uffa meg for dere.*"

Chapter 22

The Gospel is here in its fulness. The Church of Jesus Christ has been re-established. God has revealed himself anew by revelation from on high to his prophets.

"Apostacy and Restoration" in the *Missionary Handbook*

After eighteen months as the Norwegian mission president, Bjørnstjerne Bjørnson Toressen had made little headway in boosting the baptism rate. In fact, the annual number of convert baptisms had fallen from more than one hundred to fewer than fifty. Yes, he could console himself with the fact that the Norwegian members were experiencing an incredible revival, with activity rates nearly doubling in some branches. Much of the uptick resulted from his speaking tour that attracted large and enthusiastic crowds of members, many of whom had not attended church in years but who, inspired by his words, had returned to the fold. Local branch presidents said the resurgence was enabling them to fill volunteer positions and implement church programs that had lain dormant for years. But the proselytizing side of Toressen's calling was struggling, a problem that worried Salt Lake City authorities. Some had counseled him that he was too lax in his oversight of the elders and sisters in his charge. It wasn't that he allowed the missionaries to flout the mission rules, but he believed they had embarked on missions with the same righteous desire to serve as he had, and so he trusted them to follow the spirit's guidance, even if it took them in unconventional directions. "Was not the church founded on the unconventional truths and inspired guidance given through the prophet Joseph Smith?" he told Apostle Prichard.

"That sounds good in theory, but in practice too many missionaries, especially the elders, will abuse this trust, due either to immaturity or lack of true commitment to their mission calling," replied Prichard, who oversaw the Scandinavian missions. Prichard had frowned when President Toressen sent two overworked sister missionaries on a three-day holiday to Kristiansand to relax and recharge their spirits, and Prichard chastised him severely after learning Toressen had allowed several elders to train with the semi-professional Drammen soccer club. "Unless they're handing out pamphlets at every practice, they are shirking their mission duties while risking injuries that could further take them from their work," Prichard said. "No baptisms will result from these efforts."

President Toressen didn't necessarily disagree with the last statement, but so few traditional proselytizing activities resulted in baptisms that he thought it worth a try. Besides, the elders who proposed the idea came forward with such enthusiasm, especially dear Elder Creighton, whose sad demeanor belied a sensitive soul. Elder Creighton was so demoralized by his lack of success that he requested to be sent home. "The Lord called you to Norway for a reason," President Toressen told him, and though Elder Creighton appeared unpersuaded, he agreed to keep trying. When Elder Creighton suggested training with the soccer club as a way to improve the church's image and possibly find an investigator, President Toressen immediately agreed. He had no illusions that the missionaries would make inroads among the soccer players, but the effort would do wonders for building Elder Creighton's confidence.

President Toressen was sitting alone in his office, pondering how to galvanize the missionary work, similar to the revival now occurring among the member branches, when he got the idea for doing another speaking tour. *Yes, that's it. My new tour will be aimed at nonmembers and the Norwegian press.* If he could inspire and energize church members with his speeches, why couldn't he do the same for the honest-at-heart Norwegians? Like Elder Creighton, the Lord had called President Toressen on a mission for a reason. Had not God even shown President Toressen in a vision that the Norwegian people were waiting to hear him preach? The image from his vision appeared suddenly, vividly, in his mind.

"Lord, I understand now what You are telling me," he said, looking up at the ceiling. He shook his head, chuckling ruefully at his mistake. He had interpreted his vision as merely a foreshadowing, as God's way of alerting him he would be called to be the Norwegian mission president. But his vision—in which the Norwegian people begged him to preach to them—meant he was literally supposed to preach to them. That was the key to unlocking the hoped-for outpouring of the spirit among his countrymen. He had puzzled over his lack of success as mission president but saw the path forward clearly now. Success would come when he fulfilled the task foretold in his vision.

Orrin was disappointed when the assistants came to his hybel and asked him to serve as a scribe on President Toressen's new speaking tour. It was a prestigious job, one that won him the envy of the other elders, but Orrin wanted to concentrate his efforts on proselytizing in the Kjelsås area, where he and Elder Gregersen were starting to make headway. They were teaching four investigators, including Søster Poulsen, who continued expressing interest despite her nicotine addiction and increasing anxiety over her upcoming pharmaceutical exams. Orrin and Elder Gregersen were leading the entire Norwegian mission in total working hours, averaging more than seventy hours each week, and they had climbed to first place on the Mission Comparative. After hearing that two Tromsø missionaries were waking at 5:30 a.m. to increase their study time, Orrin vowed to do the same and after some pushing, persuaded Elder Gregersen to rise with him. "You can use the time to memorize more scriptures," Orrin told him.

Orrin couldn't turn down the calling to accompany President Toressen, but he convinced the assistants to allow him to continue working the Kjelsås area rather than transfer him to a new area when the tour was completed. "We're on the verge of a big breakthrough. I can feel it," Orrin told them. After the assistants left, he wrote a new affirmation: I am the hardest-working missionary in Norway.

President Toressen began his speaking tour in Oslo at the church's chapel at Hekkveien. The announced topic for the first speech was "Are Mormons Christians?" The mission printer created a flyer advertising the event, which the missionaries distributed at every door. Branch leaders placed notices in local newspapers, while the Relief Society women prepared enormous amounts of refreshments. On the day of the speech, the *Aftenposten* published a flattering story about President Toressen and the Mormons. The article quoted extensively from a pamphlet by Richard L. Evans, one of the church's apostles, touting Mormon contributions to American society. The article also praised President Toressen, recognizing him as a well-known translator of Norwegian novels and poetry, adding that some of his own poetry had been published in Norway. Members and missionaries were quite pleased with the article, which said the Mormons' cultlike reputation in Norway was based on prejudice and misconception.

The event attracted nearly one hundred non-Mormons, including a dozen reporters and a handful of investigators being taught by the missionaries. More than a hundred and fifty members from the Oslo branches also attended, flooding the noisy chapel to standing room only. Despite a predictably frantic start from the mission home, the president's entourage arrived only a few minutes late, giving the assistants time to peel bloodied strips of toilet paper from President Toressen's chin before he entered the chapel. The audience buzzed with impatient excitement when President Toressen strode down the aisle. Every member and missionary stood, craning their necks to catch a glimpse of the mission president, and this brought the non-Mormons to their feet as well, creating an electric sense of anticipation as Toressen waded through the well-wishers and climbed the stage. The congregation began by singing "We Thank Thee O God for a Prophet," and after a prayer and introduction by the Oslo branch president, President Toressen took the podium.

He began by reading a short clip from a magazine article stating that less than half of the Norwegian people professed to believe in God, and an even smaller number had read the Bible or attended church within the past year. He used this as a springboard to jump back and forth between Norwegian religious and cultural history and the history of Mormonism, as he had done in previous conference talks. It was a typically meandering speech, spoken without notes, and seemingly lacking organization or discipline. But Orrin, who had become accustomed to Toressen's speaking style, saw that Toressen selected his stories with the same care a poet selects his words, laying the building blocks of his central theme. Toressen also adhered to the philosophy that when preaching the gospel, one could serve meat as well as milk, and so he did not attempt to soften his message by dropping the church's more fantastic claims, despite the fact that many nonmembers were present. Most were learning about Mormonism for the first time, and Toressen held them spellbound by recounting Joseph Smith's first vision, in which God the Father and Jesus Christ appeared to the young prophet and told him that all Christian churches were false. They likewise marveled at the spiritual outpouring when the first Mormon temple was dedicated in Kirtland, Ohio. "Angels swept through the congregation and the Mormon faithful prophesied and spoke in tongues and the spirit of God lit up the temple as if it were in flames," President Toressen declared. But heavenly visitations occurred not only in times past, he said, but also today. He described for them many of his own spiritual experiences, including his vision in which he foresaw he would be standing before the Norwegian people this very night, preaching the gospel of Jesus Christ to them.

"Ye men and women of Norway," he said, paraphrasing Paul's declaration to the Athenians. "I perceive that in all things ye are too superstitious. The God of the Bible is unknown to you, and you worship in ignorance." Although not normally given to theatrics, President Toressen raised his hand and pointed his index finger like a lightning rod toward heaven. His face glowed as if on fire. "The State Church has played a mean trick upon the Norwegian people. Over the centuries, it has destroyed your spiritual sensibilities. This is why I love Grieg and Ibsen and Bjørnson and Hamsun and all the great Norwegian artists, because they have tried to break through this spiritual stranglehold and tap into Norway's inner soul"—and here Toressen digressed to lament Knut Hamsun's unfortunate dalliance with fascism, but he also regretted the unmerciful persecution of Hamsun after the war, when Hamsun was an old and faltering man and his past indiscretions were of no consequence.

Orrin scrambled to keep pace, not only because of Toressen's rambling detours, but also because as he watched Toressen, his mind ran to the Apostle Paul. Joseph Smith, who said he personally conversed with the ancient apostle, described Paul as short, about five feet tall, with dark hair and small black eyes that penetrated into eternity. According to Smith, Paul had a high-pitched, whining voice that when elevated, resembled the roaring of a lion. As President Toressen drew to a conclusion, he rose in majestic stature, as did Paul on Mars hill. "The Norwegian people," he said, thumping his chest to show solidarity with his audience, "will one day rise up in righteous anger against the State Church priests when they discover the cruel fraud that has been practiced upon them. As the Apostle Paul told the Athenians, in the past God overlooked your ignorance, but He now commands all people everywhere to repent and embrace truth and light."

At the meeting's end, the reporters rushed to the stage and besieged President Toressen, clamoring for more about how the Norwegian people had been deceived and spiritually enslaved by State Church priests.

Apostle Joseph F. Prichard hung up the phone, his hands shaking with righteous indignation. He had just finished a ninety-minute phone call with Norwegian Mission President Bjornsomething Bjornsomething Toressen. Egad, why didn't the man change his name after moving to America? Such a mouthful. The Norwegians probably couldn't pronounce it either. The long-distance call undoubtedly cost the church several hundred dollars. Never before had he dealt with a mission president so obtuse. *Was the man really that stupid, that oblivious to how his words would be interpreted by non-Mormons, particularly by non-Mormons from his own country?* Apostle Prichard surveyed the stack of Norwegian newspaper articles delivered by the church's translation services and now lying on his desk. Each article had a provocative headline—some on the front-page above the fold—trumpeting the most outlandish Mormon beliefs and doctrines. "Norwegian Lutherans Led Astray from True Christian Doctrines, Mormon Leader Says." "Mormon Mission President: God Speaks to Our Prophet." "Mormons Say They are God's Only True Church." "Mormons Claim Spiritual Gifts: Speaking in Tongues, Visitations from Angels."

This was not just an embarrassment for the church but also for Apostle Prichard personally. A humiliation, really. He had patiently worked with Toressen, counseling him, trying to help get Norway's convert baptisms up to the level it had been before Toressen took over as mission president—and then to be blindsided by this speech. Prichard had to confess to his colleagues that he knew nothing about Toressen's plans, that he was not attuned to his portfolio of responsibilities. Of course, he didn't need to be told the content of every speech or action by the mission presidents under his charge. You teach people correct principles and they govern themselves. But Toressen was proving to be a loose cannon, undisciplined, too confident in his calling, too willing to follow his own counsel. Prichard had dealt with many academics who tried to raise their own wisdom above that of church authorities, thinking that being learned made them wise, and he had put such men back on the straight and narrow. That's what he wanted to do with Toressen, but somehow the conversation got away from him.

"I've been reading the newspaper articles about your speech in Oslo," Apostle Prichard had said at the opening of his phone call.

"Oh, yes, isn't it wonderful," President Toressen said, his voice bubbling with optimism. "My speech was covered by all the major Oslo publications and their articles have been picked up by many smaller Norwegian newspapers."

"President, this isn't the type of publicity the church desires."

"I'm not sure I know what you mean. Wasn't getting favorable newspaper coverage one of the goals we discussed?"

"There is nothing *favorable* about these stories," Prichard replied sternly. "If you were misquoted, we can see if our lawyers can get the Norwegians to print a retraction. That's probably the best we can do at this point."

"I wasn't misquoted. In fact, I was delighted with how accurately they reported my speech. I don't mean to question your counsel, Elder Prichard, but I'm still not sure I see the problem."

"President Toressen, these articles make us look like a bunch of superstitious fanatics with all of the talk about Mormons seeing visions and angels and speaking in tongues. It's the wrong image. It's the wrong message."

"But it's all true, isn't it?"

Prichard's voice rose in volume with his anger. "You don't tell people these things right off the bat. You lead up to it. The milk before the meat. Introduce it slowly."

"I see your point, but we teach the Joseph Smith story in the very first discussion. The first thing we tell people is he had a vision in which he saw God the Father and his Son, Jesus Christ."

"But you went well beyond the first vision and talked about your own spiritual experiences. If you really had a vision, then that's something sacred and personal you should keep to yourself. 'Tell the vision to no man,' the scriptures say. If you had stuck to the advertised topic of your speech everything would have been fine. Why did you veer off course?"

"I felt inspired to deliver this message. God wanted me to be a voice of warning to the Norwegian people, so we could awaken them to their condition and shake them from their spiritual lethargy."

What errant nonsense, Prichard thought. *What arrogance!* He couldn't stand it. Prichard found himself shouting into the phone. "The only people you're going to awaken are the crackpots and kooks who'll come to Mormon chapels expecting to see angels flying across the rafters and probably a whole lot of other nonsense. But the vast majority of Norwegians, the solid, middle-class people we're trying to reach, they're going to close their minds to our message because they'll see it as the same emotional mumbo-jumbo dished out by the charlatans who preach on television every Sunday morning. And frankly, I wouldn't blame them. I wouldn't listen to that message either."

Toressen was uncharacteristically silent. "You sound upset," he said at last. "I'm sorry for the heartburn I've caused. I sometimes get so wound up that my wife will shout, 'Bjørnstjerne'—that's what she calls me when she's angry—'Bjørnstjerne,' she says, 'Why, oh why can't you be like other men,' and I say, 'I am trying, dear. I am repenting every day and trying to do better.' So you see, Elder Prichard, you are not the only one who—"

"President Toressen," the apostle said, his voice severe and strident. "Listen very carefully. Your planned speaking tour is over. Cancel your engagements. And in the future, there will be no more public speeches, not unless you get prior approval from the church's public relations department. I don't know why you didn't consult with them before organizing this tour. You should always coordinate these types of events with our public relations people. They know how to help you craft messages for public consumption. Everything must be correlated."

"Yes, sir. I understand and accept your decision. I would never go against counsel."

"Good. I'm going to have the church's public affairs representative in Norway contact you to see if there aren't some ways to minimize the damage to the church's image presented by these newspaper articles."

"Oh, I'm not worried at all," Toressen said with cheerful optimism. "In fact, this message will resonate with the Norwegian people, Elder Prichard. Not with everyone, of course, but it's going to open a lot of doors for our missionaries throughout Norway. You'll see."

Two hours after hanging up, Apostle Prichard was still fuming. Something about President Toressen's attitude was bothersome. Sure, he apologized and agreed in the future to coordinate large public speaking events with church headquarters, but unlike others whom Prichard had reprimanded for violating church protocol, Toressen seemed, well, serenely unperturbed. Prichard could not recall a time he had spoken so sternly, nor had he ever resorted to shouting, and yet, despite the sharp reproach, Toressen had remained upbeat throughout the conversation, as if he thought he knew better than the church's authorities. And he did not mind at all that the rest of his speaking had been canceled. *Had he expected this outcome all along or did he just not care? What a peculiar man!*

Orrin stifled a yawn, though he needn't have bothered, not for President Toressen's sake, because the president himself was asleep, hands on his lap, with his chin resting against his chest. They had spent the last two hours reviewing Orrin's final transcript of the president's Oslo speech. Elder Gregersen sat outside the office practicing the fifth discussion as he waited for Orrin to finish. In the quiet of the night, Orrin could hear his companion stumbling over the Norwegian dialogue, reciting it over and over until he got it right: "As our physical bodies grow, we become like our earthly fathers. And as our spirits mature by gaining the attributes of godliness, we become more like God."

Orrin was aware of the uproar the speech had ignited at church headquarters. He had wondered himself, even as President Toressen spoke, whether he had gone too far. Still, Toressen had been truly inspiring and his speech had served its purpose, jolting Norwegians with Mormonism's claims to modern revelation. Cancelation of the tour meant Orrin would not have to spend time away from his proselytizing area. For that he was grateful. He was putting the final typed notes on the president's desk when there came a loud banging on the side door.

"Bjørnstjerne, it's time for bed," Sister Toressen shouted as she swung open the door. President Toressen's head snapped back and his eyes blinked open. "You were sleeping, weren't you?" she said and then, without waiting for an answer, she turned to Orrin, "He was sleeping, wasn't he?"

Orrin looked at President Toressen for a hint of how he was supposed to answer. Toressen smiled and said to his wife, "We were just finishing up, weren't we Elder Tanner?"

Orrin shut his notebook. "Yes. We're all finished."

Sister Toressen let out a derisive snort. "I don't believe either of you." While Orrin and the president put together the final pages, Sister Toressen excoriated her husband for keeping Orrin and Elder Gregersen out late. It was now past ten o'clock and they surely would not get home before the 10:30 p.m. bedtime mandated for missionaries.

"Sometimes the ox is in the mire and you have to get it out," President Toressen said.

His wife snorted again and began haranguing him about his speech. "You're in trouble with church authorities again. If I weren't around to help you manage things, I swear, the entire mission would fall apart."

"It is true. Organization is not one of my strong suits." President Toressen smiled at his wife. "That's why I married you, dear."

"It's not a joke, Bjørnstjerne. I don't know why you didn't to do a simple thing like getting permission from Salt Lake City for your speech."

President Toressen, a mischievous glint in his eye, said something that sent his wife harrumphing from the room. When Orrin and Elder Gregersen arrived back at their hybel, they undressed quickly and readied themselves for bed. Elder Gregersen climbed sleepily under his duvet after prayers, but Orrin took out his Inspirational Thought Book and wrote, "Why risk someone saying no when your heart knows the answer is yes?"

Chapter 23

Pay strict attention to your personal and moral cleanliness. Always be courteous and kind and show your gratitude to those who assist you.
Conduct of a Missionary

After serving seven months in Stavanger, Eddie left feeling despondent and defeated, wondering how many pounds of flesh God would demand before consummating the deal. His assignment in Stavanger had begun well enough. The first week he attended a baptismal service in which a truly golden family, the Gangstads, joined the church after being taught the discussions by the sister missionaries. At a small celebration after the baptism, President Toressen told faith-promoting conversion stories, and while mingling afterward, he pulled the sisters aside for a short chat. "I want you to know the Lord chose you two to teach the Gangstads," he said. "They didn't need someone to overpower them with the discussion's logic and emphasis on the signs of the true church, because they were already believers. What they needed was someone to nurture their faith with love and fellowship, so they felt comfortable and welcome in the Mormon community. They needed the sisters' touch."

President Toressen's face lit up when he saw Eddie. "Elder Pedersen, I have to tell you how pleased I am with your work and progress. You were absolutely the perfect companion for Elder Dahle. You helped set him on a productive mission path."

Eddie flushed with pride. "Thank you, President. I really did grow to appreciate Elder Dahle's, um, unique gifts. He was a good companion for me, too, but I wish we could have accomplished more together. We were near the bottom of the Mission Comparative most weeks. I hope to do better in Stavanger."

"Oh, please, Elder Pedersen, don't place too much emphasis on the Mission Comparative. Those statistics help keep the missionaries motivated and focused, but you shouldn't use the Mission Comparative to measure your personal success."

"I've been a missionary for almost a year now and haven't baptized anyone yet. How should I measure my success?"

Toressen gave Eddie a piercing look. "You judge your success the same way the Lord does. Remember, the Lord seeth not as man seeth, for man looketh on the outward appearance, but the Lord looketh on the heart," he said, quoting the prophet Samuel. "It's what's in your heart. That's the true measure of a man. That's where the Lord looks."

"But—"

"Look into your heart, Elder Pedersen. Look into your heart," President Toressen said. He tapped Eddie gently three times on the chest, smiling and staring intently, his eyes glimmering like sapphires, as if he were also trying to peer into Eddie's heart. President Toressen excused himself to talk with other missionaries and members waiting for their moment with the mission president.

It was an exciting time for missionaries to be working in Stavanger. Now the headquarters of Norway's new Statoil company, Stavanger buzzed with entrepreneurial fervor fueled by the discovery of rich oil reserves along the rugged Norwegian coast. In the past decade alone, Stavanger's population had increased more the fifty percent to over 80,000 inhabitants, including many foreigners helping with the exploration and extraction of the oil. American companies had lobbied for permission to work the oil fields, but the Norwegian people opted to maintain control by creating the government-owned Statoil. Norwegians sought not only to retain the oil revenue for themselves and future generations but also to ensure that the nation's natural resources were protected. Newly arriving missionaries were only vaguely aware, if at all, of Stavanger's central place in Norway's burgeoning oil industry, but it quickly became apparent as they tracted among the city's residents.

"Your American companies claimed they knew better than us how to manage our oil reserves and wanted to take it from us, and now you come here to tell us you know better than us about religion. Not interested," a young man told Eddie and his companion.

Older residents who remembered gratefully the United States' role in defeating Germany in World War II were less hostile, but they still made clear Norway should be allowed to forge its own destiny in both the oil industry and religion, as if Statoil and the State Church were opposite sides of the same coin. In truth, the venting by Stavanger residents against American businesses and Mormonism reflected a widespread uneasiness about the changes their new-found oil wealth might bring, particularly to their small, picturesque city. They loved the beauty of Norway's fjords and forests and did not want the oil industry to create the kinds of environmental and social problems plaguing other Western nations. The State Church symbolized a Norway they hoped would not succumb to modernization.

The missionaries were baffled by the idea that their proselytizing represented a type of religious imperialism not unlike American economic imperialism. Many of the Stavanger missionaries saw an indirect connection between Statoil and the Norwegians rejection of their gospel message, because it played to a common complaint among the missionaries: god-less socialism was corroding the Norwegians' religious sensibilities. "The government gives Norwegians everything they need," said one elder. "Free healthcare, sick leave whenever they want, paid holidays, free college, and practically guaranteed jobs. They think they don't need God or religion because the government gives them everything."

Several missionaries nodded in agreement and offered their own critiques. "Mothers are working and sending their children to childcare instead of staying home and raising their kids like the prophet says."

"You know how in the Book of Mormon, when people become wicked, they are cursed with a famine or warfare or something to humble them, so they turn their hearts back to God, well, because of socialism, the Norwegians don't suffer want and so are not humble enough to see they need God."

"But doesn't the government have some responsibility to help reduce poverty and provide for the general good?"

"Not through socialism."

"Jesus said the poor are always with us."

Eddie got along reasonably well with his companions, especially the greenie from Denver who picked up the language quickly and didn't let rejection or the monotony of tracting discourage him. "My older brother went to Belgium, and he said if he could survive two years on a mission, he could do anything," Eddie's young companion said. "So I get up every day and say, if I can do this, I can do anything."

Eddie didn't think the Stavanger missionaries were getting rejected more often—or with any greater vehemence—than they had in Bergen. The only difference was Stavanger residents sometimes added a few observations voicing fears of expected changes to their city. His second companion, Elder Swanson, incorporated their concerns into his door approach. After introducing himself, he said, "In times of rapid change, a sound religious or spiritual grounding can help us hold onto the truly valuable things in our lives. Do you worry about any possible changes here in Stavanger that might disrupt traditional values or cherished ways of living?"

It was a brilliant approach. Many Norwegians had ready answers that led into thoughtful discussions of religion and spirituality, and some invited the elders to return and teach the discussions. Eddie touted the approach to the other missionaries in the Stavanger district, giving full credit to Elder Swanson, and the two elders cowrote an article for the *Gospel Net* about the importance of showing people how the gospel can address their everyday problems and concerns. Eddie didn't find the golden investigator every missionary yearns for, but he was making progress and holding up his end of the deal, and thanks to Elder Swanson's insight, he improved his standing in the Mission Comparative. He had not forgotten President Toressen's advice to look within his heart to measure success. *But what, exactly, had Toressen meant? Was he referring to my success as missionary or to my success in resolving my unique problem?* Eddie didn't know what his heart was telling him, and so the Mission Comparative still loomed large in his pursuit of the deal.

Eddie could tell that his third companion, Elder Ellington, came from money. Whereas most elders had only two or three suits, Elder Ellington had six, four woolen suits for the colder months and two silk suits for the summer. All tailored for an exquisite fit and with ties to match. The cuffs of his heavily starched shirts crinkled audibly when he gestured with his hands. Although he also was generous in sharing snacks and drinks he purchased during long days of tracting, Elder Ellington did not flaunt his money, nor was there anything snobbish or condescending about his manner. His pleasing smile attracted people to his side, and he carried himself with an erect posture that marked him as a leader. What Eddie liked best about Elder Ellington was his broad-minded outlook. Coming from New Jersey, where he attended a private prep school, he had been exposed to a variety of people, opinions, and ideas. Rather than disparage Norway's welfare state, he praised the government for how well it provided Norwegians with life's basic necessities, thus giving them the time and resources to pursue personal happiness. And while he obeyed the mission rules just as well as anyone, he did not have a superstitious need to roll at of bed at precisely at 6:30 a.m. or climb into it at 10:30 p.m., lest he incur God's disapproval. "The rules were made for the missionaries, not the missionaries for the rules," he liked to say. Eddie envied Elder Ellington's natural confidence and contentment with who he was.

While tracting in the Våland area, they met a man who smiled knowingly throughout Elder Ellington's door approach, as if he were already familiar with the message. After Elder Ellington finished, the man turned and called back into the house. "Tom," he said, "the missionaries from the Mormon Church have found you again." Addressing Eddie and his companion, the man said, "My roommate, Tom, took your lessons when he lived in Bergen. He said the missionaries were pleasant, intelligent young men. I'm sure he'd like to say hello." The man put out his hand, "My name is Haakon—you know, like the king."

Eddie gave the man's hand a firm grip, his heart beating with hopeful anticipation. *Could this man, Tom, be primed to accept Mormonism?*

Eddie's elation turned to alarm when Tom appeared at the door. It was Tom Haugen, the homosexual man from Bergen.

"Hello, Elder Pedersen. It is so nice to see you again. You are not stalking me, are you?" he asked in a teasing manner.

Eddie forced a smile as Tom explained to Haakon and Elder Ellington that Eddie was one of the missionaries who taught him the discussions in Fyllingsdalen. "I cannot remember the name of your companion," Tom said.

"Elder Ward."

"Oh, yes. Rather straight-laced but still charming in his own way."

"Do you want to come in and chat for a bit?" Haakon asked. "I could put on some tea."

"We are busy right now," Eddie said, a nervous quiver in his voice. "We can visit another time."

Elder Ellington shot Eddie a disapproving glance. "No, we are not. We would love to talk with you," he said, stepping into their home. Eddie reluctantly followed. As they took seats in the living room, Tom asked Eddie about his activities since their last meeting, inquiring how he liked Stavanger and talking to Eddie as if they were old friends catching up. Tom met Haakon at a nursing conference in Stavanger and they moved in together soon after. Haakon, who had never before talked with the missionaries, wanted to know all about Eddie and Elder Ellington, such as where they lived in the United States, where they had lived in Norway, and whether they were having any success. "It must be terribly hard trying to convert Norwegians," he said. "We do not go to church, except on holidays or special occasions, like a marriage ceremony. But it is the State Church where we are baptized and confirmed."

"And it is in the State Church where we will be buried," Tom added, laughing.

Haakon regarded Eddie with a familiarity that made him wonder what Tom had told him. Except for President Toressen, Tom was the only person in Norway who knew about Eddie's problem. His stomach churned throughout the conversation, fearful that Tom or Haakon would inadvertently unmask him. Tom and Haakon sat comfortably close on the couch together, and once Haakon touched Tom's leg affectionately while making a point.

Elder Ellington steered the conversation toward Mormonism. "How long did you take the discussions, Tom?"

"Elder Pedersen might remember better than I do. We met at least a half dozen times, did we not?"

Eddie replied tersely, "Yes, that is right."

Becoming animated, Tom continued, "We talked about the first Mormon prophet, Joseph Smith, and the Book of Mormon, which he translated from gold plates. That was fascinating. At our last meeting, you told me about your health code—"

"The Word of Wisdom," Elder Elkington said.

"Yes, and we read from the New Testament, where Jesus said to seek truth, and the truth will set you free. I like that scripture."

"That is in the third discussion," Elder Ellington said, nodding approvingly. After a short pause, he said, "Tom, it sounds like you enjoyed talking with Elder Pedersen and his companion about the church. Why did you stop taking the discussions?"

Eddie blanched, and he squeezed his hands into a tight ball. Tom glanced at Eddie, as if looking for guidance on how to answer. "I am a homosexual man," he said at last, "and Elder Pedersen told me homosexuals are not allowed in your church."

"They are not allowed in any Christian church," Elder Ellington said sternly. "Do you not want to change?"

"No, I like how I am."

Haakon reached over and took Tom's hand in his. "And I like how he is too."

Elder Ellington's eyes narrowed into tiny daggers. "I understand, then, why Elder Pedersen stopped teaching you." He stood and picked up his briefcase, signaling his intention to leave. "I guess there is no reason for us to continue this discussion."

Elder Ellington's abrupt change in demeanor angered Haakon, but Tom looked at Eddie apologetically and then reached out his hand. "It was nice to see you again, Elder Pedersen," he said. Eddie shook hands with both men, relieved the conversation was over, and followed his companion out the door.

"When they said they were homosexuals, you could feel an evil spirit enter the room," Elder Ellington said. "I was so . . . so appalled and sickened, I had to get out of there, like Joseph fleeing Potiphar's wife. Elder Pedersen will tell you; he was there." He pointed to Eddie but continued with his story before Eddie had a chance to answer. "I didn't even shake their hands before we left. Elder Pedersen did, but I couldn't bring myself to do it."

The Stavanger missionaries shook their heads in disgust as Elder Ellington recounted the details of their visit with two homosexual men. Elder Ellington had exploded in righteous indignation as soon as they left the men's home, and he continued venting the rest of the week, as if he were rehearsing for Sunday's district meeting. "Can you believe the gall of those perverts, living together in gross immorality as if it were perfectly acceptable," he said. "It made my skin crawl when I saw them holding hands."

"Ewwww," the sisters said, causing unsuppressed laughter among the eight district missionaries. After Elder Ellington finished his account, each missionary tried to outdo the others with expressions of horror and revulsion at the brazen display of homosexuality. One of the sisters drew a connection between socialism and tolerance of homosexuality. Two of the elders began talking about faggots and queers and mocking homosexuals in ways that elicited snickering and then a rebuke from the district leader. "Don't get carried away with lightmindedness, Elders," he said. "Joking about wickedness can invite in the evil one's spirit."

Eddie mulled silently over the fury and loathing directed at homosexuals. Such expressions of visceral distaste was common among boys and young men, but Eddie was shaken by the looks of horror and repugnance on the faces of the sisters, who he thought would be more sympathetic and forgiving. Of all the missionaries Eddie had known, he had expected Elder Ellington to be less parochial in his attitude. Eddie tried so hard, wanted so desperately to be good. The pitiless reaction of the elders and sisters crushed his spirit—it broke his heart.

Chapter 24

When entering homes, use the flannel board to arouse interest. Let contacts see how it works.

A Uniform System for Teaching Investigators

As Apostle Prichard predicted, President Toressen's controversial remarks to the Norwegian press reverberated throughout the small nation. The mission president's bold denunciation of the State Church shocked the missionaries as much as it did church authorities, perhaps even more so, because the missionaries knew they would bear the brunt of the Norwegians' furious reaction. Everyone expected the worst. A gallows humor took hold among the elders and sisters, who began speculating about how many doors would be slammed in their faces or whether they would become even more unpopular than Jehovah's Witnesses. Their district leaders, who normally kept a tight lid on lightmindedness, let the missionaries vent their fears. They, too, felt a storm coming.

Then a miracle happened. As President Toressen had anticipated, his speech spurred intense interest in Mormonism. Everywhere the missionaries tracted, whether in the larger cities or smaller towns, everyone wanted to talk about the speech. Many were stirred to anger and berated the missionaries, telling them the Mormons had no right to come to their country and criticize their State Church. "Go back to America and tell your President Nixon to stop bombing innocent Vietnamese people," the missionaries heard on more than one occasion. But the number of slamming doors and indignant rejections was no more than usual. More often, people affirmed President Toressen's characterization of the State Church and voiced complaints of their own about the state-sponsored religion. "We give the state priests our tax money and the pews sit empty on Sundays," a man told a pair of Drammen elders. "If people weren't forced to support the State Church, they would have to close most of the churches and dismiss all but a few priests." Missionaries throughout Norway got invited into homes and taught more discussions than at any time during their missions. Not everyone was genuinely interested in joining the church, but Toressen's speech had sparked their curiosity. And the missionaries, always hopeful, reveled in the opportunities to teach and perhaps bring someone into the fold. The surge in activity reinforced their belief that President Toressen was the prophet over Norway, while also reinvigorating their efforts to be inspired prophets over their own areas of responsibility.

One of those determined to be a prophet over his proselytizing area was Orrin Tanner. As Orrin moved higher and higher on the Mission Comparative, he became more confident in his role as a missionary, noting with satisfaction that he was outperforming Elder Pedersen, whose seemingly effortless achievements had stoked Orrin's feelings of envy and resentment. However, his goal wasn't to outperform Elder Pedersen but to become a missionary deserving of God's approbation and, most importantly, a tangible spiritual witness.

President Toressen's frank recounting of his visions and spiritual experiences had compelled Orrin to reflect on what, exactly, he was expecting from God. Orrin's testimony rested on the exhilarating joy, as well as the serene contentment—the welling up in his breast and tears of gratitude—he felt when he read a faith-promoting story in the church's *Ensign* magazine or listened to the testimony of someone who was once lost but had returned to the church. But those simple, quiet feelings of spiritual exhilaration were not unlike his emotional response to a heartwarming Christmas movie or an inspirational story in the *Reader's Digest.* Moreover, the spirit's stirring uplift—the burning in the heart—proved elusive under Norway's grueling and, essentially, unrewarding work. The lack of success increased Orrin's desire for a sign, something to tell him he was on the right track. Orrin's deal with God was this: complete dedication, going above and beyond the mission's requirements to outperform all Norwegian missionaries, in return for an unambiguous sign.

Is this a blasphemous desire? The ancient apostle dubbed Doubting Thomas has endured centuries of scorn for his lack of faith, and yet, did not Jesus oblige Thomas by allowing him to see and touch the crucifixion wounds upon his hands? Was not Orrin's desire evidence of faith, rather than doubt, because he believed wholeheartedly that God would make good on his promise of revelation? Grandpa Heber and President Toressen stood as examples that visions and revelations are not reserved for the church's General Authorities alone. Each man is a prophet of his own domain. And so Orrin strived for more than a good feeling. He wanted an outpouring of heavenly gifts that were so common in early church history, manifestations that brought indisputable knowledge and confirmation that he was favored of God, just as the young prophet Samuel had been. Each night Orrin laid before the Lord his sacrifices, the extra miles he trod each day. "Speak, Lord, for thy servant heareth," Orrin pleaded after a night of wrestling in prayer. In the silence, he heard only the clamoring noise of shoppers and streetcars passing below his window.

The silence drove Orrin to try even harder. He watched the Mission

Comparative closely and listened to the missionaries as they discussed the accomplishments of others. If a missionary pair in Trondheim placed ten copies of the Book of Mormon one week, he and Elder Gregersen made sure they placed eleven the next, even if it meant cutting short their free time on Saturday to work additional hours until they reached their goal. If he heard that an elder or sister was rising at six in the morning to do extra study, Orrin would rise at five thirty. Orrin harangued Elder Gregersen into rising early with him, which prompted, for the first time, some resistance from the greenie.

"I'll be too tired to study," Elder Gregersen said. "I won't remember anything."

"The Lord will bless you for your diligence and hard work. Look at me," Orrin said.

"You look tired too."

Orrin picked up a notecard and wrote, "I awake every morning recharged and refreshed and ready to study and work." He taped the notecard beside the other affirmations above Elder Gregersen's bed. "Here," he said, "read this every day and soon you'll be getting up without any trouble."

Elder Gregersen eyed the card skeptically but agreed to try waking early with Orrin. He lasted three days. Within fifteen minutes of rising, he was asleep in his chair, study materials on his lap. He slept on the streetcar going out each morning and when returning in the evening. Orrin pushed him to continue waking early, assuring him he would get used to it, until Elder Gregersen fell asleep while they were teaching a discussion. The embarrassing incident persuaded Orrin to allow Elder Gregersen to rise at the normal time, but he gave permission in a begrudging tone that suggested his companion was not fully committed to the work. Orrin's petulance was partly related to exhaustion. Had he been truthful with himself, he would have seen that not only was he getting up too early each day, but he and his companion were working too many hours. He noted that Elder Gregersen took down the affirmation about rising early in the morning and replaced it with another that said, "I love tracting." Orrin shook his head ruefully. He knew how his companion felt. Still, he never considered slowing down. He welcomed the stress and weariness, regarding it as a sacrifice that would bring forth blessings from the Lord. And so Orrin rose early and went out day after day with grim determination and cheerless optimism.

Søster Poulsen told Orrin she believed in Mormonism, but she had not received a spiritual witness of its truthfulness. She had already stopped drinking alcohol and coffee, as required by the Word of Wisdom, but she remained addicted to nicotine. "Your cigarette habit is holding you back,"

Orrin said. "The Holy Ghost cannot enter an unclean body. If you give up smoking, you will purify your body and make it a vessel worthy of a spiritual witness."

"I have tried many times, Elder Tanner, but I cannot do it. If I put my cigarettes away, I quickly start craving another. You talk as if it is easy, but it is not."

"The Lord will help you. He has helped many people overcome their addictions and other problems." Orrin then offered to give Søster Poulsen a blessing, which she readily accepted.

"I will try anything."

Orrin and Elder Gregersen returned the next afternoon with consecrated oil. They first knelt in prayer with Søster Poulsen, who asked for God's strength and guidance, and then, rising, she took a seat on a kitchen chair. Elder Gregersen anointed the crown of her head with a few drops of oil and each elder placed his hands on her head.

"Søster Siri Poulsen," Orrin began. Having never before given anyone a blessing, he paused, waiting—hoping—for inspiration. His heart was full; he yearned to discern God's still, soft voice. He felt a sensation in his breast, the same sense of wonderment as when long ago, he stared at Kolob pulsating in the night. "The Lord has heard your prayers and knows your righteous desires," Orrin said. "I bless you with the strength to overcome your addiction to cigarettes and nicotine. If you are faithful to the Lord's commandments and hearken unto His word, you will receive the spiritual witness you seek. I pronounce these blessings upon you in the name of Jesus Christ. Amen."

Søster Poulsen remained seated, her head bowed, tears on her cheeks. Never before had Orrin felt the spirit so strongly. "God has given you a great gift," Orrin said. "I am confident you will succeed in your desire to stop smoking."

"Amen," said Elder Gregersen, who regarded Orrin with awe.

The burning in his breast, a lightness of feeling, returned when he knelt in prayer before bedtime. "Speak, Lord, for thy servant heareth," he said, fervently awaiting answer. He heard nothing, but while sleeping, he dreamed of lions on a sandy beach who roared with divine thunder each time the Kjelsås streetcar screeched to a clattering halt outside his window. Norwegians bundled in hats and coats of fur stepped purposefully into the streetcars and took their seats, unaware of the glorious prize God had prepared for them at His table. And the lions roared.

While they continued teaching Søster Poulsen, Orrin and his companion met a woman, Søster Karin Ryland, who had taken all six discussion a few years earlier but had been forced to stop because her husband objected. They knocked on her door in the late morning while her husband was at work. "I would like to be baptized, but I cannot without my husband's permission," she explained. "That is the law in Norway. But I would like you to visit me. The missionaries bring a spirit of comfort and peace whenever they come into my home."

The situation baffled Orrin. The mission handbook directed missionaries to teach families, with a particular emphasis on converting husbands as the heads of households. The missionaries sometimes encountered odd individuals, misfits really, and Orrin was uncertain whether Søster Ryland was a golden investigator or an eccentric individual craving friendship. Of course, in Norway, simply believing in Mormonism marked one as eccentric. But otherwise, Søster Ryland appeared to be a rational, sober individual. About fifty years old with graying hair and conservative dress, she understood the basic principles of the gospel and had given up smoking and drinking. The missionaries who first visited her abruptly stopped coming after her husband called the then-mission president to complain. But now Søster Ryland asked Orrin and Elder Gregersen to resume their visits, suggesting they come on weekday afternoons while her husband was at work. The idea of secret meetings bothered Orrin, but in all his probing he could find no reason to doubt Søster Ryland's story or her testimony.

"We can continue visiting you," Orrin said, "but I am not sure what to teach you, given that you have already been taught all six discussions."

"Surely, Elder Tanner, there must be more to The Church of Jesus Christ of Latter-day Saints than is contained in those discussions," she replied. "Is there not more you can tell me?"

"You are right," Orrin said, chagrined by her response. "Of course, there is more to Mormonism." However, the *Missionary Handbook* stipulated that the missionaries should teach only the elementary doctrines and practices of the church. What could he and Elder Gregersen discuss with Søster Ryland? And that's when Orrin got the idea to share with her the stories from *Tanner's Faith-Promoting Series*, the pamphlets published by his father that, in Orrin's view, would illustrate and confirm Mormonism's fundamental principles for Søster Ryland without sidetracking into the obscure doctrines and teachings.

Orrin and his companion returned the following Tuesday at noon, their agreed-upon time for weekly appointments. Søster Ryland greeted them with a prim smile, dressed as if she were attending church. She was heavily painted with lipstick and makeup, had her grey hair tied in bun, and wore a plain blue dress. On the coffee table was a pot of herbal tea, *smørbrød*, and fruit. She thanked the elders as she poured the tea, saying it was a great joy to commune with the Mormon missionaries again. She set down the teapot and placed her hands in her lap. "So what will we talk about today?" she asked.

Orrin told her about his father's pamphlets containing the faith-promoting stories of everyday Latter-day Saints. "They are very popular and widely used in church talks and cited in academic books on church history and doctrine," he said, "and so they will expand your knowledge of Mormonism's basic tenets." Orrin had selected Grandpa Heber's story as the first one he would relate because it was the first pamphlet in the faith-promoting series and he knew it well, which made it easier for him to translate it into Norwegian for Søster Ryland. He read to her the following story:

The summer Heber C. Tanner returned home from his mission to France, he was shot in the face and lay comatose for three days while doctors tried to save him. The bullet entered his left temple and shredded his left eye. The side of his face was so mangled that the doctors could not tell whether the bullet was still lodged in his eye socket. Not wishing to cause more harm by searching for the bullet, they simply cleaned and dressed the wound, uncertain whether Heber would survive. The elders from the church came and gave Heber a blessing, promising if it were God's will, he would live to accomplish many great deeds in the name of the Lord. Brother Josiah Hoagland pronounced the blessing, saying Heber, hanging precariously between this life and the next, had embarked on a mysterious journey, and only God could send him back to his family and friends. "Thy will be done," Brother Hoagland said as a half dozen hands quivered on Heber's head.

While the family stood vigil over Heber, they prepared the funeral for his brother Orrin.

Heber and Orrin Tanner, the eldest sons in a family of eight children, grew up on a cattle ranch just outside the Mormon village of Seth, about one hundred miles south of Salt Lake City. Heber was born in 1880 and his brother followed a year later. By everyone's account, the two boys were inseparable companions, with Heber acting the part of mentor and spiritual guide. He taught his younger brother to swim when he was three, ride a horse when he was four, and read when he was five. As they grew older, when the two boys performed chores together, they would discuss the latest lesson, whether from church or school, and at the end of the day they would challenge each other in wide-ranging tests of knowledge. Heber was loving and solicitous in tutoring Orrin, and he took delight in his younger brother's accomplishments. Everyone in the small Utah town considered Orrin a genius, marveling at the mental

206

and physical capabilities exhibited in a boy so young. No one considered that Heber, only a year older, not only possessed the very same talents but was imparting them effortlessly to his younger brother. Orrin was not spoiled by the attention, but absorbed it naturally, as if he were destined for greatness. He returned his brother's love with equal fervor, allowing Heber to mold his receptive mind, trusting his wisdom and good intentions, never doubting the efficacy of the lessons.

Heber was dark-haired, husky, pensive, and controlled; Orrin was blond, slender, impetuous, and prone to mischief and laughter. A family photograph from when they were about eight and nine shows them posing by a river where they had been skipping stones: Heber holds several stones in one hand and demonstrates the correct throwing motion with his other hand, while Orrin, smiling wryly at the camera, tries to recreate his brother's pose. They stood next to a tall oak tree, a fitting symbol, because the brothers would grow like two oaks sprouting from different sides of a river, each standing firmly on his own; but below the river, their roots stretched far and deep, intertwined and drinking nourishment from the same moist soil. Above the river their long, sturdy branches grew together, making it hard to see where one tree began and the other left off.

When it came time for Heber and Orrin to go on missions, each agreed to drop out of Brigham Young Academy to help support the family while the other brought converts to Mormonism. Orrin intended to do so when Heber, at age nineteen, left for a mission to France, but local church authorities would not hear of it. "I have got a letter here from President Cluff, and he says they want Orrin to come with them on the school's expedition to search out Book of Mormon artifacts in South America," Bishop Miller told the boys' parents. "When the president of the academy takes notice, you know he has got talent that ought not be wasted."

With his parent's blessing, Orrin returned to Brigham Young Academy, excelling in history and church doctrine, while Heber served his mission in France. Bishop Miller opened the church's storehouse to the Tanners whenever they lacked food while the boys were away.

Heber returned two years later while Orrin was home preparing to leave on his own mission to Norway. Working the fields together, the young men fell quickly into their old relationship as Heber discoursed for hours about missionary life. Orrin, who was now an expert in Book of Mormon geography, told Heber about the ancient Nephite and Lamanite ruins they discovered on their trip to South America.

"It's truly awe-inspiring, Heber," Orrin said, his eyes wide with enthusiasm. "Fabulous cities rise from the jungles and mountains, surrounded by the

207

most primitive and uncivilized Indian natives, who today are no more capable of building these remarkable structures than they are capable of building locomotive engines or giant steel factories. You look at these ancient cities and you know without a doubt the Book of Mormon is objectively true."

The whole town of Seth came to Orrin's missionary farewell, held in late August. Most noteworthy was the appearance of Apostle Erastus G. Lyman, one the church's top leaders, who had been following Orrin's progress at Brigham Young Academy. Bishop Miller ordered all the windows of the church opened, allowing the dry desert air to flow through the one-room chapel as a hundred fans waved furiously in the afternoon heat. Women with small children stood outside beneath the windows, rocking their babies gently under the shade of the poplars surrounding the church. "Orrin is one of the Lord's special spirits, held back until the latter days to come to earth and serve the Lord," Brother Lyman declared. Lyman was short, squarely built, and spoke with the authority of one who as a young boy had crossed the plains with the early Mormon pioneers, walking the entire distance across Nebraska and Wyoming and into the valley of the Great Salt Lake. Turning to Orrin, he said, "The Lord has an important mission for you. Keep your thoughts pure and your body clean so that you might serve Him well. No matter what your success, remain humble, remembering you are a vessel through which the Lord accomplishes his sacred plans."

When Apostle Lyman finished, the congregation shouted "Amen" with a fervor that rivaled the early sermons of the prophet Joseph Smith. Apostle Lyman had admonished Orrin to be humble, but the people of Seth received no such instruction, and they puffed up in pride because a General Authority had paid homage to the town's most gifted son. Orrin's spiritual triumphs in Norway would be their own.

The next day, Heber and Orrin were laying rocks in a new well when they received word that the Seth bank had been robbed. They quickly saddled a pair of horses and rode to town, discovering that the sheriff's posse had left only minutes before in pursuit of the criminals. While riding to catch up with the posse, Heber noticed some tracks leading up a seldom-used trail through the canyon. He and Orrin decided to investigate. When the posse found them two hours later, Heber was holding Orrin's head on his blood-soaked lap, pleading furiously for God to spare his life. The robbers—there were two of them—had been hiding behind trees. They shot Heber and Orrin without warning, grabbed their horses, and left the boys for dead. Blood dripped from Heber's eye as he prayed over his brother, whose face had been blasted away by a shotgun.

"We've got to get you to a doctor," the sheriff said, trying to lift Heber to his feet.

"I can save him, I can save him," Heber said, his armed locked around his brother's neck. "I can, I can."

"It's too late, Heber, your brother is dead," the sheriff said.

"I can, I can!"

The men wept as they struggled to free Orrin from his brother's viselike grip. When Heber finally realized his beloved brother was dead, he screamed with a vehemence and pain that pierced the heavens. "Why, Lord, oh why? Why Orrin and not me?" he shouted, and then fell into a coma. The murderers escaped with three hundred dollars.

A mournful crowd gathered for the funeral. Their dark faces mocked the joyful "Amen" that only four days earlier had concluded Orrin's missionary farewell. Apostle Lyman had not yet left town when the posse carried Heber and Orrin back to Seth, and so he remained behind to preside at the funeral. The people of Seth waited with great anticipation to hear from Lyman, who, many felt, had some explaining to do. Had he not, just a few days earlier, confidently prophesied of Orrin's missionary success?

Orrin's family occupied the first three rows; his mother and father sat directly in front of the coffin. The mortician, such as Seth had, labored nearly two days with Orrin but finally concluded his face was too mangled for an open coffin, and so it lay closed. On top of the coffin, his parents had a collection of photographs dating from when Orrin was born to his last year at Brigham Young Academy.

"God moves in mysterious ways," Apostle Lyman declared as he began his sermon. His body sagged, and his fists clenched the sides of the podium as if he were trying to keep himself from collapsing to the floor. "During the past three days I have prayed to God to reveal the meaning of Orrin's death, to give me some inspiration so what I say here today will provide comfort to Orrin's family and loved ones. I regret to tell you . . ." At this point Lyman bowed his head and choked back a cry. The far-off rumble of a distant storm filled the chapel as if with a sob, and the people of Seth wondered how they would endure this terrible tragedy. Apostle Lyman raised his head and stared over the congregation, waiting, it was thought, to regain his composure, but his gaze remained so firmly fixed, his eyes burning, that the people turned to see.

There are no contemporary accounts of this event, but many of those attending the funeral left reminiscences describing the ghastly personage they saw marching toward the stand. Heber had been lying in bed at home, for Seth had no hospitals, when he awakened from his coma minutes before the funeral began. He seemed to know immediately where he was and what his own condition had been. When the lone girl left to watch over him told Heber everyone was at the funeral, he insisted on going. Despite the girl's entreaties, he dressed himself and walked half a mile across town to the church.

In their reminiscences, Heber's neighbors described him as "dreadful," "ghostly pale," and "cadaverous." Sister Floridia Robinson, an old family friend, said "he looked as one neither alive nor quite yet dead." Wrapped round his head and covering his left eye were ragged, blood-stained bandages, which the doctor had not changed for fear of causing further damage. His long, black hair, greasy and disheveled, sprouted like dark weeds through the bandages, while a three-day stubble highlighted his fearsome pallor. This seeming apparition walked slowly past the coffin to the podium, silently acknowledging his family and friends with a nod and a penetrating glance through his remaining eye, unaware he looked as dead as the man they had come to bury.

"I wish to speak," he told Apostle Lyman, who, too astonished to resist, stepped aside. Heber drew in his breath, as if collecting his strength, and began. "It is not easy to fathom the mind of God. His thoughts are not our thoughts; His ways are not our ways. When my brother was killed, I nearly cursed God, and so deep was my grief that I fell ill and was nigh unto death myself. But in my sleep, or at least my bodily sleep, I was visited by an angel, who bid me follow into the next life. He told me he was my guardian angel but otherwise said nothing. We walked for miles through a barren wilderness and then crossed a bridge spanning a large, bottomless chasm. On the other side was a beautiful garden, with flowers and trees and benches for sitting. 'Why are we here?' I asked.

"'Watch,' the angel said.

"Soon people began coming into the garden, picking fruits and berries, which they placed in baskets, and then they rested on the benches. More people entered, and they ate of the fruit and drank wine from the berries, after which they began preaching the gospel to those sitting on the benches. One of those preaching was my brother, Orrin. 'He's alive!' I shouted. I waved excitedly to him.

"'He cannot hear you.'

"'What is he doing?'

"'Christ also went and preached unto the spirits in prison,' said the angel, quoting scripture. 'For this cause was the gospel preached also to them that are dead, that they might be judged according to men in the flesh but live according to God in the spirit.'

"'But they are not in prison.'

"'There are no bars,' he said. 'But they are imprisoned by their own appetites. They hunger, but cannot eat; they thirst, but cannot drink. Only when they accept the fullness of the Gospel can they be released from the prison of their desires.'

Heber closed his one good eye and drew in another breath of inspiration. "And so it was given to me to understand that my brother Orrin was part of God's glorious plan for the redemption of man, preaching to those who died without hearing the gospel in this life, but who are given a chance in the next life to accept Christ's sacrificial gift and win eternal life. I watched Orrin preach. He is a masterful orator. And he repeated many of the sermons he practiced while we worked in the fields. The missionaries in the spirit prison—and it is a spirit prison just as the Prophet Joseph Smith said—teach two-by-two just as we do here. I saw Orrin accompanied by a young woman, who held his hand as they both preached to the spirits.

"'Your brother is serving an extraordinary mission,' the angel said.

"'I know.'

"'And you have been given a great gift. To whom much is given, much is expected.'

"'This I also know.'

"My guardian angel led me back over the bridge and pointed to the path through the wilderness. 'You know the way from here,' he said, and I began to—"

Heber stopped suddenly. He had grown stronger as he told his story, the color returning to his face, the light to his eye, but he spoke barely above a whisper when he pointed to the coffin and asked, "Who is the woman in this photograph?"

Necks strained to see, but no one answered. People looked at one another and shrugged.

"It's Eliza, Eliza Ann Martin . . . my daughter," said a woman no one knew. An unprepossessing woman, she was veiled and dressed in black, and spoke hesitantly, as if disconcerted by the attention.

"That's the woman who was preaching with Orrin in the spirit world," exclaimed Heber, again pointing to the picture of Orrin standing among his schoolmates.

"Eliza said she and Orrin planned to get married," her mother explained. "But she got influenza and died last month. Her dying words were that she loved Orrin and wished to be sealed to him. That is why we have come to the funeral."

At this moment, according to those who left a record of this event, the spirit blew through the open windows with such power that the room grew visibly brighter. The once-somber funeral turned spontaneously into a jubilant testimony meeting. Men and women, weeping unashamedly, shared their most intimate spiritual experiences and testified of God's goodness and grace and of the truthfulness of the gospel as revealed to God's latter-day prophet, Joseph

211

Smith. Instead of ending with the traditional funeral hymn, "God Be With You 'Til We Meet Again," everyone joined hands singing "The Spirit of God Like A Fire Is Burning," one of early Mormonism's most inspirational and joyous hymns.

> *The Spirit of God like a fire is burning*
> *The latter-day glory begins to come forth*
> *The visions and blessings of old are returning*
> *And angels are coming to visit the earth*
> *We'll sing and we'll shout with the armies of heaven*
> *Hosanna, hosanna, to God and the Lamb!*
> *Let glory to them in the highest be given*
> *Henceforth and forever, Amen and Amen!*

For the rest of the hour, Orrin and Elder Gregersen used dialogue from the fifth discussion to remind Søster Ryland of the scriptures and of Mormon teachings that point to preaching in the afterlife. "If a person does not get the chance to hear the complete gospel here on earth, how does he receive that opportunity?" Elder Gregersen asked.

"In the spirit world," she said, as if reading from the discussion script.

At one o'clock, Søster Ryland announced the visit must end. "I need time to clean up before my husband returns from work," she said. "That was a lovely story about your grandfather and his brother, Elder Tanner. Your name is also Orrin, is it not?"

"I was named for him."

"And now you are a missionary in Norway."

"My Grandpa Heber thinks I'm serving the mission his brother never got a chance to serve."

"Ah, great expectations," Søster Ryland sighed. "I am sure you are living up to them."

Chapter 25

Do not become idle or complacent but give yourselves in complete surrender to your missionary appointment.

Conduct of a Missionary

Something snapped in Eddie. That's how his companion would later describe it, though he couldn't pinpoint exactly when it occurred. But over a short period, the formerly restrained and polite Elder Pedersen became a strident, full-steam-ahead missionary: quarrelsome, impatient, and not at all shy when he felt the need to castigate missionaries, members, and investigators who fell short of the mark. Eddie would disagree. Nothing snapped inside; rather, a lightbulb went off in his head. It happened while he was listening to Elder Tanner drone on and on about some new missionary technique that by Elder Tanner's estimation, he had miraculously uncovered through hard work and the words of inspiration he carried around in his silly little Inspirational Thought Book. Elder Tanner was the epitome of the perfect missionary, consistently at the top of the Mission Comparative while simultaneously managing to work *and* study more hours than any other missionary. If that weren't enough, his fellow missionaries had come to regard him as a leading scholar of church doctrine and history. Elder Tanner epitomized the stick-up-his-ass missionary and so, in Eddie's mind, served as the poster boy for missionaries who cruelly reviled homosexuals. That was Eddie's lightbulb insight: if Elder Tanner, the consummate Mormon missionary, knew about Eddie, he would surely censure him with a hundred scriptures denouncing homosexuality and burn him at a thousand stakes. *Write that down in your precious Inspirational Thought Book, Elder Tanner.*

Eddie's arrest by the BYU campus police had unleashed a parade of humiliations. After being forced to confess to his bishop and parents, he underwent reparative "shock-cock" therapy subjecting him to the most degrading experimental treatment that did nothing to cure his homosexual urges. The bruises on his arm and thigh remained as physical reminders of his mortification and shame. He had done everything required, paid every price to obtain forgiveness and be cured of his sinful condition. But despite his efforts to be obedient and faithful—and he had been obedient and faithful—no change occurred, no salvation was tendered. Was God taunting him, telling him he could never change? Why else give him a companion like Elder Jensen with whom he would fall in love? And running into Tom Haugen twice, first in Bergen and then Stavanger, forcing him to repeatedly confront his homosexuality. The one golden family the Lord saw fit to give Eddie turned out to be a prank—a cosmic joke, just like his life. The final depressing blow came when the elders and sisters unleashed a torrent of hatred and abuse at Tom Haugen and his partner. But Eddie had seen the light. He vowed to outperform all the missionaries, including and especially Elder Tanner. If these preening sycophants and pretenders were God's elect few, then Eddie would show God (and them) he was made of sterner stuff. He would beat them at their own game and make it impossible for God to renege on the deal.

Eddie's companion, a greenie named Elder Steven Wilson, followed his lead. Eddie took advantage of the uproar over President Toressen's speech by scripting a new door approach that jumped right into the controversy. "I am sure you have heard about the remarks by our mission president criticizing State Church priests," Eddie would say. "Some people tell us he was too harsh and have taken offense, but other people say they agree with him that the State Church has failed to meet the needs of the people. What do you think?" For those who had forgotten or were unaware of the controversy, Eddie would show them the headlines from Oslo's major newspapers he carried in his coat pocket.

Nearly everyone had an opinion, and few had much good to say about the State Church. That's not to say they didn't take offense at an outsider taking them to task, but they were disarmed by Eddie's willingness to acknowledge their wounded feelings. Eddie and his companion listened politely, rarely interrupting or disagreeing, and eventually many people who first expressed objections talked themselves into concurring with Toressen's assertions. Invitations to come inside followed. Although other missionary pairs also experienced increased interest in the weeks after Toressen's speech, Eddie's approach stirred the pot and kept the excitement alive among Norwegians. Eddie and his companion moved quickly up the Mission Comparative until they rested in second place behind Elder Tanner and his companion. The Oslo district leader asked Eddie to give a presentation at their Sunday meeting and instruct the missionaries on how to increase their teaching hours.

Much to Eddie's surprise, the missionaries resisted his approach. "You're just reminding the Norwegians of how upset they were," said one elder.

"Yeah, we want to smooth things over so they forget about that stuff," said another. "Aren't we supposed to avoid contentious arguments?"

In the past, Eddie would have softened his response to avoid embarrassing anyone or putting them on the defensive. But he no longer cared whether other missionaries liked him. "I already told you the point is to not argue with people, but to let them state their feelings," Eddie said, adding tersely, "but go ahead and stick with your boring, ineffective door approaches if that makes you happy."

"Hold on there, Elder Pedersen," Elder Tanner said. "Elder Monroe raised a legitimate point. Your approach essentially invites people to be offended. I've had that problem when I try to discuss President Toressen's speech with Norwegians."

"Well, I haven't had any problems, so perhaps it's you and not the approach that's offensive."

Elder Tanner's face reddened. The district leader called an abrupt end to the meeting and afterward pulled Eddie aside, telling him he should apologize to Elder Tanner for speaking so harshly. "It was uncalled for," he said.

"Elder Tanner should be apologizing to me for disrupting my presentation," Eddie said. After some discussion, the district leader gave up trying to persuade Eddie otherwise. Eddie delighted in his feeling of put-upon indignation; he savored the emotion. It felt so much better to be the one sinned against than to be the one sinning, to rain down righteous condemnation rather than be rained upon.

"You burned Elder Tanner good," said Elder Wilson, who felt a defensive pride in his companion's innovative door approach. It had not been Eddie's intention to single out Elder Tanner from the other district missionaries, but it brought immense satisfaction, and so he began looking for opportunities to irritate and ridicule Mr. Perfect. The first came when he and Elder Tanner were speaking with the branch president, Bror Clausen. Elder Tanner spoke Norwegian clearly but with a heavy American accent, so while the two elders conversed with Bror Clausen, Eddie pointedly repeated some of Elder Tanner's words and phrases as if they had been incomprehensible to Bror Clausen. Elder Tanner couldn't help but be embarrassed by the implication the branch president needed Eddie to clarify his words in a clear Norwegian accent that he would never be able to master.

Eddie relished opportunities to shock the other elders, especially if he could fluster and confound the cocksure Elder Tanner. "You know, the mission rules are much like Satan's plan," Eddie remarked after their district leader reproached a missionary for failing to wear his hat during the winter season, as required by the mission rules. Eddie's fellow missionaries stared gape-faced at his assertion. "Look at it this way," Eddie said. "In the preexistence, Satan promised to save everyone who came to earth by forcing them to obey God's commandments. In contrast, Jesus said people should be free to choose right from wrong while, at the same time, he also offered to come to earth himself and provide an example for people to follow."

"But what's that got to do with the missionary rules?" Elder Tanner demanded.

Eddie smirked triumphantly. "Don't you see? The mission rules force us to be good, just as Satan's plan would compel us to follow God's commands. The prophet Joseph Smith understood this. When he was asked how he governed thousands of people in Nauvoo, the prophet said he taught his people correct principles and then they governed themselves."

"We have the free agency in the mission field to choose whether to follow the rules," Elder Tanner countered.

"Well, yeah," Eddie said, his eyes filled with derision. "We can either follow the rules or be sent home in humiliation. By my reckoning, that's not much of a choice." Much to Elder Tanner's disappointment, the district elders nodded their acceptance of Eddie's logic.

On another occasion, when Elder Tanner remarked in a district meeting that he and his companion were washing their temple garments by hand due to the mission rule against sending out garments to be washed, Eddie happily jumped in to needle Elder Tanner. "There's no rule against sending out temple garments. Lots of missionaries do it," Eddie said. Other missionaries concurred.

Elder Tanner looked perplexed. "But I was told we couldn't do it because the laundry people sewed up the sacred markings on the garments."

"That's an old wives' tale, just a bit of missionary folklore that floats around all the missions worldwide," Eddie said, scoffing and laughing in a way that encouraged the other missionaries to join in. Elder Tanner's face flashed with anger and he hung his head, chagrined.

Eddie also saw that Elder Tanner proudly rose earlier than other Norwegian missionaries, as if this represented a sign of righteousness, and so Eddie had Elder Wilson tell Elder Tanner's companion that Eddie was planning to rise at five o'clock in the morning. Sure enough, at the next district meeting, Elder Tanner reported that he had awakened at four thirty each morning the previous week. Eddie snickered when he saw the surprised look on Elder Tanner's face when Eddie reported that he and his companion had awakened at the usual six-thirty hour, though Elder Tanner's tired eyes and haggard expression were reward enough for his prank.

As Eddie and his companion continued to excel in garnering investigators and teaching discussions, the tenor of his nightly prayers changed.

No longer were his prayers characterized by self-recrimination or sorrowful pleadings for forgiveness and help in overcoming his problem. Now when he knelt beside his bed in prayer, he began by recounting the many good deeds he had performed, touting his hard work and commitment to his missionary responsibilities. He continued asking for relief, but with a tone sounding more like a demand than a request that the Lord live up to His end of the deal.

Chapter 26

Simplicity: 1) Follow the discussion dialogues; 2) Stick to the logic and scriptures given in the dialogues; and 3) Answer objections with questions. Avoid the temptation to lecture.

A Uniform System for Teaching Investigators

Missionary work slowed to a halt as Christmas approached. All of Norway went on holiday and celebrated throughout December, or so it seemed to the missionaries. The elders and sisters would bundle up each morning in hats, scarves, gloves, and layers of winter clothes, stand in sub-freezing weather waiting for a bus or streetcar, and slog through wind-whipped snow from one home or apartment building to another, only to find the people were either gone or too busy with Christmas preparations to invite them in. "Come back in January," people said, too full of holiday cheer to tell the missionaries to go away. To alleviate the boredom, some missionary pairs began playing *Trosartikler* during afternoon *middag*. Concerned that *Trosartikler* was distracting missionaries from their calling, district leaders and the assistants consulted with President Toressen, who subsequently issued an edict prohibiting *Trosartikler* at any time except on Saturdays.

"The missionaries should keep their minds focused on their work during weekdays and Sundays, but there's nothing wrong if they want to relax by playing *Trosartikler* on their Preparation Day," Toressen said. "However, Norway has so much to offer that the elders and sisters should really be spending Preparation Day visiting museums and absorbing Norwegian history and culture. That would be a better use of their time."

One of the assistants pointed out that missionaries don't have enough time on Preparation Day for museums or other activities. "Even on P-Day, we're expected to study in the morning and tract in the evening after *middag*," he said. "That leaves only a few hours free for us to write mission reports and letters to home, do our weekly grocery shopping, take clothes to the laundry, and run other errands. We often don't have enough time for even that."

President Toressen responded by formulating a new Preparation Day policy. On the first Saturday of each month, the missionaries would not be required to go out tracting and teaching in the evening, so they would have time during the day to take in a museum, concert, or other cultural offering. "These outings will serve as an essential part of your education and training as a missionary," Toressen wrote in a message to the missionaries.

"It is as important for you to know the Norwegian people as it is for you to know the scriptures."

The Oslo missionaries used their first opportunity to absorb Norwegian culture by visiting the Munch Museum. Home to the world's largest collection of paintings and drawings by the Norwegian artist Edvard Munch, the museum was located at the Toyen subway stop in Gamle Oslo not far from the Kjelsås hybel where Orrin and Elder Gregersen resided. Some of the missionaries were familiar with Munch's famous painting, "The Scream," but most knew nothing about Munch or his work. It was Orrin's first time visiting an art museum.

The grandeur and gravity of the museum intimidated Orrin. The building's two-story windowed front and high ceilings, the elegant painting frames, the plush ropes guarding the art, and the hushed reverence of the patrons made Orrin feel as if he were intruding on sacred space. He wandered hesitantly through the rooms, staring at the paintings and reading their descriptions, trying to understand what made them great works of art. Nudes made him uncomfortable. Munch's Madonna had chalky white breasts and wore a red beret. Orrin did not allow his eyes to linger. For the first half hour, he questioned whether visiting the museum was a good idea, but he persisted. Slowly his discomfort began to fade. He still hurried by the nudes, but he enjoyed the solitude and respite from the demanding grind of mission life, the rare chance to be alone with his thoughts. Orrin was as fascinated by Munch the person as he was by Munch's paintings. Anguish and grief dogged Munch throughout his life. His mother died when he was five, a beloved sister died when he was fourteen, and another sister went insane. Munch himself suffered from delicate health exacerbated by alcoholism, hallucinations, nervous breakdowns, bouts of loneliness, and a fear of going mad.

The neurotic, angst-driven artist poured melancholy into his paintings as if they were confessions, swaths and swirls of color offering a window into his existential despair. He painted scenes of jealousy, murder, psychic pain, death, and sorrow. He recreated the deaths of his sister and mother with pale mourners at their bedsides. Even when Munch depicted happy events, such as a dance or a kiss, the faces of his subjects were distorted and grotesque, even ogre-like. His brushstrokes trembled with madness.

Most compelling to Orrin were Munch's self-portraits. According to the museum's brochure, Munch painted more than seventy self-portraits over his lifetime, as if he were obsessed with understanding and portraying who he was. Each portrait offered a snapshot of Munch in a moment of time. An early self-portrait was somewhat conventional in its photograph-like details, but in his later years, Munch filled in only the barest of facial features, sometimes obscuring the eyes. Rarely did he smile or exude cheer. More often he appeared distressed or agitated. The self-portraits vibrated with emotion and mood but, from Orrin's perspective, asked rather than answered the question: who am I? Munch aimed to reveal his inner self but couldn't quite figure out who he really was. Or perhaps he knew but was afraid of who that diseased, mad, and unhappy person was. He was estranged from himself as well as others. Orrin couldn't fathom what Munch intended with his paintings, but he was seized by a curious sympathy for the man.

Eddie was not afraid to stare at the nudes. Hadn't he already viewed naked women in his reparative therapy? The other missionaries hurried past, their eyes darting quickly to their shoes, but Eddie did not fear other missionaries' disapproval as he lingered at the paintings, nor did he worry about having forbidden thoughts and being aroused. "I'd be happy if they did arouse me," he mused to himself. But there was nothing erotic in Munch's depiction of these women. His Madonna was anemic and without appeal, while the nude models posed with frumpy indifference, their flesh tired and bland. *Even a sex-starved Casanova would not get an erection from these women*, Eddie thought. Munch's women seemed to be objects of mystery and power, but not of sexual desire. A young girl who had just reached puberty sits naked, her arms crossed to cover her private parts, as if she were apprehensive or fearful of the sexual being she had become. Especially horrifying was the baby in the painting "Inheritance," which Munch depicted as alien and grotesque in its features, the consequence of sexual gratification. Eddie didn't think Munch was a homosexual—the brochure described several affairs with women—but the Victorian artist's confused, conflicted feelings about his sexual desires reflected Eddie's own about himself. Like Munch, Eddie could not suppress his desires, nor shed the accompanying guilt and shame.

Munch's subjects, like Eddie, were anguished and despairing. "The Scream" captured the immense psychological distress of a man who, standing on an Oslo bridge, emits a scream that dances and churns in a pulsating yellow, orange, and crimson sky. The scream swirls outward with increasing intensity and, in Eddie's imagination, reverberates up and down Norway's jagged coast, splitting glaciers with its shrieking wail and cry of existential pain. And yet, the two other people on the bridge seem not to even hear. *That scream could be mine.*

Eddie next found himself gazing with fierce concentration at Munch's "Self-Portrait in Hell." Munch stands naked, his face burnt red, gazing back at Eddie with a placid, sideways glance suggesting a cool acceptance of the dark, eternal flames. *This will be my fate.*

"There was an evil spirit in those paintings," an elder declared when the missionaries discussed Munch's paintings at their next district meeting.

"Did you see his self-portrait in hell?"

"That's probably where he is right now."

"I thought art was supposed to be uplifting."

"If that was supposed to help us understand the Norwegian people, I don't get it."

"Munch was literally insane," the district leader declared to near universal agreement. It was a conclusion shared by many art critics during Munch's lifetime. Eddie wasn't so sure. He regarded his fellow missionaries as Philistines no more capable of understanding Munch than they were of understanding Eddie. He tried to discern Elder Tanner's opinion of Munch, but Tanner was as much a cypher as Munch himself. Munch was clearly troubled and plagued by inner demons, Eddie concluded, but did that make him insane? Or did he just feel life more acutely and see life—his life, anyway—with more lucidity than others? And isn't being lucid the opposite of being insane? The old Eddie would have kept these thoughts to himself.

"Joseph Smith's enemies claimed his visions were epileptic seizures," Eddie said, "and the ancient Romans probably thought Jesus Christ was insane." He looked around the circle of missionaries. They said nothing, their faces blank slates. *You probably think I'm slightly insane.*

Chapter 27

Try to interest MEN, as heads of families. This makes it easy for the rest of the family also to learn the gospel. . . . During discussion, address the MAN very largely. Make him the focus of the discussion.

The Message and the Messenger

"Due to circumstances which I will explain to you when you arrive home from your mission, the Tanner Publishing Company will not be publishing any more pamphlets for the foreseeable future," Anson Tanner wrote in a short, terse addendum in a letter to his son, Orrin. "I wanted to let you know so that you could inform President Toressen of our decision and suggest that he should look for another publisher to reprint his speeches. Tell him we are sorry if this inconveniences him."

The letter left Orrin puzzled, particularly his father's uncharacteristic lack of explanation, but Orrin didn't obsess or worry until he received a letter two days later from his Uncle Porter offering more details.

Dear Orrin,

I have heard nothing but good reports from your parents about your missionary work, and I want you to know I am as proud of you as they are. Your father told me he informed you of the controversy engendered by his pamphlets, which resulted in the church's order that he cease publishing until the matter is resolved. I want to give you my perspective as a BYU professor to help ease any concerns you might have.

The chief issue is identifying which doctrinal topics are appropriate for academic treatment and which are best left to the church's General Authorities. Concerns have been voiced in some quarters that your father's pamphlets have strayed into the Brethren's domain. In my opinion, this is something your father should have addressed years ago. Being in a position where I can see both sides of the argument, I think in the long run this discussion will work to your father's benefit by establishing a clear demarcation between these two important spheres of responsibility—that is, the academic sphere for your father and the religious sphere for the Brethren. This will enable your father to conduct his research without the current cloud of suspicion or potential threat of censure that now attaches to his work.

You should not worry at all about the outcome of this matter. I have faith in the inspiration and good intentions of the Brethren involved. Our good friend Apostle Joseph Prichard is working behind the scenes to ensure that your father receives a fair hearing among the Brethren and to correct some of the

misconceptions about your father's writings, which unfortunately have been misinterpreted by those unfamiliar with his methods and purpose. I foresee a happy outcome satisfactory to all parties without any type of official discipline.
Affectionately,
Uncle Porter

Official discipline? Is Uncle Porter hinting at excommunication? Orrin wondered darkly. *What else could he mean?* Orrin rested his head on the kitchen table, his mind dizzy with shock.

Elder Gregersen, who was setting a pot of potatoes on the burner to boil, watched Orrin sit up and rub his eyes. "Is something wrong?"

"Yes, something's terribly wrong with my father's publishing business, but I'm not sure exactly what. My father told me he was planning to stop publishing his pamphlets without saying why, and now his brother, my Uncle Porter, says . . . well, I'm not sure what he's saying."

Orrin quickly dashed off a letter to his father, summarizing Porter's letter and asking him to explain more clearly whether church authorities had forced him to stop publishing. "Please tell me you aren't in danger of losing your church membership," Orrin wrote. He dropped his letter off at a post office before beginning their evening tracting. The alarming circumstances justified the breach in mission rules stipulating that letters home be written on Preparation Day. Orrin wouldn't have been able to concentrate on the work if he had waited to write the letter. Even as it was, he had difficulty focusing, given that it would still be at least ten days, possibly longer, before he received a reply.

To distract him from his worries, Orrin took up a challenge that had tugged at his conscience in recent weeks: what to do about Søster Ryland. He had no reason to doubt her sincerity. She had kept all her appointments, except once when her husband came home unexpectedly and she had a neighbor warn the missionaries to stay away. When Elder Gregersen showed up with a button missing from the sleeve of his suit coat, Søster Ryland found a replacement among the spare buttons she kept in a dresser and sewed it on the coat while they conversed. After that, she insisted that Orrin and Elder Gregersen bring with them any clothing that needed mending, saying she would count it as her contribution to the mission effort. She served delicious lunches and expressed offense if the missionaries didn't make gluttons of themselves. Orrin discussed her situation with the branch president, who said opposition from the husband was all too common in Norway. Still, Orrin wasn't sure he was getting the full story from Søster Ryland, who was reticent to talk about her husband, other than to say he disliked Mormons and had forbidden her to see the missionaries. But that had happened years ago. Maybe he had softened. Orrin felt criminal sneaking into the house when Herr Ryland was absent, especially since the *Missionary Handbook* instructed missionaries to focus on converting husbands. What a faith-promoting story that would be if Herr Ryland, after years of opposition, joined the church.

The missionaries couldn't keep their visits a secret forever, Orrin reasoned. Didn't Herr Ryland notice the large portions of food that disappeared from his refrigerator and cupboards every Tuesday while he worked? How did Søster Ryland manage to hide the church literature they gave to her? Sooner or later, her husband would stumble upon it. Or one of the neighbors might mention something about the missionaries' weekly visits—nothing sinister, just a causal, accidental remark that would arouse his suspicions. These worries manifested themselves first as uneasiness, then as irritation, like the annoyance one feels when the last piece of a jigsaw puzzle goes missing. The incompleteness got under Orrin's skin. "We need to find out if Søster Ryland is truly golden or a PFer," Orrin told his companion. "The best way to do that is by talking directly with Herr Ryland. If nothing else, it might give us some idea about how to move her toward baptism."

They got the chance to speak with Herr Ryland alone the next week when Søster Ryland took the train to Hamar to visit her sister. After praying for guidance, Orrin and Elder Gregersen tracted briefly among the neighbors before visiting Ryland, so it would appear they were just making their rounds. When they saw his porch light switch on, they walked up the steps and, hearts in their throats, gave three hard knocks at his door. Orrin was looking at the circled "X" on the doorjamb when he heard thudding feet in the hallway and the scraping slide of the door lock.

"Herr Ryland," Orrin said, offering his friendliest smile.

"Ja." The man standing before them was of medium height, stoutly built, with a brutish nose and small, rounded ears. He cocked his head and studied the missionaries through blood-red eyes.

"We are representatives of The Church of Jesus Christ of—"

"You are not from the Church of Jesus Christ. You are Mormons." Herr Ryland didn't raise his voice but spoke with bullying certitude.

"Yes, but—"

"We do not need Mormons here. Norway already has a church. I was born, baptized, confirmed, and married in the State Church, and I will die in the State Church."

"We do not want to take away your faith in God," Elder Gregersen said. "We have a message about—"

"You would destroy my home if you could," he snarled. He stretched his arms across the door, as if barring entrance, and leaned close, the smell of liquor on his breath. "Mormons are hypocrites, superstitious fanatics, and dupes, all of you," he shouted, spewing forth additional invectives, most of which neither Orrin nor his companion understood. "Go away at once or I will be forced to throw you off my porch."

The missionaries backed away, speechless, and Herr Ryland, sensing their dread, took a menacing step toward them. Elder Gregersen leaped onto the sidewalk, but Orrin remained frozen on the top step. It was neither courage nor paralyzing fear that held him there, but something more akin to curiosity, the same desire to know that had brought him to Herr Ryland's house. *Who is this man?* Herr Ryland muscled his chin under Orrin's, choking Orrin with his hot, mustard-like breath, crowding him, daring him, sneering. Orrin stared into his eyes. Staring back was a black, bottomless rage and a thousand resentments. His heart pounding, Orrin braced himself for a blow, but Herr Ryland merely snorted angrily. "Go back to America," he shouted feebly and withdrew into the darkness of his house.

Orrin watched the door slam and heard the lock being rammed into place, but he still couldn't move. Finally, Elder Gregersen reached up and pulled Orrin from the doorstep. "Man, I thought he was going to kill you."

"So did I." Orrin's hands trembled. The blood rushed from his head. He wobbled with dizziness.

"You're white as a ghost."

While they were walking to their next tracting area, Orrin's knees buckled. Elder Gregersen recommended they go home and rest. It was only four o'clock, but the streetlights were already flickering on. "I don't like to quit early," Orrin said, but he didn't protest when Elder Gregersen hailed the next streetcar. Putting a shoulder under Orrin's arm, Elder Gregersen helped him up the steps and into his seat. The sidewalk below the elders' window was still echoing with the footsteps of shoppers and people hurrying home from work when Orrin said his prayers and climbed into bed.

The next Saturday, when Orrin and Elder Gregersen were taking their weekly shower at the mission home, Elder Gregersen punctured a thumb trying to crack a walnut with a stapler. Though painful, the wound seemed minor and the bleeding was easily stopped, but within a few days the thumb began to swell and Elder Gregersen cried out miserably every time he bumped his thumb or tried to grab something with it. "I need to see a doctor," he said. "It might be infected." Orrin resisted but finally agreed that if his companion's thumb was still hurting on Saturday, they

225

would visit a doctor during their personal time. On edge and worrying about his father, Orrin was annoyed that Elder Gregersen had so foolishly injured himself. Adding to their worries, Søster Ryland wasn't home when they showed up for their weekly appointment on Tuesday. The elders told themselves she probably decided to stay longer with her sister, but neither really believed it. Thursday morning, Elder Gregersen winced in pain as he gently pushed on his throbbing thumb and saw blood and white puss oozing from underneath the bandage. "I need to have a doctor look at this today, Elder Tanner," he insisted.

Orrin exploded in anger. "Okay, but we're going to make up on Saturday any time we spend at the doctors. This is your own stupid fault."

The doctor's office was spare and clean, much like those in America, but the doctor who greeted them wore an eye patch, which was not the most reassuring look for a physician. After examining Elder Gregersen's thumb, the doctor scolded him for not coming in sooner. "This could easily have become koldbrann."

Elder Gregersen looked at Orrin, who shrugged. "Koldbrann?" said Elder Gregersen.

"It means infection. In English, you say gangrene." The doctor poured disinfectant over the thumb, numbed it with a local anesthetic, and while Elder Gregersen looked away, sliced open the wound with a scalpel to clean it out. When the doctor was finished, he sewed up the thumb with a few stitches. He summoned a nurse to put a bandage on Elder Gregersen's thumb while he wrote prescriptions for a painkiller and antibiotic pills. He also wrote up an invoice for his services but waited until the nurse left before speaking.

"Because you Americans are not part of our Norwegian healthcare system, I am supposed to charge you for the treatment I gave you today," he said. "But I know you Mormon missionaries pay your own way when you come here and do not have a lot of money, and so I'm not going to charge you the full amount. Can you afford one hundred crowns?"

Orrin calculated the amount at the current conversion rates. "That's only eighteen dollars."

"You are very generous, thank you," Elder Gregersen said.

Orrin pulled a Joseph Smith pamphlet from his coat pocket. "So you know a little about the Mormon Church?"

"Put that away," the doctor said, pointing to the pamphlet. "I am not interested in your religion or any religion. I saw too much killing and cruelty in the war to believe in God."

"If I can ask, is that how you injured your eye?" Orrin said.

"No, it is a childhood injury—the foolish kind, like what happened to his thumb. In my instance, an older brother shot me with an air gun." The doctor smiled. "The hazard of being the youngest of four boys."

Orrin tried one more time. "I know God lives. This pamphlet tells the story of a man who saw and spoke with God."

The doctor put up his hand. "No, no. I am doctor, a scientist. I trade in facts, not in superstition. I am sorry, but that is how it is." He began washing up and while drying his hands, he gave the missionaries a serious look. "When I first practiced medicine, I worked nights in the hospital emergency room. It is a job for when you are young. One time, a woman was brought in who had been in a car accident with possible organ damage and a significant loss of blood. She was unconscious and we needed to operate immediately, so we got her ready for a blood transfusion. But her husband objected. 'We are Jehovah's Witnesses and we do not believe in blood transfusions,' he said. I told him his wife would die without a transfusion, but he adamantly opposed it. 'My wife would not want it,' he contended. We did not have time to argue, so I agreed and then, when we got into the operating room, I made everyone leave except for the two nurses I needed to assist me. Then we gave her a blood transfusion. She would have died without it. I never told the husband and wife what I did. They interpreted her survival as a fantastic miracle and reward for their faith. 'See,' he told me. 'God watches over his people.' I did not say anything. They are happy not knowing. But she would have died if I had followed their superstitious beliefs."

Less than a week after receiving Orrin's blessing, Søster Poulsen began smoking again. She didn't try to hide it from the elders, not that she could have. Ashes and tobacco lay scattered about her home. She apologized, sounding more defensive than sorry when Orrin asked if she had prayed for strength when temptation came. "Maybe you think it is my fault I did not have the willpower?" she said. "My nerves were exhausted and I could not study. I have my pharmaceutical exams coming up. When God did not give me the strength I needed, I said to myself, 'Haldis, maybe this religion isn't for you.'"

Orrin invited her to attend a baptism of a single mother about Søster Poulsen's age, hoping this might inspire her. President Toressen attended the baptism, and though he was not a scheduled speaker, the branch president asked him to offer a few remarks. Speaking extemporaneously, he drew upon New Testament scriptures to talk about the early converts, likening the newly baptized woman to Martha, Mary, and the other young women who heeded Christ's words and proved themselves more courageous than some of his apostles. Orrin stood at the back door, poised to usher in Søster Poulsen. She never came. It was a lovely service that made people want to linger, but Orrin left feeling disheartened by the missed opportunity.

Despite his determination to remain focused on missionary work, Orrin could not banish his fears about his father. He dwelled on them in quiet moments, mulling over the possibilities. *Will my father be fired and banned from teaching seminary . . . disfellowshipped . . . excommunicated?* Finally, two weeks after writing to his father, he received a reply.

Dear Orrin,

I am sorry our little troubles at home have caused you so much distress. I am unhappy that Uncle Porter took it upon himself to write to you. Although he claims the best of intentions, he created needless worries for you and misled you about a few things. I suppose I should have been more forthcoming, but I wanted to spare you worry, as I am confident all will be resolved before you return home. In any case, here are the facts, which I hope will show Porter has made a mountain out of a molehill.

The initial cause of controversy was relatively minor. Your Grandpa Heber referred to his "guardian angel" in his pamphlet, which some of the Brethren took exception to, so after some back and forth, I agreed to stop publishing the pamphlets. I am confident suspicions will be allayed after those in authority have a chance to review my pamphlets.

Subsequently, another one of my pamphlets, "The Law of Eternal Progress," also rankled some of the Brethren. It has not helped that those taking offense— I have not been told their names—do not know me, and so they thought I belong to an anti-Mormon apostate group headed by someone who also happens to be named Tanner.

Thankfully, Apostle Prichard (Joe's uncle) has been able to set the record straight on this matter. Nevertheless, it is still disturbing to some that I am a teacher in the church seminary program. As you know, I have always maintained a strict separation between my research and my teaching, so I think the offended Brethren will be satisfied in this regard once they have all the facts before them.

One fact about which you were misinformed is that the church ordered me to stop publishing the pamphlets. That is not true. It was strictly voluntary. After consulting with Apostle Prichard, your mother and I decided to temporarily halt publication of any new pamphlets, as well as reprints of older ones, as a way to demonstrate our willingness to follow counsel. Remember, "to obey is better than sacrifice, and to hearken than the fat of rams."

Also, no one has mentioned excommunication or disfellowship or anything of that sort. You know what Uncle Porter is like. He thought fluoridation was the first step to a communist takeover.

I am sorry I didn't tell you more about this earlier, but, honestly, it is not that important in the vast eternity of our lives. You have more important things to worry about, so please put this issue out of your mind. My testimony remains as strong as ever. Your mother and I are very proud of you, as is Grandpa Heber, who still holds out hope that someday we might visit Riksøy together.

Love, Dad

The letter momentarily alleviated Orrin's disquiet, but as he reread it, he became agitated by two contradictory thoughts. He was angered by the anonymous church authorities who had misinterpreted his dad's intentions and doubted his faithfulness. The unfairness was difficult to swallow. Still, he questioned whether his dad was giving him the full story. Shutting down his publishing business—whether voluntarily or by order of church leaders—was an extreme reaction to a minor offense. Perhaps his father was guilty of more than being misinterpreted. Orrin prayed for understanding and comfort, that his mind would be untroubled. He thanked God for Apostle Prichard's efforts on his father's behalf and asked Him to help other church leaders see his father's righteousness and love of the gospel. Pausing briefly to listen to his heart, Orrin asked God to place upon him the burden and responsibility for his dad's troubles, that Orrin's good works and faithfulness as a missionary would be placed on the scale to balance out any unintentional wrongdoing by his father. Orrin prayed until he felt satisfied God had agreed to the bargain. During the days that followed, whenever Orrin felt tired or discouraged or was tempted to take a break from tracting, he thought of his father and soldiered on, telling himself that each additional door, each extra mile, was helping his father's case. He decided against informing President Toressen of the controversy, given his confidence it would be resolved and his father would resume publishing.

God immediately began testing Orrin's resolve. While taking the morning streetcar to their tracting area, Orrin sidled up to a man in a thin, dark tie and overcoat—just the type of family man the church was looking for. "Excuse me," Orrin said. "Do you know whether this streetcar goes to Grefsen Stadion?"

"What are you asking?"

"Whether this streetcar goes to Grefsen Stadion? My companion and I are new to Oslo, and I want to make sure we get off at the right stop. We are representatives of The Church of Jesus—"

"I know who you are," the man said curtly. "I've seen you riding this streetcar up and down the Kjelsås line for more than a month. You often get off at Grefsen Stadion, so don't tell me you don't know where you're going."

Flushed and stammering, Orrin replied, "I . . . I . . . you are correct. I . . . I am sorry."

"*Er dette en slags svindel?*" he asked. "Is this some kind of swindle?"

Flustered, Orrin saw no alternative but to be honest. "Oh, no. I was looking for a way to introduce myself and tell you about my church. Are you familiar with the Mormon Church?

"I am now. Apparently you are a religion that specializes in deception. I am not interested." The man snapped open the newspaper sitting on his lap, signaling an end to the conversation. Orrin apologized again and returned to his seat next.

"Did you give him a pamphlet?" Elder Gregersen asked.

Orrin shook his head. He opened his bible and pretended to read, hoping to deter his companion from asking any more questions.

On Tuesday, Orrin and Elder Gregersen went to their weekly appointment with Søster Ryland. They walked apprehensively up her front steps, uncertain what kind of reception they might receive after their frightening encounter with her husband. Orrin hoped Herr Ryland had said nothing to her. But just in case, he had also prepared an apology. "I will tell her I needed to know for myself. I also thought Herr Ryland might be more responsive to our message today than he was previously. But I know now I was wrong," Orrin told his companion.

"You can say 'we,' Elder Tanner. I agreed with your plan."

They stayed twenty minutes at Søster Ryland's door, knocking several times, but no one answered.

On Friday, they returned to the doctor's office to have the stitches removed from Elder Gregersen's thumb. Happily, there was no additional charge for the procedure, which a nurse handled after a short wait. They returned to their hybel earlier than usual, hoping to get in a few extra hours of study in preparation for the upcoming Scripture Chase competition. But when they got off the streetcar, they found their way into the courtyard blocked by the large truck that came each week to siphon out the contents of the outhouses. Long canvas hoses ran from outhouses through the courtyard and into the truck. As they edged their way past the truck and toward the stairwell to their hybel, a burly man with hairy arms and thick leather gloves stepped in front of them, waving a Joseph Smith pamphlet. The pamphlet was stained with urine and feces. "Is this yours?" he said angrily.

"Yes."

"Stop putting them in the toilets. Do you not know to use the toilet paper that is provided?"

"We are not putting them in the toilets," Orrin said.

"Well, someone is and they are clogging up our hoses. I pulled this pamphlet out of the hose," he said, kicking at the hose. "And this is not the first time. It has been occurring for several weeks."

"I am sorry. We did not know."

"If these are your pamphlets, then they are your responsibility. If we find any more, we are going to drop them off at your apartment door. Do you understand?"

"Yes, sir. It won't happen again."

The man unhooked his hoses and reeled them back to his truck. "*Jeg liker ikke dette sektene greier,*" he mumbled as he finished loading the hoses. "I do not like this sectarian stuff."

Chapter 28

Every missionary is expected to be a gospel scholar.
Search The Scriptures: A Missionary Study Guide

The elders and sisters gathered quarterly for training and spiritual rejuvenation. President Toressen's assistants led the training sessions aimed at improving missionary techniques, particularly when engaging people at the door. One of the highlights of each conference was the Scripture Chase, which tested the missionaries' knowledge of church history and doctrines along with the scriptures. Although a competition, the Scripture Chase was typically a low-key affair designed to strengthen camaraderie and love of learning. The missionaries good-naturedly cheered each other on, with few contestants actually concerned about winning. Besides, everyone expected Elder Tanner to win. Eddie had other ideas.

Eddie and his companion, Elder Wilson, had been moving steadily up the Mission Comparative, and the week preceding the Oslo conference had knocked Elders Tanner and Gregersen out of the top spot. Eddie's no-holds-barred—one might say belligerent—door approach fueled their success. "We are not interested," a man said curtly.

"You don't believe in the Bible," Eddie replied. It was more an accusation than a question.

"I believe in the Bible."

"So you believe in the biblical prophets like Moses?"

"Yes."

"We bring you news of Joseph Smith, a modern-day prophet."

"I belong to the State Church."

"And yet, you probably never go. Jesus denounced hypocrites, saying, 'They draw near me with their lips but their hearts are far from me.' You say you believe in Moses, but if he came to your door, would you say, 'I am not interested. I belong to the State Church.'"

At this point, people usually slammed the door, if they hadn't already. But Eddie didn't care. He and Elder Wilson relished their roles as Old Testament prophets issuing righteous warnings to the wicked. In a few cases, the person at the door would acknowledge the shortcomings of the State Church and, for reasons even Eddie didn't understand, took a liking to his brash approach and ask the elders inside. However, the people who most often invited Eddie and Elder Wilson into their homes were not State Church members but Jehovah's Witnesses and born-again Christians, not because they were interested in Mormonism but because they wanted to argue religious doctrine. Eddie was happy to oblige.

The born-agains wanted to argue in favor of salvation through faith in Jesus Christ alone. "For by grace you have been saved through faith, and not of yourselves," they would say, quoting the Apostle Paul. "It is the gift of God, not of works."

Eddie would counter by citing the Apostle James, who said, "Faith without works is dead." Back and forth they went, clubbing each other with biblical citations about faith and works. If Eddie sensed the born-agains starting to question their position, he softened his tone from chastising to sympathizing. "Of course, it is not one or the other," he said. "Man must have both faith and works. We are like a person drowning in the ocean. Christ throws us the lifeline, but we must do our part by swimming to it and holding fast. As the prophet Nephi said, 'We know that it is by grace we are saved, after all we can do.'" A few born-agains were intrigued enough to invite Eddie and Elder Wilson to return and teach additional discussions.

No Jehovah's Witness was ever interested in learning more about Mormonism. The missionaries considered Jehovah's Witnesses—or J-Dubs, as they called them—to be their chief adversaries and a major obstacle to the success of Mormonism in Norway. Like the missionaries, the J-Dubs went door to door seeking converts. They had a reputation for being confrontational and rude, often ridiculing others' beliefs and haranguing them about eternal damnation. The missionaries always knew when an area had been visited by J-Dubs because people shouted obscenities and slammed doors and told the missionaries to leave them alone. After visiting a home, J-Dubs wrote little "Xs" and "Os" on the doorjambs, which represented a code alerting the next J-Dub missionaries as to what kind of response they could expect. That was the story among the missionaries, though no one claimed to have seen a J-Dub make these markings.

Most of Eddie's confrontations with J-Dubs took place on their doorsteps, with the J-Dubs demanding to know whether Eddie knew God's name or whether he was preaching God's kingdom and a new paradisical earth. On the few occasions when the elders were invited in and set up the flannel board for the first discussion, they never got past the Joseph Smith story. A prim woman was especially dismissive after hearing Eddie recount Smith's vision. "The Bible says no man can see God and live," she said, harrumphing and twirling her glasses on their chain. "Joseph Smith is a false prophet."

Eddie countered by quoting from the New Testament. "In Acts, it says Stephen, as he was being stoned to death, saw the Son of Man standing on the right hand of God," he said. Back and forth they went, and soon they were arguing about Christ's second coming (which she claimed would occur in the spring of 1979) and polygamy and the preexistence and a score of other doctrines. They were locked in a good, old-fashioned bible bashing. Every time Eddie answered an objection, she would interrupt or change the subject. "*Dette ikke står i bibelen*," she shrieked. "That is not in the Bible."

Eddie became increasingly frustrated by her tactics but was unable to shake her loose. She moved swiftly from one topic to the next, speaking over Eddie and punctuating each condemnation of Mormon principles with the assertion, "That is not in the Bible."

Finally, Eddie stood and leaned across the table until his nose was practically resting on her forehead. "That is not in the Bible, that is not in the Bible, that is not in the Bible," he shouted, mimicking her mantra. He scowled menacingly. "Is that all you can say?"

The woman started to speak, but Eddie again shouted, "That is not in the Bible. Is that all you can say?"

When several more of her attempts to speak met the same mocking accusation, the woman erupted in furious tears. "Get out. Get out of my house."

Eddie and Elder Wilson quietly put away their materials and left. "You really burned that J-Dub woman," Elder Wilson said as he prepared to knock on the next door. "You burned her good."

Eddie's aggressive take-down of J-Dubs made him a hero among the Oslo elders. Few missionaries had the language skills, scriptural knowledge, or combative personality necessary to go toe-to-toe with J-Dubs. After one or two losing encounters in scriptural free-for-alls with J-Dubs, missionaries tended to steer clear. Reasoning with J-Dubs was impossible. While Eddie was no more successful than other missionaries in converting J-Dubs, he stood forth as their champion, giving as good as he got—and sometimes better. Nobody who knew the timid, introverted Eddie who first arrived in Norway would have thought him capable of such fiery intellectual combat. Some of the older missionaries said they could always spot J-Dubs by a certain devilish look in their eyes. "Intense and beady little snake-eyed slits," said one elder. But Eddie thought J-Dubs looked a lot like Mormons, and he never knew he was talking with one until they were all over him with their J-Dub scriptures. Yes, they liked to argue scriptures and prove their religion correct. But so did the missionaries. Still, Eddie's empathetic view didn't stop him from unleashing his wretched heartache against them, because he had something to prove to God—and to the other missionaries.

One of those missionaries was Elder Tanner. Eddie continued to look for ways to needle and upstage him. Elder Tanner had congratulated Eddie and Elder Wilson when, after inching up week after week on the Mission Comparative, they finally overtook him, but Eddie noted with satisfaction the spark of resentment in Elder Tanner's eyes. Eddie also drew praise for snaring an interview in a local newspaper. "*Unge amerikanere vil løse samfunnets problemer,*" the headline said. "Young Americans will solve society's problems." The article ran with a photo of Eddie and Elder Wilson holding a Family Home Evening manual and quoted both elders touting the church's programs aimed at strengthening families and supporting fathers as the heads of the home. The following week, many people in Kalbakken, Linderud, and other stops along the Grorud line recognized Eddie and Elder Wilson from the newspaper article and invited them into their homes. "This is the type of creative proselytizing everyone should be doing," the assistants said in the weekly newsletter to the missionaries. "Elder Pedersen and Elder Wilson have advanced the work not just in their area but in all of Oslo." Eddie smiled when he read the newsletter and saw his name, along with Elder Wilson's, at the top of the Mission Comparative. That night, he laid his accomplishments before the Lord alongside his appeal for redemption.

A soft, dry snowfall, the pleasant kind that gives off a feeling of warmth, greeted the elders and sisters as they arrived for the February quarterly conference in Oslo. The conference began with a report from the mission assistants, who both had taken to wearing black suspenders. Elder Ward summarized the progress of the mission since the last conference—fourteen baptisms—and praised the missionary pairs who had scored high on the Mission Comparative. Elder Sorensen related several inspirational stories of success, mentioning by name various missionary pairs who had developed unique methods for spreading the message. "Elder Miller has a clever way to approach people on the bus," he said, hooking his thumbs under his suspenders. "He just walks up and says, 'Do you know who we are?' He's so friendly, he almost always gets a positive response."

"*Benytt enhver anledning,*" Elder Ward said, quoting from a favorite church hymn. "Use every opportunity. "

In the last session before lunch, the assistants gave a presentation on companion relationships. "Tell your companion every day you love him," Elder Ward admonished the missionaries.

"And don't just tell him, but show him by polishing his shoes or letting him have an extra helping of potatoes or the last cookie on the plate," Elder Sorensen said.

"If you're not as happy as you'd like to be, then it is probably because you're not meeting your goals and being faithful in the work," Elder Ward concluded. He added that the missionaries should wash their hands and keep their fingernails clean, because people were always watching.

The afternoon began with the much-anticipated Scripture Chase. In each contest, two missionaries came to the stage to answer a series of ten questions. When was the church organized? Who were the eight witnesses to the Book of Mormon? Name the scriptural reference in which Jesus said, "Ye shall know the truth and it shall set you free?" What year did the first wagon train of pioneer Saints arrive in Salt Lake City? The assistants asked the questions and served as the judges, while the elders and sisters sitting in the audience shouted out encouragement, cheered when missionaries correctly answered difficult questions, groaned when they flubbed easy ones, and sometimes had to be cautioned not to give away the answers. The questions became progressively more difficult with each round as winners moved on and losers were eliminated. The missionaries watched with silent respect when Orrin took the stage and answered the questions with rapid-fire confidence. Eddie watched with trepidation. He couldn't make up his mind whether he wanted to see Elder Tanner defeated before he had his shot at him, but it quickly became clear that no other missionary would best Elder Tanner. Eddie also moved through his bracket of contestants, though not as assuredly as Orrin. On two occasions, it came down to the last question before Eddie won.

The final contest between Eddie and Orrin generated more than the usual excitement because both elders worked in the same Oslo district and were the number one and number two performers on the Mission Comparative. Neither elder was disliked, but neither did they inspire affection. Eddie's mood ran hot and cold, while Orrin comported himself like an iron-rod Mormon, with the iron rod shoved firmly up his you-know-where. The questions, now increased to twenty-five, tested the deepest corners of their memories. Orrin was asked to name the twelve apostles chosen by Jesus, while Eddie was asked to name the first twelve apostles chosen by Joseph Smith to lead the modern church. After Eddie finished naming them, Orrin pointed out to the assistants it was the Three Witnesses, not Joseph Smith, who selected the apostles. Eddie elicited laughs when, after asked to recite scriptures from the sixth discussion, said, "I just wish I could find an investigator who gets all the way to the sixth discussion."

With two questions remaining, Orrin was ahead by one point, and so only needed to answer one of them correctly to win. However, the second-to-last question played to Eddie's strength, asking each elder to recite the scriptures from the first discussion in Norwegian. Orrin's grammar was slightly muddled, while Eddie flawlessly quoted both scriptures. The elders and sisters applauded loudly when Eddie won the point and then stood, hushed, as Elder Ward asked the last question: when was polygamy officially ended in the church and which Mormon prophet ended it? Orrin's hand shot up. "It was President Joseph F. Smith in 1904."

Missionaries shook their heads in groaning disappointment. "No, I'm sorry," Elder Ward said. "That is incorrect." Orrin's face dropped, then he started to protest, but Elder Ward had already turned to Eddie. "Elder Pedersen, do you know the answer?"

"It was President Wilford Woodruff in 1890," Eddie replied.

"Correct. I declare Elder Pedersen the winner of the Oslo conference Scripture Chase," Ward said, reaching across the podium to shake Eddie's hand. Having been certain that Elder Tanner would win, the missionaries at first sat in stunned silence but soon erupted in cheers and marched to the stage to offer Eddie their congratulations.

Orrin, his face pinched, rushed across the stage to the assistants. "That's not correct," he shouted, waving his arms. "That's not correct! President Woodruff's manifesto did not end polygamy. Plural marriage continued with support from the church leadership until President Smith issued a second manifesto in 1904."

The chapel quieted down as Orrin pressed his point. "I've never heard of this second manifesto," Elder Ward said. He queried his companion, Elder Sorensen, and the other elders, but none of them knew anything about a second polygamy manifesto.

"You can look it up. It's true," Orrin said.

"We have a protest on the last question," Elder Ward announced. "We're going to make sure we have the right answer." He had Elder Sorensen review Joseph Fielding Smith's *Essentials in Church History* to see what the church's long-standing historian said about the matter. Orrin jumped down from the stage and stood next to Elder Sorensen, anxiously peering over his shoulder, while the elders and sisters milled around.

"I see a statement by Joseph F. Smith affirming that the Woodruff Manifesto ended polygamy," Elder Sorensen said. "But I don't see any mention of a second manifesto."

"Give me the book," Orrin said angrily. He scanned the index but could find no reference to a second manifesto. "Just because it's not here doesn't mean . . ." The other missionaries stared at him incredulously.

Elder Ward shook his head. "Elder Tanner, *Essentials in Church History* is the official history for missionaries. We used it to devise our questions.

Surely, Joseph Fielding Smith would have mentioned a second manifesto if one had been issued. It was his own father who was supposed to have issued it, after all."

"But it's true," Orrin said. "It's not fair. I know it's true."

"I'm sorry, Elder Tanner," Elder Ward said calmly, "but Elder Pedersen has won the Scripture Chase."

The missionaries, who had been waiting around for a final decision, began to disperse, embarrassed for Elder Tanner. His companion, Elder Gregersen, shuffled into the hall without speaking to anyone. "This was supposed to be just for fun," Elder Ward grumbled. "It's not like you get a prize for winning."

Eddie watched Elder Flossen, the Østfold district leader, put an arm around Elder Tanner's shoulder and whisper to him as he led the agitated elder from the chapel. Winning wasn't as satisfying as Eddie had anticipated. Elder Tanner's tantrum had spoiled the victory.

Chapter 29

Set your testimony apart: a) Pause slightly; b) Look contact in the eye; c) Bear testimony in a natural tone of voice.

A Uniform System for Teaching Investigators

Orrin stepped outside the chapel and into the sunshine. The brisk Nordic air caused him to shiver. (Or was he still shaking with indignation?) *Why had winning been so important?* If it was to impress the other missionaries, he had accomplished the opposite. He would never live it down, never, never, never . . . never regain the respect of the Norwegian elders and sisters. *What must Elder Gregersen be thinking?* Orrin began plotting his long-shot redemption. Reclaiming the top spot on the Mission Comparative would be a good start. Perhaps the assistants would allow him to write a brief article about the 1904 manifesto, showing everyone he had been right. They would allow it if he included an apology. Yes, combine the explanation with an apology. *That will make my boorish behavior not seem so bad.*

"What bothered you the most: that you didn't win or that you were right?" asked Elder Flossen, who stood beside Orrin, rubbing his hands to keep them warm.

"You know about the second manifesto?" Orrin said excitedly. "You believe me?"

"I remembered that you mentioned it once when we were tracting. Otherwise, I've never heard of it or read about it in any church books. But I know you too well, Elder Tanner, to think you'd be wrong about something like this. You know more about the church than the rest of us put together. So, yeah, I believe you. But—"

"But?"

"But it wasn't worth losing your mind over."

"No, but it still bothers me that the missionaries hardly know anything about church history and doctrine. How can they claim to know the church is true if they don't know anything about it?"

"Knowledge isn't necessary for a spiritual witness, not the kind of in-depth and extensive knowledge you're talking about."

"I know, but—"

"Otherwise, we wouldn't have any converts."

Orrin smiled ruefully. "Not that I've had any."

"Don't get me wrong, Elder Tanner. Knowledge is a good thing. But it shouldn't become sounding brass or a tinkling cymbal."

Orrin looked over the side rail. Two cigarette butts lay in the dirt. Orrin remembered how mortified he had been, standing here with Søster Poulsen as she smoked her hand-rolled cigarettes, oblivious to the spectacle she and Orrin had presented to the members staring at them through the chapel doors. Seeing the butts reminded Orrin that Søster Poulsen's exams had ended, so it was time to go see her. Maybe she would be ready to take another run at giving up smoking.

"Elder Tanner, it's been more than a year since I worked in Oslo, and I'll be going home in a few months," Elder Flossen said. "Why don't you and I go visit some of the members in the Kjelsås district we know? It would be nice for me to see them one last time."

Orrin welcomed the idea of absenting himself from the conference for a few hours. The two elders notified their companions of their plans and then grabbed their coats and hats. Twenty minutes later, they were ringing the doorbell of the Magnussen family.

"Oh, Elder Flossen, what a lovely surprise," Søster Magnussen exclaimed when she opened the door. "Have you been transferred back to Oslo?"

She called for her husband and daughter, Astrid, who greeted Elder Flossen with equal delight, demanding he tell them about his missionary adventures since they had last seen him. Elder Flossen recounted his activities in the different cities where he had worked, told stories of some of the members whom Bror and Søster Magnussen knew, and said a family he taught in Trondheim was planning to be baptized soon.

"How wonderful for you," Søster Magnussen said. "It is too bad you cannot be there for their baptism."

"I am just happy I helped in their conversion. They are my only converts."

When Søster Magnussen and her husband went to the kitchen to prepare refreshments, Elder Flossen and Astrid, now sixteen, resumed their familiar banter, with Elder Flossen teasing her in English and asking about her boyfriends. She smiled coyly, clearly enjoying the chance to show off her English, batting her eyelashes in an effort to get the older missionary to flirt with her.

Elder Flossen asked the Magnussen's about their son, Erik. Bror Magnussen frowned. "Erik has been difficult lately. He goes around with a different crowd now and does not want to come to church."

"There are not many Mormon boys his age in our branch," Søster Magnussen added.

"Is he still planning to go to BYU?"

"Unfortunately, no."

Søster Magnussen sighed. "We wish you could have been here to help him through this difficult period. He was eager to go to Brigham Young University and be together with other Mormons when he talked with you."

"He really liked you," Astrid said.

"And I liked him. He is not here today?"

"No, he is out with friends."

When it came time to say goodbye, Søster Magnussen became teary, knowing they would not see Elder Flossen again, and insisted on giving him a hug. Orrin said nothing, but Elder Flossen had worked with Orrin long enough to know the hug, which violated mission rules, made Orrin uncomfortable.

"Don't worry, Elder Tanner," he said after they left. "I won't take Søster Magnussen into her bedroom and start making love—at least, not while Bror Magnussen is home."

Elder Flossen received similar enthusiastic receptions at the other members' homes they visited. All wanted to know about his missionary experiences and asked for details about the new family he had helped to convert. "It is so important for us to get people who will be active and strong members," said Bror Vesberg. "It is difficult when, with so few active members in our branches, each person has to serve in several church positions. It is very sad when missionaries baptize someone who soon falls away." Elder Flossen assured them the new family would be active members.

Orrin admired Elder Flossen's genial, easy manner. He was genuinely interested in the Norwegians and they in him. Orrin learned from their conversations that when Elder Flossen returned home, he intended to study biology and become a doctor, something he and Elder Flossen had never discussed in their three months together as companions. Orrin realized he didn't have a close relationship with any church members. You weren't supposed to. That wasn't the purpose of a mission. Still, it made him sad. He had underestimated Elder Flossen. Orrin, like the Norwegian members, would miss him.

The last person they visited was Søster Halversen. They laughed as they walked up the stairs to her apartment, telling their favorite stories about her. "Hey, do you guys still pee in the basin sink like we used to do?" Elder Flossen asked.

"Yeah," Orrin said, "I bet it saves us a least an hour a day tromping up and down the stairs. Orrin told him about the embarrassing fiasco of clogged hoses after they started leaving pamphlets in the outhouses.

"*Uffa meg for dere*," Elder Flossen said.

Orrin waited with sunny anticipation after he rang the doorbell. Of all the church members in his area, Søster Halversen had been the most understanding when he told her that he and Elder Gregersen wouldn't be dropping by very often, if at all, so they could concentrate on finding investigators. He and Elder Gregersen often sat with Søster Halversen each Sunday. She would give Orrin a big smile when he slid into the pew, and they would joke and laugh before the meeting started, just like they did when they visited her home. That was early on. He had not seen her for several weeks. He decided now to resume their weekly visits. No one could brighten the day like Søster Halversen.

A stout man with tired eyes and rumpled pants answered the door. "We are here to see Søster Halversen," Orrin said. "Is she here today?"

"No," the man said curtly, closing the door.

Elder Flossen leaned forward, blocking the door. "We are missionaries with The Church of Jesus Christ of Latter-day Saints and friends of Søster Halversen. Do you know when she might be back?"

"Unfortunately, she died two days ago."

Orrin gasped, then struggled to catch his breath.

"Oh, I am so sorry," Elder Flossen said. "You must be her son, Jens. I recognize you from the photographs Søster Halversen kept on the wall. Was it sudden? I am so sorry we did not know."

"She was ill for three weeks and died here in her apartment. No one from your so-called Church of Jesus Christ came to visit her."

"Did you notify anyone in the church of her illness?" Orrin asked. "Someone from the Relief Society would have come."

"I asked her and she told me not to worry, that her boys, the missionaries, would surely come. She kept waiting, but you never came—until now, when it is too late."

The elders were too stunned to say anything except to offer their condolences, bemoaning, "If only we had known."

Jens looked at them sternly. "I did not like it when Mother joined the Mormon sect, but the Mormons I met were honest, honorable people and I saw that your religion made her happy. But I must say that abandoning her in her last days . . ." He paused, searching for the right words, and then, shaking his head sadly, said, "*Dette var veldig dårlig gjørt, gutter.* This was very poorly done, boys." Still shaking his head, he closed the door.

Orrin and Elder Flossen rode wordlessly back to the church. Orrin wiped at tears, thinking of Søster Halversen's sweet, vivacious personality, feeling guilty that she died without any visitors from the church. From the streetcar stop, the two elders walked in continued silence up Hekkveien until they reached the chapel. "Elder Tanner," said Elder Flossen, his eyes glistening with tears, "I've always thought your heart was in the right place, and so I overlooked your rigid approach to missionary work and the idea that being a missionary requires suffering and austerity. I figured that like the rest of us, you were trying to do the best you can. But this business with Søster Halversen, who . . ." Elder Flossen took a handkerchief from his pocket and wiped his eyes, stifling a sob. "Let's just say I agree with Herr Halversen. This was very poorly done, Elder."

Elder Flossen turned and walked up the steps and into the chapel.

The next day at church, Orrin informed the branch president that Søster Halversen had died. President Engelmann put a hand over his mouth, stifling a cry. The Relief Society president organized a committee of women to go to the home and offer assistance to Søster Halversen's son. "Of course, we would like to have the funeral here in our chapel, but we will support the wishes of the family," President Engelmann said. As news of her death spread among the members, just about everyone expressed sorrowful regret that they had failed Søster Halversen and her family.

President Engelmann wrung his hands in shame. At thirty years old, he was quite young to be leading the Oslo branch, the largest in Norway, but nearly all of the older men, at least those who were qualified, had already taken their turn as branch president. Some, including his father, had served two stints, and so the job fell to President Engelmann. Having studied in the United States for five years before returning home to start a construction business, his ability to speak comfortably in English helped him work closely with missionaries and visiting church authorities. He thanked Orrin for staying close to Søster Halversen, noting that Norway's branches depended on the missionaries to provide fellowship and assistance to the members. He was surprised when Orrin said he had not been visiting Søster Halversen or any of the members in his area.

"As missionaries, our primary responsibility is to teach and convert," Orrin said, sensing the branch president's disapproval. "Fellowshipping members and ministering to their needs is the responsibility of the branch organizations. That's how it's done in my ward back home."

President Engelmann frowned. "That sounds good in theory, but we do not have the manpower and resources you have. I have lived in Provo and Salt Lake City. Your wards are overflowing with people who can fill church positions. In Provo, we had so many members that people had to share church positions, just so everyone would have one. But in my branch, many members hold two positions and still, we cannot fill them all. That is why we rely on the missionaries."

"But the *Missionary Handbook* specifically forbids us to socialize with members. This was emphasized over and over at the Salt Lake City mission home and during our language training before we came to Norway."

President Engelmann rubbed his forehead and sighed. "Elder Tanner, some day you will learn that the straight and narrow path is not a straitjacket." He glanced at the front of the chapel, where a crowd of people waited to talk with him. "*Unnskyld meg,*" he said, switching to Norwegian, "Excuse me. I have other church business to attend."

Orrin wanted desperately to make a new start. He proposed to Elder Gregersen that they set aside a day for fasting and prayer, after which they would rededicate themselves and the Kjelsås area to missionary work. Elder Gregersen, whose pace had been slow and anxious in recent weeks, reluctantly agreed. They began their fast after *middag* on Sunday, planning to go without food or drink until *middag* the following day, but near morning's end on Monday, Elder Gregersen began feeling queasy, and needed to rest on a park bench.

"You look pale, Elder. Do you feel sick?" Orrin asked.

"I've never fasted for a full twenty-four hours before. I've tried, but this is what always happens and so I never finish. I really thought I could do it today."

"Lean over and put your head between your legs. That will get the blood flowing back into your head."

Orrin felt his stomach rumbling as Elder Gregersen pressed his head against his knees. A man stopped to inquire if Elder Gregersen was okay. "*Han er bare litt svimmel,*" Orrin assured the man. "He is just a little dizzy and needs a little rest." Several more people stopped and asked whether Elder Gregersen was sick and received the same answer.

"This is a great missionary tool," Elder Gregersen said, staring through his legs at the pavement. "You should give a pamphlet to people when they stop."

"Yeah, and they'll never stop to help anyone ever again."

After about ten minutes, Elder Gregersen announced he was feeling better and wanted to continue. Orrin looked at his watch. "If we hurry back to the apartment building, we won't lose any tracting time."

They had to stop three more times for Elder Gregersen to rest and regain his strength. Orrin carried the briefcase to lighten his load and even offered to go home early, but much to his relief, Elder Gregersen declined, vowing to complete a fast for the first time. Orrin admired his determination, though he wondered if Elder Gregersen wasn't being overly dramatic and somewhat wimpy. Orrin also ached for something to eat, but waiting for them at the end of the suffering and denial was heightened spiritual power. When they arrived back at their hybel at three thirty in the afternoon, they could barely drag themselves up the three flights of stairs. Once inside, they took turns praying, asking the Lord to pour forth his blessings in the Kjelsås area and allow His humble servants to find the honest in heart seeking to do God's will. They prayed especially for Søster Poulsen, that God would give her the strength to overcome her nicotine addiction, and for Søster Ryland, that Herr Ryland's heart would soften and he allow his wife to join the church. For dinner, they ate peanut butter and jelly sandwiches, too famished to take the time to prepare a normal meal. They left their hybel again at a quarter to five and went knocking on doors in the Storo neighborhood.

Orrin sought to make amends by apologizing to the Oslo missionaries at their next district meeting. His apology was sincere. He was truly mortified by the behavior he feared revealed his true character, rather than the person he aspired to be. He didn't say this. He simply said he was sorry and congratulated Elder Pedersen on his performance, all the while sucking on his lower lip to keep from saying that though his behavior was wrong, his answer was not. When he finished, the district leader praised Orrin for his willingness to lay his faults before his fellow missionaries. He extended Orrin's humiliation with a lengthy discourse about repentance being part of the divine plan. "I'm sure we all have our imperfections and weaknesses," he said.

The district missionaries concurred, saying things like "nobody's perfect" and "he who is without sin should cast the first stone," but an awkwardness remained, as if they had been complicit in a dark hazing ritual. Elder Gregersen tried to lighten the mood by telling everyone about how he and Orrin had placed Joseph Smith pamphlets in their hybel's outhouses, but later found out the Norwegians had been stuffing the pamphlets in the toilets and clogging up the cleaning hoses. "I guess it wasn't such an inspired idea, after all," he said, poking fun at himself. The missionaries laughed along with Elder Gregersen, but the more they laughed, the more Orrin thought they were laughing at him. After their meeting broke up, the district leader told other missionaries that he considered it sacrilege for church literature to be dripping in feces.

Elder Pedersen arched an eyebrow, smirking. "Well, what do you expect from missionaries who pee in their sink?"

Orrin waited one day after Søster Poulsen's last exam before going to her house. "With her exams behind her, this will give Søster Poulsen a chance to focus on her gospel studies," Orrin said. They knocked on her door for more than ten minutes before giving up. "She's probably out celebrating the end of classes and exams with her fellow students," Orrin said.

"I hope not by drinking," Elder Gregersen said.

"No, not Søster Poulsen. She has too strong of a testimony. It's only cigarettes that give her trouble."

They took the streetcar to the end of the Kjelsås line where Søster Ryland lived. Ever since their disastrous encounter with her husband, Søster Ryland had not been answering her door. They had heard of abusive husbands, and based on their experience with Herr Ryland, he appeared capable of such brutality. Søster Ryland had not spoken ill of her husband, except to say he wasn't interested, but they couldn't help but wonder. As they approached her house, Orrin saw a window curtain move. A good sign, he thought, but repeated knocks failed to bring anyone to the door. "I know someone is in there," Orrin said. He stepped off the front stoop and was preparing to knock at the window when the next-door neighbor called to the missionaries from her doorstep.

"*Er dere mormoner?*" she asked, waving an envelope in her hands. "Are you Mormons?"

"Yes."

The woman walked to where the missionaries were standing and handed Orrin an envelope. "Fru Ryland asked me to give this to you."

"Thank you," Orrin said. After the woman left, he opened the envelope and withdrew a short, handwritten note.

"Please do not come to my house. I cannot see you anymore," the note said. Orrin showed the note to Elder Gregersen.

Elder Gregersen pushed back his hat and rubbed his scalp. "Well, I guess that's that. Do you think it was because of her husband?"

"Of course, it was," Orrin said tersely. A curtain again rustled at the window, but Elder Gregersen claimed to have seen nothing.

The elders returned to Søster Poulsen's home each of the next three days, going in the morning, in the afternoon, and at night. Finally, on the third day, after pounding on the windows as well as the front door, a man living upstairs opened a window and called out from above. "What do you want?" he asked, his face full of annoyance. "Nobody lives there."

"We are looking for Fru Poulsen," Orrin said.

"She does not live here in anymore."

"Are you sure? We are friends of hers and she did not say anything to us about moving."

"If you are friends, then you know she completed her studies and returned home."

246

"To Mandel?"

"Yes. She left the day after her exams."

"Is she coming back?'

"To here? No. She paid her final rent invoice before leaving. I am just the landlord and she did not tell me her plans."

"Do you have an address? We would like to write to her." The man gave Orrin a suspicious look. "We are Mormon missionaries and Fru Poulsen has been talking with us about our religion. She asked us to come back."

"I know who you are," he said. "I saw you here with her many times. I will get her address." He went into the house and returned a few minutes later with an address torn from an envelope. He handed it to Orrin. Elder Gregersen reached into his coat pocket and pulled out a Joseph Smith pamphlet.

"Do you know anything among the Mormon Church?" Elder Gregersen asked. "We bring a message about modern day prophets."

The man took the pamphlet but declined to hear more. "I belong to the State Church."

Orrin retreated in stunned silence. "I have to sit down," he said, and so they walked to the same park where Elder Gregersen had rested just the week before. Orrin brushed the snow from the bench and patted his hands together to shake the snow from his gloves. He fell hard onto the seat, suddenly exhausted. He thought he might never get up.

"Put your head between your legs and I'll start handing out pamphlets," Elder Gregersen said.

"Very funny."

Elder Gregersen shoved his hands in his pockets and shrugged. "I thought something like this might happen. Søster Poulsen seemed golden in the beginning, but when she couldn't stop smoking, she started losing interest. That's when she started canceling appointments and putting us off. I was worried, but . . ."

Elder Gregersen continued talking, but Orrin, lost in thought, heard only the murmuring hum of his companion's voice. *Of course, Søster Poulsen was putting us off. How could I not see it? I have no powers of spiritual discernment whatsoever. And Søster Ryland. Another bad decision. I pray for guidance, I listen for the answers, but . . . am I fooling myself to think I can hear God's voice? What does it sound like anyway?* Orrin laughed at himself. Ever since he was a young boy, he had always hoped for a miraculous spiritual experience, even expected it would happen, certainly on his mission. He had wondered what it would be like to be visited by an angel or

247

whisked off into a heavenly realm like his Grandpa Heber. *I'm too dense—or too proud and sinful—to perceive God's will.*

"... anyway, I was hopeful, like you, that Søster Poulsen would come around, but I'm not surprised," Elder Gregersen concluded.

"You are more perceptive than I am," Orrin said bitterly, lifting himself from the bench. Although disheartened, the elders kept tracting until *middag*, because that's what missionaries do. Orrin's door approach felt robotic, and sounded that way too. It echoed in his head as he spoke, like the monotone drone of an actor who has no feel for his lines. After eating supper, Orrin and Elder Gregersen jointly composed a letter to Søster Poulsen. At Elder Gregersen's suggestion, they kept the letter conversational and did not press her about joining the church:

> *Dear Søster Poulsen,*
> *Your landlord told us you completed your studies and have returned home. We hope you did well on your exams and have received your license to become a pharmacist. Will you be returning to Oslo? If so, we would like to visit you again. We enjoyed getting to know you and discussing religion with you.*
> *Let us know how you are doing. We are especially eager to know whether you passed your exams.*
> *Sincerely,*
> *Elder Orrin Tanner and Elder Eric Gregersen*

Orrin wanted to add that they were interested in resuming teaching her the discussions, while also encouraging her to start reading the Book of Mormon. "This letter makes it sound like we are just her friends," he said.

"We are her friends."

"You know what I mean. We *are* missionaries, after all."

"And that's how we signed our letter," Elder Gregersen said. She's not going to forget who we are or why we pulled out our flannel board every time we came to her house."

Orrin relented. He was feeling sorry for himself. Composing a letter that went against his better judgment reinforced his self-pitying mood. The elders posted the letter on their way to their tracting area and continued proselytizing without fervor or success until nine thirty.

By morning, Orrin had willed himself to abandon his sad-faced sulk. Before going to bed the previous night, he had prayed for strength and wisdom and, more than anything else, an unmistakable sign—of what? He didn't know. Just something to bolster his morale and sustain him through his mission. When he woke up without having received the sought-after sign—other than a curious dream about lions roaming a beach—he concluded that no sign *was* a sign. God's test of his faithfulness was continuing. And so Orrin would prove himself worthy through dogged determination and obedience. He greeted the late-rising Elder Gregersen with what could only be described as a violent handshake, saying, "Good morning, Elder Gregersen. Let's make it a great day." During individual study, Orrin reread passages from *A Marvelous Work and A Wonder,* Apostle LeGrand Richards' inspirational book about Mormons and missionary work. At the end of the hour, Orrin jotted an affirmation on a notecard and tacked it on the wall next to his other affirmations: "I am a happy missionary."

Orrin worked like a man afire. He rose a full hour before the required time and pushed to start tracting as early as possible. He not only engaged Norwegians on the streetcar but also in the park and other public places, greeting people with a cheerful, "*God morgen. Hvordan star du til idag?* Good morning. How are you today?"

Elder Gregersen, however, was slow to take up the torch. He didn't rebel outright, but a weariness crept into his voice and a reluctance in his steps. He signaled his draining fervor with increasing tardiness. Elder Gregersen, who was now sleeping until the regular 6:30 a.m. wake-up time and dawdling in the mornings, laboring over breakfast dishes or fussing endlessly with the mirror above the sink, complaining that the mirror's many cracks made it impossible to shave properly. Orrin gave him an icy lecture after they missed an evening teaching appointment because Elder Gregersen wanted to change his tie right before they left. For this and countless other reasons, Orrin came to see Elder Gregersen as an albatross, a stumbling block to their success, and soon he found fault with just about everything his companion did. Elder Gregersen irritated Orrin with his slow manner of speaking, the insecure tone of his voice, the way he folded his duvet in a little square over his bed, his insistence on putting two spoonfuls of sugar in his oatmeal, his habit of loosening his soup-stained tie the minute he walked into the hybel, and his tendency to leave his dirty clothes on the floor by his bed. "Patience," Orrin counseled himself. Whenever he got really annoyed with Elder Gregersen mannerisms or habits, Orrin would repeat his affirmation: "I am a happy missionary."

Despite the constant repetition of his mantra, Orrin found himself again unhappy and out of patience by the week's end. On Friday morning, Elder Gregersen caused them to miss the morning streetcar and then, after they finished their *middag* meal and it was time to go tracting, Elder Gregersen suddenly announced he had to use the outhouse. "Okay," Orrin said, "let's go straight to the streetcar stop after you go."

"I'll need to come back upstairs and wash my hands."

"All right, but hurry." Orrin waited in the hybel for what seemed to be longer than necessary for Elder Gregersen to do his business. Orrin hurried him along when he returned and together they bolted out the door and down the stairs. "We can still make the 4:43 p.m. streetcar if we run," Orrin shouted to his companion, who was carrying their briefcase and running step-for-step behind him. Orrin was dashing out the courtyard gate when he heard a scream and a crash; he looked back to see Elder Gregersen sliding across the pavement on patch of ice, still holding the briefcase, which had popped open and scattered its contents. Orrin rushed back and began picking up their proselytizing materials and putting them back into the briefcase. Glancing at his watch, he said, "We still might have time."

Elder Gregersen struggled to a sitting position. "I can't," he whimpered.

"Are you hurt?"

"No, it's . . . I can't." Elder Gregersen started to cry, not loudly, but sniffling to himself. Orrin continued picking up their books and pamphlets. Some of their flannel board characters had spilled onto the ice. Orrin rubbed them on his coat sleeve to dry them off. One of their neighbors came out of the hallway and inquired if Elder Gregersen was all right.

"I have slipped and almost broken my neck a few times there myself," he said, pointing to the ice patch. "I have told the managers they need to do a better job of clearing the ice." Elder Gregersen assured the man he was not hurt, just embarrassed. The man waved a friendly goodbye and returned to his hybel.

"Elder Tanner," Elder Gregersen said, his voice quivering. "I can't go on like this. It's too much. You're a machine. Everyone knows that, but I'm not like you. I can't go blindly from door to door and—"

"I don't go *blindly* from door to door."

Elder Gregersen wiped his nose on the cuff of his coat. "It's like you have blinders on, like a horse or a mule that can only see what's in front of him but misses the big picture. Sometimes it seems you're more interested in DMing people and striking an X through their names than actually talking with them."

"We are called to be a voice of warning. Delivering the message is an important part of that calling."

"All I know is everyone tells me how lucky I am to be your companion and to be learning from the best, but our schedule . . . I've tried, but I can't keep it up. I'm tired. I'm nervous and stressed all the time, afraid I'll be the one to make a mistake and ruin our success. It's too much."

An overwhelming sadness swept over Orrin. Having reacted defensively to Elder Gregersen's accusations, he now saw painfully—clearly—how cruel and selfish he was. "I'm sorry, Elder," Orrin said softly. He closed the briefcase and took a seat on the steps. "I don't know why I'm always in such a hurry."

Of course, Orrin knew exactly why he was always in a hurry. He wanted to be the best missionary possible—he needed to be Norway's best missionary. But why? Elder Gregersen had called Orrin "the best." Best at what? At going mindlessly from door to door? Hah, maybe Elder Gregersen had it right after all. *Elder Gregersen says he's afraid of ruining our success? What success?* After more than a year, Orrin had nothing to show for his work. No converts. He didn't even have any investigators. *I am Norway's worst missionary.*

When Elder Gregersen stood up, his pants were torn and he had skinned a knee. The palms of his hand were bleeding, having scraped the pavement when he fell. They went upstairs so he could change. Orrin told him to take his time and, in fact, recommended they stay inside and study for the rest of the day, but Elder Gregersen insisted on going out, just as he had when he nearly fainted while fasting. They got invited in to teach part of the first discussion to a young university couple, but during an otherwise quiet night of tracting, Orrin contemplated his many failures as a missionary.

Orrin slept restlessly and awoke the next morning feeling unrefreshed. When he reached across the bed to look at his clock, it was already seven. Elder Gregersen was scurrying about in the kitchen, frying scrambled eggs and potato slices. Orrin opened his mouth to chastise his companion for not waking him but instead said a simple good morning and began his daily routine. He heated a pot of water for shaving, set the steaming pot by the sink, lathered, dipped his razor in the water, and began scraping at his face. Perhaps it was his troubled mind, but Orrin couldn't see his reflection clearly. The mirror's zig-zagging cracks created a kaleidoscope of distorted faces. Looking from one angle, he could see his upper lip and chin, but his cheeks were partitioned in quarters and his nose had completely disappeared. Changing the angle brought his cheeks into view, but his lips and chin disappeared. And his eyes, if at all visible, stared back like fractured marbles. Rising steam further obscured his reflection. The face staring back at him reminded Orrin of the grotesque, twisted faces of the people in Edvard Munch's paintings. Faces knotted in pain. As Orrin inspected more closely his own twisted features, he thought he saw Munch's self-portraits in his own reflection. Over and over Munch painted himself, forever trying not just to capture his physical self but also to understand who he was. But the ever-changing expressions in Munch's self-portraits, often conveying anguish and sorrow but never contentment, suggested he never pierced the mysterious veil masking his identity. *Who am I?* Orrin wondered, shifting his gaze to create new and changing distortions of his mirrored image. Nothing he saw pleased him.

After Orrin finished dressing and was packing the briefcase to begin their day's work, he noticed Elder Gregersen had attached a new affirmation on the wall above his bed. "I love my companion," it said.

Chapter 30

Be trustworthy. To be trusted is better than to be loved.

Conduct of a Missionary

Hearing a knock, President Toressen looked up from his desk and saw his assistants standing in the open doorway. "Elder Warden, Elder Bearensen, *god morgan*," he said, inviting them in with a cheerful wave. "How are my favorite assistants today?"

After becoming an assistant, Elder Ward had felt a surge of pride when he first heard President Toressen's effusive greeting—he had even bragged to his parents—until he learned Toressen referred to each successive pair of assistants as his favorites. Elder Ward thought about calling the mission president on his little falsehood, but not today. New missionaries were arriving from the Ricks College language training center in the morning, and they had a long day ahead mapping out companion pairs for more than one hundred missionaries. A select few missionaries would be promoted to senior companion or district leader. Elder Ward and Elder Sorensen had their recommendations in hand and expected quick decisions except in situations where the elders or sisters had not quite caught the spirit of the work or had trouble getting along with their companions. These would require some pondering and discussion.

"Here, read this," President Toressen said, handing the assistants a letter as they took seats opposite his desk. The letter contained the confession of Elder Neil Castle, who said he had fallen into temptation and had been exchanging kisses with a young woman in the Bergen congregation. "I foolishly thought I was in love and had even purchased an engagement ring," Elder Castle wrote, "but after my district leader confronted me, I realized I had made a great mistake and was dishonoring my calling as a missionary. I have broken off relations with the woman, but I realize that the process of repentance and forgiveness may require further punishment to which I will submit. I ask—please—that I not be sent home, as the humiliation would be more than I can bear."

After the assistants finished reading the letter, President Toressen handed them another letter, this one from Elder Castle's district leader. "I wish to say that while Elder Castle clearly violated mission rules and put himself in a compromising position, he is sincerely contrite and ready to put this episode behind him," the district leader wrote. "His dalliance—and that's all it was—appears to have been an attempt to find some purpose in his being called to the Norway mission. Of course, that does not excuse his behavior, but Elder Castle is, at heart, a good man and, up to this point, has been a faithful missionary."

Elder Sorensen folded the letters and placed them on the president's desk. "Are you thinking of sending Elder Castle home?"

"Not that he doesn't deserve it," Elder Ward said.

President Toressen shook his head no. "That would be much too harsh, Elders."

"But they were kissing. He deserves some type of punishment."

"Such as?"

Elder Ward had a ready solution. "We could make him a junior companion for the last months of his mission. That way he gets punished, which will serve as a warning to other missionaries who will surely hear about this through the rumor mill, but Elder Castle still gets to return home with an honorable release."

"What do you think, Elder Sorensen?" President Toressen asked.

The question caught Elder Sorensen off guard. As the junior assistant, he hesitated to disagree with Elder Ward, nor did he want President Toressen to think he was cavalier about following the mission rules. "I served with Elder Castle in Trondheim. He was one of the hardest-working missionaries in the district, and I honestly thought he would eventually be called as our district leader. I could tell he was disappointed when I was called to be Trondheim's district leader, but he didn't let it affect his work habits, and I felt, gratefully, that I always had his support."

"What's your point?" Elder Ward asked.

Elder Sorensen avoided Elder Ward's eyes as he spoke. "He's a good elder who clearly understands he made a mistake but deserves a chance to redeem himself. We need to transfer him far away from Bergen, but I don't think we need to punish him anymore than he is already punishing himself."

Elder Ward started to counter, but President Toressen held up his hand. "Let's transfer him to Kristiansand. Who's the district leader there?"

"Elder Flossen."

"Ah, yes, just the right person. We have some new missionaries in Kristiansand, including a couple of greenies, and so I'm going to instruct Elder Flossen to give Elder Castle some opportunities to teach proselytizing techniques and church doctrines to the missionaries."

"Can we be sure Elder Castle has truly repented?" Elder Ward asked.

"Have Elder Castle take the train to Oslo on his way to Kristiansand. I know it's out of the way, but I'll talk with him and make sure everything is in order. Once I'm assured of that, we'll have him finish his mission with an important leadership calling. It will give him something positive to talk about in his homecoming talk."

Elder Ward shrugged. "He'll probably think all of his troubles in Bergen were somehow part of divine plan to maneuver him into the calling."

"The Lord works in mysterious ways," President Toressen said, winking slyly at Elder Sorensen.

The three men continued working through lunch and dinner, taking their meals in the president's office, stopping only when the sister missionaries brought in a young woman investigator to see the mission home. Upon hearing the sisters in the reception area, President Toressen beckoned for them to come in. The assistants groaned, knowing Toressen never had a short chat with anyone. They were right. For more than an hour, Toressen told the woman about his first meeting with the missionaries, how he became so engrossed in reading the Book of Mormon that he did not sleep or leave his home until he finished reading it, and then he recounted numerous spiritual experiences after joining the church, including his miraculous vision that foretold of his call as mission president. The enthralled woman's eyes grew wide as saucers, and she bared her soul as she narrated her own story and quest for divine truth. The sisters left in grateful tears.

At nine o'clock, Sister Toressen knocked and without waiting for an answer, entered the side door adjoining the president's family quarters and instructed the men to wrap up their discussion. "I'm counting on you assistants to keep the president on his schedule. Doctor's orders."

"Sister Toressen likes to keep the trains running on time," President Toressen said, "Don't you dear?" He chuckled to himself. "Not that you're anything like Mussolini."

Sister Toressen's eyes narrowed. "Honestly, Bjørnstjerne. The things you say."

After she ducked back inside the family quarters, Elder Sorensen said, "President Toressen, did you know that Mussolini had a glass-bottom boat?"

"Huh, what? Why would Mussolini need a glass-bottom boat?"

"To review his fleet, sir."

A puzzled look swept over Toressen's face, and then he burst into laughter. "Ha, ha, ha. That is a good one. I must tell Sister Toressen."

"Not now, please," Elder Ward said. "I mean, we still have work to do."

President Toressen stared at his assistant. "Yes, later will do. Still, I must apologize to Sister Toressen for comparing her to Mussolini. So tell me, Elders. What's next on our agenda?" he asked, unable to hide his smile.

The last problem to tackle was what to do about Elders Tanner and Pedersen. The assistants, one after the other, reviewed for the mission president the elders' fall from grace.

"Elder Tanner leaves missionary pamphlets in outhouses, but people are using them as toilet paper."

"And he thinks that's inspired proselytizing."

"He brings investigators to church who smoke in the bathroom."

"He's obsessed with being the top-performing missionary."

"His companion, Elder Gregersen, said Elder Tanner was using his father's pamphlets to teach an investigator."

"And he's working himself—and Elder Gregersen—far beyond what's normal."

"Elder Gregersen is worn out and depressed."

"And Elder Tanner had a complete meltdown when he lost the Scripture Chase at the Oslo conference."

"He was apoplectic."

President Toressen listened in expressionless silence to the litany of Elder Tanner's transgressions. "That doesn't sound like the Elder Tanner I know," he said when the assistants had at last finished.

"Well, that's what he's become," Elder Ward said. To prove his point, he provided a detailed account of Elder Tanner's behavior at the Scripture Chase. But instead of being appalled, as Elder Ward thought he should have been, President Toressen shook his head and chortled, as if amused by the incident.

"Elder Tanner was right, you know," Toressen said. "The church didn't stop practicing polygamy until the prophet issued the second manifesto in 1904. Are you sure Joseph Fielding Smith's *Essentials in Church History* doesn't mention anything about it?"

Elder Sorensen shook his head. "No, President. We both checked."

"That is very odd. After all, it was his father, President Joseph F. Smith, who issued the 1904 manifesto. I can understand why Elder Tanner was upset."

"That's beside the point," Elder Ward said. "Elder Tanner overreacted and behaved horribly."

"Hmm, yes, you're right. Still, it's rather odd—"

Sister Toressen banged on the door and yelled from the other side. "It's nine thirty, gentlemen. Time to wrap it up."

President Toressen pretended not to hear. "Tell me about Elder Pedersen."

"I was his companion when he was a greenie," Elder Ward said. "He was quiet and kept to himself, like he was afraid to mix it up with the other elders, but boy, was he smart. He could practically speak the language like a Norwegian from the get-go."

"I've been trying to get him to open up and be more outgoing," President Toressen says. "He's got the most winning smile."

"That's the thing," said Elder Sorensen. "Now, all of the sudden, he's become a ball of fire when he's out tracting."

"But not in a good way—"

"No, not at all. He argues—"

"Delights in heated confrontation."

"And he's merciless with J-Dubs . . . I mean, Jehovah's Witnesses."

"He even made one woman cry."

President Toressen shook his head, as if he couldn't believe what he was hearing. "That's not the Elder Pedersen I know."

"But it's true," Elder Sorensen insisted.

"The strange thing is," Elder Ward added, "he has a special hatred for Elder Tanner. No one knows why—"

"Whenever they are together at their district meetings, Elder Pedersen does everything he can to rattle Elder Tanner."

President Toressen slumped in his chair and rubbed his eyes, as if suddenly overcome with tiredness. "This is very discouraging news. Very discouraging." He closed his eyes and was rocking gently when—*bang!* His eyes popped open and Sister Toressen shouted from behind the door.

"Last warning," she said. "Next time, I'm coming in."

President Toressen again ignored his wife's threats. "Let me think, Elders," he said. His chin fell to his chest. In the silence, the assistants heard a nearly imperceptible *click, click, click.*

"What's that?" asked Elder Sorensen.

"His pacemaker. You can hear it whenever he falls asleep. I'm going to wake him."

"What if he's getting inspiration?"

Click, click, click.

Elder Ward scoffed. "The man's sleeping, you dolt." He started to reach across the desk to wake the president, but Toressen suddenly coughed and opened his eyes, a cheerful expression on his face.

"Elders, let's send Elders Tanner and Pedersen to Harstad," President Toressen said. "We have an opening there, with Elder Riggs going home and Elder Crandall being transferred to a new area."

"You mean put them together as companions?" Elder Ward said.

"Exactly."

Both assistants started to object when—*bang! bang! bang!* Sister Toressen marched into the office as if her pink helmet of curlers was ablaze. "Okay, that's it. You know the rules, Bjørnstjerne. These elders have to be in bed by ten thirty sharp. No exceptions. You need your sleep too. If you've got more work to do, Elders, then you'll have to do it tomorrow."

"That's okay, dear," Toressen said. "We just finished up making our last assignment. We're all set for the upcoming mission-wide move when the new elders and sisters arrive."

Elder Ward stood up. "But President Toressen—"

"That's it. I mean it, Elders." Sister Toressen began shooing the assistants out of the office. "Even if you don't need your sleep, my husband does."

President Toressen smiled and shrugged. "Sister Toressen has spoken. It is time to call it quits." He handed the assistants the notes detailing all of the transfers and assignments. "Get started on this tomorrow." Standing between the two elders, he put his arms around their shoulders and led them to the door. Whispering conspiratorially, he said, "I'll let you know when Sister Toressen starts working on her glass-bottom boat."

Chapter 31

Prayer will keep you from sin and sin will keep you from prayer.
Conduct of a Missionary

His transfer to Harstad was punishment, Orrin was sure of that. The elders in the mission home couldn't bring themselves to look him in the eye. He could hardly look at them either. The humiliation would stay with him for the rest of his mission. Probably the rest of his life. When Elder Ward informed him of his assignment, he suggested that Orrin use the time for honest reflection. "This is an opportunity for a new start, Elder Tanner," he said. Orrin knew what he meant: "Repent and get your act together before it's too late." And so here Orrin sat, sharing an armrest with Elder Pedersen on a jet to northern Norway, two outcasts with nothing in common but their mutual animosity.

Orrin wished the assistants had been more sympathetic, but even he was appalled by his outburst at the Scripture Chase. Orrin couldn't remember ever losing his temper like that or feeling such aggrieved rage. He did not understand why it had been so important to win the Scripture Chase, nor could he explain the uncontrollable fury that came over him, an emotional hurricane determined to ravage everything in its path. Still, this was but one hiccup in what otherwise had been months of rigorous obedience to the mission rules, of faithfully going above and beyond. His intentions were good; that should count for something. Yet, what had he accomplished? He had converted no one. He had no spiritual experiences to speak of. Success appeared far beyond his grasp. *If hard work and obedience were not sufficient, what more was required?*

Before leaving, Orrin had stopped by the mission office, hoping to talk with President Toressen. "You're not going to get in to see him," said Elder Blake, the missionary secretary. "President Toressen is way behind schedule and should have left a half hour ago for a meeting in Drammen."

"I only need a few minutes."

Elder Blake was unmoved. "Even if I said yes, it wouldn't matter. Sister Toressen is on the warpath and I'm not getting in her way. When he finishes talking with Elder Castle, that's it. They're leaving—"

Just then, the president's office door opened. Toressen, his arm wrapped around Elder Castle's shoulder, ushered the young man into the reception area. Elder Castle's face beamed. "Thank you for the assignment, President Toressen," he said. "I won't let you down."

"I know you won't, Elder. That's why I gave you this calling."

Elder Blake stood and handed President Toressen a folder. "It's time to go, President. Here are the notes you wanted for your meeting. Sister Toressen is waiting in the van."

"Thank you." Toressen took the folder and was hurrying out the door when he noticed Orrin. "Why, Elder Tanner, it is good to see you. I'm very excited about your new assignment. I have great expectations for you and Elder Pedersen. It's not often we place two top missionaries together as companions."

"President Toressen, I know you're rushed, but could I talk to you for just a few minutes?" Toressen hesitated but saw the pleading in Orrin's eyes.

"Of course, Elder Tanner." The mission president turned to his disgruntled secretary. "Please go downstairs and tell Sister Toressen I will be there in five minutes."

Inside his office, President Toressen sat at his desk behind a partially eaten leafy green salad. "This will give me a chance to finish my dinner," he said, picking up a fork. "The doctors put me on a low-fat, low-salt, low-cholesterol diet to ease the pressure on my heart." He chuckled as he stabbed at the lettuce and tomatoes. "I've had difficulty strictly maintaining my diet here in Norway."

Orrin got the impression that President Toressen didn't really care for his dietary restrictions because Toressen mainly poked at his salad while rhapsodizing about the many tasty desserts filled with sugar and eggs and butter the Norwegian members cooked for him when he visited the different branches. When it appeared he might expound indefinitely on the subject, Orrin interrupted and said, "I know you need to leave right away, President, but I have something I wanted to ask you before I fly to Harstad."

President Toressen pushed aside the plate and pulled his chair forward as if he had all the time in the world. "Go head, Elder Tanner."

As best he could, Orrin described his mission thus far. Despite his desire to be a good missionary and follow all of the rules, success had eluded him. "I've been a failure as a missionary and even worse as a companion."

"Don't be so hard on yourself, Elder Tanner. You know, the Lord doesn't look at your outward accomplishments. He looks at what's in your heart."

"But that's just it. My heart . . . my heart is empty. I . . . I have somehow lost the spirit." It was a gut-wrenching confession, one Orrin had not planned on making, one that until now, he could not even admit to himself. He looked down at his hands folded neatly on his lap, not wishing to see the shock and disappointment that was surely written on the president's face. Until this moment, he had not realized how fervently he hungered for President Toressen's approbation and respect. But he had gone this far in acknowledging his weakness, so he continued. "Do you have any advice at all? Is there a secret to missionary life, something I've overlooked? I don't expect immediate results, but could you tell me something that might set me on the right path?"

"That's a big question, Elder." President Toressen straightened and looked intently at Orrin, contemplating his answer. Orrin lifted his chin and forced himself to look at his mission president. Toressen's eyes were warm and reassuring.

"The mission rules have been given to us by inspiration," Toressen said. "A missionary will never go astray if he obeys the rules. But—"

"Bjørnstjerne!" Sister Toressen stomped into the room, her arms flapping wildly. "I've been sitting in the van for fifteen minutes waiting for you and look, you've hardly touched your salad. If you keep this up, you're going to die of malnutrition or work yourself into another heart attack. Honestly, I don't know why—"

Orrin looked up, stunned. Sister Toressen abruptly stopped when she saw his face and began speaking softly, apologizing and explaining that, unfortunately, President Toressen needed to be on his way. Orrin could see Sister Toressen was trying to put him at ease, but he remained open-mouthed and mute, unsettled by seeing the mission president scolded so severely by his wife. It didn't bother President Toressen, though.

"I'm sorry, Elder Tanner, but she's right," he said. "I need to be going." He gathered his papers and started for the door. His eyes met Orrin's as he walked past, and he blinked suddenly with the realization they had not finished their conversation.

"The spirit—" he said.

Sister Toressen hooked her arm through his. "Come on, Bjørnstjerne."

President Toressen grabbed the lapel of Orrin's coat and pulled him close, so close that Orrin could smell mustard dressing on his lip and see tiny razor cuts on his neck and chin. "Remember, Elder Tanner," he said, tightening his grip, "the letter killeth, but the spirit giveth life."

He held Orrin's gaze long enough to ensure that he understood, then released Orrin's coat as his wife pulled him through the door.

Eddie had shown no emotion when his district leader notified him he was being transferred to Harstad, but his heart filled with satisfaction and optimism. Many Norwegian missionaries longed to serve in the country's northernmost districts. The natural hardships—subfreezing temperatures, relentless snowfall, oppressive winter darkness, and scarcity of church members—fed romantic notions of sacrifice and perseverance that were the staple of the faith-promoting tales told by returning missionaries. Adversity, like fasting, heightened spirituality. Eddie interpreted his call to Harstad as evidence the deal was still on, that God had not forgotten or abandoned him, that God would remove the burden of homosexuality if Eddie endured to the end. "The blissful, gratifying feeling must certainly be God's spirit," he thought. But that was before he learned that Elder Tanner would be his companion. "The cosmic joke continues," he mumbled upon hearing the news.

Was this yet a further test? Or was he being punished? Making him a co-senior companion with Elder Tanner suggested they were being equally punished, as if they were equally to blame for the Scripture Chase debacle. *But I did nothing wrong. It was Elder Tanner who lost his temper and ruined the game. I suppose I could have acknowledged that Elder Tanner's answer was correct, but that wasn't my responsibility.* Eddie reviewed in his mind all of the reasons why his new assignment was unfair. Before leaving for Harstad, he met with President Toressen.

"Am I being punished?" Eddie asked.

"Oh, no. Harstad is a challenging assignment, but you are more than capable, Elder Pedersen. Do you view it as punishment?

"You know about Elder Tanner and me, about what happened at the Scripture Chase?"

President Toressen smiled. "I know Elder Tanner feels terrible about his behavior. More importantly, I know this is promising opportunity for both of you—and for the Norwegian mission. This is the first time I've ever felt moved to put together the mission's top scholars as co-senior companions. Expectations are high, Elder Pedersen."

"Are you saying our call to Harstad is inspired?"

"That's up to you and Elder Tanner. Hopefully, you two will make me look inspired," Toressen said cheerfully. He rose and offered his hand, but Eddie merely nodded, unsmiling and slumped against his chair, his suit coat weighing heavily on his shoulders. "Is something wrong, Elder Pedersen?" Toressen asked.

Eddie wanted to unburden himself and confess that he was still attracted to men. Reparative therapy had not cured him. Prayer had not cured him. Missionary service had not cured him. God had not cured him. "What's the secret?" he wanted to ask. But he was afraid of being sent home in disgrace, of living the rest of his life as an irredeemable degenerate. And he was afraid of revealing the depth of his anger. "Wouldn't you be angry?" he wanted to shout. He thought back to his first conversation with President Toressen. "The truth shall set you free," he had said. Eddie fidgeted and pulled at his cuffs. Now is the time, Eddie thought.

Toressen sat patiently, waiting for Eddie to respond. Suddenly, his face darkened, as if he had been disturbed by an unpleasant memory. He began speaking in a grave, measured manner. "Elder Pedersen, I must ask you, are you having any problems with—"

Eddie cut him off. "No president, I've been chaste my whole mission. No touching, no kissing, no romantic liaisons."

"And what about your desires for the same sex?

"Not a problem. I've been cured."

Thinking back to the conversation, Eddie could not understand why he reacted so defensively, answered so emphatically, lied so brazenly. He could not envision a happy resolution to his predicament, only a delay to his inevitable, ignominious fate. Ha, ignominious! That's exactly the right word for it. Was it Korihor the anti-Christ or Nehor the apostate who suffered an ignominious death? Eddie couldn't remember. Elder Tanner would probably know. Eddie looked at his new companion, who was sitting in the window seat, eating the *smørbrød* brought by the stewardess and studying his scripture cards. Eddie's unhappiness wasn't Elder Tanner's fault, yet he couldn't help but be mad at somebody. It might as well be Elder Tanner.

Orrin's eyes hurt. Too little light. He put up his tray and adjusted his seat to recline. Elder Pedersen was reading a magazine article, something about the mistreatment of Laplanders in northern Norway. Orrin could see the article was too complex for him to understand, not without the constant use of a dictionary, but it posed no problem for Elder Pedersen. The only time Elder Pedersen had said anything since they got on the airplane was to ask Orrin whether he wanted an aisle or window seat. The right thing to do was to apologize for his poor sportsmanship, but Elder Pedersen didn't seem to be the forgiving kind. Orrin closed his eyes to give them a quick rest before resuming his reading, but the buzz of the cabin noise pulled him into a deep sleep. He dreamed he was standing in a grassy meadow, lush and green, watching his great-grandfather Lars Andreassen and his Grandpa Heber rocking a baby and then giving it to Orrin's father. Orrin realized he was watching the reenactment of his own father's vision or dream. "Hey, that's me! That baby is me!" he shouted to the men, but when they turned to face him, they had become roaring lions. Their roars grew louder and louder until Orrin was jolted awake by the thunderous blast of thrusting jet engines as the plane rocked and swayed on the runway before coming to a halt.

Chapter 32

Remember your calling is one of full dedication with all your heart, might, mind, and strength.

Conduct of a Missionary

Jann Harald Brevik met Elders Tanner and Pedersen at the airport gate. They were easy to spot among the handful of passengers who had flown into Narvik's small airport. Both smiled and offered firm, missionary handshakes, but their faces were tired with travel. Jann Harald also saw Herr Jørgensen walking behind the missionaries and offered him a ride back to Harstad.

"That is very kind of you," Herr Jørgensen said. "I was not looking forward to the bus ride home."

Herr Jørgensen, who was returning from a visit to his daughter in Hønefoss, sat in the front seat but rode most of the way facing the back, his thick arm draped across the seat as he talked with the missionaries. He had a square face, uneven teeth, and pendulous jowls. He wanted to know everything about the missionaries: where they came from, where in Norway they had been stationed, how long they intended to stay in Harstad, and their impressions of the Norwegian people. Jann Harald listened carefully to their answers. He had begged President Toressen to station missionaries in Harstad, even though it was a small island town and had only three members: Jann Harald and his oldest sons, Roland and Atle. The previous missionary pair, Elders Jackson and Hayden, while hardworking, had been discouraged by the long winter nights and the absence of a church organization.

"Mormonism is more than its doctrines and teachings, Bror Brevik," Elder Jackson had said when explaining their lack of success. "It is also the church programs that bring members together in fellowship and worship. That is really what makes us unique. But here in Harstad, we cannot offer that to our investigators."

"We have to start somewhere," Jann Harald countered. "After all, Joseph Smith organized the church with only six members." Though unwilling to admit the point, Jann Harald knew Elder Jackson was right. That's why he had wanted missionaries in Harstad. He himself needed the fellowship of like-minded believers, even if it was just two elders. His sons needed it even more. They were losing the church connections they had in Oslo. And if he was ever going to bring his wife around to see the truth . . . well, he needed reinforcements.

264

"You speak the language like a Norwegian," Herr Jørgensen told Elder Pedersen, "but you," he said, pointing to Elder Tanner, "you must come to my house and we will teach you how to speak like a genuine Norwegian." Seeing Elder Tanner blush, Herr Jørgensen let go a boisterous, jowl-shaking laugh. "And you can teach my daughter how to speak English like an American. She is seventeen and very pretty, but don't get any ideas. It is for English lessons only."

Roland and Atle greeted the missionaries at the door. "Welcome to the Brevik house," they said, speaking English. They bowed in unison.

Behind them stood their mother, Ingrid, holding the hand of a toddling Anne-Marie. With her faded blonde hair and loose-fitting pants, Ingrid peered at the elders through tired eyes. "Welcome," she said, extending her hand. "Jann Harald tells me you will need a place to stay until you find a hybel to rent. Our house is small, but we will try to make you as comfortable as possible."

"Thank you, Søster Brevik," Orrin said.

Ingrid spun on her heels. "*Uffa meg.* Do not call me Søster. I am neither a Mormon nor a nun."

"Thank you, *Fru* Brevik," Eddie said.

Ingrid smiled awkwardly. "That is much better." She led them to the bedroom they would share with Roland and Atle.

Over a dinner of fish balls and boiled potatoes, they talked about America and Norway. The Breviks had moved to Harstad two years earlier so Jann Harald, who served in the Norwegian military, could take a NATO posting. "His job has something to do with monitoring Soviet submarines," Ingrid said, "but Herr Top Secret will not tell me anything."

Jann Harald smiled but otherwise ignored his wife's comment. Ingrid had opposed the move due to the cold, dark, and long Harstad winters and the isolation from family and friends, which was exacerbated by Jann Harald's frequent travels to northern outposts, often for weeks at a time. "I am stuck here by myself with all of the responsibilities caring for our home and children, while also working at the hospital," Ingrid said.

"You do not have to work," Jann Harald said. "I have told you that."

"And then I would be stuck at home all the time. No, thank you."

"Then you should not complain if that is your choice."

Ingrid picked up her fork and glared at Jann Harald as if she intended to reach across the table and stab him. "What do you do at the hospital?" Orrin asked.

Ingrid relaxed the grip on her fork. "I am a nurse. It is a fulfilling profession and I can easily find work wherever Jann Harald is stationed."

The tension subsided and the conversation turned to lighter subjects until the elders had taken their last bites and Ingrid began clearing the table. Jann Harald abruptly announced he wanted to talk about
Mormonism. "We must take advantage of the missionaries' presence to
teach you more about our religion," he told his wife. Then, turning to
the missionaries, he said, "Could you teach us about the law of eternal
progression from the fifth discussion?"

"Oh, I have already heard the discussions," Ingrid said, disappearing
into the kitchen before the missionaries could reply.

"Yes, dear, but obviously you did not understand."

Ingrid turned on the water and began rinsing the dishes. "I understood everything," she called out pleasantly.

"Well, then you know how important it is for families to stay together
throughout eternity," her husband said. "Please come back, Ingrid. We
will not try to teach you the discussions. We only want to talk."

Ingrid returned, drying her hands on a towel, and took a seat across
from the missionaries. Jann Harald attempted to impress upon his wife
the importance of a temple marriage. "You see, Ingrid, The Church of
Jesus Christ of Latter-day Saints is the only church in the world with the
priesthood authority to seal a husband and wife together for all eternity."

"I have not decided whether I want to be married to you for that long.
Besides, you cannot go to the celestial kingdom without me."

"If you do not accept the gospel, I will be given someone else in the
next life—perhaps a woman whose husband would not join the church."

"Good riddance."

"We do not want another mother," Atle said, covering his mouth to
avoid spewing food.

"We want you to be with us forever," Roland pleaded.

"That is very nice, boys. I would like that too. But in the meantime,
please do not talk and eat at the same time. There is probably a rule against
that in the celestial kingdom."

Orrin and Eddie largely remained observers, though Jann Harald occasionally called on them to offer scriptural evidence or points of logic
to support his arguments. He became annoyed by the missionaries' obvious lack of enthusiasm, even resistance, to joining in the discussion. He
scowled when Orrin corrected his interpretation of the law of consecra-
tion, causing his wife to smile. It was clear that Jann Harald's earnest
proselytizing and Ingrid's bemused, ironic responses had become an established ritual the missionaries were powerless to alter. Her flippant retorts
kept Jann Harald at bay until, frustrated, he began lecturing her about

the blessings she would lose by rejecting Mormonism. "Think of your children," he said. "They will all be taken from you and given to another."

Fru Brevik stared at her husband in defiant disbelief, then put the dish towel to her face, hiding tears, and ran from the room. "What a cruel religion!"

Jann Harald gave the elders an apologetic look. "Ingrid, my wife, she is very stubborn."

The next morning, Ingrid chatted pleasantly with her missionary guests while she prepared her special *pannekaker* with strawberry jam and powdered sugar. It appeared the previous night's tension had abated, but when Jann Harald put on his hat and coat to leave with the missionaries, Ingrid harangued her husband to the door. "I suppose you are going to be gone all day while I am expected to sit home alone with the children."

"I told you I would be helping the missionaries get situated today."

"My shift at the hospital starts at four."

"I will be back by three," Jann Harald said, buttoning his coat. He wrapped a wool scarf around his neck and opened the door for the missionaries. A moist, frigid wind whipped through the entryway. Elders Tanner and Pedersen, who had watched in awkward silence as husband and wife squabbled, stepped eagerly into the Arctic air. "*Takk for frokost, Fru Brevik. Ha det,*" they called out cheerfully. "Thank you for breakfast. Goodbye."

The first stop for the elders was the police station, where a voice boomed from behind the desk: "Jann Harald, I see you have brought a new set of American spies to our town." A bearded man stood and reached out a hand to the missionaries. "I am Police Captain Aksel Hansen. Will you be staying long in Harstad?"

Elder Tanner looked at Elder Pedersen and shrugged. "Two or three months, perhaps, but we never know for sure how long we will be stationed in any location."

"We move around a lot within Norway," Elder Pedersen added.

"I guess that is how it is in the CIA spy business." Captain Hansen laughed and slapped Jann Harald on the back.

"You are too smart for us," Jann Harald said.

"Being Mormon missionaries, that is a good cover," Captain Hansen said. He turned to the missionaries. "Do not worry, boys, I will not reveal your real identities."

After they finished registering with the police and had left the station, Elder Tanner asked, "Do they really think we are CIA spies?"

"No, that is a little joke I have with Aksel. When the first missionaries came here, some people really thought they were spies, because they often came to my house."

"And because you work for NATO."

"That is right."

"We should work that into our door approach," Elder Pedersen said.

Elder Tanner laughed in agreement, but Jann Harald frowned. "Please do not do that. It could jeopardize your work, and mine too."

Jann Harald next took the elders to a clothing store to buy fur hats. "You need warmer hats like mine. See how mine has ear flaps you can pull down," he said, demonstrating by tying the straps under his chin. "Otherwise, your ears could get frostbite."

Jann Harald recommended fox fur as the warmest, but he noticed Elder Tanner was trying on hats from the faux fur shelf. "Are you opposed to hats made from animal fur?" he asked.

"No, I . . . I cannot afford them. Even hats made with rabbit fur are too expensive for me. I had not planned on this additional expense."

After spending most of his time examining rabbit-fur hats, Elder Pedersen eventually selected a more expensive hat with lightly colored red fox fur with streaks of gray and white. "Very stylish, Elder Pedersen," Jann Harald said. "You not only talk like a real Norwegian, but now you also will look like one."

Elder Pedersen beamed, as if this were the effect he was looking for. "Is that the hat you're going to buy?" he said, pointing to his companion's faux fur hat.

"Yes. Is there anything wrong with that?"

"No," Elder Pedersen said with an air of feigned indifference. "I was just curious."

The three men spent the rest of the morning looking for a hybel to rent. Armed with advertisements from the local newspaper, Jann Harald drove the elders to different locations until they finally found a suitably furnished hybel on Jørns Gate. The recently widowed owner, Fru Kjelberg, was renting the upstairs of her house. "I no longer need so many rooms, and walking up and down stairs has become difficult for me," she said. A white-haired woman with an arthritic limp, Fru Kjelberg was reluctant to rent to the missionaries. "I belong to the State Church, as do all of my family and friends. We do not go in for all of this sect business."

"I understand," Jann Harald said. "But these young men are not asking you to join their church. They only want to rent your room." He explained that the elders did not drink or smoke, would not host loud parties, and would not bring women into the house. "They will be out of the house working most days, and when they come home, they go to bed promptly at ten thirty every night," he said and, pointing to the missionaries, added. "You will feel very safe having such dependable young men living in your home."

Elders Tanner and Pedersen puffed out their chests and raised their arms to flex their biceps under their heavy coats. "My women friends will be jealous," Fru Kjelberg said. The elders drove back with Jann Harald to retrieve their belongings and moved in that afternoon.

"I hope you can come to our house for family home evening on Monday. Maybe Ingrid will be more receptive to hear the gospel after she knows you better," Jann Harald said before hurrying home to watch his children during his wife's hospital shift.

Chapter 33

In all discussions *except* the first, the contact probably should be called, "Brother Haugen" rather than "Herr Haugen." . . . People enjoy being called "brother" and "sister."

A Uniform System for Teaching Investigators

The Jørns Gate hybel offered luxurious living compared to typical missionary apartments. The eat-in kitchen had a stove and full-size refrigerator, while the bedroom had plenty of closet space and comfortable beds. In the living room, a large window provided a panoramic view of the harbor and the surrounding islands. A sliding-glass door opened to a small deck where the elders could watch boats come and go. The snow-covered deck wasn't much use now, but Orrin imagined it would offer a relaxing place to eat and study during the summer months. The missionaries' bathroom and shower were located in the unheated basement, but at least the water was hot. They could use the telephone at the bottom of the stairs, as long as they left money in the bowl whenever they made a call and did not abuse the privilege. "I am sorry, but I have only one house key to give you," Fru Kjelberg said. When neither elder reached to take it, she laid it on the table.

Alone together for the first time since being assigned as companions, Orrin and Eddie unpacked in awkward silence. Orrin wondered what he had done to earn his companion's enmity. It wasn't just the Scripture Chase. Elder Pedersen had never liked him. Orrin had overheard Elder Pedersen's mocking digs and asides to the other missionaries. He saw the self-satisfied smirks. Elder Pedersen had everything going for him. He spoke the language perfectly; he knew the scriptures and church doctrine as well as anyone, including Orrin; he had been the first in their language training group to become a senior companion; and he had, with seeming effortlessness, distinguished himself as one of the top performers in every district where he served. "Why do you hate me?" Orrin wanted to ask. Instead, he said, "Bror Brevik sure is anxious to see his wife get baptized."

"I'd say there's a better chance that Søster Brevik—I mean *Fru Brevik*—files for divorce than there is she is baptized."

"That won't look to good for us."

"We would probably get negative points on the Mission Comparative," Elder Pedersen said with his familiar smirk. "I'd say minus fifty would be about right."

"More like minus one hundred," Orrin said. *Elder Pedersen does have a wickedly funny sense of humor*, he thought. *I just wish he wouldn't direct it at me.*

Neither missionary knew how a co-senior companionship was supposed to work, but they eventually agreed to alternate weeks taking the lead in deciding where to tract and how to handle investigators. Orrin offered to let Elder Pedersen go first. Much to his disappointment, his companion accepted without any hesitation or insistence that no, Orrin ought to go first. *So this is how it's going to be.*

At each door, Orrin and Eddie vied to show who could be more sincere, more enthusiastic, more spiritual, more persuasive. Each reached deep into his repertoire to cite obscure scriptures and maxims, aiming to outshine the other. "Seek, and ye shall find; knock, and it shall be opened unto you. This is the scripture that prompted Joseph Smith to pray to God," Eddie told a Norwegian housewife.

"As man now is, God once was. As God is, man may be," Orrin repeated on several occasions, quoting President Lorenzo Snow's aphorism. He hoped to startle listeners and grab their interest by hinting at Mormonism's unique teaching that men and women can become gods and goddesses.

Eddie chastised Orrin. "You're giving people the meat before the milk. We need to stick to the basic doctrines."

"Well, that's the way President Toressen does it," Orrin countered. "And he's the prophet of Norway."

"But you're not."

Orrin got a chance to show disapproval when they spoke to a man who claimed he did not need Mormonism because he was already saved. "The Apostle Paul says we are saved by grace and our faith in Jesus Christ," the man said.

"You need works too," Eddie responded. "God helps those who help themselves."

Orrin shook his head. "*Dette ikke står i bibelen, Elder.* That is not in the Bible."

"He is right," the man told Eddie. "You are not teaching from the Bible."

A surprising number of people invited them in. They were not interested in hearing about Mormonism, but it was a simple matter of courtesy among Norway's northernmost residents that when people came to call, you didn't turn them away, especially if they were standing in a bone-chilling wind. "Would you like a cup of tea to warm up?" they would ask as they directed the grateful elders to a place by the fire. Like Herr

Jørgensen, most hosts wanted to know what the elders thought about their country. The islanders readily admitted that the frigid Norwegian winters were dark and dreary, especially in the north, but they took stoic pride in their ability to endure. Inevitably, they touted Norway's economic and social programs. "Norway is not like America where you have a few rich people and a lot of poor. We pay high taxes so we can share our wealth and give everyone a good living," said a retired fisherman.

"This is how people like us can live in places like the Lofoten Islands," his wife added. "We never have to worry about medical expenses."

"Even the university is free. Our children got very good educations and good jobs when they finish."

"And now we are pensioners. It is a good life. Would you like some more tea?"

The Norwegians watched with childlike curiosity when the elders set up the flannel board, but they rarely allowed the missionaries to get beyond telling Joseph Smith's story. "We are not interested in becoming Mormons . . . we belong to the State Church and that is enough for us . . . it is not possible to know which church is right . . . every religion has some truth . . . it does not matter which church you belong to, as long as you live an honorable life." These were the same rejections Orrin and Eddie had heard their entire missions, but Harstad's residents were more diplomatic, even apologetic. "I am afraid you will not find many converts in our town, but you are welcome to come visit anytime. It has been very pleasant talking with you boys."

"These people feel worse about rejecting us than we do being rejected," Orrin observed after spending a pleasant but ultimately fruitless evening with a dockworker and his school-teacher wife.

"Maybe if we start crying, they'll let us teach the discussions," Eddie said.

"Or at least let us finish telling the Joseph Smith story."

As Orrin and Eddie climbed the steep hill from the bus station to Jørns Gate, they joked about the different ways they could leverage the Norwegians' keen sense of hospitality to get more call backs. "If this approach works, it will prove politeness is a divine quality," Orrin said.

"You should write that in your book of inspirational thoughts," Eddie advised. Orrin couldn't tell if Elder Pedersen was serious or mocking him again.

Bror Brevik invited the elders to his home on Monday evenings to help him teach his wife how to hold a proper family home evening, though Eddie thought Fru Brevik managed fine. She prepared plenty of desserts, took her turn in leading the discussions, and on the whole appeared anxious to show she cared as much about raising a wholesome family as did the Mormons. Bror Brevik, however, made every issue a referendum on Mormonism. After his wife taught a lesson on honesty, he remarked, "I think you can see, Ingrid, how important it is to have modern-day prophets who can help us understand these important principles."

"We hardly need a prophet to tell us we should always tell the truth. The Bible teaches that."

"Yes, but the Mormon Church has given us this inspired family home evening manual to teach the children."

"Every church has books for teaching children, Jann Harald."

"But the Mormon Church teaches about the importance of families."

"You speak as if the Mormons discovered the family." Fru Brevik passed around a tray of cookies. "Here, Elders, have some treats."

Eddie was always hoping to say something that might prove inspirational or sway Fru Brevik, but he could never think of anything distinctly clever or insightful. Besides, he felt sorry for her. Bror Brevik used the church's teachings as a club to batter his wife into belief and seemed more intent on proving her wrong than fostering a loving spirit. "Ah, Ingrid," he would say, his eyes wide and smiling, "if only you could truly understand the scriptures." Fru Brevik, digging in, would smile right back. Eddie and Orrin tried to gently instruct her, bearing their testimonies of the happiness she would receive if she humbled herself in prayer, but she resisted their good intentions. With her husband, children, and missionaries arrayed against her, she inevitably jumped from the couch and fled the room, occasionally in tears.

"She runs because she knows the church is true," Bror Brevik said. "Her mother would disown her if she joined the church. That is why she is so frightened."

At the next family home evening, Eddie told Bror Brevik that he and Elder Tanner would take charge, but instead of presenting a lesson, they taught the older boys and their parents how to play *Trosartikler*. The Breviks had no trouble learning the rules, and soon everyone was throwing down cards and debating the best strategies for winning. Fru Brevik revealed herself to be devious as well as astute, often tricking the other players into laying down the wrong cards, which she pounced on with delight. Roland and Atle reveled in the chance to play and banter with their parents and the missionaries. "Be wary of too much talking and too little paying attention," Fru Brevik said with a malicious grin, and then swept up Roland's card with her joker. Her laughter was contagious, infecting everyone except Bror Brevik, who, after the fifth game, asked whether the elders had also prepared a lesson. "Family home evening must have a spiritual message," he said.

"Enjoying time together as a family is tonight's message," Eddie responded.

"There's been a good spirit here tonight," Orrin added.

Ingrid shot her husband a scolding look. "Please, Jann Harald, we are having a good time. Isn't that enough?"

"*Hei, gutter*," a boisterous voice called out. "Hello, boys." Herr Jørgensen waved to the missionaries from behind the counter, where Orrin and Eddie were examining meats to purchase for *middag*. Pointing to their fur hats, he said, "I see you are now dressed like genuine northerners."

Herr Jørgensen's loud welcome to his butcher shop turned all eyes onto the missionaries, who nodded and smiled to the other customers. "Try the whale beef," he said. "Fresh today. It is very tasty, like beef steak."

"Who are your new friends?" a thick man with a weather-beaten face asked.

"These are Mormon missionaries who have come to convert the heathens," Herr Jørgensen laughed. "Any success so far, boys?"

Orrin and Eddie shook their heads.

"I hear you are spies. Is that not true?"

"If we were, we could not tell you," Eddie replied.

"Ha, ha, ha. You are deviously clever. And you speak perfect Norwegian, just like we would expect from a spy."

"Yes, he is a spy, but as you can hear, I am not," Orrin said, prompting laughter.

"I am Peter Reissmann," the man said, extending a hand. "I am pleased to meet you. And I also recommend the whale meat. And the eel too. I brought both of them here today myself."

Herr Reissmann explained that he piloted a boat along the Lofoten Islands and down the coast, sometimes ranging as far south as Bodø, carrying supplies to the coastal ports too small to be served by the Hurtigruten ships. He outfitted his boat with compartments to hold fish, fruits and vegetables, and cheese and other grocery store products, as well as everyday supplies ranging from soap and toilet paper to trash bags and brooms. Fishermen often paid for the goods with their latest catch, fresh delicacies such as crab, eel, and whale beef that Reissmann sold at the larger ports for a hefty profit. He occasionally carried passengers as well, though the accommodations consisted of a wooden bench in an unheated hold and a cramped bathroom that sloshed water from the toilet in choppy seas. The towns and fishing villages he served were unknown to the missionaries except one.

"You say that Riksøy is one of your stops?" Orrin asked excitedly.

"Yes, the people there are regular customers. It sits off the southern tip of the Lofoten Islands, a town of about four hundred people," Reissmann said. "Do you know the place?"

"Yes, my great-grandfather Lars Andreassen came from Riksøy."

"Hmm, 'Andreassen.' There are some people there still by that name. Perhaps they are relatives."

"I hope so," Orrin said. "It has always been my family's wish to visit the island and find relatives there. My great-grandfather continued writing to them until he died. After my mission, my parents and my grandfather are planning to come to Norway and visit Riksøy with me."

"I could take you now, while you are here in Harstad, if you like," Reissmann said.

"Thank you, but I am afraid that would not be allowed, not while I am a missionary," Orrin said.

"No?"

"The mission rules require us to stay in the areas where we are called to serve. But it is nice to know there is transportation to the island."

Day after day, Orrin and Eddie obediently trudged through Harstad's snow-packed streets, each day unfolding like the last. They arose in darkness, knocked on doors in darkness, and returned home in darkness. People were cordial and many invited them in. They helped the missionaries take off their overshoes, brushed the snow from their coats, complimented Eddie's stylish fur hat, and laughed with Orrin when he made fun of his American accent. "One day," they said, "you will speak with the accent of a genuine Norwegian, just like Elder Tanner." They poured steaming tea and served *smørbrød* and sugary treats, tolerating brief discussions of Joseph Smith before steering the conversation to more general topics. When alone together, as they were much of the day, Orrin and Eddie put on a facade of politeness to cover a mutual hostility as biting and cold as the Arctic air. Eddie resented more than ever Elder Tanner's golden-boy status. Their fellow missionaries admired and praised Elder Tanner as a hardworking machine who never rested, never got discouraged, and never faltered. Eddie found him to be an utter bore. As for Orrin, he regarded Elder Pedersen as sullen and unfriendly. Even in the LTM, Elder Pedersen had rejected attempts by the other Norwegian missionaries to befriend him. *He never smiled then; he never smiles now, other than when he makes a smirking, self-serving remark.*

Orrin saw his dream of mission success fading fast away. He persevered, obedient as ever, pushing himself to the next door—there was always a next door—even when his cheeks burned icy red. On the coldest days, his fingers ached with numbness each time he took off his gloves to write in the tracting book. He wanted to blame Elder Pedersen for his misery—and some days he did—but this did nothing for getting him on the right track. Unfortunately, he and Elder Pedersen were yoked in companionship and they would rise or fall together. Orrin knew he should talk to his companion and somehow get beyond their hoary truce, but he did not know how to begin and feared a caustic rejection. On a whim, he got up early one morning and shined Elder Pedersen's shoes. He quietly removed the shoes from their closet while Elder Pedersen slept, first cleaning the scuff from the heels and toes, and then applying two layers of black polish that he rubbed in with a soft cotton cloth. He constructed in his mind the conversation of reconciliation that would ensue from his act of goodwill. He and Elder Pedersen would each admit his faults, fostering a friendship that would bring back the spirit and restore his enthusiasm for the work. With deep satisfaction, he held up the shoes to the kitchen light and admired its reflection in the smooth, black polish. He placed the shoes back in the closet and studied the Acts of the Apostles until Elder Pedersen arose.

If Elder Pedersen noticed the sparkling shine of his shoes when he took them from the closet, he did not remark upon it to Orrin. Neither did he mention it while they tracted on the far side of Harstad's *Folkeparken*. To be sure, the elders wore rubber overshoes while walking outdoors, but Elder Pedersen slipped off his overshoes when they were invited indoors. How could he not help but see the glistening shine each time he put the overshoes back on before returning outdoors? When Elder Pedersen's apparent lack of gratitude started to rankle, Orrin told himself his companion was waiting until the end of the day to acknowledge his good deed and thank him for it. But when Orrin knelt in prayer that night and still nothing had been said, a stinging bile filled his throat and choked his goodwill. The next morning, when Orrin retrieved his shoes from the closet, they gleamed with the unmistakable shine of a fresh polish.

Orrin decided that he, like Elder Pedersen, would say nothing. He smiled inwardly when, as the two elders sat side by side teaching a first discussion, he looked down to see two pairs of shiny black shoes. The next morning, while Elder Pedersen showered and shaved, Orrin ironed his companion's white shirts and hung them neatly in the closet. Elder Pedersen again said nothing, but perhaps he really did not notice this time, because his shirts were usually well pressed anyway. Still, Orrin took a long shower the next morning, just in case Elder Pedersen had noticed, so he would have time to reciprocate by ironing Orrin's shirts. Upon coming upstairs, Orrin inspected every shirt in his closet, noisily sliding hangers back and forth, looking to see whether Elder Pedersen had pressed at least one shirt. Orrin frowned when he finally gave up and unhooked a slightly wrinkled shirt from its hanger. Perhaps Elder Pedersen thought this was a much too silly game for missionaries, or too little too late for making amends. Orrin was buttoning his shirt and thinking about another cold day ahead when he caught the sweet scent of cinnamon and vanilla coming from the kitchen. He walked in to see Elder Pedersen, hot pads in his hands, setting down a warm bowl of Norwegian rice porridge.

"*Risgrøt!*" Orrin exclaimed. "That's one of my favorite meals."

"I heard you talking about it with the other elders."

"What? When?"

Elder Tanner put down a bowl and spoon in front of Orrin. "You said one of the members, that older woman you used to visit, Søster . . ."

"Søster Halversen."

"Yes, you said she made the best *risgrøt* in all of Norway."

"Oh, that brings back such pleasant memories, Elder Pedersen. She was the sweetest, kindest, and most fun-loving person I ever met. You know, she was the one who told the Kjelsås missionaries to pee in the sink rather than go down three flights of stairs. That's what she did in her hybel."

"Really, that little eighty-year-old woman?"

"Eighty-seven."

Orrin reached across the table. and spooned the *risgrøt* into his bowl. While they ate, he entertained Elder Pedersen with stories about Søster Halversen. "'*Uffa meg,*' she would say when we told her about our latest missionary mishap. '*Uffa meg for dere.*'"

Eddie had recognized immediately that Elder Tanner had polished his shoes. Only a blind man would have missed it. He also remembered the assistants' admonition to show love to your companions by performing little kindnesses. He had done the same thing in Bergen, rising early as Elder Tanner had done, to polish Elder Jensen's shoes. But Eddie's act had been one of true affection, one he hoped would arouse reciprocal feelings in Elder Jensen. That Elder Jensen had not even noticed intensified Eddie's despair at his unrequited love. He regarded Elder Tanner's gesture as gimmicky and false. It wasn't a show of real love or unselfishness but mere artifice, as genuine as the memorized door approaches they repeated dozens of times each day. *Does Elder Tanner think he can win me over with such an unimaginative ploy?* Eddie decided to pretend he hadn't noticed, hoping Elder Tanner would feel as discouraged and hurt as had Eddie when his kindnesses toward Elder Jensen went unnoticed.

Eddie's gambit had the desired effect. Several times that morning, he caught Elder Tanner glancing at his shoes and then at Eddie, searching for a sign of recognition in Eddie's eyes. Eddie wouldn't give him the satisfaction. When invited indoors, Eddie never looked down at his shoes when slipping off and on his overshoes, but instead kept up a steady banter with their Norwegian hosts. Elder Tanner left each visit crestfallen, more dismayed by Eddie's obliviousness to his shiny shoes than by the Norwegians' rejection of their message. It was exactly the reaction Eddie wanted, yet as the day progressed, he felt increasingly hollow and dissatisfied. Whatever he hoped to achieve when he accepted his missionary call, this wasn't it. Preaching Christianity with an un-Christian heart. When he prayed that night, he knew the deal was off the table. He had taken it off. And Eddie knew what he had to do to put it back on. The next morning, when Elder Tanner opened the closet and discovered what his companion had done, his eyes glimmered as brightly as his newly polished shoes.

Eddie didn't know what, if anything, would happen next. He didn't expect to find crisp, newly ironed shirts hanging next to his suits. Nor did he expect to get as much pleasure from making *risgrøt* for Elder Tanner as Elder Tanner got from eating it. And so it continued, each companion trying to outdo the other with secret acts of kindness. Well, not exactly secret, but the two elders kept up the pretense of anonymity. Continuing the kindness stretched the limits of their ingenuity. Companions are together virtually every moment of the day and night; there's only so much one can do without the other seeing. Still, they managed. One day, Elder Tanner washed the dishes, even though it wasn't his turn, while the next day Eddie took over writing in the tracting book when he saw Elder Tanner's fingers turning blue and stiff in the cold. Both enjoyed cooking special dishes, especially Norwegian treats they thought the other would like. Neither ever referred to the alternating acts of kindness, though it was clear to each that the other was paying close attention. This added to the fun, but it also meant the elders didn't have to discuss the personal disappointments and raw emotions that had fueled their spiritual breakdowns. The unspoken acts were satisfying and safe.

278

Chapter 34

Engage often in self-evaluation—watch and control trends in your life.
Conduct of a Missionary,

At Orrin's suggestion, he and Elder Pedersen made an appointment to talk with a reporter at the *Harstad Tidende* about their purpose in coming to the island town. When it became apparent the reporter wasn't interested in making his newspaper a mouthpiece for Mormonism, Elder Pedersen turned the discussion in a more general direction. "One of our prophets said the goal of our church is to make bad men good and good men better," he said.

The reporter asked the elders many questions about their backgrounds and personal reasons for coming on a mission. Given Elder Pedersen's superior speaking ability, the reporter directed much of the conversation toward him. Rather than being jealous of Elder Pedersen's language skills, Orrin marveled at his companion's command of Norwegian and the easy way he engaged the reporter. No other missionary presented such a positive image of their church. To make sure Orrin received equal time, Elder Pedersen told the reporter Elder Tanner came from a family of religious scholars, and that Elder Tanner himself was probably the most knowledgeable of the missionaries serving in Norway. This gave Orrin a chance to talk about his father's pamphlet business and offer his own view that religious scholarship was entirely consistent with secular scholarship. "There is no conflict between spiritual truths and what we learn from science and history," he said. Orrin then touted Elder Pedersen's musical prowess, listing for the reporter the many awards Pedersen had won.

"Did you know each other before coming to Harstad?" the reporter asked. "You appear to be very good friends."

Orrin and Elder Pedersen looked at each other and smiled.

"How did you know about all of my music awards?" Elder Pedersen asked after they left the newspaper office.

"President Toressen brags about you all the time, like you are the second coming of Edvard Grieg."

"How could you stand it?"

"The same way you stood for all of the bragging the president did about my superior gospel scholarship."

Elder Pedersen gave a rueful laugh. "The other missionaries must have thought we were insufferable."

"Maybe that's why he put us together."

Orrin and Elder Pedersen continued participating in the Breviks' family home evenings. Fru Brevik seemed to enjoy their company, but whenever the elders attempted to engage her in a discussion of Mormonism, no matter how mild their inquiry, she withdrew behind a wall of detached irony. Repeated efforts failed to penetrate her facade. And Bror Brevik, with his heavy-handed warnings about the eternal family, drove his wife into dispirited retreat.

"I know it is hard, but you must learn to bridle your enthusiasm and go more slowly," Elder Pedersen told Bror Brevik after one such episode. Back at their hybel, Elder Pedersen told Orrin he worried that Bror Brevik was driving his wife away from the church and, perhaps, their marriage.

The *Harstad Tidende's* newspaper article opened numerous doors for Orrin and Eddie, who now began proselytizing as a team. Misunderstanding what the elders had told him, the reporter said Orrin and Eddie had traveled more than 8,000 kilometers from their homes to serve as ambassadors for Christianity in Harstad. The story referred to Eddie as a distinguished pianist and winner of numerous music awards, and similarly touted Orrin as one of Mormonism's leading theologians. "It makes us sound like a couple of braggarts," Orrin said after reading the article. "What will the other missionaries think of us?"

"If they don't already think we're insufferable, they will now," Eddie moaned.

"And President Toressen. There's no way he will be happy about this."

But he was. "Surely, the Lord's hand was in this," President Toressen told the elders, his voice enthusiastic and cheerful. Figuring it would be best for Toressen to hear about the article from them, Orrin and Eddie had rushed downstairs and called the mission office from the hallway phone. Unfortunately, the president and his assistants had already received a copy of the article from the church's newspaper-clipping service.

"Just because you've memorized a few scriptures, that doesn't make you a doctrinal expert," Elder Sorensen told Orrin.

Elder Ward was even more scornful. "I'm surprised you didn't tell them you wrote the Book of Mormon yourself."

Orrin and Eddie offered to see if the paper would write a clarification, but President Toressen scoffed at the notion that a correction was needed. "Listen, Elder Tanner, you *are* a gospel scholar of the first order. Even if you don't know it, I do," he said. "And Elder Pedersen, you are a superb pianist, and not just because I say so. After all, music judges with far more expertise than I have awarded you prizes at numerous competitions. Don't sell yourselves short, Elders."

"Thank you, President," Orrin said. "But we are sorry the article wasn't entirely accurate about our purpose here as missionaries."

"We didn't deliberately mislead him," Eddie added.

"No need to apologize, Elders. The article quoted President McKay accurately. The Lord inspired that reporter, even if he didn't know it. It's all for the good. Now go out and knock on some hearts and prove me right."

President Toressen was right. People who had pianos invited the elders in so Eddie could play for them. Eddie played "Claire de Lune" and other classical pieces he sometimes played as interludes at church meetings, and much to the delight of their Norwegian hosts, he could play most American and British popular songs after tinkering with the keys until he found the right chords. One man pulled out music by Edvard Grieg from his piano bench for Eddie to play. "Very good," he said, sincerely impressed, "but Grieg was a Romantic and must be played with more feeling." The man gave Eddie the sheet music to several of Grieg's short pieces. "Edvard Grieg is a Norwegian hero, and so you Americans will get a much better reception if you flatter us by playing his music." Fru Kjøviksen, an older woman who lived in a bright green home west of the *Folkenparken*, allowed Eddie to take a book of popular American Broadway songs on the condition he come back once a week to play for her.

None of these people wanted to talk about religion, let alone Mormonism, which made Orrin reluctant to schedule return visits. "They're just PFers, Elder Pedersen," he said.

"Let's give it time to see what develops," Eddie responded. "After all, didn't President Toressen say the *Harstad Tidende* article was inspired? And aren't all of these invitations the result of that article?"

"Yes, but I feel so guilty," Orrin said.

"Guilty? Why?"

"Because it's all so easy. And so much fun."

"Yes, isn't it?" said Eddie, almost smiling.

Orrin's reputed biblical scholarship opened doors at the homes of Jehovah's Witnesses, but it was the same old story. Before the elders had finished recounting Joseph Smith's first vision, their host would interrupt them. "Your Joseph Smith is a liar," they would say with emphatic certainty. "The Bible says no man can see God and live."

From that point on, it was a chaotic bible bash. Orrin and the Jehovah's Witnesses threw scriptures back and forth, countering one New Testament citation with a quote from another. Rather than arguing from a defensive position, Orrin attacked the Jehovah's Witnesses' theological weaknesses. "In Matthew, Jesus said that no man knows the day or hour of the coming of the Son of Man, and yet the Jehovah's Witnesses continue to predict his coming," Orrin told one man.

"We predict the year, but not the day and hour," the man said defensively.

"And starting with 1914, every year you have predicted has been wrong," Orrin countered, reciting back to them the years of all of their failed predications.

Such arguments were fruitless, Orrin knew, and so, after a particularly acrimonious discussion about prophets, blood transfusions, and God's name, Orrin told Elder Pedersen he no longer intended to debate with Jehovah's Witnesses. "Once they identify themselves as J-Dubs, let's excuse ourselves," he said. "If we could persuade them, I'd keep trying, but I know we can't. Our arguments drain all the goodwill and spirit from me."

"I understand, Elder Tanner. But it sure is entertaining listening to you."

By March, the elders' working hours were spent primarily in daylight. They still arose in darkness, but by 9:30 a.m. when they began knocking on doors, the sun was peeking over the horizon. The sun hung low in the sky throughout the day as it circled the surrounding mountains. Still, the sun's reflecting glow on the fast-melting snow brightened Harstad's streets, as well as the town's mood. The stores bustled with shoppers and the city's harbor teemed with boats of all sizes; Harstad, like the sun, was rousing itself from a winter slumber. Herr Jørgensen bantered loudly with Orrin and Eddie whenever they patronized his butcher shop, telling his customers not to believe what they read in the *Harstad Tidende*, because the Mormon missionaries were really American spies. Whenever he saw the elders in Jørgensen's shop, Herr Reissmann would recommend the latest catch he brought from his stops along the coast. Everyone was busier now, no longer housebound by snow and darkness, so Orrin and Eddie received fewer invitations to come inside and warm themselves with tea and conversation. In mid-March, they attended Søster Kjøviksen's sixty-fifth birthday party, where they were surrounded by slightly tipsy, elderly women who teased their host with suggestive comments about her American "boyfriends" while singing showtunes to Eddie's piano accompaniment.

Orrin and Eddie also began teaching a college student Eddie met on the bus. "I read about you in the newspaper," Per Hansa said after Eddie introduced himself. Alluding to Orrin's reported biblical scholarship, Per Hansa said, "I want to learn more about the Bible and religion."

At their first appointment, Per Hansa explained he intended to get a credential as a public school teacher, but he was taking a year off and working at his uncle's concrete and gravel company. "I will be expected to teach religion courses in school, but I want to understand more about Christianity and the Bible than we learn in the State Church." Per Hansa readily accepted the logic of the first discussion regarding the need for continuing revelation and the restoration of the true church of Christ. "It would be quite odd, even nonsensical, for God to stop revelation," he said, reveling in this new way of looking at the Bible. The only time Per Hansa balked during the discussions was when Orrin asked whether he would be willing to be baptized if he received a spiritual witness that The Church of Jesus Christ of Latter-day Saints was the Lord's true church restored to earth. "Oh, I am not looking to join a new religion," Per Hansa replied, startled by Orrin's suggestion.

"He was really spooked," Orrin told his companion. "I thought he was going to tell us not to come back." Eddie agreed, and they decided not to issue another baptismal challenge until they had finished all six discussions. Other than this one wrinkle, Per Hansa proved to be the ideal investigator during the next several weeks. He was fascinated by the Book of Mormon, read it steadily, and proclaimed his belief it was true.

"There's no other way to explain it," he said.

The elders' mutual acts of kindness continued, though Orrin and Eddie became hard-pressed to come up with new ideas. There were only so many times they could shine the other's shoes or iron his shirts and pants. Cooking new meals and desserts became a regular occurrence. They constantly pressed people they met for Norwegian recipes they could try out, and they spent an afternoon with Fru Brevik learning the tricky art of making a *bløtcake*. Their extreme politeness and consideration for each other when visiting Norwegian homes did not go unnoticed. "You take the last *kjeks*, Elder." "No, Elder, I ate the last *kjeks* yesterday."

"*De guttene er for snille til å være spioner*," a woman said after watching Orrin and Eddie constantly defer to the wishes of the other when selecting meat at Herr Jørgensen's butcher shop. "Those boys are too kind to be spies."

"Ah, but what a brilliant way for spies to hide their true identities," Herr Jørgensen observed.

"Or maybe they are homoseksuell," said another customer amid embarrassed guffawing.

Weekly family home evenings with the Brevik family followed the same inevitable course: Bror Brevik would harangue his wife about the church until she fled in tears. The elders wanted to talk to Fru Brevik alone, but she turned them away whenever they dropped by during the day, insisting they come back when her husband was home. They were determined to find out how Fru Brevik really felt about the church, which meant holding Bror Brevik at bay so they could break through the emotional wall she threw up whenever the discussion cut too close to the bone. "If she says she doesn't believe, then we ought to respect her position and leave her alone," Elder Pedersen said.

"Who's going to tell Bror Brevik?"

Elder Pedersen scowled. "Bror Brevik ought to learn to love his wife."

Fru Brevik was in a festive mood when she greeted the missionaries for a family home evening to celebrate the upcoming Easter holiday. She wore a gray Norwegian sweater with bright silver hooks, while the house was decorated with yellow Easter lilies and striking purple St. Paulias. A homemade *bløtcake* rested on the kitchen table. Their two sons gave the lesson on the importance of prayer, keeping the discussion general so that Fru Brevik could participate without awkwardness, and, indeed, she offered two examples of her own in which her prayers had been answered. Fru Brevik had rarely opened up in this way or left herself so vulnerable. Eddie lifted his eyebrow and gave Orrin a sideways glance. Would she finally reveal her inner, spiritual self? But Bror Brevick seized upon his wife's admission to pointedly remark that God also answers prayers about whether the church is true. Bror Brevik leaned forward in his chair, preparing to launch another lecture, but Eddie cut him off.

"I have been coming here for nearly two months now, and you have told us many times how you feel about the church, Bror Brevik," he said. "But we have not once given your wife a chance to tell us what she believes."

Bror Brevik's jaw hardened. "What Ingrid needs to understand—"

"What she should understand," Eddie said, turning to Fru Brevik, "is that we love and respect her. You have been very kind to us, feeding us meals and sharing your home with us. It is time we listen to what you have to say. Do you not think so, Bror Brevik?"

Fru Brevik looked at her husband, baffled but amused. Never before had anyone taken control of the discussion in their house. Bror Brevik grudgingly put down his bible. "Go ahead, Ingrid," he said.

Fru Brevik began haltingly. "Well, I have always believed in God, and have always felt close to Him, that He was a presence in my life. That is why I loved Jann Harald, because he believed strongly in God and the Bible." As she continued, Fru Brevik's voice became more vigorous and her face expressive as she spoke emphatically about herself and her beliefs. Whenever she faltered, she looked to Eddie, who gave her a reassuring nod, and her courage would return. Fru Brevik said she admired the Mormons and respected her husband's faith, and that while she acknowledged the

State Church had its problems, she believed a person's relationship with God did not depend on a religious organization, and that's why she felt no need to join the Mormon Church. She also had her family to think about. Her parents objected quite strongly to Mormonism, and it would break their hearts if she joined. "This is not like America, where it does not matter which church you belong to, Elders," she said.

"Oh, Ingrid," Bro Brevik said, taking his wife's hand. "I believe you love God and are close to Him. If only you could understand how much greater your happiness would be, how much closer to God you could be."

"Yes, mother," the boys said, and they, too, entreated Fru Brevik to reconsider. If, as she said, it didn't matter which church a person belonged to, why not give Mormonism a try? Fru Brevik's husband and children pleaded with love and gentle fervor, so much so that for an instant Orrin thought she might be persuaded, but there was such a melancholy look on her face, despite her pensive smile, that Orrin felt sadness rather than joy. As Bror Brevik talked excitedly about the marvelous blessings that come from a temple marriage, her face grew passive and withdrawn. She gazed out a window, motionless and lost in thought, as if numbed by the familiar droning of her husband's voice.

"Excuse me," Fru Brevik said abruptly, standing and shaking herself from her trance. "I must serve the *bløtcake*."

Bror Brevik watched his wife drift away, then cupped his hands in grateful prayer. "Ingrid really felt the spirit tonight," he said. "Thank you, Elders. She is really thinking about being baptized."

"We will help Fru Brevik with the *bløtcake*," Eddie said and signaled for Orrin to follow him to the kitchen. There they found Fru Brevik leaning over the sink, staring into a pool of greasy water, her fists gripping the counter as if she were trying to hold it steady. She jumped back, startled, when she saw them.

"I am sorry," she said. "I was just thinking about tonight's conversation." She began looking around as if searching for something. "Where did I put my spatula?"

Eddie grabbed Fru Brevik by the wrist and held it tightly. He spoke calmly, but his words cut like razors. "You were not thinking about our conversation," he said. "You were thinking about committing suicide."

Fru Brevik's face turned ashen, then her whole body convulsed as she sobbed. "Yes," she cried. "Jann Harald will never accept me the way I am, and he has . . . even my children are against me." She threw her arms around Eddie, wailing tears of bitterness and sorrow. He gently pulled her head onto his shoulder and stroked her hair.

"I am sorry, Fru Brevik," he said. "I am so, so sorry."

When the elders told Bror Brevik about his wife's condition, he refused to believe she was seriously depressed, arguing she was probably tired or suffering from the stress of a recent illness, and that a good night's rest would set her back on her feet. But the next day, while Bror Brevik was at work and the boys were at school, Fru Brevik left her daughter in the care of a friend and checked herself into a hospital for mental exhaustion. Orrin and Eddie were the only visitors she would allow during her five-day stay.

The elders visited Fru Brevik nearly every day after she returned home from the hospital. Aside from a tendency to jiggle her legs nervously, which the doctor attributed to the antidepressants, she recovered quickly. Fru Brevik did not want to talk about her breakdown but about what she must do now to achieve peace of mind. "I have kept too much of my emotions bottled up inside for the sake of maintaining family harmony," she said. "My therapist says I need to let it out—to give it expression, he says—or I will never find happiness." Fru Brevik treated the elders as allies in the quest, especially Eddie, to whom she attributed shaman-like qualities. He had seen through her facade and had recognized her pain at the critical moment. "Elder Pedersen saved my life," she told Orrin in a private moment. "He can do no wrong in my eyes."

"How did you know Fru Brevik was contemplating suicide?" Orrin had asked immediately after the incident. Eddie answered vaguely, saying he was uncertain how he had known. Orrin dropped the matter, thinking perhaps it was inappropriate to inquire about another's spiritual experience, but he had an unquenchable desire to know. He asked again a few days later while he and Eddie studied quietly before bedtime. Orrin was reading Apostle Talmage's *Jesus the Christ*, while Eddie was jotting down notes from Apostle Richards's *A Marvelous Work and a Wonder.* "What was it like, Elder Pedersen?" Orrin said, looking up from his book. "I mean, what was the sensation you felt when you discerned Fru Brevik was suicidal?"

Eddie closed his book and looked out the window at the dark blue sea. Orrin waited for his companion to gather his thoughts. Eddie gave a long sigh. "I felt more nervousness and excitement than anything, Elder Tanner. I sensed that Fru Brevik was really upset when she ran into the kitchen. She had finally opened herself up to her husband about her religious beliefs and all she got back from him was the same old lecture about joining the church. And when we went into the kitchen to talk with her, I saw something different in her eyes. It wasn't the anger I was expecting but a dead, hollow look, like she had given up. And so I blurted it out without thinking, and it was such a frightening accusation that I almost regretted it immediately, except Fru Brevik began crying and confessed it was true."

"That's it then," Orrin said, his tone more analytical than disappointed. "No burning in the bosom or still, small voice whispering into your mind?"

"I'm not trying to be modest, Elder Tanner. I . . . I've been trying to figure it out myself. It was like I had just stepped out from a dark shadow and for one brief instant my head was completely clear and I could see life as it really was," Eddie said. "Bror Brevik was driving his wife to mental breakdown and suicide. I knew it, like I know you and I are sitting here right now talking in this hybel, and so I said what I said."

It was the kind of spiritual experience Orrin had hungered for all his life, the kind he was expecting—constantly striving for—as a missionary. Earlier in his mission, he would have been jealous—even resentful, that God had chosen Elder Pedersen as His instrument of service, even though Orrin, too, was standing right beside Fru Brevik and had looked into her face and into her eyes. Elder Pedersen had been given a gift, and Orrin admired him for the humility and purity of soul that made him worthy of it.

Fru Brevik did not look to the elders for advice or guidance but used them as sounding boards for the many complaints that had led to her unhappiness. Bror Brevik figured prominently in her list of grievances. He never helped around the house or with the children, was always busy with work or church, and didn't show any understanding of the dilemma she faced with her parents, who vehemently opposed her becoming a Mormon. "The Bible says you are supposed to honor your father and mother," she said. "Jann Harald is always nagging me about following the Bible, but only the parts that are convenient for him."

Fru Brevik twisted her wedding band back and forth around her finger. "All of our friends in Oslo disappeared after he was baptized. And since we moved to Harstad, it has been even worse. People look at me funny when I tell them my husband is a Mormon."

Bror Brevik initially tried to treat his wife more compassionately, afraid he might say or do something that would send her back to the hospital. He grudgingly accepted part of the blame for her unhappiness. "I have been more zealous than I should have been," he said. He looked at Orrin and Eddie sadly, his face pleading for understanding. "You see, I love Ingrid and want only the best for her and our family."

Bror Brevik also had a few complaints of his own. His wife, he asserted, nagged him constantly about housework, about his driving, about the church, about his job. "Nothing I do is good enough for her. She does not respect me."

Orrin and Eddie tried to mediate the Breviks' grievances and bring them back together, but the more the troubled couple talked, the wider the gulf between them became. When Ingrid poured out tales of mistreatment, rather than having a cathartic effect, it aggravated her resentment, and though she always greeted the elders with a sincere smile, she spoke of Bror Brevik with increasing contempt. She enjoyed the fact that since her hospitalization, it was now Jann Harald who walked on eggshells. A chill came into the room whenever she mentioned his name, and behind her eyes was a steely, hard glare.

Orrin and Eddie knew they were in over their heads on the day Fru Brevik complained about her husband's sexual inhibitions. They were sitting at her kitchen table, drinking tea, while Fru Brevik tapped her feet obsessively and slid them back and forth under the table in a figure-eight pattern. "We rarely have sex," she said, her voice cold and clinical, as if they were doctors discussing an anonymous patient. "And when we do, Jann Harald always feels guilty afterward because the church teaches that sex is only for procreation, and because I insist on using birth control. He says we are only satisfying our own selfish lusts."

Fru Brevik stopped and refilled the cups with hot tea, put more water on the stove, and then settled back in her seat. Her legs began jiggling as soon she spoke. "You probably did not know this, but Jann Harald and I lived together before we were married." She paused and looked into the elders' faces to make sure they understood what she was saying. "It is quite common in Norway, you know. Jann Harald felt really bad about it, even before he joined the church. But after . . . *uffa meg*, I thought he would die from the shame. He never quite got over it. And now, well—"

"Why are you telling us this?" Eddie asked.

Fru Brevik's mouth turned down angrily. "Well, Jann Harald has confessed this sin to all his leaders at the Mormon Church, even once to one of your apostles, so I do not know of any reason why I cannot tell you."

"Yes, but—"

"You do not know how it is," she said, "how undesirable and ugly you feel when you are married to someone who refuses to make love to you. You feel empty and cheated because certain expectations are not fulfilled and because certain promises are not kept. And yet Jann Harald tells me I am the one with the problem, that I cannot control my appetites and passions. Those were the words he used. Am I to go through life feeling like a sexual deviant for my natural desires as a woman?"

In the uncomfortable silence that followed, Eddie rubbed his arm while Orrin pondered how to help the Breviks repair their broken relationship. "You know, Fru Brevik," he said, "Elder Pedersen and I did not like each other when we first came to Harstad as companions."

"We hated each other," Elder Pedersen added.

"Oh, really?" Fru Brevik scooted her chair forward as Orrin and Eddie explained how they expunged their ill feelings, first by secretly polishing each other's shoes and then by performing additional good deeds that were not initially heartfelt but eventually became genuine expressions of friendship and affection.

"We understand you are upset with Bror Brevik, but this could be a way to rekindle some of those loving feelings that deep down you must have for each other," Orrin said.

Fru Brevik was unmoved. "Oh, that is a lovely story about you boys, but Jann Harald would never reciprocate. He would just take advantage of my kindnesses."

The tea kettle hissed noisily. Fru Brevik pushed herself from the table and switched off the stove. When she returned, her eyes were cloudy and moist. She patted the elders' hands. "I have been very lonely," she said, "and you boys have been the first ones to understand."

The time had come to challenge Per Hansa to be baptized. He had nearly completed reading the Book of Mormon and was eagerly studying the New Testament scriptures that showed that Mormon teachings aligned with the Bible. "You are right," Per Hansa told the elders. "The early apostles clearly talked about preaching to deceased spirits and baptizing for the dead. This is a wonderful doctrine."

Eddie suggested that Orrin be the one to deliver the challenge. "Per Hansa respects your knowledge of the scriptures and so will respond well to your encouragement," Eddie said. Before leaving for their appointment, the elders prayed that God's spirit would touch Per Hansa's heart and make him open to receiving the truth.

Per Hansa greeted the missionaries with his usual toothy smile and firm handshake, a handshake that told them Per Hansa would make an excellent leader in a country desperate for branch presidents and reliable priesthood holders. They walked him through the scriptures demonstrating the meaning of Christ's atonement and the importance of repentance and baptism for the forgiveness of sins. "That is why we are baptized in the State Church," Per Hansa said. "A priest baptized me when I was a baby."

"But you understand from the scriptures that you must be baptized by someone with priesthood authority from God," Orrin said. "Otherwise, the baptism is not valid."

"Yes, I see what you mean."

Orrin leaned forward. Clearing his throat, he looked directly at Per Hansa. The two men locked eyes. "Since Joseph Smith was given the authority to baptize by John the Baptist, the same man who baptized Jesus Christ, will you follow in the footsteps of the Savior by being baptized by that same authority."

A puzzled look swept over Per Hansa's face. Speaking hesitantly, he said, "You mean baptized into the Mormon Church?"

"Remember, it is the Savior's church, The Church of Jesus Christ of Latter-day Saints," Orrin said.

"But I would become a Mormon, right?"

"Well, yes," Orrin said, uncertain what Per Hansa was getting at. But when he saw Per Hansa's face grow ashen with apprehension, it became clear what was bothering the young man: he was afraid of becoming a Mormon.

"When I told my parents I was talking to you, they became very upset," he said. "My mother cried and said, 'We Norwegians belong to the State Church.' And my father sent my uncle to talk to me. 'What are you thinking, Per Hansa,' my uncle said. 'You are dishonoring your parents, and besides, you cannot become a teacher in Norway's schools if you are Mormon. The state will not allow it.'"

"That is not true," Orrin said, shaking his head, but Per Hansa wasn't listening.

"Norway is not like America where you have lots of Mormons and they are respected people. Did you not tell me that a Mormon was a governor of one of your states?"

"Yes, that is George Romney of Michigan," Eddie said. "He now serves in President Nixon's cabinet."

"He was born in Mexico, where his grandfather had fled to escape prosecution because he was a polygamist," Orrin added.

Per Hansa offered a rueful grin. "That could never happen here, a Mormon being elected to high office, especially not one who comes from polygamy. It would be scandalous."

"We know this is a difficult decision," Orrin said at last. "Would you pray about it? We will pray for you also."

Orrin and Eddie fasted and prayed the next two days, beseeching God to give Per Hansa the courage he needed to make the right decision, but Per Hansa greeted them coldly when they returned three days later. "I do not wish to become a Mormon," he said. Although his statement was terse and emphatic, his quivering chin pleaded for understanding. Orrin and Eddie resisted the urge to lecture and instead bore fervent testimonies that Joseph Smith was a prophet who restored Christ's church to earth. Per Hansa's face softened and he spoke with downcast eyes. "I am not like you," he said, choking back his shame. "If I join your church, my family will not accept it and my friends will think I am crazy. You have your families and missionary friends and a long tradition to support you in your beliefs, but if I become a Mormon, I would be alone."

The three men faced each other in silence. Orrin and Eddie knew what they were supposed to say—that despite Per Hansa's misgivings and fears, baptism would bring everlasting joy; that he would be rewarded with God's comforting spirit; and that, ultimately, he would experience a happiness the likes of which he had never known. But neither spoke. They couldn't. Orrin recalled his own unhappiness as a missionary. Even now, when he and Elder Pedersen were working so well together, a weary dissatisfaction gnawed at his soul. Despite his rigid obedience to the mission rules, he had not achieved any level of contentment. Did he still hope for spiritual enlightenment and serenity? Yes. But how could he promise Per Hansa something he himself had yet to find?

Eddie also contemplated his own unhappiness. Since the day he had confessed to his bishop his homosexual proclivities, he had known nothing but physical pain and mental anguish. He had demonstrated his sincere desire to repent and reform by submitting to every demand, from reparative therapy to multiple confessions and accusations of his depravity and unworthiness, but the deal that would remove his damning impulse remained elusive. Tranquility lay somewhere in the future, somewhere beyond his grasp. God had his own timeline for testing Eddie's resolve. Who was to say God didn't have a similar plan in mind for Per Hansa?

Orrin and Eddie, each on his own, arrived at the same conclusion: they had no moral standing to ask Per Hansa to make this heart-wrenching choice. Perhaps someone like President Toressen could. He had been to the mountain top and seen what lies beyond. They had not. And so they bounced and shifted nervously on their feet, watching Per Hansa's faith unravel, silenced by their own lack of conviction. Seeing that Orrin and Eddie had nothing more to say, Per Hansa said, "I am sorry, but this is the decision I have made. I ask you to respect me and please do not visit me again." He closed the door with a sorrowful look, a look not nearly as dispirited and sad as that of the two elders standing at his door.

Chapter 35

We must live the gospel we preach. Obey mission rules. Keep minds and actions clean. Give unselfish service to the cause.

The Message and the Messenger

Eddie was kneeling down to join his companion in morning prayer when Orrin abruptly stood up. "Elder Pedersen," he announced, "before we go out tracting today, there is something I need to talk with you about—to confess, really."

Eddie should have been surprised, and yet, he wasn't. In the days since their meeting with Per Hansa, Elder Tanner had been taciturn and morose, going about their missionary routines and knocking on doors with joyless diligence. Eddie understood how he felt. Per Hansa's rejection hurt like a gut punch. Still, Eddie thought Elder Tanner, of all the missionaries, would recover quickly, given his stoic faith. Eddie got up from his knees and took a seat in the green cushioned chair opposite his companion. When Elder Tanner said he had something to confess, Eddie's first thought was he had committed a sexual transgression. *Wasn't that always it—with the elders, anyway?* The tortured look on Elder Tanner's face certainly suggested a serious moral infraction. That would explain Elder Tanner's meltdown at the Scripture Chase. A delayed explosion of pent-up guilt. Eddie leaned back, apprehensive but also curious to hear what Elder Tanner had to say.

"Elder Pedersen, everything Per Hansa talked about how difficult it is to be a Mormon in Norway is true," Orrin said. "And conversely, how comparatively easy it for those of us from the United States to be Mormons. We have our parents and families and friends and all the church programs to bolster us and keep us on the right path. You know as well as I do that many missionaries go on missions not because they want to but because it's expected. For people like us who grow up in the church, it's easier to be a Mormon than not be one. But for Norwegians, it's just like the scriptures say, where you have to forsake your parents and children and even spouses, for righteousness' sake. For many people, it's not a joyful choice. I saw that when Søster Larevik was baptized in Moss, how she anticipated a life of painful rejection and isolation from friends and loved ones—and yet, she still went forward with baptism. I vowed then that no matter what the outcome or possible pain, I would try to be as honest and courageous and open to truth as was Søster Larevik and all the Norwegian people I hoped to convert."

Orrin paused and looked up at his companion. "Do you understand what I am saying, Elder Pedersen?"

Eddie nodded. "Mormonism is like our State Church. We are born, baptized, confirmed, and married as Mormons, and we'll die as Mormons."

Orrin smiled knowingly. "Yes."

"We're in agreement, Elder Tanner, if this is your point."

Orrin stood and began pacing the floor. "Not exactly, because the point I want to make—the confession I have to make—is that I have been neither honest nor courageous as a missionary. Just the opposite. I have been selfish and cowardly . . . mainly selfish, I guess. I have obeyed all the mission rules to the letter and exceeded mission requirements as much as possible."

"You're a machine, Elder Tanner. I've grown to appreciate how hard you work and how sincere your efforts are."

"But I've done it all for myself, all in hopes of having a spiritual experience demonstrating that God loves and recognizes his not-so-humble servant, Elder Orrin Andreassen Tanner. And in doing so, I've made a mess of the lives of people I was supposed to bless with my service."

Eddie was certain Elder Tanner would break down in tears. That's what most missionaries would have done. Eddie had cried many times himself—usually by himself—over his missionary disappointments. Though impassioned, Elder Tanner nevertheless offered an objective, even detached, litany of his mission failures. "I made the Mission Comparative my measuring stick, foolishly thinking God himself had written our mission rules and devised the scorecard to determine whom He would reward with baptisms and other spiritual favors. It was superstition, really, a primitive belief in how God operates. And so, in my quest to gain God's favor by being the best missionary ever, I forgot about the people I was called to serve."

Orrin continued pacing as he listed the people he had mistreated. There were the members in Oslo he refused to visit when he became a senior companion. They needed him, but he didn't need them. He neglected the needs of his companions, especially poor Elder Gregersen, whose mission he had likely ruined. Søster Ryland, a woman full of charity and faith who doted on the missionaries while also drawing strength from them, was now forbidden to see them because Orrin had insisted on talking to her husband against her wishes. The worst case was Søster Halversen, a sweet, spunky old woman who joined the church in defiance of her family, making the members and especially the missionaries, her new family. She savored the elders' weekly visits, invigorated them with her jovial spirit, offering her home as a flowering oasis of cheer amid the bumps and bruises of missionary life. Here Orrin allowed himself to shed a brief, bitter tear as he recounted his misplaced sense of duty, and how Søster Halversen died alone, waiting in vain for her boys, the missionaries, to visit her in her last days.

"I see now I wasn't being honest about who I am, Elder Pedersen. Not honest and courageous like we expect our investigators to be. I need to admit things openly that I have dared not acknowledge."

Once intrigued, Eddie worried Elder Tanner would spew forth a series of uncomfortable secrets just as Fru Brevik had done, secrets he would rather not know. "Are you sure you want to tell me and not President Toressen?" Eddie asked.

Orrin ran his hands through his hair, knotting the waving strands tightly as he fumbled with where to begin. He stopped pacing. "I hate tracting, Elder Pedersen," he said sheepishly. "I abhor it, I loathe it, I . . . I hate going door to door every day, all day. It's boring and, I'm beginning to think, pointless. I've knocked on at least fifteen thousand doors, probably more, since coming to Norway and I haven't come close to converting anyone. But even if tracting is the best way to find investigators, I still hate it. And I hate talking to people on streetcars and buses and public places. It's embarrassing. I get nervous and tense every time. And the way people react when we attempt to engage them, they look at us the same way we look at the Hari Krishna fanatics who hand out flowers at the airport. I know I've given presentations to the missionaries about talking to people on buses and making it one of the things I'm known for . . . well, I'm known for that and working like a mindless machine. But I lied. I hate it."

Eddie listened, mouth agape. *Could Elder Orrin Tanner, Norway's hardest working, most scholarly missionary really be as unhappy as all those troubled elders and sisters who are cycled in and out of the mission home in hopes of restoring their spirits and love for the work?* Eddie suspected that missionaries sometimes put on a false front of loving their missions and expressing joy in the work. He did so himself. But never did he suspect such fabrications from Elder Tanner, who, since Eddie had begun working with him, had shown himself to be nothing other than earnest and true. Eddie didn't know what to say, but it did not matter. Having begun with embarrassed hesitation, Elder Tanner had gradually wound himself up into a full-throated mea culpa, and he wasn't yet finished.

"What I'm saying, Elder Pedersen, is that I hate my mission. Sure, there have been some good parts, traveling with President Toressen and being his scribe. And being your companion. I know we got off on the wrong foot. That was my fault completely. I was jealous of you, but you've been an outstanding companion, and the fact that we haven't made any headway with the Breviks or anyone else in Harstad is probably my fault too. If I were to be completely honest, I'd have to say that despite some positive experiences, overall, I hate my mission. I'm as shocked as you are that I'm saying it, but it's true. I hate my mission."

With that revelation, Orrin fell back into his chair, not with exhaustion but relief. Eddie remained silent, wondering if his companion might still have more to say. A tense stillness filled the room. The two elders looked everywhere except at each other. "Well, Elder Pedersen," Orrin said, straightening up. "Aren't you going to say anything?"

"Are you thinking of going home?"

Orrin shook his head. "Oh, no, I'm not giving up, if that's what you're asking. I'm just done pretending that I love the work and I've never been happier and these are the best two years of my life. I hope you won't think less of me. I don't intend to cause trouble or slack off or be a malcontent, but I don't want to pretend to be feeling anything I don't feel or be anything other than who I am."

The next morning as Orrin knelt to pray, Eddie announced, "Elder Tanner, I also have a confession to make."

Orrin stood and took a seat in the green chair where his companion had sat and listened to his confession. "This ought to be good," he said. "I guess it's your turn to pace."

Orrin was in a good mood. He had been since he spilled his guts to Elder Pedersen. At first, he worried he would regret his confession, that not only would he lose his companion's respect but he would arouse God's displeasure as well (as if God didn't already know his heart and mind). But as the day had worn on, he felt a joyous release, a burden lifted. With the Norwegians who opened their doors, he conversed more naturally, simply as one person to another, rather than as God's servant on an urgent mission. He bantered, cajoled, asked and answered questions that had nothing to do with religion. He didn't neglect his duty as a missionary, but neither did he obsess or become dispirited when they sent the elders on their way. He was no more successful than he had been in the past, but no less so either. "You seem to be enjoying your mission an awful lot today," Eddie observed after the two elders completed a lengthy but fruitless discussion with a born-again woman.

"Yes," Orrin said, grinning. "I'm starting to like how much I hate my mission."

Orrin was wearing the same grin the next morning as he waited for

Elder Pedersen to make a confession, which he expected to be not unlike his own. *I bet he feels the same way about his mission as I do.*

"Elder Tanner, I have homosexual feelings," Eddie said.

Orrin squirmed, then laughed nervously. "You're not . . . are you . . . you're joking, right?"

"No, Elder, I'm not. It's something I've known for a long time."

"I'm sorry, Elder Pedersen, but this is something you should be confessing to President Toressen, not to me. It's not like hating your mission. You could be sent home for something like this."

"President Toressen knows all about it, Elder Tanner," Eddie said flatly. "So does my bishop and Apostle Prichard."

"But you can't be homosexual and serve a mission. I . . . I don't mean to be judgmental, but isn't it considered a moral sin?"

"I'm attracted to men, but I'm not acting on it. I never have, not since coming on my mission. But the point is, they think I'm cured, but I'm not. That's what I'm confessing to you. I still have homosexual attractions."

"You seem so—so normal," Orrin said.

"I am normal!" Eddie shouted, startling his companion. "I'm sorry," he said, lowering his voice, "but I am normal. I'm just like you and all the other elders in every way except this one. It's like something went haywire in my genes or I did something wrong in the preexistence, like the Negroes, and so God made me like this." Eddie proceeded to tell his dumbfounded companion the history of his compulsion, how he first discovered he was attracted to other boys but thought it was a phase that would be resolved by puberty, how he fell in love with Barry and was arrested by BYU campus police, how he confessed to his bishop and underwent reparative therapy and—

"The shock-cock treatment!" Orrin exclaimed. "I heard rumors about it in the dorms, but I thought it was a myth. Do they really shock—"

"No," Eddie said impatiently, "they don't shock your balls."

"I'm sorry," Orrin said, genuinely contrite. "I didn't mean to speak lightly of what must have been a difficult experience."

"Difficult!" Eddie scoffed, his eyes ablaze. "It was extraordinarily humiliating, worse than anything you can imagine. They even made me buy pornographic magazines of men and women."

"What? Why would they need you to—"

"The magazine photos were used to make the slides for my therapy sessions."

"But why . . . I mean, why did they ask you to buy the magazines if, you know, they're trying cure you of your, uh, homosexual situation?"

"Dr. Orlan said it wouldn't look right for someone associated with the university to be buying such material. 'It's important for our subjects to take responsibility for their rehabilitation,' he said. 'It shows you're committed. But don't worry, we can give the name of a magazine store that understands our requirements in this area.'"

"Dr. Orlan instructed me to tell the people at the store that I had a pickup for Sam Ziegler. 'You don't have to browse around or say you're a subject in the reparative therapy program,' Dr. Orlan said. 'In fact, don't mention anything about the university or the project. Just give them Sam Zielger's name. They'll have everything prepared.' And so I did it, but when I gave them the name and was handed the magazines, the store employees all turned and stared at me as if they knew all about me and the program."

"That wasn't even the worst part," Eddie said. "During the slide sessions, I had to wear this device over . . . over . . . this is so embarrassing. I had to wear this device over my penis that measured the precise level of my arousal when I viewed the slides. It had a scientific sounding name. Oh, yeah, it was called a penile pleysthysmograph, and when I got aroused to a certain level, it would trigger the shocks. When the slides of naked men dropped, I was told to fantasize about being with men—as if I knew what homosexual men did—so that I would be aroused and then shocked and, you know, so I would develop an aversion to men. Sometimes, if something went wrong with the connection to the pleysthysmograph device, Dr. Orlan's assistant had to come in and adjust it himself while I sat there with my pants down."

"Did it work?" Orrin asked.

Again, Eddie scoffed. "The program worked, though not like they intended. The shocks were so painful that after only three sessions, I was rarely being aroused by the photos of naked men. Whenever the whirring of the projector signaled a new slide was dropping into place, I thought of nothing but the impending pain. At first, I welcomed the shocks as deserved punishment for being homosexual, hoping each jolt was purging me of my sinful nature and each spasm was an atoning sacrifice. Still, I couldn't get aroused by the erotic photos of women, either. I usually vomited at the end of the sessions, but I did this out of sight in the bathroom and cleaned up afterwards. I was afraid I would be kicked out of the program if they knew it was literally making me sick. But I had no idea how Brother Orlan was assessing my progress or who, ultimately, would decide whether I was worthy to go on a mission. 'It is not enough to be repentant,' Apostle Prichard told me. 'You have to expunge completely all

homosexual desires from your mind. A mission presents unique temptations. We can't have you backsliding.'"

"But it must have worked?" Orrin repeated. "That's why they let you
go on a mission, right?"

"Dr. Orlan certified me to be cured, and so my bishop and Apostle
Prichard declared me worthy to go on a mission, but I knew, deep down,
that I wasn't cured. I don't think the program works. It didn't for me,
anyway. And so, when I came on my mission, I made a deal with God. I
would faithfully obey all of the rules and serve an honorable mission and,
in turn, He would cure me. But He hasn't. Not yet."

"You didn't get anything from the therapy program?"

Eddie rolled up his sleeve and displayed the crimson burn across his
arm. "I got this."

Orrin gasped. "Jeez. Does it still hurt?"

Eddie poked at the pinched, raw skin with a finger. "It's not hurting
me right now, but sometimes, at the oddest moments, like when we're
tracting or I'm trying to sleep, my arm will burn with the same sensation I
felt during therapy. I'm afraid the pain is a permanent part of me now, as
is this scar. It's my scarlet letter."

After Eddie finished his confession, Orrin stumbled through the rest
of the day in a daze, his mind split in two. He could hear himself conversing with Norwegians on their doorsteps, his memorized dialogue flowing
automatically from his lips; while at the same time, he carried out a separate
conversation in his head. *Isn't homosexuality a perversion, worse than masturbation or adultery? Elder Pedersen is so normal and ordinary, actually extraordinary, probably the most gifted missionary in all of Norway. Look how hard
he has worked to overcome his homosexuality. And that ugly, painful scar. His
scarlet letter, Eddie had said. More like his red badge of courage,* Orrin thought.

Orrin could not stop thinking about it, even when he and Eddie
taught the first discussion to a retired couple who had seen the elders' photograph in the newspaper. Orrin heard himself telling the Joseph Smith
story while inside his head he carried on a raging debate about the right
thing to do. *Is God testing me?* he thought as he related how Joseph Smith
saw God the Father and his Son, Jesus Christ, standing in a pillar of light
brighter than the noonday sun.

Orrin's distraction did not go unnoticed. "I know I gave you a lot to
think about, Elder Tanner," Eddie said after they finished tracting and
returned home. "Do you have any questions you want to ask me?"

Orrin had plenty of questions, but the one thing he really wanted to
know was probably unknowable: how could a man be attracted to another

man? Even Elder Pedersen was perplexed by how he had developed his . . . his condition. "When we're in the basement and undressing and shower-ing and, you know, naked in front of each other," Orrin said, "are you, well, you know . . ."

"Am I looking at you? Sneaking a peek to see what you've got?"

Orrin flushed. "Well, given what you said about being attracted to men, yes."

"I knew you were going to ask me that," Eddie said, angry and accusatory.

"It's a legitimate question," Orrin countered. "If you were girl, I'd look at you, I mean, if you were good-looking."

"Don't worry, Elder Tanner. You're not my type."

Orrin smiled, chagrined. "Ouch. You could at least let me down easy."

"It's not you. It's me," Eddie said, flashing a wry grin. "I'm sure your sweet spirit and burning testimony will one day attract someone who can bring you eternal happiness."

That night, Orrin fell quickly into sleep and dreamed he was trudging through a forest in deep, powdery snow, following a path cut by the foot-steps of others. The snow clung heavily to his shoes. He was distressed to be without his companion, as it was a violation of mission rules. Uncertain where he was heading, he hoped the path would lead to his companion. But who was it? Elder Flossen? Elder Gregersen? His anxiety grew with each step until he came to a clearing where, at the top of a hill, a group of men was standing under an apple tree, its apples gleaming a lustrous red in an otherwise black-and-white dreamscape. Orrin recognized immediately he had stumbled upon his father's dream, which had become his own recurring dream.

"That's me, that's me," he shouted as he ran up the hill and pointed to the baby being held by the men.

When Orrin reached the tree, he was greeted by his great-grandfather Lars, Grandpa Heber, and his father. Lars took the swaddled baby and handed him to Orrin, saying, "This young spirit is a child of God and precious in His sight. Unto whom much is given, much is required." Lars then removed the blanket covering the baby's face. The infant looked up and smiled. It was Elder Pedersen! Orrin was cradling his companion when he heard a low rumble and growling from just beyond a craggy peak. Still holding the baby, Orrin ran to an outcropping of rocks and, peering over the edge, saw a dark, roiling ocean extending into an in-finite horizon. "I'm on an island," Orrin said to himself. On the beach below, the waves crashed against the rocks and sand, while a pride of lions prowled the beach. Muscular and majestic, the lions pawed at the white, powdery sand, lifted their heads to the sky, and roared, broadcasting to the world their invincibility and power. In the distance, Lars called out, but Orrin could not hear amid the lions' deafening roars that continued to swell, louder and louder until Orrin awoke suddenly, jolted from his sleep by the rumble of snowplows clearing an overnight spring snow from Harstad's streets.

After morning studies, Orrin said, "Elder Pedersen, I have an announcement to make."

Eddie groaned. "Not another confession, I hope."

"No, just an announcement." Orrin paused, his eyes dancing as he took in Eddie's wary apprehension. "Elder Pedersen," Orrin said at last. "I think we should go to Riksøy."

Chapter 36

Could you gaze into heaven five minutes, you would know more than you would by reading all that ever was written on the subject.

Prophet Joseph Smith

Orrin and Eddie stepped outside their hybel, shutting the door quietly so as not to disturb their landlady. The city's streetlamps glowed like little moons in the snowy mist, casting a yellow light across the empty streets. After rising at 4:00 a.m., the elders had eaten a hearty breakfast in anticipation of a long day. Wearing heavy coats over their standard missionary dress, the young men scurried down the steep hill to the harbor below, each carrying a suitcase of clothes, proselytizing materials, and a duffel bag stuffed with bedding. Herr Reissmann was waiting inside the boat, the sleeves of his orange-and-blue overalls pushed back to his elbows, holding a coffee cup in one hand and a wrench in the other. He had shaved, but with little conviction. He shouted an enthusiastic greeting and reached out a brawny arm to haul the elders' baggage onto the boat. "Hurry up, boys," he called, his breath already smelling of sea and coffee. "I want to get to Riksøy while the tide is going in."

The wind was blowing from the east, churning up the fog and sending it over the ocean like gusts of gray smoke. Herr Reissmann estimated the temperature at about minus three degrees centigrade but said it would warm up when the fog burned off. He gave a disapproving look when he saw the elders were wearing suits and ties underneath their overcoats. "This is not the Queen Elizabeth," he said gruffly. He handed them lifejackets and instructed them on how to tie them around their waists. "You can stow your bags under the benches below."

Orrin shivered as he stepped onto the boat. Eddie gave him a look that said, "Do you still want to do this?" Orrin returned a frozen smile. Traveling on a private boat violated mission rules, as did going outside their assigned area. Orrin had called President Toressen a few days earlier to get approval, but Toressen was away on church business. Elder Blake, the mission secretary, offered a bit of mission gossip. "President Toressen is in hot water again," he said.

"Is it because of another speech?" Orrin asked.

"No. Apostle Prichard thinks President Toressen is too lenient with the missionaries, especially the rulebreakers. I overheard him chastising the president for bringing problem elders into the mission home. Sister Toressen has been ragging on him too. She's on another rampage, if you know what I mean." Orrin chuckled uneasily, wondering whether he was one of those problem elders. Hadn't President Toressen brought him into the mission office as his scribe? Elder Blake mentioned the good news about upcoming baptisms in Trondheim and Larvik, and then asked, "Do you want to leave a message for President Toressen? He's expected back on Tuesday."

Orrin let the question linger. "No, it's not important."

It *was* important, of course. They needed the president's permission, but Orrin worried he would reject their request. It was an unconventional trip and President Toressen probably wouldn't want to risk further displeasure from his church overseers. "I don't want to ask for permission because if he says no, then we're stuck. We can't go," Orrin told Eddie.

"But President Toressen might have said yes," Eddie replied. "You know how he is."

"Sure, but what if Salt Lake City authorities got even madder at him because he let us go. I'd feel really bad if that were the case."

"So we're not going?"

Neither elder wanted to give up on the idea. Orrin attached great significance to his dream, which he recounted to his companion, even the part about Elder Pedersen taking Orrin's place as the baby. He didn't fully comprehend the dream, whose meaning remained ambiguous. Still, he believed it meant something, and that something was connected to Eddie and Riksøy. After Per Hansa's rejection, Orrin had felt empty and ineffectual, a missionary without a mission. A sense that he was an unworthy emissary for the gospel message gnawed at him, as did a feeling that he lacked the moral authority to ask life-changing sacrifices of investigators. It was he who needed to change and grow. Ready to put off the old man, he was convinced that visiting Riksøy, the island of his ancestors, would be key to discovering the new.

Eddie, too, considered himself an unworthy and unfit missionary. *How can I convey God's spirit to prospective investigators when I am plagued with homosexual desires?* Yes, he suppressed them, just as the elders and sisters suppressed their sexual desires, but theirs were natural yearnings, while his were an unnatural affront to God. Eddie foresaw continued futility and disappointment in the months ahead, and that he would return home unchanged. He desperately wanted to believe Orrin's dream carried divine import. It took little effort to persuade himself that his role in the dream, which both he and Elder Tanner regarded as wondrously strange, was a prophetic sign. Pondering these thoughts, Eddie felt a searing twinge and rubbed his bicep.

The trip came together smoothly, as if guided by divine approbation. Fru Brevik accepted their explanation that they would be working in another town for a short but indefinite period of time. Like their landlady, she had grown accustomed to Mormon elders being constantly on the move. The elders felt guilty about misleading Fru Brevik, especially because she made such a fuss over how much she would miss them. Although Orrin knew it was Elder Pedersen she would miss, he did not begrudge his companion's close relationship with Fru Brevik. His resentment of Elder Pedersen had transformed into growing admiration. Elder Pedersen's homosexuality remained confusing to Orrin, but he regarded it as a mystery that would be revealed in time. As for now, Orrin felt honored to serve with him.

Little worries tugged at Orrin and Eddie as the day for leaving approached. "Doesn't Satan have control over the oceans, rivers, and lakes?" Eddie asked. "Isn't that why missionaries aren't allowed to swim?"

"That idea comes from the Doctrine and Covenants," Orrin explained. "After W. W. Phelps had a vision in which he saw the Destroyer riding on the Missouri River, Joseph Smith issued a revelation stating God has given Satan dominion over the waters."

"So does that mean we shouldn't sail to Riksøy?"

"No. Missionaries continued traveling on boats—all Mormons did— especially before airplanes were invented. How do you think missionaries used to travel to Europe and Hawaii and just about everywhere?

"Oh, yeah," Eddie said. "Still, is that the reason—"

"Missionaries aren't allowed to swim? No, that's an old wives' tale. You know, like you're not supposed to send your temple garments out to be washed because someone might sew up the sacred markings."

Eddie offered a rueful smile. "I was a jerk for calling you out on that, Elder Tanner. I'm sorry."

"I was the bigger jerk," Orrin said. "Anyway, the point is, we don't have anything to worry about if we travel to Riksøy by boat. Not from the devil, anyway."

Herr Reissmann shouted for Orrin and Eddie to unhook two thick ropes from the pier moorings, and with a belch of oily smoke from the engine, the boat rocked and bobbed its way over the choppy waves and toward the open sea. The missionaries were getting their first good look at Herr Reissmann's craft, having not thought it necessary to inspect it beforehand. It was a thirty-footer, a reliable if not particularly swift vessel, and in the ten years he had owned it, had never once had a major breakdown while at sea, at least not one he couldn't fix. But as they got underway, the boat and much of its equipment appeared distressingly worn. The seat cushions were cracked and covered with greasy stains, a fire extinguisher lay wedged under the sink, and a piece of metal that looked to be a part of the motor was shoved into a corner among some crumpled paper cups. In the hull below, the supplies being hauled to Riksøy—toilet paper, soaps of all kinds, non-perishable foods, and other everyday items—filled every available space. Eddie, the color draining from his face, went down to the cabin, saying he was getting cold, but Orrin wondered if he was going down to pray. They hadn't even left the harbor and already the boat was rocking perilously. Orrin contemplated the stories the other missionaries would tell after they drowned. "They disobeyed mission rules and the devil tipped over their boat," they would say. President Toressen would probably be sent home in disgrace. While Orrin tormented himself with these thoughts, Eddie returned to the deck, pale and tottering, and threw up.

"Go to the side of the boat," Herr Reissmann yelled, waving his arm where he wanted Eddie to go. Eddie nodded and shuffled in that direction.

"Are you less likely to get seasick by the side of the boat?" Orrin asked.

"No, but you can throw up in the ocean. I do not like vomiting in my boat."

A pungent, sour taste rose in Orrin's throat and he joined his companion by the railing. Each took turns vomiting his breakfast into the ocean. "There goes the oatmeal," Eddie said.

Herr Reissmann brought them a towel to wipe their mouths and faces. "Do you know any cures for seasickness?" Orrin asked.

"Yes. Do not go to sea." Herr Reissmann smiled to himself, then kicked aside a bag of salt and picked up a net entangled with starfish. "Here, make yourselves useful," he said, handing them the net, "and get these starfish out of here."

"You are a fisherman too?" Eddie asked.

"Yes, I do a little bit of everything on my trips."

Orrin and Eddie draped the net on the railing and began pulling out the starfish. There were at least a hundred, some bigger than their hands, others the size of their thumbnails. The starfish hardly made a splash as they were tossed into the ocean.

"I threw up my first time," Herr Reissmann said, "and it was on a ship much larger than this. A big freighter, a hundred meters long." He went back to the steering wheel and continued talking, trying to take the elders' minds off their fluttering stomachs. "Sailing is a religion in Norway. We have saltwater in our veins. When I was growing up, all the young men wanted to go to sea. There was romance and travel, and the chance of discovery."

He joined the merchant marine at age fifteen and ended up hauling Swedish iron ore from Narvik to Germany until the war broke out in Europe and the British started mining the Norwegian coast. "I hated the British and Churchill," he said. "I hoped the Germans would sink them all."

Herr Reissmann found safer work on a whaling ship, but after Germany invaded Norway and King Haakon fled to London, he signed onto an armaments ship and spent the rest of the war dodging German U-boats while shuttling arms between the United States and its European allies. "It just goes to show," he said, brushing back the hair under his cap, "that you never know which side you might end up on. One day you are cursing someone as your enemy, and the next day they are your best friend in all the world."

"Or maybe," Orrin said, "you cannot remain neutral forever, not when you have got a fight between good and evil."

Herr Reissmann pulled down a sleeve and wiped it across his nose. "It was not so simple knowing which side was good and which side was evil."

"But eventually you had to choose."

"Religion is like that," Eddie said. "Eventually you have to choose."

Herr Reissmann turned his head and spat. "Do not talk to me about religion, boys," he said, gruff and throaty, "or I will cast you Jonahs into the ocean. And you will not find any whales big enough in these waters to carry you back to shore." He pulled back the corners of his mouth, forming a thin trace of a smile, but his jaw was set firmly against the wind. He swung the boat south toward Riksøy.

They passed many mountain islands that rose with rugged majesty from an emerald sea. Green spruce and pines clung precariously to the islands' meager soil. Most islands appeared inhospitable, even angry in their defiance of human existence, but when they motored close, they could see the lights of the small harbors and houses along the shore. Seagulls followed the boat, floating on the wind, and hovered at a safe distance as if judging their intentions. Over the sound of their screeching calls, Herr Reissmann pointed out places where he used to hunt crabs as a boy, saying that during the summer months the crabs would crawl up on the rocks during the night. "We would grab them right off the rocks with our hands," he said.

Orrin walked to the back and watched the boat carve V-shaped waves in the ocean. He would pick out a wave and watch it rise and fall. Each wave begat a dozen waves, and those a dozen more, until the first was lost in a multitude of pulsating whitecaps. An hour into the trip, they slipped between two jutting cliffs of neighboring islands. The water grew turbulent in the narrow passageway, and the boat rocked furiously as waves on both sides threw themselves against the stubborn rocks. One wave would strike the cliff with an angry splash, and then another, spraying the rocks with their fury. The waves traveled with speed and powerful force, and yet, for all their persistence, the island stones remained immovable, undisturbed. Change here was measured in millennia.

Their stomachs now settled, Orrin and Eddie worked to untangle starfish from another net. "So who is this Lars Andreassen, whose homeland island we are going to visit?" Eddie asked.

Orrin tossed a spiny starfish into the ocean. "He is my great-grandfather on my father's side. He died twenty years before I was born, so I know him mainly through family stories and photographs, along with the pamphlet my father wrote about him. My Grandpa Heber says Lars was shy, kept to himself, and could go hours without speaking, but he was easy to get along with and had quite a sense of humor once he started talking. Grandma Sonya spoke of her father as the salt of the earth. Once Lars became your friend, he stood behind you one hundred percent."

"I can't believe that Mormon missionaries came all the way to Riksøy to preach the gospel."

"Oh, no," Orrin said. "Lars joined the church after a chance encounter with missionaries in Bergen and then immigrated to Utah soon after. I doubt any Mormons have ever set foot on Riksøy."

Drawing upon his father's pamphlet about Lars, Orrin continued, "At the direction of church leaders, Lars settled in St. George, where local authorities called him to be a missionary to the Indians. He teamed with Elder James Conklin, and for seven years they helped keep the peace between the Indians and Mormon settlers in southern Utah and Arizona's Little Colorado River corridor. Lars, who was seventeen when he emigrated from Norway, never shed his thick Norwegian accent, nor did he fully grasp the rudiments of English grammar, which, along with his reticence, created the impression he was slow-witted. Just the opposite was true, Grandma Sonya said. He got along best with the Indians, who came to trust this quiet, docile man, earning a reputation among the local chiefs as a tough but fair negotiator. They called him Flaming Cloud because he was so tall, nearly six and a half feet, and had thick red hair.

"Everyone considered Lars a dedicated bachelor. Conklin's wife, Mary, said Lars was happy just being a friend to all. Her children loved the affable Norwegian, called him Uncle Lars, and when he and Conklin were gone on long trips, they looked forward to Lars's return as much as they did their own father's. It was Conklin's death that turned Lars to thoughts of marriage. Lars grieved many months after his good friend was killed by a renegade band of northern Arizona Apache, blaming himself because he had miscalculated the Apaches' intentions. As an act of penance, he offered to marry Conklin's widow.

"'His was not a romantic proposal,' Mary said. She was standing in front of the cabin, her fingers wrapped around the bloody neck of a chicken she was getting ready to dress, when Lars galloped up and jumped off his horse so fast that the dust was still circling his feet when he began talking. The tongue-tied, spluttering Norwegian gazed at his boots, never once looking Mary in her eyes, and kept one hand on the saddle horn, perhaps so he could ride away as quickly as possible if she spurned the offer. He spoke movingly of Conklin, of his own loneliness since his death, and of his desire to honor his departed friend by caring for his family. As best Mary could tell, it was really her dead husband—not her—that Lars loved. But he *was* proposing marriage. Mary had three young children and a farm to run, and she knew enough about Lars, and about what was wanted in a husband and what was not, to know she should accept. She told Lars, however, she would marry him on one condition: that he must first find another wife.

"'I am married for time and eternity to Mr. Conklin,' she said. 'I and all my children are sealed to him. If you want to be saved in the celestial kingdom and have eternal increase, you must find a wife who will be sealed to you in the hereafter.'"

"I suppose he agreed," Eddie said.

"Oh, yes. With Mary's help, Lars courted a thirty-year-old spinster Martha Hennesy, who likely would not have married at all if not for Lars—or, at least, that's what Mary's side of the family said. Mary's side also said there was no man alive who could satisfy the shrewish Martha, who so jealously guarded her status as first wife that she scolded Lars constantly for playing favorites with Mary, once demanding a new pump, then a new kitchen, and finally a new house because she considered hers inferior to Mary's. Her hot temper could light a fire in a snowstorm, so when the anti-polygamy crackdown started, Lars left Martha's family in St. George and moved with Mary and their children to Mexico. Unfortunately, while visiting Martha, Lars was arrested and sentenced to three years in federal prison for unlawful cohabitation. We have a prison photograph of Lars with Elder George Q. Cannon and other church leaders, all posing stoically in their striped prison garb. Lars towered over the others, his hair tussled, his face painted with confusion, as if he couldn't believe he really was in prison. There was also sadness in his eyes. Mary teased Lars that he would have been happier if he had never married.

"'He's the only man I ever knew who wasn't lying when he claimed he got into polygamy reluctantly,' she said."

Three miles long and about half as wide, Riksøy is located among a group of islands that sit like large stones in the dark blue coastal waters. With three foreboding mountain peaks, it appears on approach to have little habitable land, but the island is blessed with a protected harbor inlet, fertile soil for garden plots, and proximity to some of Norway's best fishing areas. The harbor and village are located on the east side of the island in a crescent-shaped cove. Although they motored in under a fog and drizzle, the missionaries could see the lights of the village houses scattered in the hills above. A few boats remained tied to the docks, but most island fishermen had already left for their favorite fishing waters. In the eerie quiet of the fog, Orrin and Eddie felt as if they were explorers entering an exotic foreign land. The growing brightness of the misty village lights created the surreal impression that their boat was standing still and the island was moving toward them. Herr Reissmann cut the motor and the boat glided sideways into the dock. The island was upon them.

"Here you are, boys," he said, throwing out a rope to an awaiting group of dock hands. While the men secured the rocking boat, Orrin and Eddie went below to collect their belongings. Herr Reissmann and the men, old salts with cigarettes dangling from their lips, ignored the missionaries as they set to work unloading the boat. Herr Reissmann planned to trawl the nearby waters before returning to pick up the fresh catch that lay waiting for him on the dock. "I will return in three days to see if you are ready to return to Harstad," he told the missionaries.

"As we agreed, please do not tell anyone we are here," Orrin said. "We want to keep it secret for now."

Herr Reissmann coughed and spat into the ocean. "And as I told you boys, I will not mention your trip if not asked. But I will not dissemble if asked a direct question."

"That is fine," Orrin said as he stepped off the boat. Eddie handed over their baggage and then joined Orrin on the dock. The elders slung their duffel bags over their shoulders, grabbed their suitcases, and walked unsteadily toward the shore, their legs still swaying with the ocean waves.

Riksøy's main street was one block long. On one side was a general store and market, post office and telephone exchange, a repair shop, and two small apartment buildings. On the other side was a cafe, another business office, several houses, and a State Church. The cobblestone street led in both directions to other nearby houses. The elders passed an old man in a tattered fur cap who offered a cautious greeting, jerking his head around suddenly to watch them over his shoulder before disappearing into a doorway. Eddie remarked on various points of interest—the wooden sidewalks, the fact they had seen only two cars, both parked, the unkempt cemetery by the church, which itself was run down and badly in need of paint—while Orrin worried about where to begin. There was no Bureau of Information or any government building, other than the post office, to get their bearings. *Should we start tracting door to door and see what happens?* They might run through all the homes in Riksøy before noon, and then be stuck waiting three days for Herr Reissmann to return, while suspicious townspeople watched their every move. Orrin berated himself for not planning this better. At Eddie's suggestion, they stopped at the cafe to refill their stomachs.

Noisy conversation filled the small cafe, giving the impression of a familiar morning ritual, but the room quieted abruptly when the door swung closed behind the elders. A curly-haired woman, her hands caressing a warm coffee mug, followed them with watchful eyes as they slid into their seats. Two gritty fishermen hunched forward over their plates, their foreheads touching, and began whispering as they pointed in the elders' direction. A young father and his two sons, elbows on the table, watched intently, slurping mush and clanging spoons against their teeth. No one spoke while a man in a greasy apron limped from the kitchen and asked the elders what they would like to order. He had an island accent, one they had never heard before. The elders requested herbal tea and rice gruel. The man limped away and then returned a few minutes later with their tea, setting down the cups and saucers with some difficulty, enough to attract their attention to the stubs on his left hand where his two smallest fingers were supposed to be. They felt the cold stares of the Norwegians upon their backs, and the simple act of sliding their chairs closer to the table set off an unpleasant screech.

This is absurd, Orrin thought. *Here we are, Elder Pedersen and I, our accents obviously marking us as Americans thousands of miles from home, and yet we are trying to act nonchalant, as if we had just dropped by Riksøy for a bite of breakfast; and here are the villagers, trying to keep up the same pretense when they are aching to know who we are.* Finally, as the cook delivered their breakfast, Orrin grasped the table, pulled himself to his feet, and began to speak.

"Citizens of Riksøy," Orrin said, speaking louder than he intended. Curious faces turned and fixed their eyes upon him. His heart pounded so hard he thought it was rattling the plates on the table. He looked down and saw it was Elder Pedersen moving the teacups away from his trembling hands. "I am Orrin Andreassen Tanner," he continued. "My great-grandfather, Lars Andreassen, was born on Riksøy in 1856 and emigrated to America when he was seventeen years old. I have come to see if any of my relatives still live on this island."

Orrin stopped and looked around the room. The young boys had hopped from their chairs and were balancing back and forth on raised toes. One of the fishermen was holding his spoon upright in his palm, while the woman held her mug poised against her lips, as if waiting for a signal to drink. They stared at Orrin in reverent, astonished silence. His mouth felt dry and gravelly, so he took a sip of tea, watching the others as they watched him. *They probably didn't understand anything I said*, Orrin thought. *I should have spoken more slowly and given them a chance to get used to my American accent.* Orrin was preparing to begin again when the limping man stepped forward and set the bowls of rice gruel on the table.

"I thought you were Americans," he said. "You speak very good Norwegian."

"We are Mormon missionaries."

"Ah, I see. What was the name of your grandfather?"

"My great-grandfather. It was Lars Andreassen."

"Yes, and who were his parents?"

"Per and Bente Andreassen." Some of the people edged closer as Orrin ran through the list of the Andreassen children—Jens, Lars, Jan Karl, and Erna—and everyone nodded with recognition.

The man smiled with understanding. "I am your . . . I don't know what. He took a paper napkin from a table and drew a diagram, showing the line of descent from Per and Bente Andreassen to his parents, Inger Andreassen and Tom Jurgensen. "I am their son, Peter Jurgensen," he said, and circled the names of Inger and Tom.

"I guess this makes us cousins of some sort."

"Yes, cousins," Peter said, grasping Orrin's hand. "Look here, everybody, these are my American cousins."

"Let me see that," the old fisherman said, grabbing the napkin with Peter's genealogy. The others gathered around and traced their own connections to Peter and Orrin.

"There are many Andreassens on Riksøy," the woman told Orrin. Snatching the young boys by their coats, she said, "Go get Ole, he is an Andreassen." The boys stampeded from the room and up the street.

The Norwegians earnestly questioned Orrin and Eddie about where they came from in America and how they got to the island. Eddie attempted with only partial success to clear up the misconception that he, too, was an Andreassen, explaining his ancestors had come from Halden many decades ago. More people came into the restaurant and each time they arrived, Peter would call them over to the table. "These are my cousins," he would sing out. "Come meet my cousins from America." As Orrin shook hands with each person, Peter would say, "This woman married Henrik Olesund, who was the grandson of Jann Karl Andreassen," or "This is the great-great grandson of Lars's sister, Erna," or "This man's sister married Aksel Ingebrittsen, who . . ." Someone brought out a new piece of paper and sketched a more legible family tree. Whenever new relatives introduced themselves, their names and the names of their Andreassen ancestors would be added to the tree so all could see their relationship to Lars.

"Pedersen? There are no Pedersens on Riksøy," a man told Eddie.

"My family comes from Halden."

The man laughed and clapped Eddie on the back. "You are a long way from home, but you are still welcome here."

People came in and out of the cafe, and several times during the conversation someone would say to Orrin, "You must go see Gunnar Andreassen," which would prompt others to exclaim, "Yes, Gunnar Andreassen. You must visit Gunnar." Finally, Orrin asked who he was, and Peter explained that Gunnar was the youngest son of Lars's younger brother, Jann Karl.

"He would be—"

"Lars's nephew!" Orrin said. "He is still alive?"

Peter nodded yes.

Orrin's eyes lit up with excitement. "Be so kind as to take us to him?"

Chapter 37

Be a real and constant witness—be unafraid; be unashamed—this is a day of warning.

Conduct of a Missionary

A dozen well-wishers guided Orrin and Eddie through Riksøy's main street, past the church and up a gravel road to a square, framed house. The roof's shingles were the color of ripe cherries. Blossoming wildflowers leaned into the sun. Next to the house was a small, fenced yard with goats and sheep, and two stone huts with thatched roofs, one for the animal's shelter and the other for feed. A man named Kjel led the procession, and when the elders arrived at the house, he knocked once, opened the door, and called loudly for Gunnar. A voice from the living room invited the crowd inside.

The old man who greeted them was tall, though bent with age and thin, with slight shoulders and hips, a weather-scarred face, and a large, innocent smile. Orrin thought he was looking at Lars Andreassen. "I am Orrin Andreassen Tanner," he said, extending his hand, "my great grandfather was—"

"I know all about you." Gunnar paused and eyed Orrin dramatically. Orrin felt a tingling surge of excitement. *Had he foreseen my coming in a vision or dream?*

"News travels fast here," Gunnar continued. "There are no secrets in an island village. Welcome to Riksøy."

Orrin buried his vain hope in a smile. "Thank you."

Scattered about Gunnar's living room were various artifacts marking the place as an old seaman's home: a painting of sailors in a gunboat harpooning a whale; a model of a nineteenth-century schooner; the sharp-toothed skull of a shark mounted menacingly on the wall; a pipe and empty tobacco pouch sitting on a table by a chair. A polar bear skin rug, matted and worn, covered the wooden floor. Fifteen people crowded into the room and Orrin explained how he and his companion came to Riksøy.

"So you are a Mormon, just like Uncle Lars," Gunnar said. "My father spoke of him often, especially when he neared death. He always expected Lars to come back."

"When did your father die?"

Gunnar scratched his graying hair. "1938. Just before the war."

"Lars died much earlier, in 1924."

"All those years," Gunnar said, shaking his head sadly. "Dad kept hoping he would see Lars, and he was already dead."

Gunnar picked up his pipe and put it in his mouth. He didn't light it, just chewed on it pensively, shifting it from side to side between his teeth. "My father was fifteen years old when your great-grandfather joined the Mormon sect. Jens and Lars had gone to Bergen—it was a big trip in those days—and when they got back, Lars announced he had joined this strange and mysterious American religion. Lars's father, Per, became furious at such talk. He contended that Lars was weak-minded and malleable, like his mother, and had been duped by the Mormon charlatans.

"Although Per had previously expressed nothing but contempt for the State Church, he had the priests come and give young Lars a scare, telling him the Mormons had sprung from the devil and he would go straight to hell if he associated with them. Lars said nothing more about the Mormons, so his father thought the priests' warning had done its work, but three weeks later Lars ran away from home and the family did not hear from him until he wrote to say he was on his way to join the Mormons in Salt Lake City. Lars's mother cried at the news, but his father, his heart filled with rage, ripped up the letter and swore an oath that neither he nor anyone in the family would ever write to Lars until he returned to Norway and begged forgiveness for his betrayal.

"And that is how it remained. No one was allowed to read his letters. My father, Jann Karl, remembered vividly seeing his father wrestle one of Lars's letters from his mother's hands, who implored him to let her read it. Thereafter, Per left strict instructions with the postal agents that every letter from Lars be delivered directly to him. The letters—the 'devil's tracts,' he called them—were cast unread into the fireplace."

Gunnar paused to light his pipe. The others sat quietly, waiting for him to resume. They had all heard of Uncle Lars, but their curious, intense faces indicated they, like Orrin, were learning these details for the first time. As a result of Lars's baptism, Gunnar said, or it was more correct to say that as a result of Per's bitterness, a storm of private recriminations and regret was visited upon the family. Bente, Per's wife, withdrew into silent, steely rage as a shelter from her husband's ranting, and for the rest of her life nursed a grudge against the State Church and its priests, whom she believed drove her frightened son away. Jens alternately blamed Lars and his father for the discord, and sometimes he hated them both, though it was really himself he blamed because, after all, he had been in charge when his younger brother first met the Mormon missionaries. Gunnar's father, Jann Karl, regarded himself as disloyal to his father because he missed Lars so greatly. None dared reveal their love for Lars, lest it provoke further explosions from Per. Even Erna, who had been too young at the time to understand, absorbed the conflicting feelings of guilt and sorrow, and learned to never speak Lars's name.

Jann Karl took solace in Christ's parable of the prodigal son. When he lay in bed at night, he would think about Lars, telling himself his brother was at that very moment on a ship returning to Norway, and he imagined how Lars would look as he climbed the dirt road to their house, wearing a cap and holding an old duffel, stopping at the fence, then opening the gate and walking up to the house, knocking on the door, surprising everyone. And Per, overjoyed with happiness, would forgive his son and regain his happy temperament.

Lars, of course, never returned. Per's hatred deepened, especially after it became known the ungodly Mormons had adopted the practice of polygamy. Every evil visited upon the Andreassen family was attributed to Lars's decision to become a Mormon. And thus it was that when Jens and one of his sons drowned in a storm, Per cursed Lars; and when Erna died giving birth to her eighth child, the aggrieved Per again cursed Lars, and God, too, for sending him such a wicked son. Eventually, Per Andreassen's mind collapsed under the weight of his corrosive bitterness, and he spent his last two years confined to a bed, raging insensibly and unable to recognize even his wife or surviving children.

After his mother died, Jann Karl discovered she had intercepted some of Lars's letters without Per's knowledge. Maybe she had secretly bribed the postal agent. While going through his mother's possessions, Jann Karl found a small letter box containing her personal papers and correspondence, including a handful of the letters from Lars. She had saved them all these years but had told no one, even after Per had died. Jann Karl wrote to the address on the letters, hoping to find his brother, but never received any replies.

"Now we know why," Gunnar said. "Lars was already dead. Bente died in 1928, four years after Lars."

Orrin did not know how to respond to Gunnar's melancholy tale. Traces of Per's sorrow could be seen on the Andreassen faces, and Orrin would not have blamed them had they seized him and Elder Pedersen and driven them from their island, so awful was the misery the Mormons had visited upon their family. Gunnar put his pipe to his lips and poked at it with a little stick, shaking loose tiny bits of tobacco ash. "Please tell us about Uncle Lars," he said, running his tongue over the lip of his pipe. "We have been waiting a hundred years to find out."

Starting from the beginning, Orrin told how Brigham Young, the Mormon prophet, had personally instructed young Lars to settle in southern Utah.

"Brigham Young," said the fisherman, "you mean the one with twenty wives."

"They all had twenty wives," cried another.

"*Uffa meg*," said one of the women.

The Norwegians were enthralled by the story of Lars's life. They had seen many American western movies and were impressed he had served as a missionary to the Indians and fought in gun battles too. They marveled that Lars, a shy and contented bachelor, had married two women, laughing uproariously at his befuddled proposal to Mary. The Norwegian women thought Mary was incredibly strange to insist that Lars marry another woman. "That is how it is among the sects," one of the men said, an explanation that elicited nodding agreement. Orrin recounted how Lars moved one of his families to Mexico, how he hid from federal authorities in the Mormon underground but was arrested and imprisoned, and how he spent his last years with his daughter, Orrin's Grandma Sonya, and Grandpa Heber in Seth until he died.

"This Sonya would be your cousin, Gunnar," someone pointed out.

"Is she still alive?" Gunnar asked.

"No, she died three years ago."

"Oh . . . well," he sighed. Of all the Andreassens, Gunnar had been most affected by Lars's story. He had listened with his father's love for Lars.

"I have photographs," Orrin said, reaching into his briefcase. He spread them out on the coffee table for all to see and pointed out the various family members and Mormon authorities of note in each photo. Gunnar picked them up one at a time and carefully inspected them.

"He looks like you," Orrin said.

"He looks like my father." Gunnar motioned for someone to bring one of the photographs from the mantel above the fireplace. "See," he said, pointing to a lanky man standing next to one of the stone cribs outside the house.

The photograph was black and white. "Did Jann Karl have red hair?" Orrin asked.

"Yes, just like mine."

While the pictures were being passed around and the cousins made their own observations about which Andreassen relatives resembled Lars and his offspring, another group of relatives and curious villagers, at least ten in number, called at the door, bearing platters of *smørbrød* and pastries. Peter Jurgensen, the limping restaurant owner, led the procession.

"We must have some refreshments for our American cousins," he said, still believing Eddie belonged to the family. A fish-shaped ashtray was pushed aside to make room for the platters.

"What about the restaurant, Peter?"

"I closed it."

"He put on a sign that says, 'If you are hungry, come to Gunnar's house.'"

"A thousand thanks," Gunnar said.

Peter handed the elders a plate of bread slices covered with sardines, smoked salmon, anchovies, shrimp, and crab. "*Være så godt*," he said. "Eat."

Some of the Norwegians spooned a dark, muddy dip onto their bread. It had a pungent, fishy smell. "We call it the 'crab home,'" someone said, explaining they made it by mashing together the crab's guts. Orrin nearly gagged. "Try it," he told Eddie, pushing the black substance in his direction. Eddie choked down a bite and, smiling wanly, declared the dip to be satisfying and, yet, extremely filling.

The villagers just arriving insisted on hearing the stories of Jann Karl and Lars, stories that those who had been present the first time around retold with enthusiasm. Gunnar and Orrin interrupted only to correct misstatements of fact or to add details they previously had forgotten. There were many conversations, people talking about polygamy and the relatives in the photographs or discussing Mormonism with Eddie. "Do not smudge those photographs," Gunnar said. "They belong to Orrin Andreassen."

"I brought them for you," Orrin said. "For all of you, but perhaps you could keep them for everyone, Gunnar, because you are the closest relative of my great-grandfather."

Gunnar thanked Orrin and then went into a back room. He returned a few minutes later carrying a small wooden box under his arm. Speaking loudly to get everyone's attention, he said, "Orrin Andreassen has brought a rare and priceless gift to us today, not just these photographs, but also news of my long-lost Uncle Lars, who, we have discovered, was not so lost after all." Gunnar sat down, complaining he was too old to make speeches. He placed the wooden box on his lap, opened it, and took out a small envelope containing two of Lars's letters to his parents. He didn't know what happened to the other letters his mother had saved; these were the only ones he had. The envelopes, addressed to Per and Bente Andreassen, were plain and white, as were the sheets of paper, folded into thirds, upon which the letters were written. He handed them to Orrin, who fingered them lightly, for they were brittle with age. Orrin's Norwegian relatives gathered about, eager to inspect the letters, but he held them to his chest, reluctant to let them from his hands and risk damaging them.

"Would you read the letters to us?" Orrin asked Gunnar, hoping this would satisfy everyone's curiosity. After some encouragement, Gunnar agreed. He took a pair of glasses from his shirt pocket and began reading. The first letter, written on both sides of two pages, was dated July 6, 1879.

Dear Mother and Father,

I write in hopes you are still alive and someday you will find it in your hearts to write back to me. I have been very depressed lately about the death of my friend James Conklin, who I have told you much about. He was killed by an Indian chief named Bandera when Conklin and I tried to help Mormon settlers rescue nine Indian children who were being sold into slavery. Conklin was the only white man killed, and I cannot stop believing it was my fault because I had said we must take a hard course and not give the Indians the guns they wanted. A bullet aimed at my heart was stopped by a canteen which I had hung over my shoulder just before the shooting began.

When Conklin was killed, I lost my best friend in the whole world because, without him, I could not have survived in this new country. Everything is hot and dry and dusty here, not like Riksøy, and Conklin spoke English with me when everyone else had given up that stupid Lars could learn anything, and he taught me how to ride a horse and follow the trails and find water. It was Conklin who said to me, "Come, you can be a missionary to the Lamanites," and then I knew I had a special calling. But when Conklin was gone I cried and cried because I was all alone again like the prophet Abraham, a stranger in a strange land. I could not understand why God allowed my friend to be killed when he had a young wife and three children who loved him dearly, and at the same time God saved my own life, when I have no one to care for and no one who cares for me.

Dear Mother and Father, please do not turn away from me. Your son Lars still loves you and misses you and desires that you repent and see the light. If you will pray to God, He certainly will show you the Truth.

God's path is a lonely one. I am alone in a strange land, and Conklin's widow and children are alone, and many others are widows and orphans for the gospel's sake. I am an orphan too, cast out and despised by my family, but I love you still.

Your loving son,
Lars

Gunnar refolded the letter and placed it back in the envelope, then took out the second, much shorter letter. It was dated March 1901 and was written from Juarez, Mexico.

Dear Mother and Father,

I am writing to let you know your son Lars has married again. I have three wives! The United States government is arrayed in all its corrupt power against the Church on the subject of polygamy, but we know it is a True Principle and it cannot be abandoned except at our Eternal peril. I am now quite settled here and rarely take visits to my Martha's family in St. George. I once spent two years in prison and do not wish to repeat that experience. We have quite a growing Mormon colony in Juarez, and I would not be surprised if this part of Mexico someday becomes one of the United States of America. I have become quite settled and content with my families and children—I even have a grandchild on the way—but I never stop missing my mother and father and brothers and sisters.

Your loving son,

Lars

Gunnar sighed and put away the letter. "He lived quite a life," he said. "Who would have thought that a little fisherman's boy would grow up to have such experiences—a Wild West cowboy, Indian fighter, and husband to three wives."

"Yes, three wives," Orrin exclaimed. "We only knew about two. This will come as a big surprise to everyone back home."

"It surprised us too," said Peter, laughing, and everyone began speaking at once, anxious to express their admiration and astonishment for long-lost Uncle Lars. Their lives, they said, have been commonplace and dull compared to his. They remarked on Lars's loneliness, his devotion, and his bravery. "Lars's father should have forgiven him," someone said, "even if it was the Mormons."

Chapter 38

Do not socialize. Social life is not a part of your missionary assignment. Do not call anyone by his or her first name or in the personal form if you are speaking in a foreign language.

Conduct of a Missionary

Herr Reissmann finished his cigarette and crushed it under his foot. "Here is your mail and the key to your hybel. I knocked, but Fru Kjelberg was not there so I got your mail and left the envelope with your rent payment, as you asked." He spat on the dock and began rolling another cigarette. "Are you boys ready to come back?"

"We are going to stay one more week," Orrin said. "Elder Pedersen has a big musical performance with the school children next Saturday evening. Can you come on Monday?"

Herr Reissmann's callused fingers pinched the ends of a new cigarette. "I will be here about noon. Please be ready."

"We will," Eddie said. He handed Herr Reissmann several envelopes. "Here is our weekly report to our mission president and letters to our families."

"You are mailing these as soon as you arrive in Harstad, right?" Orrin asked.

"Yes, yes." Reissmann put the cigarette to his lips, struck a match, and cupping the flame in his hands, lit the cigarette. He inhaled slowly, savoring the nicotine-induced adrenaline rushing through his bloodstream. He would need the extra boost for the long trip home. "I did not expect you boys would stay here so long."

"Neither did we," Orrin said. "It is not a problem, is it?"

"No, no. It is none of my business, of course, but you have been here three weeks already and if you want to keep your trip a secret, well—"

"We appreciate your discretion, Herr Reissmann," Eddie said. "We plan to return to Harstad next week, absolutely."

Herr Reissmann rubbed out his cigarette, grinding it with the ball of his foot, and climbed into the boat. "Unhook those ropes and throw them aboard, boys," he said, starting up the engine. "See you next week."

Orrin and Eddie had spent three eventful weeks in Riksøy without, as far as they knew, arousing suspicion at mission headquarters, but both elders knew they risked being found out by staying a fourth week. Bror Brevik would be returning from his NATO assignment in a few days and might come knocking at their door soon after. Still, the cover story they left with Fru Brevik about visiting other towns would satisfy him until they returned. They would confess everything to President Toressen. Surely, he would applaud their resourcefulness, even audacity, and after hearing of their experiences, he would congratulate them on their inspired undertaking. That is what they told themselves during numerous late-night discussions in which they sought to reassure themselves they had made the right decision to travel secretly to Riksøy.

"I can hear President Toressen chuckling, his face lighting up with that look he gets when things are going well," Orrin said.

"You know him better than I do, Elder Tanner. I hope you're right."

Orrin and Eddie had not arrived in Riksøy with a plan for how long they would stay. They had brought their flannel board, Joseph Smith pamphlets, and extra copies of the Book of Mormon in case they met people wanting to hear the discussions. Orrin had entertained romantic notions of effecting mass conversions, as did early church missionaries when proselytizing remote villages and towns. But upon meeting Gunnar Andreassen and other distant relatives, he recognized this as the same selfish desire that was poisoning his mission and causing him misery. *I won't preach or proselytize again until my heart is pure*, he told himself. Still, that left unanswered the question of what they would do in Riksøy.

Gunnar had invited the elders to stay in his home. His wife had passed away many years ago and his two sons were married and living in Oslo, so he had an extra room—if they didn't mind sharing a bathroom and were not bothered by an occasional goat wandering into the house. The next morning, Orrin and Eddie were finishing up a breakfast of *smørbrød* and lox when they heard a loud knocking and a shout of "*God morgen.*" In stepped a man wearing a black bowler and an agreeable smile.

"Hi, Gunnar," he said, poking his head into the kitchen. "I hear you have relatives visiting from America. I have come to meet our town's new celebrities."

"Please, come join us," Gunnar said, gulping coffee.

The man removed his hat and coat, which he hung in the entryway. "Ah, that is better," he said, rubbing his hands together for warmth. He wore black pants and a black shirt and looked to be in his mid-thirties with sandy hair well over his ears. His large, round glasses gave him a pensive, owlish look. A white collar encircled his neck.

"*Si hei til sognepresten vår,*" Gunnar said. "Say hello to our parish priest, Pastor Einar Carlsen."

Orrin and Eddie both stood to shake his hand. "You are a State Church priest?" Orrin asked.

"Yes, and I presume you are Mormon missionaries."

"You have not come to harass my guests because of their religion, I hope," Gunnar said.

"No, no. I was just curious. We do not often get Mormons visiting Riksøy, you know."

"Probably the last Mormon to set foot on Riksøy was my great-grandfather Lars Andreassen," Orrin said.

Pastor Carlsen and Gunnar let loose a burst of laughter. "Yes, I am afraid that is so," Gunnar said.

Pastor Carlsen grew serious. "Do not let my position as a State Church priest intimidate you boys. I am not here to discourage you or drive you away. I am not afraid you will steal sheep from my flock, if that is what you might think."

"Hah," Gunnar smirked. "That is because he has none to steal."

Pastor Carlsen smiled. "Gunnar is correct. In Norway, Christ's servants toil on rocky soil."

"We understand that all too well," Eddie said.

"I only wanted to find out why you came. If you want to proselytize, I will not stand in your way. In fact, I will be curious to hear what you have to say."

"You may be the only one," Gunnar said.

"No, we did not come to proselytize," Orrin replied. He gave Elder Pedersen an apologetic look, knowing they should have discussed this decision together. Elder Pedersen looked puzzled but not unhappy. "I wanted to visit my Andreassen relatives and . . ." Orrin's voice trailed off.

"And we wanted to see if we could be of any help to the people here," Eddie said.

"Help?" Pastor Carlsen said.

"As missionaries we are charged with serving the people," Eddie continued. "We can do that in many ways."

"It is fortunate you came over today, Pastor Carlsen, because you might know better than anyone how we might be of service," Orrin said.

"How long are you boys planning to stay?"

Gunnar waved a spoon at the two missionaries. "As long as they like or until my food runs out."

"We could stay a week, if that is okay with Gunnar," Orrin said.

"That is a nice offer," Pastor Carlsen replied. "I will check around the village and see if we can put you to work."

Eddie didn't know how he felt about Elder Tanner's abrupt announcement they would not be proselytizing on Riksøy. Eddie's confession to

Elder Tanner that he was homosexual was really an acknowledgment to himself of that fact. And with that acknowledgement, Eddie was now looking at life—and at himself—from a new but unclear perspective, as if through a glass, darkly. *What did it mean to be a homosexual Mormon? Is it even possible to be both homosexual and Mormon?* Until he figured out his relationship with God and the church, he did not feel it appropriate to continue teaching the discussions. That was *his* reasoning for not wanting to proselytize. But what had prompted Elder Tanner's decision? *Does he consider me unworthy to preach?* It made Eddie's heart ache to think Elder Tanner viewed him this way, even if Eddie thought the same thing himself.

"Do you think Pastor Carlsen is as friendly as he appears?" Orrin asked as the elders finished up their daily studies.

"I don't know. I've only heard bad things about State Church priests, though I've got to admit I've never actually met one."

"Me either," Orrin said. "It's the Norwegian people themselves who are always complaining to us about their priests."

Both elders also acknowledged they knew little about the Norwegian State Lutheran Church or its doctrines, let alone anything about its priests. "We preach that State Church teachings are false, but we don't even know what those teachings are," Orrin said.

Amid the elders' banter, Pastor Carlsen knocked and opened the door. "Are you boys still here?" he called. "If so, I have found a job for you."

Pastor Carlsen explained that Riksøy's school had been without a qualified English instructor since the new year began. The previous teacher left after she married, and it was difficult for a small island town like Riksøy to attract new teachers, especially those specializing in language instruction. A science instructor who had gained some knowledge of English while working at sea in his youth had taken over English instruction, but his skills were limited. He readily agreed when the principal asked if he would like help from the American missionaries. No teaching of Mormonism would be tolerated, of course, but it would be a great service to the students. Orrin and Eddy hurried down the hill with Pastor Carlsen to the village school; before they had a chance to catch their breath, they were standing in front of the class.

"I am Elder Pedersen and this is Elder Tanner," Eddie said. The students laughed and whispered among themselves. "Did I say something wrong?" Eddie asked.

A student's hand shot up in the air. "It is funny you both have the same odd first name."

"Oh no, these are not our first names. They are religious titles. Just like you have pastors, we are called elders because we are missionaries for

The Church of Jesus Christ of Latter-day Saints. You have heard of the Mormons, right?"

Before the students could answer, Orrin interjected, "But we are here to instruct you in the English language, not religion."

"Yes, thank you, Elder Tanner," Eddie said, again causing laughter. Eddie flushed. "Have I said something wrong again?"

Another student raised her hand. "Is his name really 'teeth'?"

"Teeth?"

"Yes, tanner means 'teeth' in Norwegian."

Orrin flashed a toothy grin. "I show you these so you will always remember my name."

For the rest of the hour, Orrin and Eddie conversed with the students in English and Norwegian, having them recite simple English phrases to gauge their proficiency and establish a rapport. Marte, the girl who had raised her hand, was a ringleader among the girls, while eleven-year-old Steinar, a boy with dirty boots and greasy pants, ruled the boys. The elders worked hard to get Marte and Steinar on their side, and when Steinar expressed interest in Orrin's upbringing in the West, Orrin promised to tell the students in a future class about the experiences of his great-grandfather Lars Andreassen. "And if you are diligent in your studies, I will teach you how to speak American," Orrin said, emphasizing his thick rural "r," much to the delight of the students, who recognized the familiar accent from American movies and television shows.

After teaching the class, Orrin and Eddie helped Gunnar clean out goat and sheep excrement from his barn. "We had a particularly harsh winter this year. It was hard for me to keep up," Gunnar said apologetically.

"It doesn't smell any worse than Grünerløkka's outhouses," Orrin remarked as he wheeled another load of waste to the pasture.

As it turned out, there was plenty for the elders to do in Riksøy. Several widows needed help with mending and painting fences, and many others asked for assistance preparing gardens for the spring planting of vegetables. Having worked on his grandparents' farm, Orrin had little trouble assisting the Norwegians and directing Eddie in their efforts, though Eddie struck a thumb with a few errant hammer blows. "You stick to painting and I'll do the hammering," Orrin said after the third such incident. "We can't afford to damage any of those precious fingers of yours."

Orrin was referring to Eddie's piano playing abilities. The elders had found a spinet piano in the school gymnasium which, with the help of the janitor, they moved into the classroom where they taught English. After a few days, Orrin and Eddie developed a routine that used music to make language instruction more interesting to the students. In the mornings they taught two separate classes from the *barneskole* (elementary school) of twenty students each and after lunch, they taught another class of seventeen students from the *ungdomsskole* (lower secondary school). After finishing the standard lesson for each day, Eddie would accompany the students in singing songs in English. The elders taught the younger students songs sung by all American children, such as "Three Blind Mice," "The Farmer in the Dell," and "Happy Birthday," as well as songs from popular Disney movies. The older children soon tired of the simple songs, so Eddie encouraged them to suggest American and English pop songs they had heard on the radio. After school, Eddie would work out the chord changes to recommended songs while Orrin wrote the lyrics on the blackboard. The last fifteen minutes of class were always spent singing and going over the pronunciation of the words. If the students successfully completed their weekly assignments, all of Friday was devoted to singing in English.

The elders spent their nights preparing their next-day lessons and songs, though they also received several invitations to dinner. People knew of Orrin's connection to the island, but they also were curious about why the young Mormon men had come to Norway. "We are already Christians," they would say.

Neither Orrin nor Eddie felt ready to pull out their flannel board and begin teaching discussions, but this did not mean they shied away from conversations about religion. To the contrary, they readily answered questions about Mormonism and, much to their surprise, found themselves engrossed with their hosts in far-ranging discussions about God and religion. The elders discovered that when they asked islanders about their beliefs without an ulterior motive to drive them to the "right" conclusions or, especially, toward baptism, people no longer answered from a defensive posture but often revealed deep and well-thought-out ruminations on life. The Norwegians were not biblical scholars—few had even opened a Bible since their confirmations—but they enjoyed exploring their own beliefs against both the teachings of the State Church and of the Mormon missionaries. Most regarded the concept of a pre-earthly existence to be highly logical and did not need the elders to offer scriptural proof telling them so. They also liked Joseph Smith's teaching that everyone will receive some level of heavenly reward in the next life based on their faith and actions.

"I hope you Mormons are right," Herr Hendriksen told the elders. "I may not go to the top-level celestial kingdom with you boys, but I will be in a happy place nevertheless, probably with my friends who drink and smoke a little too much."

"Ugh, I am not sure I want to be in the same place with those friends of yours," Fru Hendriksen said, elbowing her husband.

"Thank you for suggesting that I will go to the highest level of the celestial kingdom, Herr Hendriksen," Orrin said. "But there is no guarantee I will get there."

Herr Hendricksen clapped Orrin on the back. "Then you can be with me and my friends."

"I think they would rather be in my heavenly kingdom," Fru Hendriksen said. "Much quieter."

At the home of Herr and Fru Aarnes, whose two children attended the *ungdomsskole*, Fru Aarnes expressed surprise at some of her husband's views. "I did not know he had such a strong belief in God," she told the elders.

Herr Aarnes offered a rueful smile. "You Mormons will probably think this odd, but it is the first time Siri and I have ever had a serious talk about our religious beliefs."

"I would like to do it more often," Fru Aarnes said, reaching for her husband's hand.

People invariably asked how long the elders planned to stay. "Not long," Orrin told them. "Probably a week. Herr Reissmann returns next Monday."

"Oh, that is too bad," Fru Aarnes said. "You boys should get to know some of our young people who come home on the weekends." Because of Riksøy's small population, the island's older boys and girls attended the upper secondary *videregående* school on the mainland. They left early each Monday morning on the ferry and returned on Friday afternoons. "There are some pretty girls among them."

"We are not allowed to date," Orrin said.

"What? Young Mormons cannot go out together?"

"It is because we are missionaries. Only missionaries are not allowed to date. Otherwise, your beautiful Norwegian daughters would be too tempting for us American boys," Eddie said, grinning slyly.

"Ah, I understand," Fru Aarnes said. "Still, that is too bad."

On Saturday, Orrin and Eddie were slated to help the Hendriksens clear away a rat-infested brush pile in a field behind their house, but Herr Hendriksen canceled due to a heavy rain, and so the elders wandered over to the school's gymnasium to get some exercise. There they found the *videregående* schoolboys practicing basketball. "You must be the Americans who are teaching English," a muscular boy named Geir said.

"Yes, may we shoot baskets with you?" Eddie asked. The Norwegian boys, eight in number, agreed. They were amazed by the shooting skills displayed by the two missionaries.

"Our coach says basketball is now an international sport, so we Norwegians must learn to play basketball. But we cannot shoot the ball like you. What is your secret?" Geir asked.

Eddie, who was more experienced than Orrin, saw at once the problem. "You are shooting a two-handed set shot like this," Eddie said, demonstrating their form. "No one shoots like that anymore. Here, watch how Elder Tanner and I shoot. This is how everyone in American shoots baskets these days."

For the next two hours, Eddie and Orrin worked with the Norwegian boys, helping them not only with their shooting but also with dribbling, rebounding, and other skills. Eddie drew from his experience playing on his high school team to run the boys through a variety of drills that developed court awareness and coordination. After lunch, the boys returned for more drills and shooting exercises and then formed teams to scrimmage with Orrin and Eddie. At the end of the day, the Norwegian boys asked if the elders would help them practice again on Sunday. Orrin and Eddie stepped aside to discuss the matter. On the one hand, it was the Sabbath. And they *were* missionaries, after all. But the Riksøy boys would be leaving the next day. There would be no other time for them to practice. Eventually, the elders decided it was an ox-in-the-mire situation and agreed to train with the boys on Sunday. However, they would not be able to start until noon because they were going to attend the morning service at the State Church.

"Why are you going to the State Church. Are you not Mormon missionaries?

"Yes," Orrin replied, "but Pastor Carlsen has been very nice to us and we want to hear what he has to say."

"Okay, but you might be the only ones there," Geir said, drawing laughter from the other boys.

Geir exaggerated only slightly. When Orrin and Eddie slid into a pew for the ten o'clock service, they counted only fifteen other people in a chapel that could hold nearly two hundred. The elders nodded to the people they knew, including an older couple who had hosted them for lunch earlier in the week. Pastor Carlsen acknowledged the elders with a brief smile when he took his place at the front of the congregation. Orrin found his sermon on the beatitudes to be heartfelt and moving, but the echoing grunts and coughs among the congregants made him question whether anyone was paying close attention. "That was a wonderful sermon," Eddie told Pastor Carlsen after the service.

"I agree," Orrin said, adding, "It is unfortunate more people did not come to hear it."

"I am not disappointed. In fact, we had a slightly larger turnout than usual because of the rain. People cannot work outside, so some of them came to church instead." Pastor Carlsen lifted off his vestments and folded them over his arm. "I hear you have drawn a good crowd of boys at the gymnasium. I would like to watch, if that is okay."

"Put on your gym clothes and you can play too," Eddie said.

"No, no. I understand nothing about basketball. Besides, it is not good for my congregation to see their pastor running around with his skinny legs in little shorts. It undermines the aura of divine mystery I am cultivating with my flock."

Chapter 39

The missionary must always be a gentleman. Now this includes gentlewoman.

Conduct of a Missionary

Orrin and Eddie did not return to Harstad on the first Monday, as they initially planned, opting instead to stay a second week. They enjoyed teaching English classes and felt as if they were providing a needed service. In addition, an oppressive weekend rain had prevented them from completing the growing list of chores they had agreed to perform. When Herr Reissmann arrived at the dock with his boat, they gave him their weekly reports to the mission president and a handful of letters to home. "It is important you mail the letters as soon as you return, so they are postmarked as coming from Harstad," Orrin said. He also gave Herr Reissmann a key to their hybel, so he could bring back their mail. "Fru Kjelberg places our mail on a table at the top of the stairs, just outside our door."

"Does that mean you intend to stay even longer than another week?" Herr Reissmann asked.

"We do not know, not for sure," Orrin said. "Is that okay with you?"

Reissmann smiled as he took a drag from his cigarette and blew smoke from the corner of his mouth. "I am always glad to participate in God's divine machinations."

After staying the first week with Gunnar Andreassen, Orin and Eddie moved into the clapboard home of Georg Tungsten and Olav Berg so they could be closer to the town center and have more living space. Olav, who taught math and science at the *ungdomsskole*, invited the elders to stay after getting to know them through his students. Olav and Georg grew up together in Riksøy. Georg, a fisherman, never left the island; when Olav returned after earning his teaching credentials, the two men purchased the house together. That was twenty years ago. The longtime housemates bickered and bantered like an old married couple.

"Where is the *ostehøvel?*" Georg would say as he rummaged through drawers looking for the cheese slicer. "Why have you moved the *ostehøvel?*"

"If it is not there, it is because *you* have moved it," Olav would reply. "You used it last."

"I did? When?"

"Just this morning."

"This morning?"

"Yes."

"No."

"Yes."

And on and on they went, arguing about *ostehøvels*, dirty towels, missing keys, empty coffee containers, a door hinge that needed fixing, and other minor aggravations of daily life. But there also existed a gentle affection between the two men. An early riser, Georg would leave a bowl of cut fruit and a hot pot of coffee on the counter for Olav before leaving for his boat, while Olav would have frothy beer and a light snack waiting for Georg when he returned at the end of the day. Georg was stout with dark features and thick hands that had gutted tens of thousands of fish, while Olav, though not tall, was slender, even delicate, with skin as white as the blackboard chalk dusting his pants and shirt. Olav did not smoke, but Georg enjoyed his pipe, and while Georg fussed with the tobacco, constantly refilling and relighting his pipe, the two would talk animatedly about the island's latest gossip. Georg often went to bed early, especially if the weather portended a promising day of fishing. On those nights, Olav would stay up talking with the elders while he fixed a meal, which he put in a metal lunch box in the refrigerator for Georg to take with him the next morning. "I wish the Breviks could see how well these two men get along," Orrin told Eddie.

The English classes grew in popularity. The school children enjoyed the novelty of speaking with young Americans well versed in a popular culture that was carving inroads into everyday Norwegian life. Orrin and Eddie achieved authoritative stature in the eyes of Riksøy's youth by virtue of their ability to decipher the meaning of American and English idioms. The Norwegians could not understand why being "out of sight" was a good thing; nor why a T-bird was fun, fun, fun; nor what it meant to "get down" when dancing, all of which were easily explained, though Orrin blushed and feigned ignorance when a student asked what Tommy James meant when he said his baby did the hanky-panky. "We do not know, but it probably is not good," Eddie finally said. The older students nodded knowingly without pressing further.

"Apparently, we should have spent more time watching television and going to movies, and less time reading the scriptures," Eddie joked after a class with the ungdomsskole students.

"Watch more television?" Orrin said. "I will put that in my Thought Book of inspirational ideas . . . right next to outhouse tracting."

The skies cleared on Tuesday just as the local fisherman had predicted, allowing the elders to resume their general handyman work. They performed well on all of the projects except at the Hendriksens, who lived at the top of a hill on the southern edge of town. When the elders arrived, Herr and Fru Hendriksen were standing beside a brush pile where several families of rats had taken up residence and, in recent months, had fulfilled the biblical admonition to multiply and replenish the earth. Fru Hendriksen was kneeling on the ground, striking a match, while her husband stood beside her holding three shovels. "Ah, just in time," Herr Hendriksen said as he handed each elder a shovel.

"What would you like us to do?" Orrin asked cheerfully.

"My wife will set the brush on fire and when the rats run out, we will—WHAM!—hit them with our shovels."

"Hit them?"

"Kill them."

Orrin blanched. "Is that not, um . . ."

"*Grusom*, Herr Hendriksen," Eddie interjected. "Is this not cruel?"

Fru Hendriksen, who was blowing on pieces of kindling she had shoved under the brush, looked up at the elders. "You would not think it so if you saw the rats running across your kitchen floor."

"Or eating the feed you have set out for your sheep," her husband added.

Orrin tugged at Eddie's coat. "I thought we were just going to clear out the brush where the rats were living."

"So did I."

"This isn't the kind of thing—" Before Orrin could finish, a juvenile rat whose body was no longer than a finger darted out of the smoldering brush toward Orrin.

"Get it," Herr and Fru Hendriksen shouted in unison. "Get it."

Panicking, Orrin swung his shovel at the scurrying creature. BANG! The shovel's metal blade vibrated with the cracking bones. The tiny rat, its back legs broken, valiantly tried to pull itself forward with its front legs. "Hit it again!" Herr Hendriksen cried. Orrin raised his shovel but could only stare, mesmerized at the struggling rodent. Seeing Orrin's hesitation, Herr Hendriksen rushed forward and struck the rat with his shovel, smashing its lifeless body into the ground. "There, this is what you should do. It is cruel to let them suffer." Herr Hendriksen looked up to see tears streaming down Orrin's cheeks.

"I am sorry, Herr Hendriksen," Orrin said. "I should not have volunteered for this job. I know the rats must be killed, but I cannot do it."

Orrin handed his shovel to Herr Hendriksen and walked away, wiping his eyes. As the fire spread, more rats dashed out of the brush pile. "Here, I will take the shovel," Fru Hendriksen said, and with her husband began pummeling the fleeing rodents.

"I, too, am sorry," Eddie said, laying down his shovel, "but I must go with my companion." As he walked away, Eddie could hear the loud clanging of shovels announcing each rat's demise.

"I will be the laughingstock of the island," Orrin lamented after he and Eddie had returned to the house. "Not just of the adults, but also the children we teach." Orrin recalled the rite of passage when he and his boyhood friends went hunting with their fathers for the first time. The boys who hung back or cried watching the men kill and gut deer were mocked and teased as being no better than the farm girls who wept when a beloved calf was designated for slaughter. "No one will respect me," Orrin said. "I'll be the Andreassen everyone on Riksøy will be glad to see go."

"Don't be so hard on yourself, Elder Tanner," Eddie replied. "I didn't want to kill those rats, either—not by bashing them over the head, anyway. That was brutal."

"Yeah, but the way I cried and carried on like some prissy girl," Orrin said, "you would think that between the two of us, I was the one who was—" Orrin abruptly stopped, but not before a look of pain swept across his companion's face. Eddie rubbed his arm but said nothing, his mouth agape. "Oh, Elder Pedersen, I'm so sorry," Orrin said. "I, I didn't mean it that way. I was just trying to make a joke and . . . oh, please forgive me."

"We have never discussed my homosexuality, not since that first day I told you about it," Eddie said, speaking in measured tones. "It's like this gigantic weight the two of us carry together but never speak about. I have wondered what you think of me. Now I guess I know."

"No, that's not it at all. I didn't think it was my place to initiate a discussion about . . . you know. And since you never did, I thought *you* didn't want to talk about it, at least not with me."

A knock at the door interrupted the elders. "Hello, is anyone home?" Pastor Carlsen called. He stepped into the house without waiting for an answer and greeted the elders. "I hear you boys had a rough time at the Hendriksen's today."

"It was me, not Elder Pedersen, who behaved badly," Orrin said. "I do not know what came over me. I grew up in a farming community where people raised and slaughtered their livestock, and I have killed deer and elk myself. And so my reaction to killing those rats does not make sense, even to me. I have embarrassed myself, which I have done a lot since becoming a missionary. I apologize to you, Pastor Carlsen, because you gave us this project to perform. And I will also go and apologize to the Hendriksens."

"Please, Elders, let us sit," Pastor Carlsen said, pointing to the couch and chairs in the living room. After the three men had taken seats, Pastor

Carlsen placed a hand on Orrin's knee. "It is I who should apologize. In fact, that is why I came here. I should never have given such an assignment to ones with your calling. It was not a proper use of your talents."

Orrin's emotional outburst reminded Eddie of the time when he had broken down sobbing after Elder Ward and other Bergen elders had played a prank on him. He thought the humiliation would follow him throughout his mission and even beyond. And yet, he had nearly forgotten it until now. He would tell Elder Tanner about it later. As the men conversed, there came another knock; before the elders could answer, the door swung open and they heard hesitant greetings from Herr and Fru Hendriksen. The husband and wife hung close together and cast their eyes on the floor when they saw the elders.

"We are sorry to disturb you," Herr Hendriksen said, holding his hat in his hand. "But we came to apologize for what happened today."

"Yes," Fru Hendriksen added. "We should not have asked you to do something so upsetting to you. We did not know."

Orrin and Eddie jumped to their feet. "No, no, please," Eddie said. "You have nothing to apologize for."

"It is us, especially me, who should apologize," Orrin said. "I am embarrassed for myself, but we hold no ill will toward you, do we Elder Pedersen?"

"No, none at all. But it is so kind of you to come and see us."

The elders rushed forward to shake hands with the now-smiling Hendriksens as everyone continued offering apologies, each seeking to absolve the others of blame, until Pastor Carlsen suggested they continue their conversation in the living room. "When I was a boy, I had a favorite lamb that I raised to be a fine sheep," Herr Hendriksen said. "I thought my father would let me keep it as a pet, but no, that was not the plan."

"What did you do?" Orrin asked.

"I tried to run away with the sheep, but on an island, there are not so many places to hide. I cried and cried for days."

"Everyone who has grown up on Riksøy can tell a similar story," Pastor Carlsen said.

"Yes, but I bet they did not cry over a rat," Orrin said, still chagrined.

"That is true," Herr Hendriksen observed. "You are the first one."

Fru Hendriksen affectionately tussled Orrin's hair. "There is no shame in being tenderhearted, Elder Tanner."

The elders served their guests tea and were setting out a plate of cookies when Olav arrived home from work. "Hello, Olav, we are in here having a party in your home," Pastor Carlsen shouted when he heard the door swing open and the thud on the floor as Olav took off his shoes. Olav smiled broadly and took a seat with his guests as Eddie poured him a cup of tea.

"This is a nice surprise, Jakob and Hilde," he said to the Hendriksens, cupping his hands around the warm tea. "Is there an occasion for your visit?" The Hendriksens looked at the elders, wondering how they should answer the question. Olav lifted the tea to his lips, testing it, and then exclaimed, "Oh, yes, I remember now. The Mormon boys were going to help you today with your rats. How did that go? Did you get them all?"

Olav waited for an answer, but his guests pretended to be too busy eating or sipping tea to speak, each one looking to others, back and forth, none looking eager to answer. "Well," Olav said. "Did you kill the rats or not?"

Orrin cracked first, emitting a muffled laugh. Fru Hendriksen snickered and her husband chortled, first separately, then merrily together. Eddie and Pastor Carlsen joined in and soon the five of them were howling, their eyes moist with laughter. Olav stared at them, stone-faced and confused. "We have a story to tell you, Olav," Orrin said, wiping away tears.

Friday evening, the older Riksøy boys came back with exciting news. Their coach at the mainland school wanted Orrin and Eddie to come to their school and teach all the boys, as well as the coach himself, their basketball drills and techniques. "We were the best players," Geir said, referring to the Riksøy boys. After just one weekend under the elders' training, they had become the school's best players and had even drawn attention from a local club team that competed in a league along the northern coast. The elders, having finished their second week on the island, had planned to return home on Monday but told the boys they would consider the request.

They met the boys early the following morning at the gym to continue their weekend training. A number of parents and townspeople also came to watch, having heard about the boys' prowess at their school. The younger children played along the sidelines and vied with each other to catch and return balls that were knocked out of bounds. A few of the *videregående* girls sat in the bleachers and yelled encouragement to the players. Orrin saw that Fru Aarnes had been right: the older girls *were* pretty, especially the one in a blue skirt with strawberry hair and an ever-present smile. Orrin tried not to pay attention, but every time he looked in her direction, she seemed to be looking at him. He knew it was foolish, even dangerous, to allow himself to feel any attraction toward her. Yet he couldn't stop his gaze from wandering to where she was seated. *Did she just smile at me?*

During their break for lunch, Pastor Carlsen, who had also been watching the practice, came over to talk with the elders. "You boys have gained quite a following. Half the town must be here," he said. "You are our most popular entertainment." They conversed a short while and after the pastor excused himself, the strawberry-haired girl walked up to the elders and stood beside them until she caught Orrin's eye.

"Excuse me," she said. A gaggle of her friends stood a few feet away, watching.

"Yes?" Orrin said.

"My name is Anna-Britt Tessem. I was wondering if you would like to have dinner at my house tonight?"

Orrin blushed. He was flattered and he wished he knew the Norwegian word so he could tell her so, but with his limited language, all he said was, "I am sorry, Anna-Britt, but because I am a Mormon missionary, I am not allowed to go out with girls."

Anna-Britt smiled and whispered something to her friends, who covered their mouths to stifle laughs. "You do not understand. I am not asking you to go out with me. It is my parents. They want you and your companion to come to dinner with our family."

Orrin felt his face flush again. "Yes, of course. We can come."

Orrin and Eddie attended State Church services the next day, as they had the previous Sunday. They counted more than thirty parishioners and, having been in Riksøy fourteen days now, they knew many by name. They shook hands vigorously with Peter and thanked him for his hospitality at his restaurant the day they arrived, saying he had set in motion a heartwarming welcome to the island. The Hendriksens clapped their hands and rushed to greet the elders when they saw them. "How are my tenderhearted Americans today?" Fru Hendriksen asked affectionately.

"Pastor Carlsen was lying when he claimed last Sunday's turnout was a good one," Eddie whispered to Orrin as they slid into a pew. "There are at least twice as many people here today."

"Yes, but it's still quite empty," Orrin said, gesturing to the vast chapel that surrounded them.

Basketball practice after Pastor Carlsen's sermon was a festive community affair. A rainy spring Sunday, which the Norwegians said was all too common, normally kept them shut up at home, so they were happy to have a place to go with friends. The novelty of watching basketball kept them entertained, though many were perplexed by the rules, and so the elders stopped the scrimmaging on several occasions to explain a particular foul or violation to the spectators. Conversations about basketball stretched the limits of the elders' Norwegian, but the townspeople, especially the young people who had been studying English for many years, were happy to interpret and help the elders learn the correct words. The enthusiasm for basketball among the island's residents made the elders believe they had no choice but to agree to go to the mainland and coach at the *videregående* school.

Orrin and Eddie met Herr Reissmann at the dock the next day and informed him of their plan to stay a third week. He expressed no surprise as he handed over the letters he had collected from their apartment and took from them the letters and reports to mail from Harstad. "Same time next week?" he asked.

"Yes," the elders said. They unloosened the ropes holding the boat against the dock and threw them onto the boat, then waved goodbye as Herr Reissmann motored away from the sheltered cove and onto the sea. They took the ferry the next day to the mainland.

Egil Ellefsen met Orrin and Eddie as they exited the ferry. Egil, who insisted the elders call him by his first name, was a tall man in his sixties, gray-haired but not yet bent with age, trim and athletic-looking, and eager to speak English that he learned serving aboard a merchant marine ship during the war. "I made many crossings of the Atlantic Ocean and escaped death when many of my friends and shipmates did not," he said. He learned to play basketball from the American sailors who recruited him to play center because of his height. "I could not shoot or dribble so good, but I could grab the ball when players missed the basket," he explained.

The elders trained the boys in five consecutive gym classes. Not all of the boys were skilled athletes or interested in becoming basketball players, but Egil told them it was important to learn the American sport as Norway expanded its international profile. "We have for many years been an isolated people, especially those of us who live on the northern islands, but those times may soon end," he said.

"Do you think that is a good thing?" Eddie asked.

"Now that we are becoming an oil nation, it is inevitable," he replied. "Maybe we will become rich like Americans."

After school ended, Egil assembled the best players for a basketball team that would scrimmage the local club team the following afternoon. He again turned the coaching over to the elders, who taught the boys to play defense, switch and double-team opponents, and set up an offense. They practiced simple plays with an emphasis on passing and moving without the ball. "Keep your spacing on the court, don't dribble too much, and whatever you do, don't dribble the ball into the corner," Eddie advised.

They stayed the night with Egil, who regaled the elders with stories of when he served in the merchant marines. "They do not want to hear those old stories, Egil," complained his wife, a kindly woman who served the elders beef patties, sauerkraut, and potatoes. "I have heard them every day for more than twenty years."

"But they have not," Egil replied, undaunted, and proceeded to tell how he had become a sailor at an early age and was at sea on a cargo ship when the Germans invaded Norway. His ship was enlisted in the war effort and carried arms and supplies to allied fighters throughout the war, crossing the ocean in large convoys for protection. "Of course, we never saw the U-boats and only knew they were lurking close by when we heard the explosion of their torpedoes hitting one of our sister ships. Thousands of Norwegian sailors lost their lives," he said. "Twice after I was billeted to a new ship, the ship on which I had served was sunk. I became a good-luck charm. All the sailors wanted me on their ship and no one wanted me to leave."

"God protected him. That is what I think," Fru Ellefsen said as she cleared away dishes. "He should thank God every day for keeping him safe."

"He saved me for you, my dear wife," Egil said. "Perhaps *you* should be the one thanking God."

Fru Ellefsen gave a disdainful snort and carried the plates into the kitchen. When Egil was certain his wife was well out of hearing distance, he scooted back his chair and began unlacing his shoes. "You want to know how I was protected during the war? I will reveal it to you," he said, and proceeded to take off his shoes and socks to show the elders his bare feet. On the top of each foot was a colorful, beautifully drawn tattoo. A pig decorated his left foot and a rooster his right. "A pig and a rooster. A rooster and a pig. They bring sailors good luck," he said, rubbing the tattoos as if they were talismans. "Some sailors had their hands tattooed with a pig and rooster, but tattooing your feet is better."

"What is the significance of the pig and rooster?" Eddie asked.

"In the old days of sailing, having pigs and chickens on board your ship was considered good luck because they were kept in wooden crates, and if your ship went down and you could not get to a lifeboat, you could keep afloat by hanging onto one of the crates. Modern ships do not carry farm animals, so we sailors tattoo them on our feet so the good luck continues."

"That is an interesting story," Orrin said, "but you do not really believe this superstition, do you, that your tattoos brought you luck? Did not some of the sailors who drowned also have the same tattoos?"

Egil put back on his socks and shoes with pensive deliberation. "That is true, Elder Tanner. But many of those sailors who drowned also prayed to God to save them, so I think there is as much evidence in favor of tattoos as there is for God."

The afternoon basketball game featuring the *videregående* schoolboys against the local club brought out the entire student body as well as local sports fans interested in seeing how well Norwegians could play the American game. Egil asked Eddie and Orrin to coach the boys, saying he would help if communicating in Norwegian was a problem for the elders, but otherwise the team was better off in their hands. The players on the club team were no taller than the schoolboys, but they were stronger and more experienced and dominated early with their aggressive play. Eddie, who assumed the role of head coach, called two timeouts in the first quarter to settle down the boys. The quarter ended with the boys scoring only four points and falling behind by ten.

Disheartened, the boys began arguing among themselves during the quarter break. "Do not you missionaries have some special connection with God that can help us?" Geir asked.

Eddie laughed, breaking the tension. "We do have a special connection to God, as do all of you. But unfortunately, God does not care who wins or loses basketball games, so it is up to you. But do not be discouraged, you were getting better with each minute, especially your defense. We just need to score some points." Eddie inserted Geir and one of the other Riksøy boys into the game and diagrammed a play to get them open shots. "Square up and set your body, just like you did in practice," Eddie told them. "You will surprise them."

Eddie was right. Geir made three quick baskets, boosting his team's morale, and by halftime, the boys were only four points behind. The club team adjusted their defense to counter the boys' shooting and increased their lead to eight points as the third quarter ended. But the boys gained confidence throughout, receiving constant encouragement from their many fans, and while the club team's play improved, so did theirs. Halfway through the last quarter, Eddie walked to the scorer's table to check the score. The scoreboard showed zeros for each team. "Is something wrong with the scoreboard?" Eddie asked.

"No," Egil replied. "I have stopped keeping score."

"What? Why?"

Egil smiled and pointed to the court. "The score is not important. Look how beautifully our boys are playing together."

On the ferry ride home, Eddie and Orrin stood together at the rail, watching the sun's rays shimmer and dance across the darkening sea. A pod of whales appeared in the distance. Their long, arching backs were barely visible above the surface, but the spray from their blowholes sparkled in the reflected sunlight. The breach of a large whale sent waves of churning foam in all directions. Eddie couldn't help but feel pleased with the success of the basketball team. *Would it lead to any baptisms?* Eddie hesitated to guess. "Egil Ellefsen is quite the character, don't you think, Elder Tanner?" he said.

Orrin nodded without elaboration. Eddie tried several more times to engage his companion in a discussion of their experience coaching basketball, but Orrin responded with little enthusiasm. Orrin had seemed happy when they first boarded the boat, but now he stared ahead, mute, absorbed in dreamy melancholy. Eddie worried that because he had the primary coaching duties, Orrin perhaps did not share Eddie's feeling of triumph but instead felt slighted and underappreciated. "Is there anything wrong, Elder Tanner?" Eddie asked. "I hope I haven't offended you in some way. I am sorry if I dominated the coaching and didn't allow you equal chance to lead the team."

"Oh, no, that's not it at all," Orrin replied. Turning to his companion, he continued, "It was a wonderful experience, even inspirational, and I shall never forget that delightful man, Egil Ellefsen, and his wife." Orrin looked back at the flickering lights on the mainland. "It's just that I've been thinking . . . we will probably never see Egil or most of those people ever again."

Chapter 40

Have the "Attitude of Success. . . . Motivate your contacts by expressing confidence in their ability. Do not rely on forceful speech or logic alone.

A Uniform System for Teaching Investigators

A mild spring morning had Riksøy's residents sweeping off their porches in anticipation of noonday lunches under a radiant sun, but a sudden wave of turbulent clouds darkened the sky, and by early afternoon drenching rains and gale-like winds began lashing the island. Fishing boats operating nearby made their way quickly to Riksøy's small harbor. Their crews reported violent squalls and in one case, powerful waves that nearly capsized a boat. A radio operator called for any remaining boats to return home or find shelter immediately, and islanders kept track of which boats had returned and which remained at sea. Peder Mjøs called from his boat radio to report that he and two others were safely harbored at Sørland. Eventually, all the Riksøy fisherman were accounted for—except Georg Tungsten.

By tradition, the crews that had safely returned went to Peter's restaurant and waited until all boats were reported safe, standing ready to return to sea and look for any missing boats when the storm passed. They smoked and drank coffee and spat tobacco and exchanged stories comparing today's storm to those of years past, recounting dangerous escapes and rehashing the island's folklore of those who never returned. They hushed when Olav entered the restaurant, distraught, asking where they had last seen Georg's boat. They tried to reassure Olav, telling him Georg was a fine sailor, more skilled than any of them, and that he was probably safely harbored at a nearby island. But when talking among themselves, they worried. Georg had not called in on his radio, nor had they been able to reach him. They apologized to Olav because they could not immediately go out to look for Georg, though no apology was needed. Everyone who grew up in a fishing village understood you did not risk lives trying to save someone who may already be lost. Still, Olav closely monitored the weather reports and repeatedly asked when the others thought it might be safe to start searching for Georg.

Orrin and Eddie had stayed home, not wishing to get in the way, but at sunset, they walked to the restaurant to see if there was any news of Georg. Most of the fisherman had returned home to rest, pledging to return at morning's first light. Pastor Carlsen was making lunches for the sailors who would go, while Olav had taken up vigil on the dock. The rain was now merely a drizzle, though the wind still blew fiercely in gusts. Pastor Carlsen said Olav had gone out with a lantern, acting as a lighthouse. When told there were plenty of lights on the dock to help Georg find his way home, Olav said he just wanted Georg to see he was waiting for him. Eddie grabbed a lantern and said he would wait with Olav. Orrin slipped behind the counter with Pastor Carlsen and began cutting up bread, while the pastor sliced up tomatoes and cucumbers for the *smørbrød*.

"So, Elder Tanner," Pastor Carlsen said. "I hear you and Elder Pedersen have been discussing religion with many of my parishioners."

"Is that a problem?"

Pastor Carlsen laughed. "Not at all. I am glad to hear they are interested in such matters. It is just that you have never discussed Mormonism with *me*."

"What would you like to hear?" Orrin replied. "I can talk all night." As the two men continued assembling *smørbrød*, Orrin told the story of Joseph Smith's first vision and explained some of the church's main doctrines and practices.

Pastor Carlsen gave Orrin a puzzled look. "Do you mean Joseph Smith, from that one vision, was able to start a church with all of those teachings and theology?"

"Oh, no," Orrin said. "Joseph continued receiving revelations over a period of twenty years, learning step by step as he put in place the organization and revealed doctrines we have today."

"That makes more sense to me. God does not reveal himself all at once. Discovering the divine is a lifelong journey."

"I hope it does not take me that long," Orrin said.

Pastor Carlsen smiled. "Elder Tanner, you and Elder Pedersen have come to hear me preach. When will I have a chance to hear you?"

Orrin contemplated his answer as he helped Pastor Carlsen wrap the slices of *smørbrød* and place them in a bag. *Should I confess to a State Church priest my spiritual weaknesses?* Orrin wondered. *What will he think of me when he knows what I am really like?* Orrin felt as if he were struggling with his heart as well as his mind. Orrin remembered his vow to be honest and courageous in speaking with the Norwegian people, even to a priest from another religion. "It is difficult to explain and even more embarrassing to admit, but I have not attempted to preach or convert people since I have come to Riksøy because I do not feel worthy of my calling."

Pastor Carlsen looked at Orrin with great surprise. "You do not feel worthy?"

"No, I do not," Orrin said. "I have been a fraud, pretending to be someone I am not." Orrin told Pastor Carlsen about his desire from early childhood to receive revelation and become a man mighty in the Lord, and that as a missionary, he had worked extremely hard, but he had done so not for the benefit of the others but for himself, always with an eye toward receiving the ultimate spiritual reward. All his misadventures as a missionary spilled out, how he had neglected members and companions, lost his temper, and strained out the gnat while swallowing the camel. "I came to Riksøy to rid myself of those selfish desires and make a new start."

"I see. And what about Elder Pedersen? Does he also feel himself unworthy?"

Orrin pondered what to reveal about his companion. "Yes. Yes, he does, though there is not a more honorable or righteous missionary in all of Norway. Not one I have met, anyway. But I promise you, Pastor Carlsen, we will send someone to preach to you after we return to the mainland."

The two men finished their work in silence, loading the bags with food and filling thermoses with coffee. They carried the refreshments out of the kitchen and placed them on a table for the rescuers to pick up at sunrise, now only two hours away. "Tell me about yourself," Orrin said to Pastor Carlsen. "Your accent tells me you are not from Riksøy or from anywhere in the north. How was it you came to work here? This cannot be a prize position for a State Church priest, can it?"

Pastor Carlsen shook his head. "No, it is not. There was a time I never wanted to work in a place like this, not with my background and ambitions. I grew up in Oslo. I like city life, the theaters and music and lofty cathedrals and intellectual stimulation of academic life. I was happy too. I married a lovely woman I met while studying for the priesthood. Birgit was her name. We had two children, Anders and Solveig. Ours was a happy life. Mine especially. I was moving up in the priesthood, recognized by my superiors as one with promise. And then one day, while driving to a church service to hear me preach, Birgit hit a patch of ice and skidded off the road. She was killed instantly, as were Anders and Solveig. My happy life was gone in an instant."

"I am so sorry, Pastor Carlsen. Was it long ago?"

"Six years. The accident wrecked me. I could not work. For months, I could not even get out of my bed in the morning. I had counseled many people through their grief, but I could not counsel myself, nor would I allow others to counsel me." Pastor Carlsen avoided his duties for an entire year, believing he could not give solace when he had none, nor could he preach joy when he felt none. Finally, the bishop of the Oslo synod gave

341

him an ultimatum: return to his work or be removed from the priesthood. "'Your grief will always be with you. I am sorry but that is so,' he said. 'But you will not regain your thirst for life by lying in a darkened bedroom with curtains that shut out the world.' It was an act of kindness by the bishop," Pastor Carlsen said, "because I should have been removed long before that. Seeing the bishop was right, I chose a position far away, in Riksøy, where, as you said, few priests want to serve. And so, not unlike you, Elder Tanner, I came to Riksøy to find myself again."

"And have you?"

"I am finding little pieces of myself nearly every day. I find respite from my grief and contentment in my work. I truly love the people on this island."

"But very few come to your services."

"I am disappointed, yes, and I wish it were not so," Pastor Carlsen said. "But my work is also outside the chapel. That is what I have discovered. Where is your work, Elder Tanner?"

"It is supposed to be with the Norwegian people," Orrin replied, "but the people are like Norway itself, a hard rock that I chip away at without success. Instead, it chips away at me."

"Is that so bad?"

Orrin frowned. "I am afraid I will leave Norway without making any kind of mark. I will be like a clamorous wind or turbulent sea that beats against the rocky shore without effect. I will return home after two years and it will be like I was never here."

"If we are not mindful," Pastor Carlsen said, "that is the story of our lives."

Light came to the island shortly after two in the morning, and soon the restaurant was buzzing with fishermen who awoke to blue skies and a calm sea. They grabbed lunch bags without stopping to talk and hurried to their boats. The roar of their engines reverberated up and down the fjord. Orrin followed the men to the dock, where he found Eddie lying on his back, looking up at the sky. Olav was talking to the boat owners, thanking them, alerting them to the places Georg liked to fish. "Elder Pedersen, I have brought *smørbrød* for you and Olav," Orrin said.

Eddie yawned and sat up. "Thanks. I'm as hungry as I am tired."

After they finished eating, the elders lay back down and without intending, fell asleep to the rhythmic murmur of waves lapping against the shore. They awoke hours later to the blaring of horns. Jumping to their feet, they saw several boats rounding a jetty of rocks that protected the harbor. Olav stood at the edge of the dock excitedly waving his lantern, though its light was virtually invisible in the morning sun. Amid the flotilla of boats, Georg's boat followed in tow. Georg stood at the helm, a triumphant smile on his face, waving earnestly to those on shore. Upon seeing his housemate, Olav swung his lantern back and forth with even greater enthusiasm, tears covering his face.

The first arriving crew told the story. The storm hit as Georg was anchored and checking his eel traps. He was just starting for home when a crashing wave sparked an electrical shortage causing a complete loss of power to both his motor and radio. He worked for hours on his backup generator but could not get it to work. Olav shook his head disapprovingly. "Georg knew the generator was unreliable, but he had put off replacing it," Olav said. Georg occasionally saw the lights of other boats in the distance, but the wind and rain made it impossible to catch their attention. Meanwhile, the storm and tide pushed Georg's boat closer and closer to a rocky shoal and so he dropped anchor again, hoping it would hold him in place for the night. He knew his friends would come looking for him when the weather cleared.

When Georg hopped from his boat onto the dock, his triumphant smile had turned to a sheepish grin. He tried to assure everyone his night alone on the tempestuous sea was a minor inconvenience, but his uneasy stare and the weary lines etched across his face revealed what everyone knew: he had spent the night grasping the rails of his boat, white knuckled, willing his boat to stay away from the shoal. Olav rushed forward and kissed Georg on both cheeks. Embarrassed by Olav's outpouring of emotion, Georg tried to appear stoic, but he did not resist, and while they hugged, he whispered to his friend, "It was your lantern I saw first when we approached."

After the men finished pumping Georg's hand and pounding his back, they headed up to Peter's restaurant, where they boisterously picked over details of Georg's rescue, each man embellishing his own role in finding Georg and bringing him home. They refueled themselves with *fiskeboller* and coffee for what everyone agreed would be a fine day of fishing.

Olav and Georg did not join the celebration. As soon as Georg's boat was safely tied to the dock, the two men walked up the hill and past the school to their house. Sunlight at their back, they wordlessly followed their shadows along streets still wet with rain. Olav, though smaller, supported Georg with a shoulder under his arm, holding onto his friend as if he intended never to let go.

Following a longstanding Norwegian custom, the missionaries left their bedroom window open during the day to keep the room alive with cool, fresh air from the sea. They would close the window at bedtime, but not all the way, leaving a slight crack that kept the invigorating air flowing. After prayers, Orrin and Eddie climbed quickly into their beds and wrapped themselves in their down-filled duvets, shivering until the cocooned covering warmed their bodies. "Elder Tanner, I have a confession to make," Eddie said as the young men were drifting into sleep.

"Ha," Orrin laughed, thinking Elder Pedersen was joking, but sensing in the silence his companion was serious, said, "This hasn't got anything to do with . . . you know?"

"No, no, it isn't anything like that," Eddie assured him. "It's . . . I don't know how to put this. It's just that I don't care if any of these people on Riksøy are baptized or join the church. I know that makes me a bad missionary, but I don't care about that anymore. All I want is for them to be happy."

Orrin pondered Elder Pedersen's confession. "Now that you mention it, that's the way I feel too. But I feel guilty because, if they don't join the church, well, that means they can't go to the celestial kingdom and will instead be relegated to one of the lower kingdoms."

"The way you and I are going, we'll be right down there with them," Eddie said. "Maybe we all will be happy there together."

Eddie reached his hand from under the covers and stretched it across the darkness to Elder Tanner's bed, knowing instinctively his companion's hand would be there. It was. "Happy together," Eddie said, gently squeezing Elder Tanner's hand.

Orrin returned the affectionate squeeze. "Yes, happy together here—and in the hereafter."

The window rattled as a chilled wind forced its way into the bedroom. The elders pulled their arms back and wrapped the covers tightly around their bodies. Turning over on his side, Eddie said, "Goodnight, Elder Tanner."

"Goodnight, Elder Pedersen."

Chapter 41

Immorality is the bane of missionary life. . . . Avoid taking pictures of the opposite sex. Don't become too familiar in the homes you visit whether member or non-member.

Conduct of a Missionary

The elders' decision to stay a fourth week on Riksøy could be traced to their dinner the previous Saturday with the Tessem family. When they arrived at the Tessem home, Orrin was still feeling embarrassed that he thought Anna-Britt had asked him on a date. He hoped she would not be home. But when Herr Tessem answered the door, Anna-Britt was standing by his side, as was her brother Steinar, whom the elders knew from the *barneskole*. Herr Tessem looked the elders over and, frowning, turned to his daughter. "Which one of these young men wanted to take you on a date?"

Anna-Britt's freckles disappeared behind a rosy blush that spread across her cheeks. Orrin, seeing her embarrassment, stepped forward. "It was me," he said. "I am sorry if I offended you."

Eddie pulled Orrin back. "To be completely truthful, Elder Tanner thought it was *your daughter* who was asking *him* on a date."

Herr Tessem eyes took on a mischievous glint. "Well stated, Mormon missionaries," he said, taking their coats. "Come and sit." As they sipped cups of tea, Herr Tessem explained that he had invited the elders to dinner because Steinar had spoken so fondly of them. He and Fru Tessem had never seen their son so enthusiastically embrace his schoolwork, and so they wanted to thank the elders for their efforts. "We do not speak English and need the Norwegian subtitles when we watch American television programs, but we can tell Steinar is beginning to understand very well."

Over dinner, they learned that Herr Tessem worked as some kind of a fish broker—*fiskemegler*—who negotiated prices for Riksøy's fishermen and helped them get the best prices for their daily catches. Herr Tessem shook his head with a scoffing laugh when the elders asked if he worked with Herr Reissmann. He called Herr Reissmann a minor player among the buyers but also a shrewd bargainer who had a knack for swooping in when an abundance of one kind of fish or another meant he could purchase them at a steep discount. "Some on the island resent him, but he provides a good service. Otherwise, some of the fish would go unsold and rot in their boats," Herr Tessem said.

Anna-Britt was completing her last year at the *videregående* school and was applying for acceptance into a nursing program. "We do not have any doctors on Riksøy, but I would like to work in a doctor's office or nearby hospital, so I am not so far away from home," she said.

When the table was cleared after dinner, they retired to the living room, where Steinar prevailed upon Eddie to accompany him on the piano so he could show off his singing skills in English. The piano was slightly out of tune but serviceable, and Steinar had a strong voice and knack for showmanship that provided much appreciated entertainment for his proud parents. His audience grew when some of Anna-Britt's friends came over; though they intended to go visit other friends, they soon found themselves requesting that Eddie play popular American and British songs they knew, singing along amid laughter and lively conversation. With Eddie concentrating on getting the melodies right, Orrin helped the Norwegians with their pronunciation of song lyrics and explanations of their meaning. Anna-Britt, like her brother, had a lovely voice, so she and Orrin would often sing difficult parts of songs as a duet before her friends joined in. The singing continued until Fru Tessem brought out warm Norwegian pancakes and lingonberry jam.

"You should put on a show with the school children," Fru Tessem said.

Herr Tessem's echoed his approval. "Yes, all of those songs you are teaching to Steinar and the other children would make an entertaining program. Their parents would love to hear their children sing in English."

Eddie and Orrin agreed, but as they were discussing a possible format for the program, Anna-Britt interrupted. "We want to be in the program, too," she said, gesturing to her friends, who signaled their agreement. "You could hold it on the weekend when we are here."

"But how would we practice?" Eddie asked. "You are gone all week."

That could be easily addressed, Anna-Britt said. The students who attended the mainland school could practice when they returned home for the weekend and then perform the following Saturday evening. Anna-Britt became increasingly enthusiastic as she outlined a practice schedule. Herr and Fru Tessem also threw their support behind the idea. Including the older students would bring out the entire town. Eddie hesitated to agree. Staying a fourth week was problematic enough, but he also worried whether the children could sing at a performance level, especially with so little time to rehearse. Singing in the classroom, while fun, was sometimes a ragged affair.

Orrin knew they needed to get back to Harstad, but singing with the young Norwegians had been invigorating. And though he was not ready to admit it to himself, Anna-Britt's coy beauty was proving irresistible. *I bet she's probably only two or three years younger than me.*

"Please, Elders," Anna-Britt said. "You would bring so much happiness to our island."

"Yes, I think we should do it," said Orrin, having been won over by Anna-Britt's charm. "What do you think, Elder Pedersen?"

Eddie looked at Orrin and then at Anna-Britt. Unlike his companion, Eddie was not taken by her allure, but he was willing to follow Orrin's lead. "I will do my best to help everyone get ready," Eddie said.

"Oh, thank you, Elder Tanner," Anna-Britt cried, clapping her hands. She reached out as if intending to give him a hug. Orrin dutifully stood back and grabbed her hand, giving it a warm shake.

"It will be our pleasure."

Orrin and Eddie immediately had second thoughts about staying a fourth week. Bror Brevik would return from his NATO assignment at the beginning of the week and would probably check in on them right away. Their absence would be quickly discovered. They intended to call off the planned musical event, but the following day, the school's principal called at their house. "I think it is an excellent idea, especially including our older students," he said. "You tell me what you need and I will have everything set up and ready for the performance in our gymnasium."

The elders still thought they might be able to call it off when the older students returned from the mainland over the weekend. "They probably will lose their enthusiasm for it during the school week when they realize what a lame and amateurish affair it will be," Eddie said.

Orrin agreed. "They won't want to be considered small island rubes."

Just the opposite happened. When Anna-Britt and the other Riksøy students arrived on Friday evening, they brought with them many of their mainland friends, all of whom wanted to participate in the *sangfestival*, particularly the girls. And where the girls went, the boys followed. At an impromptu gathering at the Tessem home that night, Eddie sat at the piano and took requests from the young people, which enabled him to begin compiling a repertoire of songs for the *sangfestival*. Orrin and Anna-Britt reprised a few of their duets, eliciting a few sideways glances that got Orrin wondering whether he was interfering with designs that other young men may have had on Anna-Britt. But that didn't stop him from enjoying the moment. *I'll soon be gone forever and they'll have their chance again.*

Rehearsals began in earnest on Saturday, with Eddie running the show. During rehearsals with the elementary-age children, Orrin organized basketball scrimmages with the older boys, an activity that again brought out the entire community to watch and kibitz along the sidelines. "*Hurra for dommeren*," Olav shouted as he watched Orrin run up and down the court, whistle in his mouth, calling fouls and instructing the players. "Hurray for the referee."

During a break in play, Olav marveled to Orrin about the large crowd of islanders gathered in the gymnasium. "This is the first time I can recall that students from the mainland wanted to come to Riksøy for fun," he said. "Usually, it is our young people who want to escape to the mainland."

Following morning rehearsal at the school, Pastor Carlsen brought over *kjøttkaker*, or meatballs, and potatoes and then helped Eddie prepare his classroom for the older students. "I have been meaning to ask you about my housemates, Olav and Georg," Eddie said, somewhat hesitantly.

Pastor Carlsen smiled as if he knew already the question. "Yes?"

"Are Olav and Georg homosexuals?"

Pastor Carlsen nodded. "It is plain to see, is it not?"

"Yes, and I have only been here three weeks. And so, if it is obvious to me, does that mean everyone on Riksøy sees it as well?

"Norwegians are very accepting of homosexuality, at least when it involves consenting adults."

"But no one says anything, as if it is tolerated but still is what in English we would say, 'taboo."

"We also say *tabu*," Pastor Carlsen said. "And you are correct. We Norwegians are not as tolerant as our Swedish neighbors, who legalized homosexual activity in the mid-1940s. But we are moving in that direction, even the older people. And the people here on Riksøy, they have watched Olav and Georg grow up together and know their hearts, that they are good, decent men. No one remarks upon it because, for us, it is unremarkable, and because no one wants to bring attention to a situation that might cause an outsider to raise trouble, especially for Olav, who teaches in our school. We are very protective of these men."

"I see," Eddie said as he scraped a few last bites of meat, potatoes, and peas onto the back of his fork.

"Why do you ask, Elder Pedersen?" Pastor Carlsen said, trying to assess his demeanor. "Does it bother you and Elder Tanner to be living with two homosexual men? Perhaps it offends you?"

"No, but it surprises me, because I am a homosexual too."

"What? You and Elder Tanner?"

Eddie laughed. "No, just me."

"But still, your church allows homosexuality?"

"No, but I am cured—or, at least, I am supposed to be," Eddie said, and then he recounted for Pastor Carlsen his experience undergoing reparative therapy and the conditional approval that allowed him to serve a mission. "It is all because they think I am cured."

Pastor Carlsen frowned. "But you do not really think you are 'cured'?"

"No, I do not."

"I did not think so. One does not cure homosexuality. It is not an illness or disease."

Eddie put down his knife and fork and leaned forward over the table. "So what it is then?"

"It just is," Pastor Carlsen said. "You could ask the same question about heterosexuality, and the answer would be the same. It just is."

Eddie shook his head sadly. "I wish I could believe that."

Orrin and Eddie again attended State Church services. This time, even more people filled the chapel, including Olav and Georg, school children from both Riksøy and the mainland, and Gunnar Andreassen, Lars's nephew. After taking a seat next to Orrin, Gunnar said he was not surprised to see so many people now attending the services. Whispering into Orrin's ear, he said, "Well, Elder Tanner, we thought we should come hear the preaching by Pastor Carlsen that is so captivating that even the Mormon missionaries are coming to hear his sermons."

Orrin leaned over to his companion. "Did you hear that, Elder Pedersen? We're boosting attendance at the State Church."

"How many points on the Mission Comparative do you think we'll get for that?"

In his sermon, Pastor Carlsen likened the community of believers to the parable of the blind men and the elephant. Everyone experiences God in their own unique way, but having one spiritual experience or reading one scriptural passage doesn't tell a person everything there is to know about God or provide complete, universal insight in life. Like the blind men, we need multiple and repeated touches of the divine, and so we must be humble in our quest for knowledge and accept truth from wherever it comes.

"As the Apostle Paul says, 'Whatever things are true, whatever things are noble, whatever things are just, whatever things are pure, whatever things are lovely, whatever things are of good report, if there is any virtue and if there is anything praiseworthy—meditate on these things.' And ultimately, Paul says, we should 'prove all things and hold fast that which is good.'"

On Monday, Orrin and Eddie informed Herr Reissmann they were going to stay one more week to put on a musical program. After that, they would return to Harstad. "Next week for sure," they said.

Chapter 42

Be consistent and faithful in your work, give a good account of your stewardship every day, every week, every month you are in the mission field.

Conduct of a Missionary

"Shut up, Porter. Just shut up." Those were Anson's last words to his brother before slamming down the phone. Sometimes he regretted those harsh words, other times he wished he had said them years ago. Anson pulled up the shade and peered ahead over the jet wing, catching a glimpse of the sun's morning light. They would be landing at Fornebu Airport in less than an hour. What irked him most was that Sarah took Porter's side yet again.

"How can you help find Orrin when you don't speak Norwegian?" Sarah said. "Meanwhile, you'll leave me here to explain why you've gone."

"You don't have to explain anything to people at church," Anson replied.

"They'll know just by the fact you're flying to Norway that Orrin is in some kind of trouble."

Anson knew Sarah was right. Bishop Pulsipher would want to know what was going on, of course, under the guise of providing spiritual assistance to the family, all the while enjoying with smug satisfaction that all was not right with the Tanner family. Anson had agreed to follow Bishop Pulsipher's guidance in shutting down his publishing business, but he had not reconciled himself to the bishop's questioning of his loyalty. Nor could he shake the feeling: *Orrin's disappearance is my fault.*

Sarah called Porter, hoping he could persuade Anson to cancel his trip. Once on the phone with Anson and Sarah, Porter eagerly pointed out the many ways Orrin had likely gone astray. Every scenario cast the blame on Anson. "You foolishly exposed Orrin to the mysteries," Porter said.

"But—"

"I know your intentions were good, Anson. But not everyone has a strong testimony like yours."

"But—"

"The Brethren have made it abundantly clear our focus as teachers should be on the fundamental principles of the gospel. Many of my fellow religion professors will not even allow themselves to read your pamphlets, let alone give them to their students."

"Is that what happened to Orrin?" Sarah asked Porter. "I'm starting to worry Anson pushed the boundaries a little too far with his pamphlets."

"Orrin wouldn't be the first one to go off the deep end after getting his head mixed up by the mysteries."

"Will you listen to me, Porter?" Anson said, his voice animated and strident. "We don't know that Orrin has done anything wrong. After all, he and his companion are still sending in their reports. They're still proselytizing and teaching."

"Porter," Sarah interjected. "Don't you think Anson should stay at home and leave it to the church authorities to sort this out?"

"Orrin's mission president says Orrin has been an exemplary missionary, one of the best in Norway," Anson added.

"*Has been*," Porter emphasized. "*Has been.* No missionary in good standing goes proselytizing outside of his assigned tracting area without permission, not for three weeks anyway."

"But—"

"I hate to be the bearer of bad news, Anson, but you should brace yourself. This has all the telltale signs of a sexual transgression."

"What?"

"We've seen it happen many times."

"Shut up, Porter. Just shut up!" And with that, Anson slammed down the phone. Even after the call was disconnected, Anson continued muttering to himself. "Shut up, Porter. Just shut up."

Marie Pedersen and her husband, Don, struggled to comprehend what Eddie's disappearance meant. After speaking to Eddie's mission president, Don angrily gave Marie the details. He immediately assumed the worst about Eddie, then refused to discuss the matter.

"What's there to discuss? He broke the rules. He left his tracting area without permission and took another young man with him. We should never have sent him on a mission, not after he became involved with . . ." Don couldn't bring himself to finish the sentence.

Marie tried to speak calmly. "But that isn't what the mission president thinks, is it? Didn't he tell you—"

"I have no idea what Eddie's mission president thinks," Don snarled. "He is a very odd man, if you ask me. And irresponsible too, sending missionaries off on their own into such remote places, especially a young man with Eddie's . . . I don't know, proclivities or condition or whatever euphemism you want to use."

Don glared at Marie, daring her to defend Eddie. Marie stared right back, grimacing, and then left the room. There was no talking to Don after he started one his rants. When they drove to BYU to pick up Eddie after his freshman year, they were, of course, shocked by his confession. Well, shocked was not a strong enough word to describe their feelings. No single word was. They were horrified, sickened, despondent, bewildered, terrified. But on the drive home, they decided to meet the challenge head on and to have confidence in Eddie's sincere contrition and trust in God. Hadn't they always been faithful? God would bless and help Eddie because of their good works.

They also vowed to do everything they could to support Eddie. Back in Glendale, they assiduously researched everything they could find on the causes of and remedies for homosexual proclivities. Marie poured over the latest psychological studies, while Don consulted the writings of church leaders to gain their insights, hoping to combine the best spiritual and secular wisdom to aid their effort. They also sought to protect Eddie by telling no one about his experimentation. No one else needed to know. They were glad he had remained at BYU for the summer. Had he come home, his bishop in Provo would have been required to notify the Glendale stake president and their ward bishop. Because Eddie was on probation, everyone in their ward would have noticed he hadn't been given any church assignments and wasn't taking the sacrament. "It's a black mark that would have followed him from ward to ward, wherever he went," Don said. Having served as both a bishop and stake president, he knew. That's why they held Eddie's missionary farewell in Provo rather than at home. "Our friends will get to see the best side of Eddie when he returns home from his mission and has all of this experimentation business behind him," Don said.

Marie's research brought only confusion. There was no scientific consensus on the causes of homosexuality and no proven cures. Psychology's so-called experts offered a multitude of theories and explanations, some more reasonable than others, but Marie was disturbed by the explicit discussions of male sexuality and blunt references to "sexual deviance" and "mental illness" and "oral fixations" and "stunted psychosexual maturation." She hated thinking about her son in this way. Besides, the Eddie she knew was none of these things. He was kind, intelligent, amiable, extremely talented, and well-adjusted in every way except this one. None of the authors provided any real guidance for parents as a way forward, though many vilified parents for the long-term damage they inflicted on their sons as a result of the mother's domineering and smothering personality and the father's passive submission to his wife. The only ones who offered any kind of optimistic outlook were those few who claimed homosexuality was innate and unchangeable, and thus something that should be tolerated. Marie did not see how she or Don could ever accept that. The church certainly would not. Eddie wouldn't either.

The lack of unanimity among psychiatrists, not to mention their hare-brained theories about causes and cures, persuaded Don that he and Marie should look to the church to both understand the problem and help Eddie overcome it. But the more Don learned of the church's views, the more pessimistic and upset he became. Not only was homosexuality the worst of all sexual transgressions, but once started, it became a compulsion that was difficult to stop. Like cigarettes and liquor and heroin, once a person got a taste of it, he struggled to give it up—even if he wanted to. This meant Eddie's experimentation with homosexuality, however slight, could have the same crippling effect on his soul that experimentation with drugs has on the mind and body. Despite Dr. Orlan's optimistic pronouncements about Eddie's recovery, Don had no such confidence in Dr. Orlan or the Reparative Therapy Institute. It was all secular nonsense, as far as he was concerned. Instead, Don foresaw a lifetime of struggle for Eddie against this awful sin.

Marie, who had become discouraged by the academic literature on homosexuality, was frightened by her husband's attitude, and tried to persuade him to consider whether they had done something to trigger Eddie's compulsion. "We should at least explore the possibility for Eddie's sake, so we can make the right changes," she said.

"Are you saying it's our fault? Don exclaimed. "Tell me: what did we do wrong? We have four other sons. Why didn't any of them turn out that way?"

"Maybe we treated Eddie differently without knowing it."

"If anything was different, it was that you babied Eddie. He was the youngest, and so you coddled and obsessed over him, just like you're doing now."

"You don't really believe that, do you?"

"No, but that's what all of your psychological literature says, doesn't it? See my point?"

"Don't you think—?"

"I'll tell you what I think," Don exclaimed. "It was that Barry boy, that's what it was. He's the one who set Eddie on this path. And now it's out of our hands. It's up to Eddie now."

After Eddie left on his mission, Don and Marie settled into a persistent, unspoken worry. They set aside the subject of causes and cures. They filled their letters to Eddie with upbeat news about his brothers and inspirational homilies and scriptures, all the while scouring his letters for signs he was doing fine. They relaxed a little after Eddie made it through his first year without incident. And when they learned that not only were Eddie and his companion routinely among the top performers on the Mission Comparative, but that he also had won the Scripture Chase, his parents finally allowed themselves a measure of genuine hope.

"He'll come back a good boy, just like the Eddie we've always known," Don said. He refolded the letter and, before handing it back to his wife, kissed her on both cheeks.

A few months later, President Toressen called to say Eddie and his companion had disappeared. Don's pent-up anxiety and fear exploded in a furious diatribe detailing the ways Eddie had let them down. "What's wrong with that boy?" he said.

Anson called the Pedersen family before leaving for Norway to see if they had any information that might help him find their sons. Elder Pedersen's father was not home, so Anson spoke only to the boy's mother, Marie. She was a pleasant woman with a friendly but anxious voice. "Don wouldn't want me to tell you this, but since you are flying all the way to Norway, you probably should know about Eddie's problem," she said, and proceeded to tell Anson about Eddie's confession and the reparative therapy that cured him and his subsequent approval by church leaders to serve a mission. "I tell you this in strictest confidence and, so please don't tell your son or even my husband that I told you, but I didn't want you to find out later and think we were withholding any relevant information from you, even though I doubt this it has anything to do with our sons leaving their tracting area. In fact, we don't really know whether the boys have done anything wrong, do we, Brother Tanner? It all may be a big misunderstanding."

Anson said nothing. His mind was still reeling from Sister Pedersen's revelation that her son was a homosexual. *If it's not relevant, why did she tell me?*

"Eddie is fundamentally a good boy, Brother Tanner," Sister Pedersen continued. "I've been trying my best to understand him, but my husband says there is nothing to understand. Sin is sin."

"I wish I could say something that would bring you solace, Sister Pedersen. I will pray for you."

"I love Eddie," Sister Pedersen said. "I pray God will help me understand and accept him."

Anson could see that Eddie's problems were driving a wedge into his parents' marriage. The Pedersens were on the verge of a breakup, though

Sister Pedersen never said as much. Anson worried about his own marriage. He had tried to assure Sarah that Orrin had done nothing wrong. As Sister Pedersen had said, it was probably a misunderstanding.

"So why then are you rushing off to Norway?" Sarah said.

Anson didn't know why, not at the time. But now, as his jet approached Fornebu airport, the answer came suddenly to him. If it was the pamphlets, if Orrin had lost his testimony because of doubts and questions put into his mind by the pamphlets, then Anson wanted to tell Orrin this: "Whatever your doubts, you can rely on my testimony, Orrin. Grab hold of my testimony. Lean on my faith." But what if it had nothing to do with his pamphlets and everything to do with Elder Pedersen's problem? The thought unsettled Anson and deepened his uneasiness. He didn't tell Sarah about Elder Pedersen's experimentation with homosexuality.

Before Anson left for the Salt Lake City airport, he asked his father to give him a blessing. He was feeling closed off, crushed by the family turmoil, and needed reassurance. "A blessing will calm my mind," he said. With his hands resting firmly on Anson's head, Heber Tanner felt inspired to say Anson should not worry, that all was right with Orrin, and promised God's help in finding him. When the blessing was completed, Anson stood and hugged his wife. "I love you," he said. Her eyes were cold and black, and he could not tell whether she had been mollified by the blessing.

Chapter 43

Be missionaries of honesty and integrity with yourself, with the Lord, with your companion, with the Mission President, and all the others to whom you are responsible or represent.

Conduct of a Missionary

Kristina Toressen had never seen her husband look so depressed. He had just received a call from Salt Lake City mandating a meeting with Apostle Prichard. Bjørn said they were calling it a performance review. "I've never heard of such a thing for a mission president," he said.

"Are you going to be released?"

"Yes, I am afraid so." President Toressen slumped dispiritedly into his chair. "I never thought Apostle Prichard would do it, but it's really going to happen. I have displeased the Lord and failed my missionaries." Toressen covered his face with his hands. "I don't know how I failed."

Don't know? Kristina fought an exasperated urge to say "I told you so." Hadn't she warned him this would happen if he didn't get his act together? She had foreseen this day, imagining when the time came that she would explode in anger. But now, seeing her husband beaten and despairing, she felt only sorrow, because she also knew how much this calling meant to Bjørn, to the person he saw himself to be. *Still, you don't know? I could have told you. I did tell you. Dozens of times.*

"I need to be alone for a while," President Toressen told his secretary, Elder Blake, and for the first time since his mission began nearly two years ago, Toressen canceled all of his appointments and refused to see visitors.

Kristina searched her feelings. Previously, when contemplating Bjørn's possible release, she had anticipated disappointment and shame, while rehearsing in mind the furious tongue-lashing she would give her husband. Instead, she felt numb relief. The mission had exhausted her. *Did I really sign up for this chaos?* She loved Bjørn, but that didn't mean she understood him. There was an impenetrable strangeness about him, an inner drive she could not fathom. He was like a rudderless ship, driven by spiritual winds but lacking discernable direction. Add it all together and she was ready to go home. *The release will be humane, something said about his health and his heart. No one but us will know the truth. I need to rest. Bjørn needs to rest too. And we need to get our kids back in American schools. Once we're home, I can salve his psychological wounds and nurse him back to his old self.*

Having persuaded herself the mission release was for the best, Kristina decided to tell Bjørn she was reconciled to it and that he need not worry about its impact on her. She would survive, he would survive, their family would survive. Without knocking, she entered his office through the side door from the family quarters and found Bjørn on his knees. She gasped, thinking he had suffered another heart attack or had fallen ill. She took a step toward him with the intention of rousing him, but then stopped, realizing he was praying, praying so intently that he did not hear her enter. Not wishing to interrupt, she retraced her steps and was quietly closing the door when she heard her husband pleading.

"I have failed thee, oh Lord," Bjørn said, audibly sobbing. "Please give me a second chance and show me what I must do to serve thee and fulfill the mission to which thou hast called me. Please help me."

"Please help me." Wasn't this the same plea Kritina had heard twenty-five years earlier when the young Elder Toressen had been scolded by his mission president? "Help me," he had cried to the Lord and there was Kristina, standing by to help him. Here he was again in the same mission office, making the same plea; and here she was again, listening to his plea. Kristina ruminated on the odd coincidence, and suddenly it became clear what she must do. *This is my purpose. This is what I signed up for when I agreed to marry Bjørn. I married him because I believed in him and wanted to be part of his life's mission in all of its wonderful, unfathomable, frustrating eccentricity. And that includes this, his mission presidency in Norway.*

Kristina quietly closed the door and went directly to the mission secretary's office. "Elder Blake," she said, "get me the phone numbers of President Toressen's counselors and of all Norway's branch presidents and Relief Society presidents too."

"What about the places too small to have branch presidents. Do you also want the phone numbers for those leaders, Sister Toressen?"

"Hmm, yes, good idea." Kristina pulled up a chair and took a seat next to Elder Blake. With an uncharacteristic cheerfulness that startled the mission secretary, she said, "Here, I'll help you compile the list."

Within minutes, Kristina had more than two dozen phone numbers in hand and was sitting at her kitchen table dialing her phone. "Hello, President Alnaes," she said. "This is Kristina Toressen, President Toressen's wife. Listen, I want to talk to you about President Toressen. What I am going to tell you is in the strictest confidence, but he has got himself into some trouble and could use your help. Here is what I need you to do."

Apostle Joseph Prichard watched Apostle Hiram G. Bingham un-wrap a chocolate candy and pop it into his mouth. "It's my mid-morning pepper-upper. Keeps me going until lunch. It's the sugar rush," President Bingham said. "Want one?"

It's probably the caffeine rush, Apostle Prichard thought to himself. Still, if chocolate was an acceptable stimulant for the President of the Twelve Apostles, he was not going to object. "That looks delicious. Thank you, sir," he said, reaching out his hand.

Prichard loved the welcoming spirit of Bingham's office. He admired the plush leather chairs and fine-grained mahogany desk that conveyed the significance of Bingham's position in the church hierarchy, but the office decor showed he was a man devoid of pomp and self-importance. While many church authorities would have displayed diplomas and awards and photographs of themselves with prominent civic and religious leaders, Bingham filled his walls and desk with photos of his children and grandchildren, many dressed in temple whites for family portraits. It was an everyman touch that Prichard made a note to emulate. Prichard was also feeling good about the impromptu meeting called by Bingham, who said he wanted to talk with Prichard about the Norwegian mission. Prichard regarded it as inspiration on Bingham's part, because it gave Prichard a chance to discuss his planned "performance review" with President Toressen, particularly the expected outcome of the review. Although Bingham was ninety-three years old, his mind was as sharp as a steel trap. "You wanted to talk with me about the Norwegian mission," Prichard said.

"Yes, I do," Apostle Bingham said, his voice suddenly stern. "What in the Sam Hill is going on over there?" Bingham paused to wipe chocolate from the side of the mouth, keeping his eyes glued on Prichard. "In the past several days, I've been getting all sorts of phone calls from Norwegian leaders and rank-and-file members asking me not to release the mission president there, that Toressen fellow you've been complaining about."

Prichard blanched, flustered. "Yes, I . . . I mean. . . . This is the first I—"

"And it's not just me. The First Presidency is getting many of the same calls, all from people afraid that their beloved mission president is going to be unceremoniously dismissed from his calling. Are you planning something we don't know about? It would not reflect well on our purported prophetic powers if everyone in Norway knows about something this important but we do not."

"I can explain," Prichard said, irritated that he, in fact, had to explain. Over the next thirty minutes, he described the many problems President Toressen had created with his public comments and leadership style. "I've worked with a lot of mission presidents, but never have I come across one so resistant to counsel and difficult to work with. The man is an administrative disaster and simply not up to the task."

"Well, the information I've been given tells me otherwise," Bingham said, tapping a long, bony finger on his notepad. He adjusted his glasses and began reading from his notes. "The branch president in Oslo says church attendance has increased by twenty percent since President Toressen assumed his position. In Trondheim, it's nearly twice that number. Other branch presidents also report increases, not just in Sunday attendance, but in activity rates across the board. And whenever Toressen speaks, well, the numbers go even higher."

"But his speeches," Prichard exclaimed. "They're public relations nightmares, just terrible for the church's image."

"All I know is he is inspiring the members while also generating interest in the church among nonmembers."

"But the baptism numbers are way down—nearly fifty percent. You can't call that success."

President Bingham sighed. "Yes, you're right. That is a problem. But you're too emotionally wrapped up in the issue and not looking at it objectively. By my calculations, we now have fifty fewer convert baptisms each year, but we also have at least two hundred and fifty more active church members. And that's just so far. I will take that trade-off any day. Moreover, it's active church members who will do more to bring in converts than door-to-door proselytizing." Bingham shook his head ruefully. "It has been more than seventy years and I still remember how much I hated tracting when I was a missionary."

Prichard continued pressing his case, but Bingham kept bringing him back to the statistics and testimonials provided by Norwegian members. "It seems to me," President Bingham said, "you've been looking for reasons to get rid of President Toressen rather than for ways to help him magnify his calling. What would it take for him to stay?"

"I've tried. I really have."

"What would it take?" Bingham said, tapping his desk and glaring at the junior apostle.

"First, President Toressen needs to find those missing missionaries and discipline them. They probably need to be sent home. And no more coddling of rulebreakers. He needs to deal more directly with any problem elders and sisters who are hindering the work."

Bingham nodded. "I'm with you there."

"And no more public speeches without first vetting them through my office."

"A good precaution."

"And finally, he needs to listen to counsel and set an example for the missionaries. I'm not surprised that a couple of elders would think they can ignore the rules and work out of their assigned area, given the example of their mission president. Rules are rules, not guidelines or recommendations."

Bingham smiled. "We're in agreement there too." he said. "Now let President Toressen know he's got your support, provided he adheres to the conditions you've laid out here. Tell him it comes from my authority."

"Thank you, sir." Apostle Prichard stood and shook President Bingham's hand. It was not exactly the outcome he had hoped for, but he felt a measure of relief that he wouldn't be releasing Toressen. Charity and forgiveness; repentance and second chances. That's what the gospel was all about. Besides, President Bingham had given him the backing he needed to come down forcefully on Toressen. His performance review would have real teeth.

"So tell, me," Bingham said, "do you think President Toressen himself started this campaign of phone calls?"

Prichard rubbed his chin. "No, he wouldn't do something like that. President Toressen has too much confidence in his own counsel and calling. It was probably his wife, Kristina. She's the one who keeps the trains running there. The mission would probably fall apart without her administrative skills."

Bingham laughed. "I know a lot of Relief Society presidents like that, women who would make exceptionally effective bishops."

A look of concern swept over Apostle Prichard's face. "President Bingham, you're not suggesting . . ."

"Oh, no, don't worry," Bingham said, waving a dismissive hand. "Our positions are safe."

President Toressen tiptoed into the bedroom and quietly slid open the closet door. He hung up his suit coat, brushing lint from the shoulders as he placed it on the hanger. He loosened his tie and was pulling it through his collar when his wife called out from the bed. "I'm still awake, Bjørn," she said. "You can turn on the light."

Bjørn switched on the light and continued undressing wordlessly until he had slipped on his pajamas and was buttoning up the top. "Was it you, darling?"

Kristina Toressen gave her husband a puzzled look. "Was what me?"

"Were you the one who called the Norwegian branch leaders and told them to tell church authorities in Salt Lake City not to release me?"

Kristina wasn't sure how to respond. She had hoped her behind-the-scenes effort would remain anonymous, but she didn't want to lie or pretend she had not been concerned. "People are calling Salt Lake City?"

Bjørn chuckled. "I just got off the phone with Apostle Prichard. We had my performance review."

Kristina sat up in the bed and tried to read her husband's expression. "Don't play games with me, Bjørn" she said impatiently. "What did he say? Are you still the mission president or not?"

A wide smile spread across Bjørn's face. "Yes, yes I am, thanks to you and to all of the wonderful Norwegian people who supported me in my hour of need. But I know it was you who put everyone up to it. Apostle Prichard knows it too."

"Was he angry?"

"Only at me. He said I should buckle down and exercise my priesthood better, so I don't have to depend on my wife to save my bacon."

"Did he really say that?"

"Not exactly in those words, but yes," said Bjørn, who again began chuckling to himself. "But don't worry, dear. I will still depend on you. Always have, always will."

Kristina scowled. "Don't make light of this, Bjørnstjerne."

"You are right, as always, dear," Bjørn said, now growing serious. "Apostle Prichard made clear that from the Brethren's point of view, I am still on probation and must follow Apostle Prichard's counsel to the letter. I realize now I was not humble but thought 'I know who I am,' that I was following the Lord's wishes, but it was hubris thinking I could know the divine will when He has chosen servants, men wiser than me, to oversee my work."

"And are you . . . will you follow their counsel?"

"Yes, I have my marching orders and know what I must do." President Toressen turned off the light and climbed into bed next to his wife. "Remember how I used to sit up nights trying to memorize every missionary's name?" he said, staring at the darkened ceiling. "I really thought I could make a difference in their lives, that even something as small as remembering their names would help them become their better selves."

"You can't fix everyone, Bjørn."

President Toressen sighed, filling the room with dispirited gloom. "I guess I must first fix myself," he said.

The assistants returned from Harstad the next morning and gave their report. All signs indicated Elders Tanner and Pedersen were working in a nearby area and returning occasionally to send in reports and pick up their mail. "But for some reason, they are keeping their whereabouts a secret," Elder Sorensen said. "No one knows where they are."

"At least, no one who knows is willing to tell us," Elder Ward added.

"Thank you, Elders," President Toressen said. "I'm glad you think the elders are safe. I'm going up there myself later today, and with the work you've done, I am confident I will be able to finally get to the bottom of this."

The president's planned trip was almost cancelled when Elder Tanner's father showed up unexpectedly at the mission home, suitcase in hand, disheveled and forlorn, saying he wished to help search for his son and the other missing missionary. Sister Toressen castigated her husband for allowing the boy's father to come to Norway, but President Toressen pointed out that Brother Tanner had not made known his travel plans. "Besides, I do not have the authority to forbid his travel if he chooses to come here," Toressen said. He initially invited Brother Tanner to stay at the mission home while he traveled to Harstad but after getting to know the man, Toressen decided to bring him along.

"You don't want him with you," Sister Toressen cautioned. "He's obviously distraught and even troubled, like his son. And if you have to send his son home, as Apostle Prichard recommends, then if you do find him, there's no telling what kind of emotional fireworks it will set off between the two of them."

President Toressen acknowledged the risk, but he found Brother Tanner—despite his obvious worries about his son—quite reasonable and genuinely looking to help, apologizing for the trouble his son had caused and repeatedly expressing gratitude for the mission's efforts to find him. In response to President Toressen's inquiries, Brother Tanner talked openly and without bitterness about the controversies surrounding his pamphlets, and said he was doing everything he could to make things right with the church. As they talked, Toressen felt a growing affinity with Orrin's father, whose troubles mirrored his own. Both men had flown too close to the sun, as far as church authorities were concerned. And now each man was repenting and trying to make amends. However, Toressen knew these arguments would not sway his wife, so he pointed out that Brother Tanner was close friends with Apostle Prichard. "The Tanner and Prichard families share pioneer roots going back a hundred years," President Prichard said. "It would be helpful to have Brother Tanner in our corner, given his special relationship with Apostle Prichard."

Sister Toressen agreed and the two men took the first flight to Narvik, arriving in Harstad that evening. Early the next morning, Bror Brevik picked them up at their hotel, and together they drove through nearby Lofoten Island towns searching for possible locations where the elders had gone. They knocked on numerous doors in the towns and rural districts they visited, but by mid-afternoon, they had come no closer to discovering where the missing elders had gone. The men talked of finally asking the police to step in and cast a wider net with their nationwide resources, but none relished doing so. "The elders will certainly be sent home if we have to do that," President Toressen said.

"Not that they wouldn't deserve it, after what they've put you through," Brother Tanner asserted.

Toressen tapped Bror Brevik on the shoulder. "You know, Jann Harald, we have driven up and down all of the places that can be reached by car or bus. Could they have taken the Hurtigruten boat somewhere further from Harstad?"

"We checked with their local office and even their headquarters, and they found no record of Mormon missionaries from Harstad or anywhere else purchasing tickets in the last several months," Bror Brevik said.

"Is that the only company offering boat or ocean service?" Brother Tanner asked.

"It is possible they arranged a private excursion with a local boat owner," Bror Brevik replied. "There is one man in particular, Herr Reissmann, who travels up and down the coast. He mainly delivers supplies but occasionally takes on passengers as well. I have wanted to talk with him, but he has been away since I arrived home last Saturday."

President Toressen climbed back into the car. "Let us go to the harbor and see what those men know."

Herr Reissmann had just finished washing down his deck and was pulling out the fishing nets to clean and repair them in preparation for his next trip when he saw three men walking along the pier. Two of them were dressed in suits and coats and looked out of place on the wet, slimy docks along Skoleveien. He watched them stop and talk with Magnus Oftenbrø, who shook his head and then pointed down the walkway in his direction. Reissmann knew at once who these men were and what they wanted.

"Are you Herr Reissmann?" asked a slight man with dark hair and deep, penetrating eyes.

Reissmann put down his net and stepped out of his boat. "Yes."

"I am Bjørnstjerne Toressen, president of the Norwegian mission for The Church of Jesus Christ of Latter-day Saints," the man said.

"Mormoner," said a man he recognized as Jann Harald Brevik, a local military man.

"Yes, I know who you are."

"And this is Anson Tanner. He has come all the way from the United States to look for his son, Elder Orrin Tanner, who is a missionary serving here in Harstad. Elder Tanner and his companion, Elder Edward Pedersen, have left their assigned proselytizing area in Harstad without telling anyone where they were going. Do you have any knowledge regarding where they might be?"

Reissmann eyed the men carefully, pondering what to say. He was slated to pick up the elders on Monday, which was only two days away. He could say he didn't know where the missionaries were and simply deliver them back on Monday and let them deal with the consequences. But these men waited for an answer with desperate, pleading faces. Reissmann rubbed his hands together and spat on the deck. "Yes, I know where they are," he said. "They are on Riksøy, a small island about six hours south of here."

"Riksøy!" the young man's father exclaimed.

"Ah, I should have known," Toressen said, and then, pointing to the father, "Can you take the two of us there?"

"I intend to go there on Monday."

"We would like to leave immediately."

"I suppose we could go tomorrow morning, but they will not be expecting us."

"All the better," Toressen said.

"We found them. We found them!" Kristina listened with growing relief as her husband recounted how they found Herr Reissmann. "Surely it was the Lord who led us to Herr Reissmann," he said. Kristina was inclined to agree, especially because Bjørn and Brother Tanner would be retrieving the missing elders tomorrow. Perhaps it was providential after all that Brother Tanner had come to Norway. "And guess what," Bjørn said, "Elders Tanner and Pedersen have been working in their new area all along, just as I thought."

Kristina snorted derisively. "They broke the rules and caused everyone a lot of trouble—you, me, their parents, church authorities in Salt Lake City, and people here in Norway too. Don't go soft. They must be punished. You know that, don't you?"

"Yes, dear. I only meant—"

"Listen to me, Bjørnstjerne. Elder Prichard needs to see that you mean business, that you have changed your ways. That's the deal. Many people stuck their necks out for you. You can't let them down."

"Yes, yes, I know." Bjørn acknowledged his shortcomings, that he needed to repent. And no, he didn't want to jeopardize his calling.

There was sadness in his voice, a recognition that he must shed the old Bjørn. But isn't that what repentance is, casting off the old man and putting on the new? The important thing was Bjørnstjerne was now doing as directed. "I will tell Apostle Prichard the good news," Kristina told her husband.

"Tell him I will be back in Oslo with the missing elders tomorrow night."

Chapter 44

Remember the Lord is depending upon you to be faithful and true to your calling.

Conduct of a Missionary

An hour before the *sangfestival* was set to begin, Eddie suffered an attack of nerves manifested by trembling hands. He could not stop them from shaking. Sitting down at the piano only made it worse, so much so he didn't even try to play. "In all my years of performing, this never happened to me," he told Elder Tanner. "I saw it happen to others, saxophonists who squeaked their way through recitals and pianists who got the yips."

"Yips?"

"Their fingers stiffened, like they had arthritis, so they couldn't play. Others had their minds go blank. They froze in the middle of their sonata, unable to remember what came next. They had to start their piece all over again and hope their fingers would remember what their brains could not."

Eddie would get nervous, of course. Butterflies were natural. Everyone got those. But that kind of nervousness—an excited anticipation—heightened concentration and enhanced rather than hindered performance. Rehearsals with the students had gone well. He had no fears for them. He doubted himself. His expertise as an accompanist—his ability to carry them through the songs, keep them on tempo, and cover up their mistakes—was the linchpin holding everything together. Never before had the success of others been so dependent on him; never before had he wanted success not for himself but for others.

Those others were the people of Riksøy. The distance and distrust that typically separated missionaries and Norwegians had dissipated during the four weeks they had spent on the island. *Was the Norwegians' acceptance of the elders conditioned on the fact we were not preaching or teaching discussions?* Maybe. Yet, Eddie also sensed an intimate connection with these people, a mutual respect and compassion. He wanted tonight's performance to lift their spirits as they had lifted his.

It wasn't just for the Norwegians that Eddie wanted the performance to go well. He understood Elder Tanner's devout yearning for a spiritual breakthrough, a unique mission experience that would affirm his self-worth and make him feel the Lord accepted his sacrifice. By all appearances, Elder Tanner looked past Eddie's condition to see and appreciate his real self, but Eddie was afraid to ask Elder Tanner directly how he truly felt, because, unfortunately, he already knew the answer—the answer that any believing Mormon must give. Still, Elder Tanner did not shrink from him in horror, and for that Eddie was grateful. He wanted this to be a special night for Elder Tanner. As the two elders were preparing for the performance, Eddie asked Elder Tanner to give him a blessing to help calm his nerves.

"Isn't a certain amount of nervousness to be expected?" Orrin asked.

"This is completely different than the typical pre-performance jitters," Elder Tanner said. "My fingers are like weighted stones that I can barely lift across the keys."

Orrin watched sympathetically as his companion rubbed and clapped his hands together, trying to stir them to life. Orrin had to admit he had never seen his companion so agitated. In fact, one of the things he had always admired about Elder Pedersen was the serenity with which he carried himself. It followed him into the room and touched those around him. Orrin himself felt it, an aura of calmness and confidence that everything would be all right. But Orrin had also noticed how hard Elder Pedersen worked, his ability to concentrate his energies on whatever task was at hand. He had seen it in their language training when Elder Pedersen sat alone, blocking out all distractions, and practiced pronouncing the Norwegian words over and over until he mastered the sing-song accent. And this past week, Elder Pedersen had worked into the night practicing the musical numbers, working on phrasing and tempo, making sure he got it just right. He was a perfectionist, but it was his perfectionism that made him both calm and confident, because he knew his preparation would carry him through.

Elder Pedersen's situation confused Orrin. Orrin had never thought about homosexuality, never engaged in the banter about homos and perverts that occupied young men insecure about their own sexuality. He supposed he should be disgusted by his companion, but Orrin was not confronting a hypothetical homosexual but Elder Pedersen himself, and there was nothing disgusting or abhorrent about him. Just the opposite. Elder Pedersen was the most kind and patient missionary he knew. The perfect missionary, really, except for this one major flaw. He believed Elder Pedersen was telling the truth when he claimed he had always been attracted to boys and then to men, that there was no traumatic event or sexual experimentation or extraordinary experience that would have caused his condition. But why? *It was a mystery.* The church was too clever for its own good, trying to carve out rules and allowances and exceptions for homosexuality, tying itself in theological knots like the Sadducees and Pharisees, whose obsession with regulating every aspect of life drained the spirit from their religion. But Orrin had one vital piece of information that others did not: his dream in which Elder Pedersen was presented as a person who should be nurtured and loved, just as he, Orrin, had been presented to his father in a similar manner. Let church leaders sort out the rules and policies regarding homosexuality. As for Orrin, he would nurture and support his companion, whose only sin was being who he was.

Elder Pedersen took a seat in front of Orrin, rubbing his arm, waiting for a blessing to relieve his anxiety. Standing behind his companion, Orrin let a drop of consecrated oil spill from the vial onto the crown of his head. He placed both hands on Elder Pedersen's head, felt the moist oil about his fingers, and began his prayer: "Oh, God, the Eternal Father . . ." Orrin knew what he wanted to say. He had mulled over the ideas in his head, envisioning the words, hoping for a profound result, not for himself but for Elder Pedersen, who so desperately needed God's love and approbation and help.

It would be a simple prayer. He would ask for the Lord to infuse Elder Pedersen with His calming spirit so he might perform tonight to his highest ability, that he would be rewarded for his hard work and preparation, and that God would touch his heart so he knew he was loved and counted among the Lord's sheep. But when Orrin began, he froze. He searched his mind. What had he intended to say? All was blank. His thoughts drifted to his recurring dream of lions roaring on the beach and Elder Pedersen's role in his dream. *Why did it pop up just now?* His mind wandered, though he did not know how long. Was it two seconds or two minutes? He couldn't say. And so he started over. "Oh, God, the Eternal Father . . ."

After Orrin concluded his blessing, Elder Pedersen stood and shook his hand, blinking back tears. "Thank you, Elder Tanner. That was beautiful."

"You are welcome." Orrin said. His mind was an empty vessel and he did not know—could not remember—what he had just said.

Nearly everyone from Riksøy attended the *sangfestival,* along with a fair number of mainland families. Every seat in the gymnasium was filled and people stood along the walls. Pastor Carlsen estimated at least three hundred people attended. What surprised Eddie and Elder Tanner was that many of the women wore *bunad* dresses and the men matching *bunad* suits, traditional Norwegian folk costumes from the region where they were born or, in some cases, where their ancestors came from. Many people wore Lofoten *bunads* with their distinctive wildflower embroidery. "I thought people only wore their *bunad* costumes on special occasions," Eddie said.

"That is true," Pastor Carlsen replied. "And for us, this is a special occasion. We do not have many celebrations that bring out everyone in the village."

The school principal called for everyone's attention and the festive buzz grew quiet. He introduced Eddie and Elder Tanner to a loud applause and in that moment, as the crowd cheered and Eddie looked upon the sea of smiling faces, his agitation dissolved into calm anticipation. He nodded to Elder Tanner, letting him know he would be fine, and took a seat at the piano. Elder Tanner led the first group of performers from the youngest class onto a wooden stage built for the performance, and the concert began. Eddie would have been the first to admit there was nothing special about the songs he chose or his arrangements. It was enough to get the children to memorize the words in English. And so the first group opened with "The Wheels on the Bus" and continued with "The Farmer in the Dell," "John Jacob Jingleheimer Smith," and "Three Blind Mice," which they performed as a round. Eddie wondered whether their parents would be disappointed by the simplicity of the songs, but he need not have worried. The children's enthusiasm and evident joy enthralled the audience, who clapped and laughed as the children twisted their mouths into odd shapes to enunciate the foreign words. The older children came on and sang more complex songs recognized by many in the audience, including "Supercalifragilisticexpialidocious" and the "Do, Re, Mi" song from *Sound of Music*.

Before the older mainland students came out to perform, Eddie had the children sing "Happy Birthday" to Peter, the restaurant owner. Eddie played the song twice, inviting everyone in the audience to sing along the second time. "Your children will help you with the words," Eddie said. The Norwegians sang with fervor equal to that of their children.

At the end of the song, Peter stood and announced, "I have baked for myself a big cake for my birthday, which I will share."

"It better be a big cake," someone shouted, eliciting clapping and laughter.

The audience took a break as the children marched off the stage and the mainland teenagers gathered for their performance. Orrin got the students lined up and then shook their hands as they mounted the stage. "*Lykke til*," he said to each one. "Good luck." When he reached out his hand to Anna-Britt, she grabbed it firmly and pulled it to her lips. "A kiss for good luck," she said, her eyes dancing. Still holding Orrin's hands, she lifted her hands to his lips. His heart pounding with blushing delight, Orrin gave her hands a quick peck. "*Lykke til*," he said, and watched her skip onto the stage. *I will never be able to explain this to President Toressen*, he thought. Nevertheless, his feelings of guilt did not stop him from plotting his return to Riksøy—and to Anna-Britt—after his mission.

369

When Eddie played the first notes of "Breaking Up is Hard to Do" and the student chorus sang, "Do do do down dooby doo down down," the audience broke into unrestrained applause. It wasn't just the familiarity of the song, but the quality of the performance that surprised and delighted. The students did not disappoint, singing well-known songs by the Beatles; the Beach Boys; Peter, Paul and Mary; and other popular music artists. Pastor Carlsen introduced the last number. He wanted the audience to know it was a Mormon hymn, but he had listened to the lyrics and considered the song to be appropriate for a State Church youth gathering and, in fact, for any Christian denomination. "The Mormon elders asked me beforehand to make sure it was okay, and I approved the song," he said. "I think you will like it."

The students sang "I Am a Child of God," a children's song that was popular among missionaries because of its sweet sentiments and the comforting feeling it brought to young Mormon men and women living away from home for the first time. The students sang the first verse in English and then in Norwegian, so the audience could understand the lyrics. Everyone stood and clapped loudly at the conclusion. Eddie took several bows, all to wild cheering, especially from the students, and he called for Elder Tanner to share the stage. Then he asked for the audience to quiet down and announced, "We have an encore to perform." He led the students in a rousing performance of the Beatles' song, "Ob-La-Di, Ob-La-Da."

Eddie and the students had fun rehearsing the song. Neither he nor Elder Tanner could explain what the title meant, if anything. "It's just nonsense syllables," Elder Tanner said. Likewise, neither knew the meaning of the phrase "Life goes on, brah." The large number of verses allowed for some of the more talented students to take turns singing the main sections as solos before the chorus came in on the familiar refrain. The song was well known among the adults, who stood clapping to the beat throughout and, midway through the song, singing the refrain. The gymnasium echoed with the joyous voices of people singing nonsensical lyrics as loudly and passionately as their throats allowed.

Orrin clapped and sang along with the crowd. He could not recall a time he had been so happy. He looked over at his companion at the piano. Elder Pedersen was singing along with everyone, his face beaming with a dazzling, wondrous smile.

Chapter 45

As missionaries, you are now building the spiritual foundation [for]
character, virtues and values of your lives.
Conduct of a Missionary

Orrin awoke earlier than usual the next morning, roused by the exhilarating joy still present from last night's *sangfestival*. He set the kettle
on a burner and began measuring out the ingredients to make a *bløtcake*.
It would be a thank-you present for Olav and Georg. He pulled back the
kitchen curtains. The early rising sun illuminated a light blue sky. Would
he see Anna-Britt at the State Church service? He certainly hoped so. She
would be gone early tomorrow morning, off to school, while he and Elder
Pedersen would be returning to Harstad.

During breakfast, Orrin and Elder Pedersen took turns recounting *sangfestival* highlights. "It is something neither I nor the students nor anyone on
this island will ever forget, Elder Pedersen," Orrin said, heaping praise upon
his companion. "They will be talking about this for years to come."

The two elders were cleaning up the dishes when there came an urgent
knocking at the door. It was Knut, a young boy from one of their English
classes. "Herr Reissmann sent me to tell you he has arrived and is ready to
take you back to Harstad."

"What? Are you sure?" Orrin said. "He told us he was not coming
until tomorrow."

"It must be someone else," Elder Pedersen said.

"No, it is Herr Reissmann. He has two men with him who said they
have come to bring you back. But you must hurry, they said, so you can
fly back to Oslo tonight."

Orrin's euphoria melted into panic and fear. "Okay," he told Knut.
"Tell them we will pack as quickly as we can and meet them at the dock."

The elders pulled their suitcases from under their beds and began filling them with clothes. "Who do you think those two men are, I mean, the
ones who came with Herr Reissmann?" Orrin asked.

"Maybe the assistants," said Eddie.

"Or policemen. If they were really worried about us, they might have
sent the police."

Orrin thought about all the ramifications of their disappearance,
dredging up worries he had buried in the feel-good story he had concoct-
ed in his head. Church authorities would be understandably disappointed
and angry. They faced certain punishment. He worried most about Elder

Pederson, whose special circumstances would likely bring harsher punishment. Whatever happened to Orrin would be doubly worse for his companion. "Elder Pedersen," he said. "I'm sorry I roped you into this. I will tell them it was all my idea—which it was—and you agreed to come to Riksøy because I told you I had received permission from President Toressen."

"But you didn't get permission."

"I know, I know. But see, you didn't know that. That's why you came along with me."

Elder Tanner buckled his suitcase and began stuffing his bedding into his duffel. "But I did know. I knew you didn't ask and didn't get permission."

"But they don't know that. That's the point."

During a last inspection of cupboards and closets to make sure they had not left anything behind, Orrin was overcome with profound sadness. He would not have a chance to say goodbye to Gunnar Andreassen or Pastor Carlsen or Anna-Britt or Georg and Olav or anyone. He would be leaving without a trace. Maybe not immediately forgotten, but soon enough. "Are you sorry we came, Elder Pedersen?" he said. "We could get into a lot of trouble, even be sent home."

Elder Pedersen replied without hesitation. "No, are you?"

Orrin smiled weakly. "Ask me when this is all over."

The two elders swung their duffel bags onto their shoulders, picked up their suitcases, and hurried down the road, scattering dust as they ran.

"That's my father," Orrin shouted to his companion as they neared the dock. President Toressen and Orrin's father stood beside the boat, arms folded across their chests, their faces etched with anger. Herr Reissmann was leaning against the front of the boat, casually tapping ashes from his cigarette into the ocean. He caught Orrin's attention with an amused grin that said, "You're in for it now."

"Hello," the elders said sheepishly. Neither dared smile.

"You know why we're here, don't you?" asked Orrin's father, who without waiting for a reply, berated the elders for the various deceptions that kept their trip to Riksøy hidden from church authorities. Herr Reissmann apparently had told President Toressen and his father everything—about having their letters and reports sent from Harstad, about Reissmann sneaking into their apartment to collect their letters and pay the rent, about their plan to return to Harstad in secret. Orrin gave Herr Reissmann an accusatory look, but in response, the boat captain merely shrugged and rolled his eyes as he took a drag from his cigarette. "Has it all been lies," Orrin's father asked, "including everything you wrote in your reports to President Toressen?"

"No, all of that was true," Orrin replied.

"Yes, the people and activities we described, it all happened just as we reported," Elder Pedersen said, adding, "this week's report will have news of even more exciting activities."

President Toressen put a hand upon the boat's rail, as if needing to steady himself. "I put a lot of faith and trust in you, both of you, when I sent you to Harstad. And then you reward me with . . . with this," he said, spreading his arms in bewilderment. "Why did you do it, Elders?"

Orrin and Elder Pedersen looked at each other, trying to decide who should explain. "We felt inspired." Orrin said. "Yes, we felt inspired. I had been having this recurring dream, a dream that in many ways resembled a dream my father had, and as I contemplated its meaning, Elder Pedersen and I thought—"

"But you couldn't have been inspired to break the rules," Orrin's father said. "If you really felt inspired and really wanted to come here, why didn't you ask your president?"

"It's . . . it's just that I knew in my heart the answer was yes."

"That's nonsense," Orrin's father snorted, but from the corner of his eye, Orrin saw President Toressen stifling a smile.

"We thought it was the right thing to do," Elder Pedersen said.

"That's the kind of thinking that will get you in trouble," Orrin's father countered.

He sounds like Uncle Porter, Orrin thought, but not wishing to antagonize his father any further, he kept this observation to himself. Herr Reissmann continued tapping ashes into the ocean with a bemused expression that seemed to say, "*Slik er det med sektene.* This is how it is in the sects."

While the men were conversing, Pastor Carlsen appeared at the top of hill outside of Peter's cafe, followed closely by two dozen townspeople. Pastor Carlsen hailed the missionaries and ambled toward the boat while the townspeople remained on the hill, watching intently the scene below. "*God morgen,*" Pastor Carlsen called out when he reached the dock. Orrin introduced the pastor to President Toressen and his father. "We are honored that your mission president and your father have come to Riksøy, Elder Tanner," Carlsen said, now speaking English. "But does this mean you and Elder Pedersen are leaving us now?"

"Yes."

"Well, I'm sorry we never got to hear you preach or teach your discussions."

"What?" President Toressen said. "You were here for four weeks and did not teach anyone the discussions?"

"No, I'm afraid we didn't teach the gospel at all," Orrin said.

Orrin's father frowned. "So you did everything *except* teach the discussions?"

"And exterminate rats," Pastor Carlsen added.

"Exterminate . . . what?"

"Exterminate rats. That is another thing your Mormon missionaries did not do. They didn't exterminate rats," Carlsen said, winking at the elders. "But they promised to send someone to come and preach to us after they returned to Harstad. We would love to have you stay and preach. As you can see," he said, pointing to the gathering crowd whose numbers continued to grow, "these young men have made quite an impression. Can you stay?"

President Toressen shook his head. "No, we have to be going," he said emphatically. "Many people are worried about Elder Tanner and Elder Pedersen—"

"Including Apostle Prichard," Orrin's father told the elders. "He is expecting a full report."

A man broke from the crowd and made his way slowly to the dock. "This is Gunnar Andreassen, Lars Andreassen's nephew," Orrin said, introducing Gunnar to his father.

"I wish to talk with you before you leave," Gunnar said. He pulled an envelope from his coat. "Your son read to us your fascinating pamphlet about my Uncle Lars. I want to give you these letters from Lars to his parents. I have kept them all these years; for what reason, I did not know, but now I think you should have them. You can also publish these in one of your pamphlets, like the one Orrin gave to me."

Orrin, stirring with excitement, translated for his father. "We surely can print these letters. They would fit in well with our pamphlet about Lars. Isn't that right, Dad?"

Orrin's father opened the envelope and unfolded the letters. He fingered the tattered sheets with astonished reverence, then handed them back to Gunnar. "These letters are precious, but I am sorry," Orrin's father said, "I cannot accept them because I am no longer publishing pamphlets."

Orrin translated his father's words for Gunnar. Seeing the disappointment in Gunnar's eyes, Orrin impulsively reached out for the letters. "Yes, these *are* precious," he said, "and should be published for the whole world

374

to read. I might start my own publishing business when I get home. I will take them, if you will let me, Gunnar."

"I would be honored, Elder Tanner. These are my gift to you, just as you brought the gift of news about Uncle Lars to me and all his relatives on Riksøy."

Gunnar shook hands with everyone present and returned up the hill. The men looked up to see that the crowd had grown to at least one hundred. Orrin saw Olav and Georg and many of the students he and Elder Pedersen had taught at the local school, as well as the older students. Standing among them was Anna-Britt. She caught Orrin's eye and waved. Not wishing to raise suspicion with President Toressen or his father, Orrin pretended not see her, but when she smiled, he could not help but smile and wave back. *I can't get into any more trouble than I'm already in.*

"Before we go," Elder Pedersen said, "I have something I wish to tell you, President Toressen."

Orrin raised a skeptical eyebrow. "Are you sure? Perhaps it would be best discussed in private."

"Thank you, Elder Tanner, but no. I don't mind if others hear. It will be good for them to know." Turning to his mission president, he said, "President Toressen, I am a homosexual."

President Toressen and Orrin's father gasped. Herr Reissmann continued blowing smoke rings and tapping ashes over the side of the boat.

Catching his breath, Orrin's father said, "Oh, Orrin, you're not . . . ?" He couldn't bring himself to finish the sentence.

"Don't worry, Dad," Orrin said, grinning slyly at this companion. "Elder Pedersen says I'm not his type."

President Toressen was not amused. "This is very serious, Elder Pedersen. Are you saying you have—

"Oh, no, President. I have done nothing wrong. I am just saying that I'm not cured. I don't think I ever was. This is just the way I am."

"I can vouch for him," Orrin said. "Elder Pedersen's conduct has been exemplary."

A look of relief swept across Toressen's face. "Well, if you have not committed any sin, then you can still stay on your mission as long as you don't say anything about being homosexual. That is our agreement with Apostle Prichard."

"But that's just it. I am homosexual. I fooled myself for many years, telling myself I really wasn't this way, not if I didn't act on it. But I'm finished pretending to be something I'm not. I am no longer going to deny it."

"But you know this means—"

"I have to go home."

President Toressen continued to counsel Elder Pedersen, trying to persuade him to stay, to not say he was homosexual, knowing what the admission would mean not just for his mission, but for his future in the church. Finally, Elder Pedersen held up his hand. "It's okay, President Toressen," he said, his voice ringing with conviction. "I know who I am." Elder Pedersen had spoken, more sharply than he had intended, but now, contemplating what he had just said, he repeated the words to himself, in a whisper, "I know who I am."

"Time to go," Herr Reissmann called from his boat. He stamped out his cigarette and pointed to the elders' suitcases and gear. "Hand those over, boys, and we will get underway."

Orrin turned to pick up his bags just in time to see President Toressen's knees buckle and his face turn ghostly pale. "I think I lost my sea legs," Toressen said as he started to swoon.

Orrin and Elder Pedersen rushed to his side, each taking an arm, and lowered him to a seat on one of the suitcases. "Take slow, deep breaths," Pastor Carlsen advised. "Everybody, let us stand back and give him some air."

"Is one of those people standing up there a doctor?" Orrin's father asked.

Carlsen shook his head. "No, I am afraid the nearest doctor is across the sea on the mainland."

"Give him a moment," Orrin said. "Perhaps he is just exhausted."

As the men mulled around, wondering what to do, an eerie calm descended on the inlet. The salty wind, almost a constant force along the shore, disappeared, while the splashing of the sea against the rocks and pilings faded away. Not even a ripple troubled the bay. A lone seagull flew overhead, flapping with uncharacteristic sluggishness, because there was no wind upon which to soar. The clouds disappeared, revealing a perfectly blue sky. *Click, click, click.*

"What is that?" Pastor Carlsen asked.

Click, click, click.

"It is President Toressen's heart, or rather, it is the pacemaker attached to his heart," Orrin explained. "It grows louder when he is tired and falls asleep. I have seen this happen before."

Pastor Carlsen suggested that Herr Reissmann take President Toressen directly to the mainland, just as a precaution, but before Reissmann could answer, Toressen's eyes blinked open. He looked around and smiled. He appeared completely refreshed, the color having returned to his face.

Before anyone had a chance to help him up—or to insist that he remain seated—Toressen was standing and walking about. And in the brief time between when his eyes opened and he rose to his feet, the cacophony of ocean noises returned—the wind, the lapping sea, the squawking seabirds, and even the barking of seals in the distance.

"What was that all about?" Orrin's father wondered.

"It was the shifting tide," Herr Reissmann replied. "And that is why we must shove off and take advantage of the change."

The elders once again picked up their bags. "Just a moment," President Toressen said. "Pastor Carlsen, does your invitation still stand? I would like to stay and preach."

"Why, yes."

Orrin's father erupted with surprised alarm. "But President Toressen, we have to get back. You told your wife we would have the elders back in Oslo tonight."

"Brother Tanner, this is a rare and wonderful opportunity."

Orrin's father continued to object. Was not their goal to find and retrieve the two elders? Was not everyone expecting their return? Staying would make it appear he approved of the elders' actions. Apostle Prichard would be extremely unhappy. Wagging his finger, Orrin's father warned, "You are jeopardizing your calling as the Norwegian mission president."

"Stop! Stop right there, Brother Tanner," President Toressen said, his eyes blazing with righteous anger. "Don't tell me how to go about my business." He glared at Orrin's father, daring him to speak again, but he bowed his head and remained silent. Speaking calmly, Toressen said, "Brother Tanner, do not worry. It will be all right. I want you to take Elder Pedersen back with you to Harstad and then fly with him to Oslo tonight, as we had planned. When you get to Harstad, you can call and inform Sister Toressen of the change in plans. Tell her I will return in a few days. I'm sure she will understand."

President Toressen offered Orrin a mischievous grin. "Elder Tanner, how would you like to be my companion and help me preach to these people?"

"As your scribe, sir?"

"I think it is time for you to start preaching again, don't you?"

"I would love that, President," Orrin said. He turned to his father. "Dad, thank you for coming to find me. I am sorry to have caused you and Mom so much worry. But I'm all right. Please tell Mom I'm all right."

Elder Pedersen stepped toward Orrin, "I guess this is goodbye," he said, reaching out to shake Orrin's hand. Orrin brushed aside the extended hand and pulled his companion close, wrapping him in a bear hug. Elder Pedersen returned Orrin's hug, hesitantly at first, then with gusto. "Uh, you know how this looks, don't you, Elder Tanner?" Elder Pedersen said.

"I don't care," Orrin whispered in his ear. "I don't care."

The young men stepped back, still holding each other's arms. Elder Pedersen spoke hesitantly. "I guess this . . . being homosexual, that is. I guess this means—"

"We'll be happy together in a lower kingdom," Orrin said.

Elder Pedersen smiled. "Yes, happy together in the here and the hereafter."

Herr Reissmann picked up Elder Pedersen's suitcase and started for the boat. "Okay, young man. We must get underway if we want to go with the tide."

Orrin nodded to his companion, grabbed his suitcase and duffel bag, and hurried to catch up with President Toressen and Pastor Carlsen, who had already begun the long walk up the hill. "I was wondering, Pastor Carlsen," Toressen said. "Has Elder Tanner told you about the remarkable vision I had foretelling of my mission call to Norway? I had forgotten until now that I was preaching on an island just like this." Orrin heard the familiar shudder of the boat's engine, followed by a thunderous blast and belch of smoke as the engine roared to life. He stopped and turned, his suitcase still in hand. Elder Pedersen stood at the back of the boat, smiling sweetly, waving goodbye. A low, translucent fog was creeping in, floating just above the water. Elder Pedersen disappeared into the mist.

The trip back to Harstad was uneventful. Upon their arrival at the apartment, Brother Tanner sent Eddie upstairs to collect the rest of his belongings. Hurry, he said, because Bror Brevik would be arriving soon to drive them to Narvik. In the meantime, Brother Tanner intended to call Sister Toressen and inform her of the change in plans. Eddie wanted no part of that conversation, though he wished he could listen in. Eddie gathered a few souvenirs from the places he had lived: a poster of the view from Bergen's Mount Fløyen; a print of an Edvard Munch painting; a T-shirt from his climb up Preikestolen while he was stationed in Stavanger. He and Elder Tanner had each left a suit, several white shirts and ties, and a pair of shoes in their closet. Eddie made room for his shoes in the suitcase and placed his suit and shirts in a garment bag. He took off his hat and felt the contours of its soft fur. *I won't have much use for this in southern California,* he thought. He placed the hat on the closet shelf for the missionary who would be called to replace him. Eddie returned downstairs and put his suitcase by the door.

"Brother Brevik is on his way," Brother Tanner said. He tapped his left foot nervously as the two men waited in silence.

"Just a moment," Eddie said, racing to the stairs. "There's something I forgot."

Brother Tanner looked at his watch. "Don't be long."

Once upstairs, Eddie rummaged through the bedroom dresser until he found what he wanted. He worked furiously, knowing he didn't have much time. First one, then the other. He began a second application. Bror Brevik's car pulled up outside.

"He's here," Brother Tanner called from the bottom of the stairs.

"Almost finished," Eddie yelled. And a minute later, to himself, he said, "Ah, perfect."

The room is too dark, Eddie thought, and so he pulled open the curtains. He marveled that the sun shone brightly this late at night. Eddie paused to admire his handiwork and then hurried down the stairs. Bror Brevik was already loading his suitcase and gear into the car.

"Hello, Bror Brevik," Eddie said as he climbed into the back seat. He wondered how much Brother Tanner had told Bror Brevik about his situation. Bror Brevik returned his friendly hello, but Eddie discerned a cold distance in his eyes, a look mixed with revulsion and pity. It was a look Eddie knew he must get used to. He would have to find a way to see past it or ignore it. For now, he would just close his eyes. Bror Brevik put the car in gear and they sped away.

Eddie tried to sleep, but his mind, though burning with anticipation of what lay ahead, drifted backward to his mission. It began as a deal with God: complete dedication in return for a cure. *Oh Lord, remove this cup from me.* A promising sign of redemption turned out to be a prank. And Eddie cried. Elder Jensen won his heart and, inevitably, broke it. Again, Eddie cried. Incredibly, God seemed determined to lead Eddie to homosexual Norwegian men: Georg and Olav, and Tom Haugen—twice! *Is God sending me a message?* The revulsion and furious contempt aimed at homosexuals by the elders and sisters shocked and sickened Eddie. *Is this how they would see me—if they knew?* Disheartened, Eddie had unleashed his own furious anger and despair at Elder Tanner, who served as a stand-in for all straight-arrow missionaries who would condemn and reject Eddie—if they knew. But Elder Tanner, by taking the first step toward reconciliation, proved himself to be anything but small-minded or judgmental. Was the *sangfestival* the highlight of Eddie's mission? It certainly sparked the most joy. Still, Elder Tanner's unspoken acceptance of Eddie, of Eddie the man, was a precious gift that gave Eddie the courage to acknowledge and accept himself as well. Would he be able to summon up that courage when facing Apostle Prichard, his parents, his brothers, and his many friends back home? Eddie closed his eyes and prayed for courage and strength. A kaleidoscope of jumbled images spilled forth, their meaning unclear. He was standing in front of Munch's icy-pale Madonna when the slushing of the car's tires, rhythmically beating against a virgin snow, lulled him into a soothing sleep.

Upstairs in the Jørns Gate hybel, a pair of Elder Tanner's black dress shoes sit on a chair, buffed and polished with a luminous, mirror-like shine. The shoes glimmer under golden rays streaming through the window. The sun rises higher each day now, hovering insistently on the horizon. Soon it will remain visible throughout the day, giving his shoes an eternal shine.

Acknowledgments

I was fortunate to have many colleagues and friends read various drafts of my novel and offer suggestions and encouragement. Those deserving my thanks include Simon DeGroot, Jason Farr, Steve Gregory, Barbara Haugsoen, Craig Jolley, Sandra Jolley, Daniel LeSueur, Jeff LeSueur, Dean Rehberger, and Rick Sorenson.

I owe a special debt of gratitude to David Kranes, a writing coach extraordinaire who helped me keep the novel focused on its main characters and themes.

Loyd Isao Ericson, managing editor at Greg Kofford Books, provided encouragement and superb editing while also fast-tracking my book into production. Raistlyn Camphuysen, an editor at Greg Kofford Books, fixed numerous typographical errors while also enhancing and clarifying my prose where necessary.

A dear friend, Steve Quinn, who is now deceased, read the earliest drafts of my novel. Steve proved a generous reader, offering reassuring support as well as helpful advice. I wish he were here to see the fruition of our work together.

Finally, I must thank my wife, Kathy Reeder, who read numerous versions of my novel. She did so cheerfully, offering sound advice and encouragement at each step in the novel's development.

Also available from
GREG KOFFORD BOOKS

Life and Death on the Mormon Frontier: The Murders of Frank LeSueur and Gus Gibbons by the Wild Bunch

Stephen C. LeSueur

Paperback, ISBN: 978-1-58958-772-4

In *Life and Death on the Mormon Frontier*, historian Stephen C. LeSueur delivers a gripping and meticulously researched account of a brutal chapter in Western history—one that has long been overshadowed by the romanticized legends of outlaws. On March 27, 1900, a sheriff's posse set out to track five suspected criminals linked to Butch Cassidy's Wild Bunch gang. By the following day, two young men—Frank LeSueur and Gus Gibbons—were found murdered in cold blood. As the great-nephew of Frank LeSueur, the author brings a deeply personal perspective to this tragedy, shedding light on the true cost of outlaw violence. Using firsthand accounts, newspaper reports, and historical records, LeSueur reconstructs the harrowing events and dismantles the myth of noble bandits, exposing the Wild Bunch for what they truly were—ruthless killers.

Set against the backdrop of Arizona's White Mountains, this compelling history also explores the struggles of the Mormon settlers of St. Johns, whose resilience was tested by both a hostile frontier and the unchecked brutality of outlaw bands. The LeSueur and Gibbons families, early colonizers of the region, faced relentless hardships in their efforts to build a community, but the senseless murder of two of their own sent shockwaves through the town. With vivid storytelling and sharp historical analysis, *Life and Death on the Mormon Frontier* offers a fresh perspective on the realities of frontier justice, the perils of lawlessness, and the lasting scars left by one of the West's most infamous gangs.

Praise for *Life and Death on the Mormon Frontier*:

"Stephen LeSueur takes the reader on a ride into the dark, murderous world of the Wild Bunch in the Mormon settlements of the Utah-Arizona frontier. A compelling, deeply researched, and well-written study that will grab the attention of Old West historians." — Daniel Buck, co-author of *The End of the Road: Butch Cassidy* and *The Sundance Kid in Bolivia*

The Garden of Enid: Adventures of a Weird Mormon Girl

Scott Hales

Part One ISBN: 978-1-58958-562-1
Part Two ISBN: 978-1-58958-563-8

Fifteen-year-old Enid Gardner is a self-proclaimed "weird Mormon girl." When she isn't chatting with Joseph Smith or the Book of Abraham mummy, she's searching for herself between the spaces of doubt and belief. Along the way, she must grapple with her Mormon faith as it adapts to the twenty-first century. She also must confront the painful mysteries at the heart of her strained relationship with her ailing mother.

This edition of The Garden of Enid: Adventures of a Weird Mormon Girl recasts the award-winning webcomic as a two-part graphic novel. With revised and previously unpublished comics, it features the familiar story that captivated thousands online, yet offers new glimpses into Enid's year-long odyssey.

Praise for *The Garden of Enid*:

"Enid brings something real, something faith-affirming, something beyond Happy Valley and seminary videos and Saturday's warrior to the LDS audience." — Sarah Dunster, author of *Lightning Tree* and *Mile 21*

"This book is a classic whether you rush through it from cover to cover or linger over each moment, as the original readers did, at a pace of a few comics a week." — James Goldberg, author of *The Five Books of Jesus*

"Hales has created a world that will be an enduring addition to Mormon Literature. Don't miss this delightful work." — Steven L. Peck, author of *A Short Stay in Hell* and *The Scholar of Moab*

"There is much that Enid does not understand, just as there is much that I do not understand. But she makes me laugh, gives me hope for the future, and teaches me that it's okay to be myself: a weird Mormon girl." — Jana Riess, author of *Flunking Sainthood* and *The Twible*

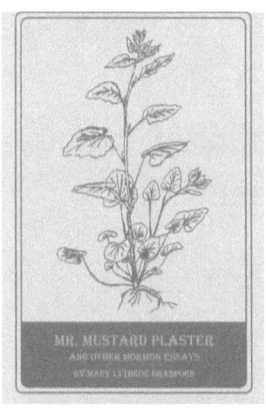

Mr. Mustard Plaster
and Other Mormon Essays

Mary Lythgoe Bradford

ISBN: 978-1-58958-742-7

"Mary Bradford is the original literary 'Mormon Girl.' Long before anyone even imagined the bloggernacle, she believed that writing about everyday Mormon life—especially women's lives—could be beautiful and powerful. In her own essays, she brings unparalleled power of perception, generous humanity, and quiet humor to bear on even challenging Mormon subjects. This book is an incredible opportunity for a new generation of Mormon readers to get to know one of our faith's wise women elders. Don't miss it." — Joanna Brooks, author of *The Book of Mormon Girl: A Memoir of an American Faith*

"Mary Bradford believes that the distinctive nature of the personal essay originates from what she calls the three "I's" ("I's," eyes, ayes)—the authors' first-person perspective, their clear and rich vision, and their honest and affirming testimonies of life. Mary's own essays are true to form: her essays are vibrant portraits of a kind and loving soul, a rich and unique perspective, and a life well-lived and deeply loved." — Boyd Jay Petersen, author of *Dead Wood and Rushing Water: Essays on Mormon Faith, Culture, and Family*

"Mary Lythgoe Bradford offers her autobiography in personal essay—revealing a lifetime that bridged generations and pioneered the power of essay in Mormon literature. Since the first issue of Dialogue in 1966, Mary's wisdom and presence as an editor, writer, poet and biographer have linked us together, reaching back to women like Virginia Sorensen and moving us forward into feminism. Today at 84, Mary is still helping 'Mormon women speak.'" — Maxine Hanks, editor of *Women and Authority: Re-emerging Mormon Feminism*

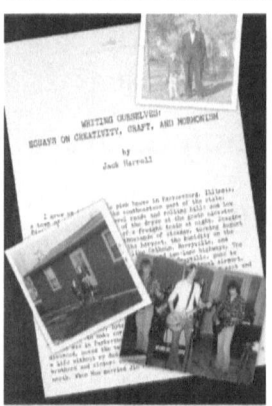

Writing Ourselves:
Essays on Creativity, Craft,
and Mormonism

Jack Harrell

Paperback, ISBN: 978-1-58958-754-0

Continuing a conversation as old as Mormonism itself, Jack Harrell explores the relationship between Mormonism and the writer. Mormons see the universe in mythic proportions. Their God is a creator, their devil a destroyer. This makes meaningful conflict fundamental to their worldview, and begs the terms for religious redemption, as well as the redemptive power of art. Harrell urges writers to be authentic as they embrace the difficulties inherent in the creative process. His essays blend faithful intellectual inquiry, personal narrative, research, and application to offer insights for anyone who cares about writing, creativity, and the human condition.

Dead Wood and Rushing Water: Essays on Mormon Faith, Culture, and Family

Boyd Jay Petersen

Paperback, ISBN: 978-1-58958-658-1

For over a decade, Boyd Petersen has been an active voice in Mormon studies and thought. In essays that steer a course between apologetics and criticism, striving for the balance of what Eugene England once called the "radical middle," he explores various aspects of Mormon life and culture—from the Dream Mine near Salem, Utah, to the challenges that Latter-day Saints of the millennial generation face today.

Praise for *Dead Wood and Rushing Water*:

"*Dead Wood and Rushing Water* gives us a reflective, striving, wise soul ruminating on his world. In the tradition of Eugene England, Petersen examines everything in his Mormon life from the gold plates to missions to dream mines to doubt and on to Glenn Beck, Hugh Nibley, and gender. It is a book I had trouble putting down." — Richard L. Bushman, author of *Joseph Smith: Rough Stone Rolling*

"Boyd Petersen is correct when he says that Mormons have a deep hunger for personal stories—at least when they are as thoughtful and well-crafted as the ones he shares in this collection." — Jana Riess, author of *The Twible* and *Flunking Sainthood*

"Boyd Petersen invites us all to ponder anew the verities we hold, sharing in his humility, tentativeness, and cheerful confidence that our paths will converge in the end." — Terryl. L. Givens, author of *People of Paradox: A History of Mormon Culture*

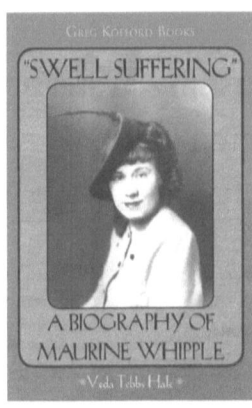

"Swell Suffering":
A Biography of Maurine Whipple

Veda Tebbs Hale

Paperback, ISBN: 978-1-58958-124-1
Hardcover, ISBN: 978-1-58958-122-7

Maurine Whipple, author of what some critics consider Mormonism's greatest novel, *The Giant Joshua,* is an enigma. Her prize-winning novel has never been out of print, and its portrayal of the founding of St. George draws on her own family history to produce its unforgettable and candid portrait of plural marriage's challenges. Yet Maurine's life is full of contradictions and unanswered questions. Veda Tebbs Hale, a personal friend of the paradoxical novelist, answers these questions with sympathy and tact, nailing each insight down with thorough research in Whipple's vast but under-utilized collected papers.

Praise for *"Swell Suffering"*:

"Hale achieves an admirable balance of compassion and objectivity toward an author who seemed fated to offend those who offered to love or befriend her. . . . Readers of this biography will be reminded that Whipple was a full peer of such Utah writers as Virginia Sorensen, Fawn Brodie, and Juanita Brooks, all of whom achieved national fame for their literary and historical works during the mid-twentieth century"
—Levi S. Peterson, author of *The Backslider* and *Juanita Brooks: Mormon Historian*

www.ingramcontent.com/pod-product-compliance
Lightning Source LLC
Chambersburg PA
CBHW020811020726
47495CB00008B/2683